JEWISH BLOOD

Jewish Blood

A Novel

Edward Schwartz

iUniverse, Inc.
New York Lincoln Shanghai

Jewish Blood

iUniverse books may be ordered through booksellers or by contacting:

iUniverse
2021 Pine Lake Road, Suite 100
Lincoln, NE 68512
www.iuniverse.com
1-800-Authors (1-800-288-4677)

This is a work of fiction. All of the characters, names, incidents, organizations and dialogue in this novel are either the products of the author's imagination or are used fictitiously.

ISBN-13: 978-0-595-40184-0 (pbk)
ISBN-13: 978-0-595-84561-3 (ebk)
ISBN-10: 0-595-40184-8 (pbk)
ISBN-10: 0-595-84561-4 (ebk)

Printed in the United States of America

This book required research on the recent history of Germany and Israel. There is no possibility that persons living today will see them or be mistaken by the public as characters in the novel. With the exception of actual historical personages, characters are entirely the product of the author's imagination, and have no relation to any person in real life.

For David

PART I

▼

DARK TIME

"When meanness of men's souls elevates, sinners saunter around."

—Teghilim, 12.

CHAPTER 1

▼

For the last several years, nothing had changed in the hotel; the same owner napped on the counter, the same walls featured unmentionable stains, and the same decaying rooms. They had sinks but no toilets. Bathrooms were at the end of the long hall. Sometimes they were all busy; prostitutes used them to avoid paying for a room. And of course, no one required a reason for staying there.

Rupert rose from the bed and pulled the curtain aside. But it did nothing to bring more light in; the narrow window looked at a brick wall wet from rain that glistened in the glow of a nearby streetlight. He turned and looked at the young man lying on the bed. His freckled face, with a blade of a snub-nose that had apparently been broken once, sharply contrasted with two deep wrinkles on his forehead and the scar on his cheek, obviously earned in a drunken fight.

"Get out of here," Rupert growled. Taking twenty crones out from his wallet, he put them on the night-side table.

A wondering look flared across the man's face. Then he quickly dressed, took the money, and disappeared without saying good-bye.

Rupert looked at his watch. It was too early to pick up his wife at her cousin's house. He had told Eliza that he was meeting some old military friends, and such meetings never finished any earlier than midnight.

Gulping down the rest of the beer in the half-empty bottle by the bed, Rupert threw himself on the rumpled sheets, and closed his eyes. In the nothingness that surrounded him, he felt lost in the vast present. Memories flashed through his mind…

He could not complain about his fate after the war was over, but his military service in the 16th Bavarian Reserved Regiment had been the best part of his life. He wasn't eager to lose the military barracks's atmosphere, its unique form of relationships with the others who served. He felt very cozy in the company of those men. Plus there, near him, was his beloved friend Adolf Hitler, his lover. They were like a single person for five years, from the summer of 1914 to 1919. Up until that point, he had never experienced a closer man than Adolf. A year into the relationship, after their unit lost almost half its men, he had even refused a promotion to sergeant because his beloved Adolf wasn't included on the advancement list. So they both remained as private first class. Those years were unforgettable! He had so many pictures from that time—Adolf Hitler, Erich Bruchner, Gustav Koor…The melting gladness of old remembrances filled him. Rupert sighed and smoked a cigarette.

The Peace Treaty of Versailles had destroyed Germany, and also the unforgettable military brotherhood. Life scattered everybody. Gustav had tried to rob a bank, and was killed committing the crime; Eric had married, and now tried to keep a distance from old friends; his beloved Adolf, as well…They said Adolf had unsuccessfully tried to sell his wonderful pictures, and then he began playing politics: he talked to youngsters about the future of the German army and the unification of

Germany and Austria. Young people always adored him. If he, Rupert Menke, weren't married, he would have joined Adolf's movement. But maybe not, Rupert sighed again. It would be too painful to see Adolf, and not to be with him. Alas, he, Rupert Menke, is an old-fashioned man, a one-love-in-a-life-time man. With a vicious wrench of his thoughts, he returned to the present.

The bitter taste of cheap cigarettes made his stomach roll. He needed a drink. Remembering enervated him. He glanced at his watch again. The hands were both on eleven. He washed his face and dressed. It's time to get out of here, he thought.

When he tossed the room key on the front desk downstairs, the owner did not bother to open his eyes; Rupert had paid for the room in advance.

When he reached the street, he inhaled sharply, invigorated by the cold, bracing air, and turned in the direction of a pub at the end of the street. The rain had stopped, and the street was buried beneath a carpet of slick leaves. A three-quarter moon had risen and it laid a silver swath across the sky.

Once inside the pub, Rupert perched on a high stool at the end of the bar. "Schnapps," he ordered.

The expression on his face made it clear that he did not wish to talk to anyone. After the bartender filled a small glass, Rupert took a long thirsty drink in one gulp and felt better. After the second drink, Rupert's thoughts returned to his marriage.

Who could have imagined that he would marry? Yes, Germany defeat had destroyed the usual life of a private first class Rupert Menke. His house was the barracks, and his house was destroyed; his family was the group of his fellows-in-arms, and his family was also destroyed. He had remained alone.

Maybe loneliness led him to marriage. Did all his fellows feel the same loneliness? Maybe he felt it sharper than the others did.

The Empire's collapse, the revolution and the following chaos had opened a way up for some of them, but for most it was a way down. Gustav Koor had been the first victim. But weren't all of them victims?

Rupert reached for his glass and drained the last of the liquid from it. He wanted to order another, but changed his mind when he remembered that he had to drive Eliza home. He raised a finger to the bartender and asked for a beer instead. Munich's beer is the best in the world, he thought, as he tasted it. It could make you sober in minutes, and always dispel your gloomy ideas.

He grinned at his thoughts. Every period tests the heart in its own way. Perhaps it was true that our generation is spoiled. We looked in the eyes of a rifle at a time when we should have glanced at the eyes of a beloved girl or a boy. Rupert grinned again.

Why did he marry Eliza if women didn't interest him? He remembered their first meeting in the church, at Christmas dinner. Eliza seemed plain looking, but she possessed a natural charm. And she was a good listener. What more did he need? Many people thought that he had married for her dowry, but they were wrong. Perhaps he simply tried to avoid loneliness.

His mother died when he was ten, he almost had no memory of her. As he could see on the photos in their family album, she was a small, brittle blonde, delicately boned, and with big blue eyes on a piquant face framed by a cloud of hair. On one of the photos she sat at a piano. Later Rupert could not understand what forced her to marry his father, a rough, uneducated man. Obviously they had very little in common.

Rupert took after his father in body. But he inherited his mother's passion for music, and her weakness. Perhaps because of it, he preferred the company of men. In any case, traditionally, a man had to show his strength to win a woman's heart. A man had to be better than others in her eyes, but when in the company of other men, he was just like the others, an equal among equals. A fleeting memory of the recent past slashed through him as he scrawled wet rings on the bar with the bottom of his glass.

His father was a big, noisy man who owned a pub. He paid no attention to Rupert. Almost every month he brought another woman to the house. Before he hired a waitress, she had to sleep with him. Why were they so compliant? Rupert did not understand it. Father wasn't good-looking—short, with thinning blond hair, and a squat wrestler's physique gone soft with debauchery. Years of working in the pub made him stout; he weighed no less than two hundred forty pounds, with at least hundred of it in his belly.

At sixteen, Rupert hated women. For him, a woman's origin was always cowardice, obedience and unreliability. Still maybe he would have remained an ordinary man, with the ordinary sexual orientation, if a chance occasion hadn't interfered with his life; his first sexual experience turned out to be homosexual.

One day, marching along the street after the usual shouting match with his father, Rupert stopped in front of the brightly lit window of a travel agency that was decorated with posters of Vienna's sites. With the sun gone, the air had suddenly turned cold, but Rupert didn't want to return home. His thoughts dwelled on his father. "He is a bunch of bullshit," Rupert muttered, remembering that yesterday he had seen a prostitute, taller than he was, with dark hair and crimson lips, hanging on his father's arm.

"I see you enjoy sightseeing in Vienna."

Rupert turned and saw a smiling, handsome man. He was a slender, delicate build, well under six feet tall, with short-cropped hair, pale skin, eyes of brilliant blue, and a straight nose. Rupert made no reply, but nodded nonchalantly.

"It's a wonderful city," the man continued. "I lived there for several years. This is one of the most beautiful cities in the world." He looked at Rupert and saw interest in his eyes. "My name is Iowan," he added. "I teach German history at the university."

"I am Rupert." The words trickled from his throat with a slight smirk. He looked flustered and uncomforted.

As a light rain began, Iowan invited Rupert to the nearest café. Smiling broadly, he escorted his new friend to a table where he continued his story. "You have to visit Vienna to appreciate its beauty, Rupert. Let's stop by my apartment if you don't object," Iowan offered. "I'll show you some books on Vienna." Iowan's smile was affable, confident. "Interesting?" He stretched backward.

The words hung between them. Rupert kept silent, indicating neither denial nor confirmation. Drinking his coffee, Iowan did not interrupt silence, eyes observing Rupert's hesitation.

"Yeah, maybe." Rupert tried to swallow, but his mouth was dry.

In Iowan's apartment, they sat side by side on the sofa, looking at books about the beautiful city. After a few minutes, Iowan draped his arm around Rupert's shoulders.

There was something feminine in Iowan's way of eating and gently bringing his glass to his lips, and Rupert liked it. The man's fingers were soft; their touch was pleasant. The feeling of pleasure that came over him was new and unfamiliar. Rupert admitted to himself that he actually was harboring a secret hope that Iowan would ask him to stay.

Over a second cup of coffee and a second glass of wine, Iowan managed to steer the conversation to love and friendship. "Friendship is a much deeper feeling, Rupert," Iowan said carefully. "When you experience it, you will be another man." He looked at Rupert's face and saw a flicker of sympathy and understanding in his childish face.

As the hour was late, Rupert eagerly accepted Iowan's offer to stay over. The next morning Rupert had no regrets for any actions of the night.

For that fleeting instant, Rupert's thoughts flew backward, into the past, and returned to the present. He drank his beer and felt sober. He peered at his watch and thought it was the proper time to pick up Eliza.

CHAPTER 2

▼

Eliza Menke was thirteen years older than Rupert. At forty-three, she was a plain flabby woman, although she had begun life with a body as thin and flat as a boy's. The type never to attract the attention of men, she had lived in her parents' home for over forty years. More accurately, it was her father's house; her mother having escaped with a lover before Eliza was fifteen years old. But at that age, she never thought about her parents' personal life.

A bright, smart child, Eliza was always at the top of the class' list at school. Since childhood, she could read beyond her age level, and she had a sharp eye.

A mystery surrounded Eliza's birth, and one scorching day when she was fourteen years old, she became aware of it. Left alone in the house when her parents went out to celebrate her father's birthday, Eliza amused herself. Loneliness never scared her, and that day she was happy to have the opportunity to do anything she wanted. Firstly she read a little in a book she found in her mom's bedroom, but had quickly grown bored with the descriptions of sexual escapades of the young hero. Eliza wasn't still ready for such a literature. Next, to kill time, she went upstairs to her father's study. She had never been there alone; it was forbidden.

Eliza sat at her father's desk. Its surface was empty, decorated solely by an inkstand and a blank sheet of white paper. Why was a blank sheet there? She pulled at one of the drawers. It was locked. Another was locked as well. But the lowest drawer opened to her tug. A gun! Her hand moved to slam the drawer shut, but hesitated. Instead, very carefully, with two hands, she took the gun out and put it on the table. Then she rifled through the papers in that drawer. Among the faded birthday cards, there were two items that perplexed her. One was a photograph of a beautiful, naked woman lying on the sofa. It wasn't her mother; she had never seen the woman. The other strange article was an officially looking document.

Eliza learned in seconds that it was a marriage license bearing her parents' names and a date years previous on it. Eliza knew that her birth certificate was dated two years earlier than the document in her hand. How could she have been born before her parents married? Her face wrinkled like a confused infant's. What could it mean? Only one thing; Daddy wasn't her real father.

Then Eliza pondered the photograph. But no reasonable explanation about who the woman could be came to Eliza's head. So she carefully put everything back in the drawer, and then went to her bedroom.

For months, Eliza intended to ask Mother about the discovery she had made. But almost six months passed until, when her father was away on a business trip and they were home together, she asked Mother the question.

"My father is my stepfather, right?" Eliza asked in a small, quiet voice as they finished supper.

Mother smiled. "If you are so inquisitive, honey, you are my daughter. Does it make a big difference to you? You're mine," she repeated.

That night she put Eliza in her bed. As was her custom on hot nights, Mother was nude.

"Take off your nightgown, honey. It's too muggy to fool with clothes," Mother said casually, and switched the light off. For an instant, they lay motionless. Then Mother said, "Sometimes life isn't easy for a woman, honey. Not everybody is happy." She sighed. Her kind, gruff voice soothed Eliza.

"You aren't happy with Father?" Eliza's face crumbled, and her eyes filled with tears.

Mother embraced her and smiled tenderly. "Who knows what a woman's happiness is? When you are with me, I'm happy." She enfolded Eliza in her arms again, and kissed her cheek.

Eliza was pleased that Mother needed her. She returned the kiss and was ready to turn to the wall to fall sleep. But Mother took Eliza's hand and placed it on her breast.

"Do you hear my heartbeat, honey? When a woman loves, her heart beats faster, and I love you." She kissed Eliza on the mouth; her nipples suddenly stood erect. Her head dipped lower and she began tenderly licking the girl's small breasts.

The kisses were pleasant Eliza, and she also wanted to please her mother in return. So she touched her mother's breast.

Mother pressed Eliza's head close and moved lower. And lower..."Kiss me, honey, kiss," she whispered passionately. At last a moan of satisfaction accompanied her body's convulsions.

The feelings Eliza experienced that night were very nice, and not talking about the fact that she and her mother now had one body, each joined to become one.

Less than a year later, her mother escaped with a lover, an event that Eliza had not anticipated. After all the intimacy that had taken place between them, Mother had abandoned her like a useless kitten. When Eliza learned of the desertion, she dropped her head into her hands and wept desperately in her room.

"The bitch has abandoned us," Father said the next day, in an amazingly flat tone as if guessing Eliza's thoughts. He was a quiet man by nature, and did not seem to ever find the need to make small talk to his daughter about her stepmother.

Eliza realized that the woman whom she considered her mother had lied to her. At that point, Eliza hated all women, and clutched the arm of the first man she met in the street. He was a soldier who made love to her quickly. But Eliza wasn't in a hurry to leave the motel room. She pleaded to him to come inside her the second time. When he did, she jerked and fell forward on his chest, her body damp with sweat. For the first time in her life, she experienced an orgasm, and it was a wonderful feeling.

Since then, Eliza never missed a chance to repeat that satisfaction with casual partners. Eventually her luck ran out, and she was not only pregnant, but also sick with a venereal disease. Having no other options, she planned to go to her father and confess everything; he was the only person who could help her.

She expected that her father would kill her, but he remained surprisingly calm. He drove Eliza to the family doctor who aborted her and treated her for the venereal disease. The doctor was not an expert at abortions, and later Eliza discovered that she had lost her ability to have children.

After the abortion, she lost all interest in sex. It was the most surprising to Eliza fact. Sometimes, remembering the magnificent flight in which she experienced orgasm, she asked why it had happened. But she had no answer until years later she knew that the doctor, at her father's request, had cut her clitoris off. Her father had just received a large contract for soap production for the German *Wehrmacht*; he dealt with conservative people, and a daughter-whore could spoil his reputation.

At the beginning of the WWI, Eliza's father could be considered a rich man, but after Germany defeat and the following inflation, he lost most of his wealth. By the time he reached his seventies, he realized how stupid he was to be angry with his daughter, and felt a prick of conscience for his daughter's broken life. He remained an old-fashioned man and wanted to see his daughter married before he died. As a dowry, he was ready to give her future husband a factory still manufacturing soap, and $20,000, a much more stable currency than deutsche marks. His business logic was impeccable; the deutsche mark was on the verge of collapse.

By that time, Rupert Menke had inherited the pub, and one of his regular customers told him about the large dowry he could receive if he married his distant relative Eliza.

Seduced by the dowry, Rupert turned out a lucky man. He met Eliza at the right place at the right time—at Christmas dinner in the church where Eliza was a parishioner. At first glance, Rupert didn't impress her. He was short, heavy, and looked as he could break a brick wall with his face. But she felt Rupert's weakness; he touched her with his sincere fantasies and his love of Wagner's music. She couldn't say she fell in love with Rupert, but she did like him; they felt a mutual sympathy for each other.

After several short dates, Eliza took him home to introduce to her father. When Rupert left, Father tapped his cheek and said, "This man may be a jerk, but he looks like the kind of man who could go off the deep end. If you like him, dear, marry him. I don't object. He survived the war, maybe he will be a good husband."

They married and created a strange family—a husband who was indifferent to women, and a wife who was indifferent to men.

And now, sitting in the dining room of her aunt's house, with a half-empty cup of cold tea in her hands, Eliza passively waited for Rupert to pick her up. Certainly she knew that his "meeting with old friends" was a myth, but she was absolutely indifferent about where and with whom he spent his time.

Contemplating their life, Eliza decided to talk to Rupert about adopting of a baby, one of the war orphans. Rupert wanted a dog, but she had read that the average dog only lived about fifteen years. Why don't adopt a baby?

When Rupert honked from the street, she kissed her aunt, yawned, and then said, "Bye, love. It's late."

Downstairs, Rupert's Benz was already near the front door. It was a big, two-door convertible car. Eliza liked to sit in it, especially in the summer when the top was down. She knew cars were Rupert's main weakness. After meeting her, Rupert had still doubted if it made sense to marry her, but he discarded all reservations as soon as he saw the Benz. It was a dream car, regardless of which woman was sitting near him on the passenger seat. If he could only invite Adolf for a ride!

As Rupert held her door open, Eliza climbed in. Rupert then trotted around to the driver's side.

"How was the party?" Eliza asked as she made herself comfortable on the passenger seat.

"Nice as always," Rupert replied. "I think there's nothing better than military brotherhood."

"I think you are right. Women cannot understand it," she agreed.

Rupert looked at Eliza with a grateful smile, switched on the headlights, and turned onto the main road. Usually everything about his wife irritated him: her round face, her colorless eyes, and her flabby body: But today, after she understood his feelings about the brotherhood, that emotion was absent. She even seemed attractive; fair skin, blue eyes, and brown hair.

A strange feeling of harmony filled Rupert. He had no idea what caused it. Rupert didn't try to understand that strange feeling; he wasn't accustomed to analyzing and finding reasons. He simply was in harmony with himself, with his memories, with the car, and with the road. He pressed the accelerator down, enjoying the speed. What a wonderful car the Benz was! Almost seventy kilometers per hour!

The moon disappeared behind a cloud, and it grew suddenly colder. He glanced at the sky and frowned. "It's going to rain again soon," he said. The road was dark and empty. A wonderful feeling of freedom totally flooded Rupert. He drove with careless ease, relaxed, fingertips barely touching the wheel. His foot pushed the accelerator to the floor.

When he saw a small Opel coming in the opposite direction, it was too late. Eliza's hysterical cry deafened him, and he slammed on the brakes, jerking the steering wheel in an attempt to avoid overturning.

The Opel's driver was less lucky. The Opel flipped end to end down the road and came to rest on its roof. Everything happened in seconds, so Rupert did not even understand what had really happened. But the adrenaline vaporized the alcohol from his body; he was sober.

Rupert ran to the Opel and tried to open the driver's door. But he failed. With his final mighty jerk, the door almost twisted off, and a body tumbled to the soil. Rupert had seen many deaths in his life; with his first glance, he knew the driver was dead. He glanced inside and saw a woman whose face was covered with a waterfall of blood. She was still alive but unconscious. As Eliza crouched to peer in the Opel, Rupert looked wildly at her.

"We need to take the woman to the hospital," he yelled with a frown.

"Are you crazy? Do you want to go to prison? You've killed them!" Eliza jumped up and brushed the dirt from her clothes, dragging her husband away from the wreck.

"The woman is still alive," Rupert whispered. He was thin-lipped with terror. As he lit a cigarette, some of the fear evaporated from his voice.

"She'll die," Eliza said firmly as she analyzed the situation. "What has happened has happened, and no amount of mourning would bring them back."

At that moment, they heard a baby's cry. Eliza rushed back to the Opel to find an infant under the woman's body. Without saying a word, Eliza grabbed the baby and dashed back to their car. Sitting on the back seat, she examined the baby nervously. Then she clutched the baby to her chest.

Rupert slid back in the driver's seat. His palms were so wet that he had to dry them on his handkerchief before putting his trembling hands on the steering wheel.

"Drive!" Eliza squalled. Her composure cracked. Her cry was almost hysterical.

CHAPTER 3

As soon as they reached home, Eliza took the baby to her rooms. Rupert went to the kitchen to find a bottle of schnapps. Alcohol dispelled the pricks of his conscious, and he slept like a child.

But with the early morning light, a splitting headache returned his thoughts to the previous day's accident. He felt like a piece of shit. In his soul, Rupert still was a soldier. To help a wounded comrade was one of the main commandments. The woman in the car had been injured but still alive when he drove away, and he had not helped her. Rupert clenched his teeth in self-contempt. If only Eliza had not forced him to drive away! A woman is the base of evil, he thought. He opened a new bottle and drank until his eyes closed, and his head hit the table.

Unshaven, with a sallow face, Rupert sat at the kitchen table, emptying one glass after another, losing his sense of time. In the breaks between forgetfulness, Rupert caught the thought that if he had a gun, he would shoot himself. But returning home after demobilization, he had thrown them all out; guns had caused his aversion.

When Eliza put her hand on his shoulder, Rupert shuddered and opened his eyes.

"Yesterday's *Deutsche Allgemeine Zeitung*," she said, her voice descending a full octave. She handed him the newspaper that was open on the page of criminal reports. Then Eliza sat next to him.

Rupert read the article marked with a red pencil.

At the 27th kilometer of the Munich highway, police discovered yesterday an overturned car. The driver was dead. A woman was found alive, but she died on the way to the hospital. Obviously help came too late, and she had lost too much blood from her injuries.

The driver was identified as Michael Ginsberg, a Munich attorney, and the passenger was his wife Esther. On the eve of the tragedy, she had been discharged from the hospital where she had given birth. However the baby's body was not found. Evidently the baby became a victim of a wolf or a bear.

Police suppose that Herr Michael Ginsberg could not control his car due to slick roads in the rainy weather.

During the World War, Herr Michael Ginsberg was a lieutenant in the 3rd Bavarian Regiment. He was noted for valor in the battle for Werden, was wounded, and decorated with the Big Crest for Bravery.

Rupert read the article and dropped his head to his hands. "We killed her." He said it very soberly, very reasonably. His teeth snapped with an audible click.

"Be a man, Rupert," Eliza said in a determine tone. "It was an unfortunate accident." She refuted his self-accusation. "But it was never ever your fault. Forget about it." Her grin disappeared as suddenly as it had come.

Rupert's face turned red, and then something approaching purple as Eliza spoke. "It doesn't matter whose fault it was." Rupert gave a nervous, low, harsh laughter. Then he rolled his eyes. Bitch, he thought looking at her. Silence came.

He had been frowning, but now a slow smile came over his face. "The boy is a Jew," Rupert said, his voice growing grave. He leaned slightly forward. Then he erupted from his chair, incoherent with fury. "A Jew!" His tone grew sharp. It was Jews who sold Germany out to the Allies at Versailles. "A Jew!" he repeated bitterly. His voice broke and fell away in silence.

"So what?" Eliza asked defiantly, narrowing her gaze. "He's five days old. Make him German. Now he's your son." She pressed the nails on her left hand into her palm, reminding herself to stay calm.

Rupert was silent, thinking over what she just said. "You could never give birth," Rupert said impersonally, but his tone was suddenly bitter. Then he grinned, pondering the possibilities.

"I'll go to my uncle's house in the Alps and stay there for three or four months," Eliza explained, looking patiently at him. "You'll tell our friends and neighbors that you sent your pregnant wife there because of the pure air, and in four months, I'll be back with a newborn baby." Eliza stood up, forcing him to look up at her. Then she walked out.

"Bitch," Rupert muttered at her disappearing back.

Rupert seemed to hear the sound of her laughter. The bitch gives a plausible scenario, he thought. Well, at least that will smoke her out of my eyes for four months. He came out of his trance to light a cigarette. Then he shoved his chair back and stood up.

In the darkness of a rainy evening, Rupert drove Eliza and the baby to the train station. As he watched the train depart, he felt much better. Yes, he'd make the boy German, he thought. Everything depends on him. He had lost nothing, but may gain much.

After Eliza's departure, Rupert's constant dissatisfaction didn't spoil his life. He felt comfortable, and even visited his factory although he had never done this before. The manager politely explained all the technological process, but Rupert understood nothing. Chemistry was too complicated for him. But surprisingly, the trip opened an interest in business for Rupert. He left the factory so quickly that the manager's face betrayed his astonishment.

Rupert tried to avoid staying home alone. Being alone depressed him. Once he spent the night with a pleasant young man who vaguely resembled his beloved Adolf. A lock of hair constantly fell on his forehead, and he moved it with a feminine gesture.

Unexpectedly Rupert decided to write Adolf a letter and ask him to be the newborn baby's godfather. It would be a wonderful chance to see his old friend again. He sat at his desk and wrote:

"My dear, old military friend Adolf;

I've allowed myself to bother you because memories of the past live forever in my heart. People always remember their history with love. The past is full of youth and hope.

But our yesterdays were cemented by war, death, and the friendship of men. What can be stronger than military brotherhood?

Frankly about myself…I think the strange composition of different features makes my life difficult. One day I need a harmonic atmosphere, wanting to live calmly, without politics. I dream about Richard Wagner and the piano. But the next day, I despise everything that was dear to me. Today I am supersensitive, tomorrow—cruelty. I do not know what to do with myself…

But the reason I'm bothering you, my dear old friend, is not just a wish to talk to you. My wife Eliza has given birth to our son, and I have a dream to see you as his godfather. I would be honored if you could find the opportunity to make my dream true.

Your devoted military friend,

Rupert Menke."

Rupert rewrote the letter and sealed the envelope.

Adolf Hitler remained no less sentimental than he was seven years ago; he has accepted Rupert's invitation. When Eliza came back, the boy was baptized and called Heinrich Menke.

Embracing Rupert after the baptismal ceremony, Adolf said, "I am happy for you, my old friend."

That day Rupert joined Adolph's National Socialistic Party, and made his first lavish political donation—20,000 deutsche marks. But he had no idea of course, that it would be a very perspicacious step.

His new interest in business kept Rupert from political adventures. He had joined Adolf's party, but didn't take any active part in its activities, referring to lack of time, as he was the official soap supplier for *Wehrmacht*. When he read in the newspapers that on November 8, 1923, Munich's Nazi party tried to capture power in Bavaria, but the plot failed and its leaders were arrested, Rupert praised himself for being so perceptive. But he couldn't stop admiring his beloved Adolf who was among the arrested leaders.

Rupert couldn't have known that jailed Nazis lived in privileged conditions. During the day, they had physical exercises outside, in fresh air; in the evening, they had friendly chats, like in the 'gold time' of the brotherhood at the front. The warden asked only that they not walk naked along the jail corridors. For all of them, including Hitler, jail wasn't punishment. If Rupert had known it, he willingly would have exchanged his place in the family bed with Eliza for a narrow bunk near Adolf. But Rupert knew that for a long time, Adolf's close friend was Rudolf Hess. No one could return to the past.

On January 30, 1933, Adolf Hitler became Chancellor of Germany. And on that day, Rupert Menke, together with pride for his former lover sharply felt acute fear. Going upstairs to his study, he opened the safe, took out an envelope, and looked through the old photographs it contained. What a nice time they had while at the front! Rupert narrowed his eyes, searching his memory.

Rupert understood that now, having become the Fuhrer and Chancellor of Germany, Adolf would prefer to terminate the image of his past that contradicted his image as the nation's leader.

Rupert opened another bottle. Clutching the dear-to-his-heart photos to his chest, he sat at the table for a long time, drinking one glass after another. Eventually his head nodded and slowly fell to the table. He jerked awake only when he heard Eliza's mocking remark. "Nice photos!"

Rupert winced. Then he quickly turned the photos face down. "If you open your mouth, bich, I'll kill you," he said quietly but calmly. He didn't try to hide his anger.

Not saying a word, Eliza turned on her heels, and walked out. She believed him.

Full of gloomy thoughts, Rupert was about to put the photos back in the safe, but hesitated. Changing his mind, he decided to find another place for them. He put in the safe only one innocent photo in an envelope—he and Adolf, both in military uniforms. Serious faces, no smiles. Soldiers of *Wehrmacht.* Defenders of Motherland.

Next, he opened his checkbook to write a 50,000 deutsche marks check to the Nazi Party. He was only forty-seven years old, and wanted to die in his own bed. After putting the check inside the envelope, he added a letter addressed to the boss of the regional Nazi Party division, Herr Frakenlobb. In the note, Rupert expressed his wish to be elected as the *Oberburghomaste*r of *Murnau,* and asked Herr Frakenlobb to support his candidature.

It's high time to become an active member of the party, Rupert thought as he mailed the envelope. The most important thing is to keep my mouth shut.

CHAPTER 4

▼

The pub was a fern-and-antique-bricks place called GRETHEN'S KISS, down the block from the Municipal Building. The pub had creaky wooden floors, rough brick walls, and framed reproductions of German sporting prints. There was a sign near a cash register PLEASE WAITE TO BE SEATED. But most of customers preferred not to wait a waitress. They stood along the counter or sat on high stools. In the corners of the pub, there were several booths, permanently reserved. One of the booths was always at Rupert's disposal.

Today Rupert scheduled here a meeting with a guy named Hence Hoffmann, his potential political rival in the coming elections. He owned the car body shop, and also dreamed of moving to the *oberburghomaster's* office. Rupert hasn't yet received the response to the letter he sent to Herr Frakenlobb. He wasn't sure he would be able to fight against the Hoffman's gang.

Going to the pub, Rupert always took Heinrich with him and forced him to drink beer. Heinrich hated this noisy place, and hated beer; he could hardly stand even beer's smell.

But today Rupert took Heinrich to the pub not only to get him into the habit of drinking. He was afraid of the open confrontation with Hoffman who was well known by his criminal connections. Being drunk, he could initiate a fight.

In the nervous expectation of the future talk, Rupert tried to force Heinrich to drink a glass of beer. But after the first gulp, he pretended to be drunk. He put his head on hands, and closed eyes.

A tall man with a gloomy face came to the pub. The sleeves of his shirt were rolled up, showing tremendous elbows. The waitress came toward him, carrying a tray with full glasses of beer, and showed him to the Rupert's booth. He sat and put his hands on the table.

"Hi, Rupert," he said amiably. "Your pub is the best place in the town."

Surprisingly, Hoffman wasn't aggressive, and looked nervous. Rupert didn't know that yesterday Hoffman had a long talk to Herr Frakenlobb. Summing up the conversation, Herr Frakenlobb lifted his chin slightly, and then he said, "This is our country. We advice you, Hoffmann, to support Herr Menke's candidature." He said it slowly and softly. Hence Hoffman was not a stupid man. He understood what meant *our country.*

"I think you don't want the Fuhrer be upset, Herr Hoffmann." Frakenlobb froze his look on Hoffmann's face. He was as calm as Hoffman was nervous.

Hoffmann felt compelled to answer. Obediently, as a first-grader, he whispered, "No, Herr Frakenlobb."

Rupert and Hence drank enough beer, but Rupert still avoided a frank talk; Hoffman was still sober. Suddenly Hoffman said, "We have to drive the same wagon, Rupert. Can I hope to be your deputy?"

Rupert couldn't believe what he was hearing. Involuntarily he slid down in his seat at too a weary glance at Hoffmann. Hoffmann stared at Rupert without any expression at all. He stared at him long enough for the silence to envelop them.

"With your help, Murnau will belong to us, Hence," Rupert said at last. *"Prozit!"*

"Prozit! You are absolutely right, Rupert. You are right as rainwater." He made a big sigh. Then he drank his big glass to the bottom.

Only now Hoffmann paid attention to Heinrich sleeping at the table. "You're bastard, Rupert. Your son will get drunk," he said indifferently as he pushed frantically between two chairs, trying to free himself for the ride to the bathroom.

"A German must be able to drink." Rupert grinned wryly, looking at Hoffmann's back.

"You're dirty rotten bastard." Which was all Heinrich could think of to call his father; only he wasn't really saying it, only thinking it, recalling his mother's words.

When Hoffmann returned to the table, Rupert was far from sober. "Fly away, your house is on fire," he told the man with a drunken smile.

"Damn you," Hoffman said mildly, drinking another glass with a slurp and a smack.

"It's a game, idiot," Rupert said thoughtfully.

"What's the game?" Hoffman didn't understand him, but Rupert didn't explain. His concentration was already obscured by alcohol; some nonsense amused him.

He looked at Heinrich, and he seemed him different. Did this bastard become German? He glanced at Heinrich again, but his aggressiveness has gone. He became almost sober. Yes, it's a game, he thought. Isn't a game—to grow a German from a Jew?

Ever since that car accident occurrence, he had watched closely, cautiously, alert for signs of remarkable changes in Heinrich. But he had witnessed none, only the growing perception of an unusual mind, which might be nothing more than the extreme vividness of his imagination. Growing a man, what could he not do in the world? It was for this Eliza said her prayers each night. Children must grow up. Must they? Now Eliza adores indulging Heinrich, delighting in his fancies, his alluring make-believe; she loves his fackin' Jewish face, eyes wider widened. And in time, surely he would outgrow it the way children outgrow Santa Claus.

Rupert looked at Heinrich who still sat, put his head on hands. He knew Heinrich always pretended to be drunk to avoid drinking. He grinned. Childhood lasts only a few brief summers; then lifetime winter comes. But if he is not a German in his childhood, how can he be a German when he is grown?

"What's the game?" Hoffman asked with the drunken insistence. "What game are you playing?"

"The game?" Rupert re-asked, and shut him a vacant glance. "Ah, the game! The life game," he said, and then he added after a pause, "A boring game." Rupert drank his glass and suddenly felt homesick for a place he had never been to—Paris, a town without Eliza and Heinrich. "How many kilometers are to Paris?" He asked Hoffman.

Hoffman shrugged. Then he again nodded to Heinrich. "Your son is drunk," he said matter-of-factly. Then he waved a waitress for another glass of beer.

Rupert pushed Heinrich's shoulder. "Go home, bastard. Tell your mother I'm gonna be late." There was a strange look in his eyes.

CHAPTER 5

▼

The night of March 9, 1933, Rupert was already in bed when the door flew open and he saw a gun directed at him.

"What do you need?" Rupert croaked, his throat sore.

"One more word, and you'll get a bullet in your head," said the invisible man, his voice neutral.

In the darkness, Rupert saw two men in the party uniform, standing near the bed. A man in civilian clothes behind them said quietly but politely, "You'll come with us, Herr Menke. Please put your clothes on."

They led him downstairs, and outside. The night was moist, heavy, and unseasonably warm. Before they got in the car, Rupert turned his head and saw Eliza's face in one of the windows. The driver started the engine, and in just a few minutes they were on the road.

"We are going to 'The Brown House?'" Rupert asked, his voice trembling. He had the Gestapo in mind.

"No," the man in the suit answered, "To police headquarters."

Rupert was led into an office and left alone. Sitting down on the chair, he felt that his body was wet with sweat. The same civilian, a large, plump, bald man, came in and sat at the desk.

He was extremely polite, but he neither introduced himself nor mentioned his rank.

"We invited you here, Herr Menke, to discuss a very 'ticklish' item," he said in a neutral tone.

Rupert felt a prick of relief when the man had said "invited" instead of "arrested." Because the man hadn't introduced himself, Rupert did not know that in front of him was Kurt Dilmann, Deputy *Oberpolitzymaster* of Munich. He was a confidant of the Austrian Chancellor Engelberd Dolfus who had given him the task of collecting documents that could compromise Hitler.

But on the other hand, the same Kurt Dilmann had received an order from the Fuhrer's aid-de-camp *Obergruppenfuhrer* CA Wilghelm Bruchner to eliminate all documents that could compromise Hitler.

Dilmann found himself between two fires, but he played on two fronts and transferred documents to both. Unfortunately for Dilmann, Chancellor Dolfus was a 'chatterbox.' He showed the file to his friend and ally, Benito Mussolini, in June 1934. Several days later, Chancellor Dolfus was killed. Several weeks after that, Wilghelm Brukhner's people put a dot on Kurt Dilmann's career. He was found strangled to death in his bedroom.

But on that day, March 9, 1933, Kurt Dilmann hadn't yet known his fate. In front of him, there was a piece of paper with five names on it. In the past, all these people were Hitler's lovers, and were therefore worth terminating. One of the names was Rupert's. But unlike the other names, Rupert's had a mark nearby—"A blindly devoted admirer. Be careful."

The remark meant that Rupert Menke's termination could cause Hitler's anger—he kept an unexpected attachment to some of his former lovers.

"Herr Menke," Kurt Dilmann continued, carefully choosing his words, "we Germans are getting sentimental with the years; we want to see in front of us everything that reminds us of the past. Some of us try to use any opportunity to meet old friends. But the people who occupy high-level positions are too pressed for time. So they'd like to see even half-forgotten letters and photos, for instance." Dilmann paused. Then he offered Rupert a cigarette. Rupert could not allow himself to refuse. He smoked one. But his fingers were visibly shaking, and Dilmann saw it.

"As we know, Herr Menke, you keep some of those half-forgotten photos. We'd like you to give them us voluntarily." There was a long, significant pause.

Sticky sweat covered Rupert from the head to the toe. Even though he wasn't the most intelligent man, he understood that now his life was on the table. If he gives the photos to this man, he is done. They would simply kill him. How smart that he'd hidden the pictures in a different place the day after Eliza had seen them! But if they press her…Rupert was terrified. Drops of sweat fell on his trembling hands. No, she'd keep her mouth shut, she doesn't like Nazis, Rupert thought. He remembered the following day he had told Eliza that he'd destroyed the photos.

"But I don't have the photos any more, Herr Officer," Rupert whispered. His face was red. "When I got married, my wife found them, and we tore them up. She was jealous of my past." He swallowed and shook his head.

Kurt Dilmann kept silent, analyzing Menke's answer. Perhaps, he thought, this Menke lies, and he kept the photos. A search of Menke's house was underway, and obviously would give the answer. His people were professionals; if photos were in that house, they would definitely find them. In that case, this Menke was a dead man. But there was also the possibility that he told the truth, and photos had already been destroyed. Let's wait until the search is done, Kurt Dilmann decided finally.

"It would be better Herr Menke to think twice longer than to quickly give a wrong answer," Dilmann remarked philosophically. "Think longer. I'll see you tomorrow."

He pressed a button on his desk, and a policeman showed Rupert to a cell. If there weren't that fuckin' remark near his name, Dilmann thought, it would be much easier to make the right decision.

Within two hours, one of Dilmann's men reported that the search had negative results. They found only two friendly letters from the Fuhrer, addressed to Rupert Menke, and a photo in which they both were in the military uniform. The result of the search only justified the remark "to be careful."

Rupert had spent an awful night in the cell. Obviously in the case of torture, he would have given them the photos, but he was lucky to avoid it. When he was transferred to one of the small concentration camps in Berlin's suburbs, he realized that Dilmann's people had found nothing. It was a camp for "privileged citizens." It looked more like a sanitarium, with only one restriction—'patients' weren't allowed to leave. His imprisonment was only a warning to keep his mouth shut; Rupert Menke understood it.

Within a month, he returned home, obedient and silent. The past did not exist any more, he told himself. The world had changed; it was high time to realize it. Do not talk, do not see, do not remember, and you'll keep your life.

But soon Rupert Menke was called to Berlin. This time fate prepared a present for him—he was awarded with the gold sign of the Nazi Party. After the decoration, Rupert had a three-minute chat with Hitler. He curved his lips slightly when Rupert reminded him of an old soldiers' joke. He wasn't Adolf from Rupert's past; he was the Fuhrer—powerful and unpredictable. Now Rupert Menke hated him.

Soon after Rupert returned home, he was 'elected' the *Oberburghomaster* of Murnau.

CHAPTER 6

▼

A little town in Bavaria, Murnau, was a few minutes from Garmish-Partenkirchen, and about an hour from Munich. *Oberburghomaster's* duties did not take too much of Rupert's time; he officially approved only decisions that were already made by Nazi Party officials. But he tried to spend as much time as possible in his office in order to see Eliza as seldom as possible.

For a long time, Eliza had been drinking excessively. Half prostrate, hair across her face, she looked for bottles all over the house. Not always finding them, she gave Rupert noisy arguments. However, not even a bottle would always shut her mouth. In such moments, Heinrich was afraid of his parents' eyes. He used to lock his room's door, and sat quietly, trying to read a book or to think about something pleasant, remembering his recent past.

One of his first memories was his first impression of a railroad. It was evening, and the locomotive, with its great lights rolling to a stop, created an unforgettable impression. Listening to his parents' arguments, Heinrich often dreamed about that locomotive which would take him far away from Murnau, from the house where he lived, and from his parents.

Although Heinrich was not a particularly unruly child, he was very independent, and took a certain delight in shocking Murnau's respectable citizens. One Sunday morning, he had ridden into a church on the back of his St. Bernard dog. This produced a complete panic, when some of the engrossed worshipers mistook the harmless animal for a wild beast. Women fainted; men rushed outside shouting. But the uproar didn't disturb the calm of Heinrich's St. Bernard, which ambled through the church and delivered him to his mother's side. Surprisingly, Heinrich survived this desecration without any particular harsh punishment. He didn't hear Rupert told Eliza, "Your fuckin' Jew will never be a German, I knew it!" The next day Rupert sold the dog, and when Heinrich learned that he had lost his only friend, he silently cried in his pillow for days.

At school, he wasn't considered a very capable student; the situation at home prevented him from concentrating on his studies. But being the *Oberburghomaster's* son, he always received good grades. The school's atmosphere changed imperceptibly, but drastically. Old teachers who had taught traditional, conservative knowledge vanished. Young, self-confident teachers changed them. They knew their subjects much less well, but spoke a great deal about the grandeur of German nation. For Heinrich, the grandeur of the nation was connected with the names of father-*oberburghomaster* and mother-alcoholic. He never doubted in the grandeur of the nation, but would have preferred to have calmer atmosphere around him.

At fourteen years old, Heinrich was a reserved, unsociable boy—the result of the eternal bitter disagreements between his parents. At school, he kept a distance from other students and never had friends. But neither did he support his more aggressive schoolmates who tried to compensate for a lack of knowledge with ultra-patriotism. However, nobody wanted to spoil his relationship with Heinrich. Everybody knew he was not only the *Oberburghomaster's* son, but also the godchild of the Fuhrer himself. Knowing Heinrich's biography, the new school teachers-guards already worshipped him.

Heinrich's class was extremely Aryan, extremely blond, and extremely dull. The only exception was Arnold Goldberg, the son of the rich Munich merchant who sold furs. In Murnau, all respectable mothers wore Goldberg's fur coats.

The whole class tried to humble him, but Arnold was patient and never expressed any emotion. The boy who tried more than any others to humiliate him was Otto Lickner, a stocky blond, with colorless, fish eyes. He often provoked Arnold, but Arnold, who was physically very strong and obviously could easily have beaten Lickner, preferred to endure the insults.

Although Heinrich never felt any particular sympathy for Arnold, his obedience irritated him.

"Why can't you beat up Lickner, Arnold?" Heinrich asked him at their break. "Don't be a piece of shit. Be a man!"

Arnold looked at Heinrich with surprise, and then stepped aside without words.

The next day, in answer to the habitual of "fuckin' Jew," Arnold, to surprise of the whole class, punched Lickner and broke his nose. Crying Lickner run away to complain to a teacher, and Arnold was immediately called to the principal's office. He was expelled for two weeks.

When he came back to the class, nobody greeted him with mocking *"Guten morgen,* fuckin' Jew," but it turned out there was no free school desk for him; every student had placed his school bag on surrounding seats, effectively demonstrating that they did not want to sit near him.

At a loss, Arnold stood at the door until Heinrich waved him over, pointing to a seat near him. Heinrich's behavior was so defiant that he obviously would be shunned. The whole school knew what had happened, and everybody condemned him. But Heinrich wasn't just "a student"; not every school could boast that they had among its students the Fuhrer's godchild.

The principal called the *oberburghomaste*r and had a long talk with him.

When Heinrich came home, Father met him in the entry and, saying nothing, gave him such a box on the ear that Heinrich fell to the floor. Having heard a noise, Mother rushed out.

"Don't touch him!" she yelled, alarm, self-pity, fury, trembling as she supported her breasts with a shaking hand.

She wasn't entirely sober as she dashed at her husband with her fists. The usual fight began between them and Heinrich, using the excuse, ran upstairs to his room, locking the door. But he heard Mother scream that, in any case, Father's "*blodes Nazischwein*" would not keep him alive.

Heinrich fell on his bed. Tears of powerlessness and anger fell from his eyes as somebody had opened the valve in his soul. The sobs last for a long time but produce few tears. His shudders weren't from sobbing. Heinrich's tears were tears of angry calmness. Drowning in his sea of tears, Heinrich fell asleep at last.

The next day, on the way to school, he waited until he saw Arnold, and approached him. "Sorry, Arnold," he said gloomily. "I'm the same piece of shit as everybody else."

Arnold looked at him with a wide-eyed gaze, but Heinrich had already stepped aside. Then he stopped, turned around, and repeated one more time. "I am very sorry."

Entering the classroom, Heinrich sat at another desk.

CHAPTER 7

▼

Eliza was becoming more uncontrollable with every day. Her predilection for alcohol helped her stun the pricks of her conscience that woke up in her soul.

Everything began five years previously when, sick with pneumonia, she lay on the bed, delirious with a high fever. In her delirium, she saw the bloody face of the woman in the car crash. The woman held out her hands to Eliza, trying to clutch her throat and crying, "Give me back my son."

After three days hovering between life and death, Eliza recovered consciousness. In a week, thin and silent, she went to church and prayed for forgiveness. She stayed in front of the crucifixion for a long time as she hoped to hear the Lord's words. But the Lord kept silent. Eliza left the church only after the priest told her that they were closing.

At that moment, Eliza realized that there would be no forgiveness. Since that day she drank heavily. Alcohol used to bring relaxation and oblivion. Sometimes, an unexpected tenderness to Heinrich fulfilled her soul. She passionately pressed him to her breast and whispered, "God's with you, my boy." During those moments, she looked at his face so steadfastly as if she had never seen him before.

Heinrich was far from a stereotypical German Jew. He had a straight nose, rigid hair, cat green eyes, and long, fluffy eyelashes. Looking at him, all the neighborhood girls lost their heads.

Heinrich tried to put his mother off gently—the odor of alcohol was too strong. Eliza felt his intuitive reaction and it often turned her tenderness into rage.

She pushed Heinrich away, and hurried to the kitchen to drink another glass of schnapps. In such moments, she always muttered some insulting words, but Heinrich could never understand them.

Mother's hard drinking usually continued for seven or eight days. After that, she would again become indifferent to everything. Unfortunately, with the years of hard drinking, the periods when she couldn't control her behavior became longer and longer. She loudly abused "all Nazi homosexual shit," including "the beloved Fuhrer."

While Eliza and Rupert were at the Munich Opera listening to Richard Wagner's *Tannhausen* performed by the famous conductor Herbert von Karajan, Eliza felt her heart beat like a bird in a cage.

At first Eliza told herself, "It's not a big deal. It's just too stuffy in here." But minutes passed by, and her heart beat faster and faster. She was drenched in sticky sweat. Frightened, Eliza tried to concentrate on the opera and to dispel her fear. But following the events on the stage became more and more difficult. She suddenly laughed without any reason, and Rupert looked at her surprisingly. "What's funny?" He asked, but she didn't respond. For Eliza, it seemed that she came to a different, absurd reality that she'd never experienced before. Now her eyes were full of tears, she felt dizziness.

"Rupert, I'm not quite well," she told him and blinked. "I have to go out."

But Rupert didn't want to follow her; he liked Wagner's music. It was rare that they went to the opera together.

"Get out of here and sit outside to take a fresh breath," he advised her.

"Sorry, but I cannot reach the exit alone," Eliza whispered as she staggered.

But as Rupert looked at her pale, moist face, he agreed, "Calm down, Eliza. Let's go out, and I'll call for a doctor."

They stood and went slowly from their seats to the door with a red 'exit' sign above it. Eliza's heart beat as if it were ready to jump out of her breast. She had no doubt that she would die in a moment. The panic seized her but she knew she was alive; she had a feeling she could even touch life as if life was a solid thing, like a ring on her finger. She has never had such a feeling before in her life. Then the unexplainable fear flooded Eliza, panic that Rupert would kill her as soon as they reach the exit door; she knew definitely that it wasn't the exit door but a door to another world full of emptiness and death.

By a force of all her will, Eliza tried to calm herself, and her world began to fall back. But when they reached the hall, her panic returned. Automatically Eliza marked one strange thing; the field of her vision narrowed to a very small, bright disk, and all the rest was foggy. Around her, she saw a mass of crying women's faces. But only one of them was bloody; it was the face of the woman from the car crash.

For several minutes, the color returned to Eliza's face; her heartbeat was normal as before; and her panic disappeared.

"Sorry, Rupert," she said as they got in the car to drive home. "I spoiled your evening."

"Don't mention it." Rupert leaned back in the seat, smiling gently. He was still under Wagner's influence.

But four days later, the feeling of death flooded her again. Colors became sharper. Eliza picked up a bottle of wine and, convulsively, drank it in several large gulps. Her panic had gone, but all things around her seemed now funny and absurd. She came to the mirror and studied carefully her face. Why do people need to see their reflections if they wear such ugly faces, she wondered. She looked at the clock hanging in the hall and mused on why the clock's hands were running from the left to the right but not vice versa. They would show the same time, she thought absent-mindedly. She opened the wardrobe, looked at her dresses and wondered why people needed to cover their bodies if they were born naked like animals. In any case, they behave like animals, she thought.

Eliza's panic attacks became as habitual as a runny nose, but she always felt it was approaching. The only treatment to escape that fear was alcohol.

One of such hard drinking period coincided with the *Oberburghomaster's* party at City Hall, dedicated to the Fuhrer's birthday. So Rupert Menke wearing a black suit coat, with a gold Nazi pin on the lapel, was alone. With a glass of champagne in his hand, he talked to one of the local businessmen, a man interested in acquiring a haberdashery factory. The owner, a Jew, had left the country. The businessman hinted openly about Menke's profit from the deal.

At that moment, *Shturmbanfuhrer* SS Manfred Rilbachter, the boss of a local SD, came up to them. With a glance at the bald, round-faced, haughty newcomer, the businessman quickly stepped aside. Rilbachter had climbed up his career ladder of command because he possessed the habit of weighing what a word was going to cost his bosses. Rilbachter and Menke were sympathetic to each other.

"*Heil Hitler*, Rupert." Rilbachter's round face grew even rounder with a smile, displaying his yellow front teeth, with a wide gap in the middle.

"*Zig Heil!*" Rupert shook Rilbachter's hand; the grip was strong.

"I see you're alone today. Frau Menke isn't well?"

"She's sick." Rupert sighed deeply.

"Unfortunately, she *is* sick," Manfred agreed. "And when she's sick, she compromises you as an official." Manfred's cold glance shrunk Menke. An awkward silence came, and then Rilbachter added, "And not only you, Rupert, unfortunately. I think you understand who we're talking about?"

Rupert's mouth grew dry, and he looked at Rilbachter in an earnest, deranged way. "She is sick," he repeated quietly as if Eliza's sickness could defend her behavior.

"That's why we recommend that you, Rupert, to take care of her treatment." Rilbachter leaned forward in a friendly, confidential manner. He again called Menke "Rupert" instead the official "Herr Menke."

Like a schoolboy standing in front of his teacher, Rupert kept gloomy silence. Rilbachter took his elbow. "You have to take care of Frau Menke's health. Why not send her to the sanitarium in Badenzee? It's not cheap of course, but I think you can afford it, can't you?"

"I can." Everything was for the best, Rupert told himself. Maybe it would be the best decision. "It's not a matter of money," he added.

Rilbachter nodded. "That's right. It's not a matter of money. It's more a matter of life." He winked at Rupert. They understood each other.

In a fortnight, with the help of Rilbachter's protégé Doctor Tichter, Rupert persuaded Eliza of the necessity of admitting herself to a drug and alcohol rehabilitation clinic. Eliza had listened to Dr. Tichter with disbelief, her hands clasped under her chin. Then she gave an exhausted nod, and turned to Rupert. "Do it." Her eyes filled with a sort of tearful fury. Eliza was a clever woman; she understood everything with half a word. Then she turned abruptly and left Dr. Tichter's office.

The next day, Rupert drove her to a special sanitarium, a place where, for last five years, no patient had ever left alive. Eliza Menke was not the exception. She died seven months later.

CHAPTER 8

▼

Learning of Eliza's death, Rupert Menke felt a mixture of relief, grief, and mild sadness. Although their marriage had never been one in the common sense of the word, Eliza, for many years, was his life partner. Even if she had not been a devoted wife, she had never betrayed him. He knew that when he was arrested, she had kept her mouth shut. Otherwise, he would be dead. When Heinrich appeared in their family, Rupert and Eliza grew closer. Perhaps they both realized they became co-conspirators in a murder case.

But Rupert had no paternal feelings for Heinrich. It had nothing to do with the boy. Obviously, even if Heinrich had been his biological son, nothing would have changed.

Sometimes Rupert thought if his indifference to women was debauchery or God's punishment. His mother was a pious woman, and he knew that homosexuality was one of the deadly sins. But wasn't it an even bigger sin to pour innocent blood in the war?

The first of Rupert's decisions was to bury Eliza quietly at the sanitarium's cemetery. But her father who was still alive, but in a wheelchair, insisted that she be buried at home, in Murnau. Rupert could not refuse his father-in-law who had never interfered in his and Eliza's family life, so he called to have the body delivered to Murnau.

To his surprise, at the cemetery Rupert saw Eliza's Cousin Katherine with her husband. Katherine, in her late forties, was a well-preserved, very tall, very haughty woman. Rupert considered her good looking, but there was too much of her to take in at one glance. Her husband, Berlin University Professor Otto Dornberger, was a lean man, with a deep voice, thick glasses and crumpled face. While in Berlin, Eliza sometimes had visited them, though they were never very close. Rupert had never been in their home, considering Katherine's husband a snob. There was too large a gap in education and life perception between them.

The day of the funeral was gloomy. A light rain had ended, and the weak sun shone through broken clouds. Burying procedures did not take too much time. A priest read a short prayer, and the gravediggers quickly finished their work. There were no speeches, no tears, no sobbing. One unhappy woman had left this world.

After the funeral, as usual in such cases, serving a short meal and drink, Katherine said, "I think Rupert, now it will be a very difficult time for you. Heinrich's already getting to be a teenager and he needs much attention." She spoke carefully.

Rupert nodded. His face was red from the schnapps he had drunk. "There's nothing to be done," he said. "God gives, God takes."

"Without a woman at home, it's impossible to bring up a son," Otto Dornberger said, nodding his head in agreement.

"Do you want me to marry someone the day after Eliza's funeral?" Rupert asked brusquely, and grinned wryly.

"Don't pretend to be worse than you are, Rupert," Katherine said mildly. She came to him with a smile of someone who had achieved a goal. "We only want to help."

Rupert glanced at her questioningly.

"Let Heinrich live with us until you regain your soul's calmness after Eliza's death," Katherine said.

The offer was unexpected. But Rupert didn't think long. He looked at her attentively, wondering as if they could guess that he had no paternal feelings for Heinrich. After all these years, he still couldn't call him son.

"Won't Otto object?" Rupert raised an eyebrow.

"No. I've talked to him. We have two daughters, but Otto always wanted to have a son. He would be happy if his nephew lived with our family. It will be good for all the children too."

"Okay," Rupert said, "I think life in Berlin will be good for Heinrich. Frankly, here in Murnau, he had nothing in common with most of his classmates. Heinrich isn't very sociable. And I'm too busy with my o*berburghomaster's* duty."

"We understand that official duties take all your time, Rupert." A brief glint of mockery sparkled in Katherine's eyes, but she rapidly extinguished it.

"Heinrich!" Rupert called for his son and, when he came in, said, "Your aunt and I have decided that you would live with them in Berlin for a while."

Heinrich kept silent, but his heart jumped with joy. He always dreamed of leaving this house where he felt unreasonable fear. It was the fear of feeling the hatred in Father's eyes, or the strike of drunken Mother's eyes in his back. He could only dream about it—not going to Murnau School and not seeing all the disgusting faces around him. Had his dreams really come true?

"As you wish, Dad," Heinrich said and glanced at Aunt Katherine. She smiled him softly, and he loved her at first sight.

"I think you'll like your new sisters, Heinrich," she said. "They're almost the same age as you, and you'll have a lot in common."

Dornberger shook Heinrich's hand. "At last I'll see another man in my house." He gave Heinrich a friendly smile. "You can't imagine how it is difficult to take care of a family consisting of three women."

Heinrich returned the smile. In his home, he was unaccustomed to experiencing a sense of humor.

CHAPTER 9

▼

The Dornberger family occupied a huge five-bedroom apartment on the third floor of an ancient six story building in the center of Berlin, on the tree-lined *Lentzealle,* a block from *Kaizerstrasse.* Otto Dornberger was a famous professor at Berlin University, head of the Department of Molecular Biology.

The atmosphere at Dornberger's home sharply differed from that of Heinrich parents' house in Murnau. In the evenings, Professor Dornberger's colleagues often gathered there to discuss medical problems, as well as to exchange opinions about Germany's political issues. All the visitors were talented people, but ultra-chauvinistic.

Professor Dornberger himself was one of the initiators of "Manifesto 300," in which three hundred leading representatives of the German scientific community appealed to the world's common opinion to understand the aims of the German nation.

Otto Dornberger's daughters Martha and Eva, blond, good looking, and intelligent girls, became quickly Heinrich's friends. Martha was barely five feet four, with a soft curving body, curly, light brown hair, and hazel eyes. Eva was taller and slender than her sister. Blue-green eyes, lighter, long hair. For the first time in his life, Heinrich experienced an atmosphere of benevolence, coziness and of family.

The school that he now attended also substantially differed from his previous one. Instruction was on a higher level; even the ultra-patriotism seemed Heinrich at a less hypertrophied level. In Berlin, he even had casual relationships among some of his schoolmates. He did not befriend everybody, but now he didn't need school friends. He spent all his free time with Martha and Eva. Together they read verses of Heine and Goethe or in rapture listened to Wagner's music.

Once Heinrich found in the sitting room an open book. He looked at the title: '*The History of Anti-Semitism in Germany.*' Why do we hate Jews? Heinrich pondered the thought as he sat on the sofa and read a page:

> "*The reasons of our hostile attitudes toward Jews come from ancient times. It's worth remarking that before Christianity spread over the world, persecution of Jews was sporadic and short-lived, although rather cruel as they were under the rule of the Emperors Caligula, Domitian, and Adrian. Christian campaigns sharply reinforced anti-Jewish tendencies in the Christian world. Many Jewish communities in France and Germany were totally destroyed.*
>
> *As ideology and a political movement, anti-Semitism was born in Germany at the end of 1870s. A preacher of King Wilhelm the First, Adolph Schtekker, turned his Social-Christian party in 1879 into an anti-Semitic party. It's worth mentioning here that the famous composer Richard Wagner also contributed to spreading anti-*

Semitism in Germany by publishing in 1869 his pamphlet "Jews in Music." Political aspects of anti-Semitism figured also in the works of the German journalist Wilhelm Marr. He was the first to use the term "anti-Semitism," by naming the group of his adherents "Anti-Semitic League."

Why was Professor Dornberger interested in this matter? Heinrich wondered. Perhaps using a case, I'll ask him the question, he decided. But as soon as Heinrich closed the book, it left his mind.

For Heinrich, his relationship with his father narrowed to sending and receiving Christmas cards. Obviously Rupert Menke had long recovered from his wife's death. But he had not the slightest wish to insist on Heinrich's return home. In his soul, Heinrich could not imagine returning home; he was accustomed to thinking of the Dornbergers house as his own.

Time in Berlin passed very quickly, and Heinrich arrived at his final examinations for his diploma. The exams consisted of two parts, oral and written, but Heinrich distinguished himself in the written portion, and was exempt from the oral. This suited him very well because preparing for orals demanded work such as learning poems by heart. But Heinrich had always had a poor memory for routine things and quickly forgot numbers, addresses, and the like. His memory was much more apt at retaining ideas, experiences, and books.

At last his graduation ceremony came, and Heinrich was chosen to deliver a speech for his class. He wasn't the best in his class, only one of the best, as the director said; and his choice was defined by patriotic considerations, by taking his godfather, the Fuhrer, into account.

The subject of his speech was Nietzsche. When he spoke, he added a few words to his prepared version, telling the audience about the conflict between teachers and students, the eternal conflict of generations; it produced considerable astonishment. Heinrich said that while they had admittedly been undisciplined and rebellious, this was attributable to their age, rather than to ill will. "We understand," he said, "the great aims of our great German nation."

At the banquet afterwards, Otto Dornberger was more than satisfied when parents of the other students congratulated him for having such a great nephew. He embraced his nephew. "I would be happy if you, Heinrich, joined the biology faculty," he suggested as if the question of Heinrich's future was already settled.

Several days later, he explained to Heinrich that he led a secret laboratory group doing research for *Wehrmacht*. "I hope that after you get your advanced degree from the university, Heinrich, you would join me in the 'family business.' You are my only hope. Serious medicine is not for girls." He smiled. "Martha attends the Berlin Conservatory, and Eva is now only choosing her way."

"It's a long way, Uncle," Heinrich agreed. "All the way to five years from now."

"Time flies, my boy." Dornberger's face was wreathed with a big smile.

Heinrich didn't object to becoming a doctor, and soon he entered Berlin University. For almost two full semesters, he attended lectures. But then he saw that bright, scientific researchers who were famous all over Europe had almost vanished, not to speak of the Jewish professors, most of whom had left Germany. They had been changed into colorless people. The new instructors wore civilian suits, but they looked more like *untersharfuhrers SS*. More and more every day, Heinrich was losing his interest in his studies. Now the university reminded him of the Murnau School.

Once, after the Sunday's family dinner, he surprised everybody at table by announcing his decision to quit the university and join the Cadet School.

"Now it's not the right time for studying, Uncle," he said, addressing Otto Dornberger. "The Fuhrer needs soldiers, not scientists."

Dornberger smiled. "I think he needs soldiers and scientists. Plus, Heinrich, the word 'scientist' can have different meanings. For somebody it can say only that a person studied science, nothing more. Alchemists also studied science, but for the sake of pure science. We German scientists do research for the sake of the German nation. There's a big difference. We are 'the brain center' that defines the policy of any state." He took his glasses off and peered at Heinrich. "I cannot agree with you, my nephew, but I respect your decision. This is a decision of a German patriot and a clever man," Otto Dornberger finished with a smile.

Heinrich understood what his uncle was trying to tell him.

CHAPTER 10

---▼---

When Heinrich expressed his wish to serve his motherland as a reason to join the army, it was the truth, but only half the truth.

The real reason for leaving the Dornberger house was truly another. For more than six months, Heinrich was like a man who received shelter, and then stole from his host.

Everything had begun on one Saturday evening when Otto and Katherine had already gone up to their bedrooms, but Martha, Eva and Heinrich continued their lotto game. Heinrich wasn't lucky, and on his card almost all the numbers were empty. Suddenly Martha joyfully clapped her hands; she had won the main prize of thirty marks. After passions leveled, everybody went to their room.

For several minutes before falling asleep, Henry had been reading *Zaratustra*; he liked Nietzsche's philosophy. At last he switched off the lamp and closed his eyes. Just as he was about to fall asleep, he heard someone quietly opened the door of his room. A dark, silent figure slipped into his bed, and he heard Martha's whisper. "I'm cold, Heinrich, make me warm!"

Heinrich was speechless. Such a scenario had never entered his mind—even in his dreams. Martha's hand rose to his cheek. Long fingers traced the contours of his face, touched his lips, and caressed his eyelids. She bent her head to touch her lips very lightly to his.

Heinrich was still a virgin, and a shiver ran through him. Martha kissed his trembling lips, and Heinrich could not control himself reaching for her naked body. Then she groaned so loudly that Heinrich was afraid she would be heard all over the house. He pressed his palm to her lips so forcefully that Martha almost choked. But it only increased her satisfaction. Finally Heinrich shuddered and groaned, pulling her against him so hard that at that moment Martha could not breathe.

Speechless, they lay silent for minutes. Everything had happened so unexpectedly for Heinrich that he could not find words. Did he like Martha? He considered her a relative. What could he say? That everything was wonderful, and Martha was the first girl he had? Then he realized that Martha was not a virgin. Swarm of thoughts passed through in his mind, but he could not find any words for her. Not breaking the silence, Martha slid her nightgown on and slipped away.

In the morning, all drank tea and chatted about innocuous things. Martha's blue eyes sparkled with innocent purity.

Heinrich spent several sleepless nights in expectation of Martha's next visit. Black circles under his eyes betrayed his expectations, but Martha did not come. At last the door of his room quietly opened, and a woman's figure slipped again into his narrow bed. He gave her a nervous smile, but she could not see it in the darkness. Then Heinrich moved toward her in a dreamlike way, covering her by kisses. She expressed little emotion today, and Heinrich thought she might be upset. Entering her, Heinrich felt tears on her face. Surprised, he switched on the lamp and saw…Eva. She smiled at him through her tears, and switched the light off. Later, leaving the room, Eva said quietly, "Thank you, Heinrich." She was a polite German girl.

L'amoure aux troix continued for several months, but with each day Heinrich grew gloomier. At the base of his irritation was the contempt he felt for himself—the "innocent" girls simply used him for their sexual satisfaction. But he could not break the vicious circle.

The only right decision he could find was to enter a military school. It would be a plausible explanation. And he made his choice.

Heinrich informed his father of his decision to enter a military school, and received a letter indicating that Rupert was proud of him. He always knew that the Fuhrer's godchild would be a devoted servant of the Fuhrer. As a sign that he approved Heinrich's decision, Rupert Menke sent him a watch that had belonged to Eliza's father, recently deceased.

Military School did not leave any bright memories for Heinrich. Only two years of routine military studies. His superior officers knew that he was the Fuhrer's godchild and did their best to create a German idol from him—they facilitated Heinrich's life as much as possible. It didn't cause any love from the other cadets, but Heinrich, as in school and the university, had no close friends.

On August 28, 1939, on the eve of the beginning of the World Was II, Heinrich was promoted to the rank of lieutenant. Rupert Menke, in a black suit, with a gold Nazi emblem on the lapel, and Otto Dornberger who now wore a black uniform of the *schtandartenfuhrer* SS, attended the ceremony. Rupert pumped Dornberger's hand in greeting. Recalling Verdun, he said that the war was more awful when they worried about it than when they were at the front. "It's only due to your influence, Otto, that my son became a man," he said. "Believe me; I'm very grateful to you."

"He's our son," Otto Dornberger responded, indulgently. "We have both done our best."

However Lieutenant Heinrich Menke was not sent to a *Wehrmacht* unit. *Schtandartenfuhrer* SS Otto Dornberger recommended him for the Main Headquarters—*Reichschancellery*; he was sent to the department of coordination for scientific work for *Wehrmacht*. Otto Dornberger wanted to have his own man in the headquarters, and the head of the department, *Gruppenfuhrer* SS Zigfrid Schwartzkopf, was Dornberger's university friend.

The Fuhrer's godchild did not require a special clearance check, and soon he was introduced to Hitler.

"Heinrich Menke? Of course, I remember," Hitler said and tapped Heinrich on the cheek. "With such long eyelashes, you have a dangerous appearance for attracting girls, my boy. I am afraid all the women at my headquarters will be mad for you. Be very afraid of being raped!" he added, being in good spirits.

Hitler proceeded further, and the people around him smiled politely. Then they followed him away.

Hitler was right. The lieutenant with long eyelashes soon became famous all over the entire headquarters for his amorous adventures. Every secretary or receptionist dreamed of finding herself in Heinrich's bed, not only because of the rumors about his numerous victories had reached every office, but also because it was very flattering to sleep with the Fuhrer's godchild. All of them were very patriotic ladies.

Headquarters did not suffer from Puritanism if the affairs didn't touch the purity of the Aryan race, and Heinrich turned out to have been a good student learning the lessons of Dornberger's daughters.

Within two years, rumors of Heinrich's affairs reached the Fuhrer. Once, when they met in the hall and his godchild was frozen in "*Heil,*" Hitler stopped and again tapped his cheek. "They say, Heinrich, that you have spoiled almost all my female personnel. But I'm not angry at you." He smiled, being on the top of his spirits. His troops had conquered almost all of Europe. He took a step aside, and then stopped again. "Don't be in a hurry to be married, my child. Women kill a man." The retinue that accompanied him politely smiled.

PART II

▼

FORGET YOUR NAME

"…And bones of Baal's priests He burnt on their altars."

—Divrai Aiamim, II. 34.

CHAPTER 11

▼

The unlucky blitzkrieg in the war with the Soviet Russia, the defeat of the German armies in Stalingrad, the capture of Field Marshall Paulus, and the defeat of Field Marshall Rommel's army in Africa had already put its print on Germany. Berlin was not an exception. Air raid sirens accompanying bombardments of allied flights became as normal as the destroyed buildings in the center of the city.

Heinrich Menke's life did not change much although there were already captain's epaulettes on his shoulders. He spent all his free time in a rented apartment, not too far from headquarters. Tired of "patriotic girls," he preferred being alone, reading a book.

In all those year, he had not seen Uncle Otto often. Almost a year previously, Dornberger had sent his wife Katherine and both daughters to the Alps; it turned out all three had weak lungs and needed the treatment of fresh mountain air. Occasionally Otto Dornberger invited Heinrich to dinner. The meals were always enriched by a few bottles of old Bordeaux or Courvoisier. After he smoked a cigar, he remembered the "golden old days" when Germans were the "true people." At such moments, his cold eyes behind tinted lenses became sad as he exposed another layer of emotion.

Otto Dornberger's offer via the telephone to celebrate Christmas together wasn't unexpected; Heinrich knew that his uncle loved him. He reciprocated the warm feelings.

"Neither Katherine nor the girls are coming, so we'll chat a little together. Do you object?" He sighed on the other end of the line. Images of his wife and children flashed through his thoughts.

Heinrich did not object. Having a chat with Professor Dornberger was much more pleasant than an aimless party at one of the officers' clubs. At any rate, while talking to his uncle, Heinrich needn't be afraid of every spoken word, especially now, when defeatism was felt everywhere.

"No objection, Your Honor." Heinrich smiled.

"Thank you, Heinrich. You are the best nephew in the world." Dornberger hung up. He sat in the chair and began rubbing his forehead.

He felt a strange attraction to this young man. Really they were not relatives. The son of Katherine's cousin, Heinrich was nobody to him, but he felt more than the usual relative's emotion for the young man; it could be called closer to a father's love. Perhaps it had happened because Professor Dornberger, even after he became a scholar, had no scientific pupils-followers. Maybe he didn't acquire pupils because he didn't create his doctrine?

But hadn't his hard work led him to the point where he had collected unique scientific data that gave a push to developing many new directions for medicines of the future? Medical liberals in white gloves could judge him because he experimented on people. But he only used the unique opportunity that the war had given him. Scientists did not begin wars. They took part in them. Nobody could live in a society and be free of it, as fairly said the Russian Communist leader. He, Professor Dornberger, lived in German society. He was also not free of it.

Dornberger sighed and opened a folder with the information about the patients delivered recently from the concentration camp. He read the names of the prisoners:

- Aaron Goldberg, 57, engineer, imprisoned for 3 years;

- Baruch Melman, 64, shoemaker, imprisoned for 2 years;

- Sarah Meir, 41, bookkeeper, imprisoned for 1 year;

- Rachel Gecht, 18, pianist, imprisoned for 3 years.

After the last name, there was a remark *'she is the daughter of Arnold Gecht, Chairman of the German Zionist Organization. He was terminated in 1942.'*

Otto Dornberger marked the last name with a red pencil. The rest, he thought, were useless material. He reread the girl's name one more time, and closed his eyes.

Why did he choose only Jews for his experiments? It was understandable that *Schtandartenfuhrer SS* Otto Dornberger was an anti-Semite. But why must professor Otto Dornberger be an anti-Semite?

Many times throughout his life, he had tried to find the answer that question. He was not a genetic anti-Semite. Neither his mother nor his father had that feeling; the atmosphere of anti-Semitism never existed in his family.

Moreover, little Otto knew that his mother's grandfather was a Jew. Dornberger grinned. As a *schtandarterfuhrer SS,* he was not crystal clear on his race estimation although such distant

Jewish blood hadn't been really taken into account. With the same success, *Obergruppenfuhrer SS* Heidrich could be blamed for not being a pure Aryan because his grandmother's second husband wore the last name Zuss.

For all his life, he had hated Jews although none of them had ever done anything bad to him. In his scientific career, he was cleverer, more educated, more talented, and more purposeful than all his equals, including Jews. He became a tenured professor at Berlin University at age twenty-six, the youngest for all the centuries of the university's history. But why, in such a case, did he hate his Jewish colleagues so much that he could not calm himself until old Chancellor Michael Schechtel was imprisoned in a concentration camp and soon died there?

Otto Dornberger tried to understand the source of his anti-Semitism. Not understanding hurt him as a scientist because consequences could not exist without reason. At last, many years of soul digging has brought results; he has found the reason. It turned out to be a ten-year-old girl named Dora Leibman who had lived next door. She had not invited little Otto to the party to celebrate her 11th birthday. Otto was so upset that he sobbed behind his closed bedroom door. When his tears dried, he realized that he hated Dora.

For the first time in his life, conceited Otto was painfully rejected. Despite the fact that in the future he had never experienced anything similar, the feelings of rejection, humiliation, confusion and injustice created an indelible track in his soul; he hated all Jews considering them the source of all German misfortunes.

'*Post factum*,' he always found confirmation of his negative feelings. Wasn't the Jew Karl Marx equipping plebes with his harmful *Capital*? Weren't the Jews leaders of the German Revolution Karl Libcnecht and his *comrades* who tried to export a Russia-style Communist revolution to Germany? Wasn't the Jew Sigmund Freud debauching Germany with his sexology?

Otto Dornberger stood up and restlessly walked to a window to open it. Far away, just above the horizon, the half-moon was glistening on churning waves. He had the sickening feeling of hearing that little girl's voice, the one who didn't invite him to her birthday party fifty years ago. Maybe she was among his patients, he thought. Returning to the desk, he opened the lower drawer and took out a bottle of cognac. He poured a little in a small glass and gulped it down. Then he again picked up the sheet of paper with the names on it. It's worth sending all of them back, except that girl, he thought. They're human garbage. Like a harbinger of the rain, a drop of sweat plopped from his forehead onto the paper he held in hands, blurring a name. "I have to visit the camp myself before Christmas and select the proper material for my experiments," he muttered.

Dornberger wiped his forehead and squeezed his eyes shut, making the darkness darker, but menacing images were still harbored there. He was torn by longing and loneliness.

CHAPTER 12

In the office of his old comrade *Schtandartenfuhrer SS* Zigfrid Kuchlitz, the commandant of the concentration camp, Otto Dornberger relaxed in a comfortable armchair. The office was furnished in an academic style: a fireplace with a picture of Lucas Cranach above it, (Otto didn't doubt it was an original) two big, soft armchairs, and a huge desk. From ceiling to floor, the walls were covered with bookshelves filled mostly with books on philosophy. Before the war, *Schtandartenfuhrer SS* Zigfrid Kuchlitz had been a doctor of philosophy at Heidelberg University.

"The last time you sent me nothing but human garbage, Zigfrid!" Dornberger glared at Kuchlitz.

"Be afraid of God, Otto." Kuchlitz smiled. "Himmler requests so many prisoners to be exterminated that I don't have time to select the people who could be useful for your experiments or our mutual purposes." He took a piece of paper from the table and handed it to Dornberger. "Look. Here's the yesterday's schedule. From Poland, we received 1037 Jews; 950 were terminated and eighty-seven remain. We're way behind schedule, but what can I do? The oven's capacity is about 1,000 people a day. I don't have time to choose people for your experiments." Kuchlitz paused, and then he poured cognac in their glasses while Dornberger looked through the papers, with the inscription *Geheim* printed across the top of them—Most Secret. "For a moment, let's forget about our job, Otto. How are Katherine and your charming girls?"

"They're fine. You know, doctors have recommended that my girls change climate because of their asthma. I sent them in Baaden."

"In that case, give Katherine my best regards. I think the mountain air will be good for all of them." Dornberger couldn't miss mockery in Kuchlitz's voice. "What's new in our world of science? Since I am doing the dirty work, I am way behind."

"I cannot believe that." Dornberger smiled, pointing to the books around.

"That's not all science; this is my lifelong hobby." Kuchlitz stood up and went to one of the bookshelves. He chose a book and read aloud; '*When you look into the abyss, the abyss also looks onto you.*'"

"Nietzsche's genius did forecast the future. Can anybody consider himself a philosopher after him? Let's drink to the philosophy that rules the world!" He took a small gulp. "In what direction does our science go, Otto?" Kuchlitz licked a piece of lemon.

"In the direction all of us go—to the dead end." At seeing Kuchlitz's raised brow expressing open surprise, Dornberger explained, "Science always comes to the dead end, and later always seeks an exit from it." The devil knows Kuchlitz, he thought. Despite the fact that he's my friend and a business partner, it's best not to be too frank with him. After von Schtaufenberg's plot against the Fuhrer failed, even a devoted Nazi was afraid of his shadow.

"That's right, Otto," Kuchlitz agreed. "All of us are seeking an exit from the dead end. But do we find it?" He fell into a speculating silence.

There was a hint to the frankness in his question, but Dornberger pretended not to understand it.

"At the beginning of 1943 I attended a coordination meeting at the department of scientific research for the *Wehrmacht.* There the Fuhrer verified two main directions; the first was von Braun's research and the production of FAU; the second, Dr. Heisenberg's work on creating of the atomic bomb." Dornberger said with a bland face.

"Alas, the Allies has destroyed all our heavy water stock in Holland," Kuchlitz remarked, and Dornberger understood that his friend wasn't behind the news at all.

"Alas," he agreed quietly. "That's why this work is off schedule."

"The atomic bomb was the only thing that could save Germany," said Kuchlitz. "Of course *Wehrmacht* will kill hundreds of thousands more of our enemy's soldiers, and people like us will terminate hundreds of thousands of civilians in the ovens. But frankly speaking, our work already has lost its sense. We understand the miracle will not come; the war is going to end."

Dornberger sighed deeply and gulped his drink. "We are Germans," he said. "We have to continue even a useless job as forcefully as before until we receive an order to stop. Unfortunately we will never receive that order. We are a nation not of creators, but of destroyers. By the way Zigfrid, we've already come so far in our eagerness that there is no way back. If, having terminated hundreds of thousands civilians, tomorrow you would save a thousand, it won't play any role in the estimation of your personality; if tomorrow several dozen of my patients remain alive, it wouldn't change anything in my estimation. The problem is who would be the judges? If Germany judged us, we would be heroes; if the Allies, we would be criminals."

"Damn the Allies!" Kuchlitz gulped his cognac. "Don't think about tomorrow. Today, von Braun's rockets fall on London and even reach New York. I think we still have some time at our disposal not to think about tomorrow." There was a hopeful note in his voice. "Let's go, Otto, I'll show you material that can interest you." Kuchlitz raised his heavy body from the chair.

"Zigfrid is too optimistic with his forecast." Dornberger grinned, following him.

CHAPTER 13

The laboratory where Professor Dornberger worked was located in a small suburban town, a forty minutes ride from Berlin. The day was gray and rainy, and Heinrich was not afraid of the Allies aviation blasts. The highway was empty. Twice the SS patrol stopped his car, but upon seeing the pass signed by Heinrich Himmler that allowed the owner free movement all over the Reich, the SS soldiers froze in a "Heil Hitler." Heinrich would have had trouble finding the laboratory if not for the second motorized patrol that accompanied his car to the entrance.

The laboratory was perfectly camouflaged as a destroyed factory behind a tall brick fence. It was surrounded by barbed wire, with guard towers on the perimeter corners, and SS guards near the entrance. The whole complex reminded Heinrich of a small concentration camp; it was a real one, a special one.

Heinrich visited one such camp a year ago when he had accompanied a delegation of the International Red Cross headed by a Swiss Count Folke Bernadotte. In that camp, everything was very respectable: flowers on the windowsills, clean white linen on beds. And nobody complained.

It was 'a slow death camp.' Here prisoners were not asphyxiated with gas; they don't die of hunger, thirst, dysentery, consumption, and dystrophy. They didn't work until they dropped.

They were not guarded by the fierce police dogs, and guards, in most cases, didn't wear the SS uniform; instead, they wore white medical gowns.

But the prisoners wore the stripped clothing of convicts, and they fought death every day, every hour: they died being victims of 'scientific experiments.' What death was more painful?

"*Schtandartenfuhrer SS* Dornberger expects me." Heinrich handed his ID to the duty officer.

"I'll report about you right away, *Herr Hauptman*."

The *unterscharfuhrer* called, and in a few minutes another officer who had *oberscturmfuhrer's* epaulettes showed Heinrich into the administrative building.

"My name is Ditrich Reckmann. I'll personally let the *schtandartenfuhrer* know about you, *Herr Hauptman*." He saluted and left.

Heinrich looked around. Except for two big leather armchairs and a large picture of the Fuhrer, the walls were empty and sterile white, like in an ordinary medical institution. Tired of looking at the Fuhrer's face that was much younger and fresher on the portrait than in real life, he sat in an armchair.

Two people in white lab jackets have passed by—a man and a woman. They were forcefully discussing something understandable only to them. For the first time since he entered the building, Heinrich felt the atmosphere of a medical laboratory. At last the door in the far corner of the room opened, and he saw Uncle Otto's smiling face. He also wore a white coat, and Heinrich had the thought that no scientist in the world looked better than Professor Dornberger.

Dornberger embraced Heinrich. "At last I see you in my house of science, Heinrich! It's wonderful that you came this morning. Obviously you haven't had breakfast, so we'll have coffee in my study." He turned to the officer accompanying them from a distance. "Please set a table for two for breakfast." The officer silently disappeared.

Professor Dornberger's office in the lab was as similar as two drops of water to his office in his Berlin apartment, as Heinrich remembered it. The same photos of Katherine and his daughters were on the desk, the same lithographs by Dourer on the walls. Dornberger liked Dourer more than any other German painter. The only difference was a large portrait of the Fuhrer on the wall, but it was a necessary tribute to the society in which they lived.

They relaxed in the armchairs. Dornberger offered Heinrich a cigar and he did not refuse the Havana. Releasing a ring of smoke, Dornberger said, "I'm glad, Heinrich you visited my lab at last." He smiled. "You are such a nice looking man."

"I am in a *Wehrmacht* uniform; it creates a nice look." Heinrich returned the smile.

"And I think that in a white lab coat you would look even better." Dornberger laughed.

"Hospital attendants also wear white jackets, but I wouldn't like to be one of them."

"Dear Heinrich, I was one of the first who marked your ambitions. That's why I persuaded you to enter the medical faculty of the university. Even now, I think I was right. Frankly, your decision to enter military school surprised me."

Heinrich blushed, remembering both of Dornberger's daughters in his bed.

"Each of us makes the decision he considers right. Everything depends on obstacles."

"Everything depends on obstacles," Dornberger agreed.

They heard a knock at the door, and then Ditrich Reckmann pushed a wheeled table into the room, with breakfast for two on it, a bottle of cognac and two glasses attached. Dornberger took the bottle in hand and looked at the label. He liked Curvousier more than other French cognacs although Heinrich considered Martel was softer. Dornberger poured the cognac into their small glasses.

"Perhaps you want to ask me a question Heinrich, what am I working on here, in this lab?" he asked, pouring coffee in the small cups near the cognac glasses. "It's better black coffee, with lemon," he advised Heinrich, "if you want to drink cognac before breakfast." He held the cognac in his mouth for some time, and then swallowed. "I like to drink a small glass in the morning. It works as a stimulator for me for the whole day."

Heinrich followed his advice. The cognac was nice, soft and aromatic.

"What am I doing here?" Dornberger re-asked himself. And then he answered, "I'm studying the effect of cold on the human body. That's one of the directions of my research. Another direction, without any connection to the first, is my attempt to find the genes for geniality." He drank from his glass and licked a piece of lemon with sugar on it. Then he sipped his coffee and ate a small piece of bread with black caviar. "Don't take me as an example, Heinrich." He smiled. "I'm already an old man, but old people don't eat too much."

Schtandartenfuhrer SS Otto Dornberger definitely had no problem with delivering delicacies to his table. For some time they ate silently. At last Dornberger wiped his mouth and again smoked a cigar. Then he continued in the same manner in which he delivered his captivating lectures to his students at the university, "Ancient medical doctors were very much aware about cold's capability to decrease pain and inflammation, decrease the body's temperature, increase the resistance of the human body to unfavorable external influences. Hypocrites and Galen, Celsius and Abby Henna widely used cooling to treat different illnesses of the joints. For a long time, European people considered such treatment an eccentricity. They sharply changed their opinions in 1886, when the Bavarian Pastor Sebastian Knieppe published a book with the title *My Water Treatment.*" Otto Dornberger paused and released a mouthful of aromatic smoke. Then he smiled. "As you see Heinrich, in this field of science, we Germans were the ancestors of progress."

"What was amazing in his book, Uncle? Was in it anything that gave a push to scientific research?" Heinrich asked.

"Pastor Knieppe described that when he was very sick with pneumonia and exhausted with a high fever, he jumped into the icy cold water of Danube River; and how after that, he had quickly recovered."

"It contradicts everything that we're accustomed to," Heinrich remarked, "since we treat with heat."

"Heat's only the absence of cold, as cold is only the absence of heat," Dornberger explained indulgently. Then he sighed and added, "As evil is only the absence of good, and good is only the absence of evil." He again released a smoke ring. His cigar had burnt down a third of the way but the ash had not fallen off. At last Dornberger noticed it and shook it into an ashtray. "Knieppe's scientific method," he continued the lecture, "became the first codex of rules for cooling therapy; and what is remarkable, it hasn't lost any actuality even today. And today I continue the research that was begun by Pastor Knieppe. I study influence of the effects of temperature on the treatment of different diseases and injures in different age groups."

"How can you create statistics involving sick people with specific diseases, if the diseases don't become epidemics? Every case is an isolated one." Heinrich surmised.

"We have to create a disease to find a way to treat it." A weak smile touched Dornberger's lips but his eyes behind the glasses remained cold. "To find an antidote to a poison, we have to use the poison," he explained.

After those words, Heinrich felt a twinge of discomfort.

Dornberger recognized the change in his mood. "Later we'll return to the moral aspect of this," he said, "but now let's take a break. I want to show you my new device; I call it 'a cryogen cell.'"

Heinrich put on a lab coat and followed Dornberger to an adjacent building. Dornberger led him to a large, ugly metal construction. Then he explained, "Cooled, dry air gradually goes through one of the walls as a soft laminar flow, and then it is exhausted through the opposite wall. The temperature here remains no lower than minus 110 degrees Centigrade because we've not found any difference between hyper low cold, minus 180 degrees Centigrade, and ultra cold, about minus 110 degrees, in its affect on the human body."

"Those techniques are like a dark forest for me," Heinrich remarked, "but it's very interesting."

"It's *really* very interesting, Heinrich." Dornberger smiled. "As you understood, here we study a whole complex of problems, not only the medical but also physical and technical. We experiment with different carriers of the desired temperature—

cold water, ice, cooled liquids, gases, and so on. For example, the boiling temperature of liquid nitrogen is minus 196 degrees Centigrade. Such cold does not exist in nature on our planet."

"Can a man or a woman in a cell breathe nitrogen vapor?" Heinrich's face reflected his surprise.

Dornberger laughed. "Of course they cannot, Heinrich. In the experimental cabin, the entire body of the patient is experiencing the temperature of minus 140 C, but his head's at room temperature. As a result, the temperature gradient in different points of the body can reach 160 degrees Centigrade. This is still a field not well studied; of course we have a lot of technical problems, such as purification of the nitrogen vapor after using it. But these are problems for my technical associates. My problems are medical—research on the influence of extreme cold on the human body. I have already collected unique statistics on a wide age range from ten to sixty years old."

Heinrich imagined a ten-years-old child in the experimental cell, and was nauseated. "I need a drink, Uncle Otto," he said. "You flew such a volume of information at me that I need time to understand it all."

"Okay." Dornberger agreed indulgently. "Now I think you have an idea about my research. Sometimes it seems to me that this is Sizeuph's work. But when I look through the scientific data that I've received, I think that as a scientist, I hadn't lived vainly."

"What can I understand about science?" Heinrich said, and shrugged his drooping shoulders. "I'm only a *Wehrmacht* officer." Despite the fact that the walk through had taken no more than an hour, he felt exhausted.

They returned to Dornberger's study. A glass of cognac removed his tension, the thoughts of those ten years old children in the nitrogen cell departed.

The sharp sound of telephone interrupted silence.

Dornberger picked up the receiver. "We'll start in an hour, Willy. For today, use only sixty years old. I think we don't have any older at our disposal." He hung up.

"Let's get back to the moral aspect of my work," Dornberger said. He had not forgotten Heinrich's reaction. "I feel it worries you."

"I am an officer," Heinrich said matter-of-factly. "An officer cannot discuss the morality of war. Obviously from the point of view of morality, all wars are immoral. But an officer must accept war as it is." He took a big gulp of cognac.

"Morality!" Dornberger exclaimed bitterly. "What does 'morality' mean in science? There are two types of morality— morality as a harmony with myself as a scientist; and morality as a harmony with the society that science serves. Society changes, and that's why this type of morality also changes. This is bad morality because it easily turns into amorality if society is immoral. I don't serve society. I am a servant of science. As a scientist, I am in harmony with myself; and that's why my work is moral." Dornberger poured cognac into his glass and took a big swig. "Yes, I do experiments on prisoners, and hundreds of patients die during them. Do I feel sorry for it? No! Does the surgeon in the OR think of his patient as a human being? No. During surgery, the patient is only a work material. My patients were also only work material for me.

Peace, Heinrich, is a narrow path of progress; war is its highway. I move along that highway because the war gave me the unique opportunity to make progress in gigantic steps. If I had lived in peaceful Germany, I would experiment on dogs and monkeys. But I would get the same results I have received in my laboratory in five years, in the best case, in fifty years."

Heinrich had kept silent. He didn't know how he could object. Dornberger accepted his silence as agreement with his point of view. He took another drink of cognac, and continued his monologue, "I know that today's humanists can call my work criminal. But from another angle, it could be called a scientific deed. Everything depends on the point of view, and that point is totally subjective. If today's humanist read the results of my work, he would destroy them squeamishly as well as fifty or a hundred years of scientific progress. Yes, due to my work, several hundred people have died; but also due to my work, in the future you or another researcher will save thousands of lives. This is the positive balance in favor of future humanism.

In gas chambers, prisoners are terminated uselessly, for the sake of the advantage of German race. Most of us understood from the beginning that it was baloney; but it was pleasant to consider ourselves 'chosen people.' We consciously closed our eyes that we were the self-made 'chosen people' while God may have chosen other people. Maybe this is the starting point of hatred?" Dornberger closed his eyes and spoke as if he were talking to himself, as if he wanted to persuade himself about something understandable only to him.

Heinrich sipped his cognac and thought about how lonely his uncle was. The reason for today's frankness seemed to be the absence of friendly interlocutor.

"I'd like, Heinrich, you to use the results of my research in future, when you graduate," Dornberger continued. "Not for the sake of Germany and her future—all that's baloney—but for the sake of scientific progress. After the war, you'll graduate from the university and, with pure hands, will serve the same focus of science that I served with dirty ones." Otto Dornberger stopped talking and opened his eyes.

"Why do you think Uncle that I want to pursue medicine? I'm a military man."

"No, you are not, Heinrich." Dornberger laughed. "Your decision to join *Wehrmacht* was the spontaneous decision of a young man, made on the eve of war. Now the war is approaching its end and, unfortunately, not in our favor. You must think about your future."

"Don't think about tomorrow." Heinrich tried to joke but Dornberger didn't support it.

Silence came. It was interrupted only by the monotonous sound of the wall clock standing in the corner of the room. When it began to strike the hour, every sound reflected in Heinrich's head like a thunderstorm. At last the clock silenced.

"I'm glad that you came to my lab. I feel that the first visit remained a twofold impression in your soul. But the more you visit me the more you'll understand me." He poured cognac in their glasses and proposed a toast. "Let's drink to our mutual understanding, Heinrich."

Heinrich drank. The cognac gave him his heat and Heinrich felt comfortable. At any rate Uncle Otto was the only relative he enjoyed visiting. He was definitely not the worst man around. He looked at Dourer's lithograph on the wall, and pointed to them. "They remind me of those I've seen in your study in Berlin, Uncle. Are they the same?"

Dornberger smiled. "That's right. I think nobody but Dourer illustrated *The Divine Comedy* better. The difference is negligible. In Berlin, it was the illustrations to Paradise, here—to Purgatory." He looked at his watch. He was a punctual person and had not forgotten that he promised his assistant that he would be in the lab within an hour.

Dornberger embraced Heinrich and showed him to the door. *Oberschturmfuhrer* Ditrich Reckmann was waiting for him. Once outside, Heinrich looked at the sky. The gentle rain had stopped, and the moon peeked through broken clouds. They started walking.

"It's a great honor for me to serve *Schtandartenfuhrer* Dornberger," Reckmann said on their way. "He is a great German scientist." He hoped Heinrich would transmit his words to the *schtandartenfuhrer*.

They crossed the yard and came to the checkpoint. But a big military truck, with a closed tent over the back, blocked it and they had to wait until the guards pulled the prisoners out. Heinrich struggled to light a cigarette while they waited, succeeding after two minutes of contorting his body against the wind. One of the prisoners caught Heinrich's attention. It was a young girl who had hurt her leg jumping down from the high truck. She fell down to the ground and screamed with the unexpected pain. Her eyes began to tear, and she used every ounce of self-control in her possession to keep from crying. The SS guard ran to her, ready to strike her with his rifle, but Ditrich Reckmann stopped him. "Easy," he said impersonally. "This isn't the concentration camp, but Professor Dornberger's special laboratory."

"*Yavol, Herr Oberschturmfuhrer,*" the guard responded indifferently, and stepped aside.

The girl stood up and looked at Heinrich. She had the short black haircut of a prisoner and hectic, large sparkling eyes; they blinded Heinrich by hatred with such force that he began to shake.

Ditrich Reckmann referred the tremors to the cognac that Heinrich drank, and supported his elbow. Not to dissuade him, Heinrich cast him a thin smile and said, "Curvousier is a good cognac, goddamnit!"

"The best," Reckmann agreed.

Heinrich turned, but the girl's face had already mixed with the others. The truck moved away from the gate, and he extended his hand to Reckmann. "Thank you," he said, climbing into the car. "See you later, Ditrich."

On his way to Berlin he came across an air strike, and there were no SS patrols on the highway. He drove the car like a madman, pushing the accelerator to the floor, and recovered his wits only when he stopped the car at his house.

He felt so exhausted that he collapsed on the first piece of furniture he came to. He would willingly attribute his condition to the cognac he had drunk, but he felt absolutely sober. In front of him, he saw a room full of amazingly beautiful girl's eyes blazing with hatred. To drive them away, he went to the kitchen to get a bottle of schnapps from the refrigerator. Not taking his mouth off to top, he drank almost half of the bottle until he crashed down unconscious.

CHAPTER 14

The next day Heinrich felt like a piece of shit. Obviously he did not look any better. Colonel Schurke, the senior officer in charge for the department of medical research for *Wehrmacht*, was the first to meet him in the hall and asked, "Are you okay, Heinrich? You look sick. I think you should go to the doctor's office."

"I am all right, *Herr Oberst*," Heinrich said.

For the entire day, he did his work automatically and met surprised glances from the other officers; for the first time, he was unshaven. At last he left headquarters and walked home, looking around as if he were a stranger who was visiting the capital for the first time.

Armed detachments marched through the streets. Proclamations were posted on walls, calling for a purge and the search of traitors. A loud air raid siren broke silence, and Heinrich stepped into a half-demolished, abandoned house. The walls were hung with color photographs of Vienna, a yellow ivory crucifix, and a portrait of a lady in a russet dress. On a green, velvet armchair, an aged fox terrier squatted, forgotten by its master. The dog neither barked nor whined, but merely cocked its head inquiringly. Heinrich picked up a book lying open on the floor. It was a small volume of poems. "*I disturbed the profound slumber of the rose,"* he read but couldn't remember who wrote the verses.

An explosion took place quite near, and Heinrich headed down to the basement. There he found women, children and several old men. They are too old to be afraid of death, Heinrich thought. They were sitting among empty barrels, and every time a shell burst nearby, the women exclaimed, "Lord Jesus!" Nobody paid attention to Heinrich although he was in the military uniform.

The air raid was only for a short time—maybe the unexpected thunderstorm helped, maybe the *Luftwaffe* destroyers frightened the Allies' planes.

Heinrich went upstairs and saw the *Wolksturm* unit coming along the street. What could they do, he wondered, children with rifles?"

"Everything comes to the end," Heinrich muttered. "All of us come to the end." He almost stepped on a young girl.

"Does *Herr Hauptman* want to rest?" she asked.

"No, thank you, dear."

In his pocket he had a chocolate bar, and he quickly slipped it in her hand.

"Danke schon, Herr Hauptman!" She rolled her blue eyes in surprise, and then dashed away.

Unexpectedly he remembered the hate filled eyes of the young prisoner at his uncle's laboratory. He shook his head trying to push the daydream away. But he failed; it seized him. He saw the girl in Professor Dornberger's cell, and heard his calm voice. *"The difference in temperature of different part of a human body can reach minus one hundred sixty degrees Centigrade."* Heinrich imagined the girl's frostbitten body and felt nauseated.

He had to stop and lean on the wall. Fortunately his flat was around the corner.

Neglecting to take his coat off, he took three huge gulps from a bottle of schnapps that was standing on the table. He felt better. For several minutes, he sat motionlessly in the chair. Then Heinrich decided to call his uncle.

After several seconds he heard, "*Schtandartenfuhrer SS Dornberger.*"

"Good evening, Uncle Otto. It's Heinrich."

"Heinrich! I'm glad you didn't forget me."

"Uncle Otto, I'm sorry to be worrying you. You know, in several days it will be my birthday. Would you do me a great favor for a birthday gift?"

"If it's in my power, consider that you've already received my gift," Dornberger said, and Heinrich felt his smile on the other side of the wire. "What would make you happy?"

"I want you to give me a girl that I've seen among your...patients." Heinrich was about to say 'prisoners,' but closed his mouth in time.

"You know, Heinrich, in general I am not in favor of using my patients for sexual purposes. But for you, I'll make an exception." Unexpectedly Otto Dornberger laughed. Then he said, "How can I know what your taste is, Heinrich? Today among my patients there are thirty-seven females from ages twelve to sixty years. You have to come and show me who your choice is."

"If it is not too late, I drive out now, Uncle Otto."

"For you it's never late, Heinrich. The lab is my home. After I sent Katherine and girls to Alps, I live alone."

"Thank you, Uncle Otto." He hung up.

Heinrich went to the bathroom, took a cold shower and shaved carefully. In an hour he came to Dornberger's study.

"I thought my laboratory wasn't that close to Berlin," Dornberger smiled. "It seemed to me that I've just hung up."

Dornberger offered him supper but Heinrich refused. "I had some already," he lied. "I'm full but I don't mind a small glass of cognac," he said to please his uncle. He understood Dornberger did not like to drink alone.

While Dornberger poured the cognac, he said, "An hour ride from Berlin is a huge difference. Here I feel that the war is far away."

"The war is always inside us." Dornberger grinned. "If the war that's inside us harmonizes with the war outside, we survive. If there is no harmony, this will be the end." He looked at Heinrich's face. "I don't like the way you look; I think you're on the edge of nervous exhaustion. It's not dangerous but unpleasant. Maybe my gift will allow you to find the soul's equilibrium. Who your choice is?"

"I don't know. I saw her face for a second in the yard."

"Don't worry, we'll find her. One of thirty-seven isn't such difficult task, is it?" He laughed and took a big gulp of his drink. "Show me her face, and she'll be prepared for you the next day."

Pouring cognac in his glass, Heinrich tried not to look in his uncle's face. He threw his drink down his throat in one gulp, and then said, "I want to take her with me, Uncle."

Otto Dornberger did not respond. "Let's go and look at your choice," he said, his voice neutral.

They went through the courtyard to the female barracks. A burly woman in a lab coat was sitting in front of the closed door. Seeing the *schtandartenfuhrer*, she jumped up. If not for the club in her stout hands and the pistol on her belt, she could be considered a nurse at a psychiatric clinic.

Dornberger silently pointed her to her place. She opened the door and sat back down. The barrack was clean to the point of being sterile although it didn't remind Heinrich of the camp he had visited with Count Bernadotte.

They had walked to the end of the barracks, but none of the frightened faces he saw reminded him of the one that had impressed him so much. He suddenly thought that maybe she was already dead, and terror possessed him. After that thought, the wave of cold in his heart changed to such heat that he had to unbutton the collar of his uniform.

Then the bathroom door opened, and Heinrich saw the girl. She stood there in her nightgown but didn't lower her eyes before the officers who were staring at her. In her eyes, Heinrich saw the same hatred that had blinded him before.

"Sorry," she said at last, and went between them to her bed.

Heinrich saw the number on her bed and, turning to Dornberger, said quietly, "Number seven." He went to the exit, not waiting for his uncle's response.

As they left, Dornberger told the guard to send a patient number seven to his office. Thrusting her huge breasts at him, the female guard answered in an unexpectedly low voice, "*Yavol, Herr Schtandartenfuhrer.*"

Dornberger looked at her, disconcerted. In his lab, he didn't like to be called *schtandartenfuhrer*; he preferred to hear "professor."

They returned to Dornberger's study where he smoked a cigar while Heinrich poured himself a cognac.

"You drink too much," Dornberger remarked matter-of-factly. "I think it's because you try to understand the reasons for our defeat."

"But we haven't yet lost the war," Heinrich objected weakly.

"C'mon, Heinrich! Here you are in your home, and you need not be afraid of your own shadow. Where did we blunder? What was the rougher mistake—an attempt to destroy England after we have invaded France or in hurrying to the East? Dornberger extinguished his cigar and rummaged through the papers on the desk. He opened one of the folders and read aloud, "Rachel Gecht. Born in Dresden, in 1926. Since 1939, imprisoned with her family in Buchenwald." He closed the folder and looked at Heinrich. "You've got good taste, Heinrich. But don't you think that the first SS patrol that stops your car will see that she is Jewish? She looks as much like Eva Braun as you look like the Fuhrer. She has the tattoo with her camp number on her hand. In the best-case scenario, she would be sent back to the camp; in the worst case, not to lose time, they'll shoot her on the road. You wouldn't be shot but degraded to private and sent to the front; in the best case, to the East against the Allies; in the worst—against the Russians." Dornberger paused.

"You have painted too gloomy a picture, uncle," Heinrich attempted to joke.

"But I need you here," Dornberger continued, paying no attention to Heinrich's last words. "You have to continue my work." He sighed heavily. "You are the only one who can continue it." Silence came; Heinrich did not interrupt it. "If you still wish, she will be prepared for you by tomorrow." Dornberger repeated his offer.

"Uncle Otto, you promised to do everything that's in your power. This is in your power. Give me this girl, and I'll be your debtor." Heinrich was insistent.

Then, after a short thought, Dornberger agreed, "Okay. If you like to play with fire, play. But when you're tired of her, send her back; you'll perhaps save her life. Maybe your life too. Have you seen hatred in her eyes? She would kill you before committing suicide."

"Thank you Uncle Otto. I'll take care of myself, and return my debt." Heinrich smiled. "You have given me an unforgettable gift for my 25th birthday."

"Your happiness is my happiness, Heinrich. The only difference between us is the fact that youth's charm cannot be replaced by age's experience." He paused and then said, "Regarding your debt...You can pay it earlier than you think."

Heinrich looked at him with surprise. Dornberger continued, "Favor for favor. I want you to go to Baaden and visit Katherine. I cannot," he explained. "It's too close to the Swiss border. Some of my colleagues, who do not care for me too much, will think I decided to escape."

"I am entirely at your disposal, Uncle," Heinrich said sincerely.

"That's fine. I think that in one or two weeks I'll agree with *Obergruppenfuhrer* SS Gerlach that he'll give you a week's vacation with all the proper papers." Dornberger smiled. "And while you're there, you will be able to ski; it will be good for your health and strengthen your nerves. Returning to your girl...I'll give you an official paper saying that you are accompanying the prisoner for the Gestapo. Please Heinrich, be careful."

Dornberger went to the desk and filled in the paper. Then he sealed it and handed to Heinrich. "If you reach your place without needing it, please burn it. The Gestapo is still a big fire."

Without glancing at the paper, Heinrich put it in his pocket. "Thank you, Uncle Otto. How can I express my gratitude?"

"Divert!" Dornberger grinned. "If you want the girl to satisfy you, you have to feed her properly." He opened the refrigerator and took out a can of black caviar. "Take this; it will help her recover." Then he sharply changed the topic. "She will be led to your car. By the way, the prisoner's name is Rachel."

He called inside security. "I am sending a prisoner number seven to the Berlin Gestapo. She will be accompanied by Captain Menke," he said to the duty officer. "Prepare her immediately. That is all."

By the time Heinrich reached his car, two guards had led Rachel there. She was handcuffed and barely held a small suitcase with both hands. Heinrich's first thought was to take her suitcase, but he rethought the inclination. He opened the trunk and ordered, "Put her luggage here and get the prisoner on the back seat."

Once that was accomplished, he started up the engine and moved out of the gate. When the laboratory building vanished, he stopped the car and removed the girl's handcuffs.

The night was dark, and the highway was empty. In any case, Heinrich didn't exceed the speed limit. Approaching the SS checkpoint, he ordered the girl to lie on the floor between the seats. She obeyed, and her brittle figure vanished from his view when he glanced in the rear mirror. He had hoped to pass this point without any trouble, but he had to stop; the crossing arm was down.

Not waiting until the SS patrol reached to the car, Heinrich got out and shouted angrily at the soldiers who were slowly approaching him, "Are you blind, you dope? Don't you see this form signed by Heinrich Himmler? Or do you dream of being sent to the front?" He thrust the paper in the *scharfuhrer's* face, and the soldiers froze, raised their hands in "Heil Hitler!" Then one of them rushed to the gate and lifted it.

Heinrich hurried to the car and sped through. Gradually the tension left him, and he shivered. He was nearing his home when an air strike began. Happily for Heinrich, when the night concierge heard the first sounds of the siren, he had hurried to the bomb shelter, and nobody saw Heinrich lead the girl into the apartment.

Rachel stopped on the threshold.

"Come in," Heinrich said. "Now you'll live here."

In the kitchen, he placed on the table bread, butter, ham, and the can of caviar his uncle had given him. "You have to eat, Rachel," Heinrich said softly.

Rachel began cramming food in her mouth. Uncomfortable at seeing her eat this way, he went to his bedroom and took his uniform off. When he returned to the kitchen, the plate was empty.

"Can I take a shower, *Herr Hauptman?*" Rachel asked.

"Here you can do anything you want, Rachel." He showed Rachel to her room. "You'll live here," Heinrich repeated tenderly. He rubbed his forehead, feeling a headache coming on. Rachel went to the bathroom.

Heinrich ate a quick sandwich and went to his room where he put Bach's *Mesa* on the record player. Bach was his favorite composer, and the music always made Heinrich calmer. It seemed that he lay, with closed eyes, for a long time. When he opened them, to his surprise he saw Rachel standing at the door. In a nightgown, eyes down to the floor, she whispered, "If *Herr Hauptman* wants to have my body, he can take it."

Heinrich could see she really wanted to tell him to go to hell. He jumped from the bed as he was jolted by a concealed spring. He grabbed his robe lying on the chair, ran to the girl and, forgetting that he was in his underwear, threw it on her shoulders. He felt Rachel's shudder. Then he led her to her room, murmuring, "No, no, Rachel. No one will hurt you. You will live here."

He closed the door to her room and returned to his bedroom. The record had stopped. He switched it on again, and tried to concentrate on Bach's music.

Unexpectedly Heinrich felt tears on his cheeks. For several minutes, he struggled silently, trying to suppress them. But he failed. Uncontrolled tears poured from his eyes as if he had kept them hidden for the last ten years of his life and only now released. Trying to halt the waterfall, Heinrich hid his face in the pillow. But they did not stop. They transferred to sobbing shaking his entire body. Afraid that the girl in the adjacent room could hear him, Heinrich made the music as loud as possible.

CHAPTER 15

▼

Three days later, Otto Dornberger called Heinrich. "I'm glad you're alive, nephew," he said and laughed in the receiver. Then he explained, "If I hear your voice, it means that there no longer is hatred in the eyes of your girl." Then he quickly changed the topic and asked Heinrich to come to his office.

When Heinrich reached his uncle's complex, the laboratory seemed to him more like a concentration camp than ever. Otto Dornberger was in the uniform of the *schtandartenfuhrer SS*.

It was already the end of February 1945, and the first tank units of Russian Field Marshall Ivan Konev's army were observed twenty-three kilometers from the lab. Dornberger realized quite clearly that the war was approaching the end quicker than he thought. Sometimes this thought made him madder than hell; sometimes he accepted it calmly.

When Heinrich sat in the chair, he was offered cognac and a cigar.

"You look much better than last time, Heinrich." Dornberger took his glasses off and looked at Heinrich with shortsighted eyes. "Have you thought what you would do after the war?" he asked Heinrich after brooding silence.

Heinrich shook his head. "The Bible says 'Don't think about tomorrow because tomorrow will take care of itself.'" Heinrich answered in his usual cryptic way.

"This is a harmful philosophy," Dornberger remarked without a smile. "Despite the fact that we Germans have accepted Christianity, in our souls we remained pagans. That's why our wars were always barbaric—in the First World War we were the first to use poison gas; in this war—we used gas chambers. Will people judge us based on the philosophy of forgiveness? It's hardly to be expected. As a *Wehrmacht* officer, you can hope to be forgiven. I, as a *schtandartenfuhrer SS,* cannot. Everybody deserves his fate, and it's fair." Frowning in concentration, Dornberger took a gulp of cognac, and then continued, "I have finished my experiments. My lab is not functioning any more. I sent my patients back to the camps. The whole complex of buildings will explode as soon as Russian tanks reached the gate. I think it'll happen within several months.

I cannot leave this place now because it would be considered desertion; my friends will be the first who'll pin me to the wall. I want you to go to Katherine in Baaden." He shook his head and sighed deeply. Then Otto Dornberger opened the wall safe to take out a big leather briefcase and a small package. He put them on the table.

"In this package is money," he said. "I think it will be enough for Katherine after the war. The briefcase is for you, Heinrich. Here are the results of my research, the result of my scientific life. I do not want them to be fall into the hands of foreigners; I do hope that after the war my scientific life will continue in you," he added. A smile crept slowly into his lips. Dornberger gulped his cognac again and lit the extinguished cigar.

"Tomorrow a SS transport plane will fly to Baaden," he continued. "*Gruppenfuhrer SS* Orlendorf has arranged for the crew to take you to Baaden and back. But it can also be a one-way ticket. It's up to you." He put his glasses on and glanced at Heinrich sharply. Heinrich shrugged and said nothing. Dornberger again brooded for a time. Then, as if he was back to reality, Dornberger offered Heinrich a cigar. Heinrich took it and smoked. He did not interrupt his uncle. He felt Dornberger would like to tell him something important, but was still hesitating. At last Dornberger finished his cognac and discarded his hesitations. He made the final decision. At any rate, he had no one but Heinrich to rely on.

"To visit Katherine is only a part of your mission, Heinrich," he said quietly. "You must also visit a Zurich bank, put the briefcase in my security box and," Dornberger made a pause, and then he continued," renew my bank account number."

Heinrich looked at him questioningly but again did not ask questions.

"My Swiss bank account is my security; I'll use it to pay the Allies in exchange for my life." Dornberger explained with a cynical expression. "Americans are business people, and we'll be able to find a common language with them. My life is in your hands, Heinrich. The account number I give you is not my personal account. It's a joint account known to several people in the SS leadership. I want you to understand me correctly. I only want to extract my part of the money—two hundred and seventeen thousand. No more. You will have to put the money in a separate account." Naming the amount, Dornberger grinned, now acknowledging that over the last years he had become an adept of handling such large amounts of money.

Heinrich had kept silent; he only raised a questioning brow. He still did not understand what money his uncle spoke of.

Dornberger paused and gulped his cognac again. Then he continued, "This is a dangerous mission, Heinrich, and I don't want to keep you in the dark about what money we are talking about. There are a lot of stupid idiots in the SS, but there are also some smart people who understood that it was stupidity to burn money. Frankly speaking, it was my idea to liberate the prisoners who could afford to pay for their freedom. Among hundreds of thousands of prisoners, hundreds who had rich relatives in the USA and Britain could afford it. If it were official government politics, it could bring the Reich millions of dollars, and we could spend them on scientific research, for instance. Unfortunately for the SS leadership, the fanatical idiots prevailed; for them, only statistics are important. The more prisoners terminated the better for the Reich. Hundreds of redeemed prisoners—this is a private business for me and several of my partners among the high rank SS officers. If you noticed, there were three barracks in my lab. In two of them, I've kept the patients for my experiments; in the third there were always several people, the fate of whom depended on negotiations with the World Zionist Organization based in Switzerland. By the way, your girl was one of them. We intended to negotiate her fate because her father was one of the leaders of the German branch of that organization. Unfortunately the stupid idiots killed him before we knew who he was." Dornberger grinned. "So my gift for your birthday wasn't cheap."

Heinrich stared at him. Dornberger's face was dark gray, and its expression corresponded to his SS uniform. For the first time

Heinrich thought that a scientist's analytical ability lived in his uncle in total harmony with a burger's practicality.

"Now you know the true aim of your mission." Dornberger's words barely had the energy to be heard. "It's a dangerous mission, Heinrich. If anybody knows about our conversation, you're a dead man. Not only because we cheat the SS, but also because in revealing the truth, the SS people would realize what idiots they. Please, Heinrich, be careful. Whatever happens, keep your mouth shut. It can save your life. And mine as well."

"I'll be careful, Uncle Otto," said Heinrich at last.

Dornberger wanted to pour more cognac in their glasses but Heinrich stopped him. "I need to be sober, Uncle," he said.

Dornberger embraced him. "Good luck, my boy. I always loved you as a son, Heinrich." His shoulders slumped slightly.

"I love you too, uncle." Heinrich tucked the package under his arm, picked up the briefcase and, without looking back, left.

After Heinrich returned home, he told Rachel that he had to go on a business trip and that she would be staying alone for several days. Fear flashed in her beautiful eyes, but she said nothing.

"Don't worry, Rachel," he said. "Nobody will come in here while I'm gone. The apartment will be locked from the outside and sealed. The refrigerator is full, so you won't have to worry about dying from starvation." He tried to joke but saw tears in her eyes. "Don't worry," he added, "I'll be back."

"I don't worry *Herr Hauptman*," she said softly, her voice thin, strained, and unnatural.

"My name is Heinrich," he reminded her. He made a small, breathy sound in the back of his throat.

"Your name is Heinrich, *Herr Hauptman*," she repeated obediently.

Heinrich went to his room. To concentrate, he put a record on to play Bach. He brooded for some time.

Otto Dornberger's offer—as a matter of fact, it was not an offer but an order—was more dangerous than thrilling. The mission could result in tragedy not only for him, but for Rachel also. If the Gestapo arrested him, nobody would pay any attention to the fact that he was Hitler's godchild. Heinrich reached for his cigarettes.

But he could not refuse the mission. By giving him Rachel, Dornberger had tied his hands. The price of this gamble was two lives—Rachel's and his own.

Then the wild idea came to his mind—to take Rachel with him to Baaden and then to escape to Switzerland. But he immediately discarded it. To take a girl with such obvious Jewish appearance on board a SS plane was not only crazy, but also a stupid idea. So he had to come back despite all the possible obstacles, in defiance of the fate.

The next morning, having shaved carefully, Heinrich went to the kitchen to drink a cup of coffee before his departure. To his surprise he saw Rachel.

"Good morning, *Herr Hauptman*," she said quietly. "I've prepared breakfast for you." She stood at the door, hands behind her back as she had for many years.

"Thank you, Rachel," Heinrich said softly and added, pointing to the other chair, "Take a seat, please. Drink a cup of coffee with me."

Rachel sat. He poured coffee in her cup; she didn't touch it. Several times he tried to catch her glance but couldn't. He sipped his cup of coffee and ate the food she had prepared. At last he moved the cup aside and wiped his lips. Glancing at Rachel again, he sighed.

"I do hope everything will be all right. I'll be back in five or six days. But anything can happen, Rachel. Humans suppose, but only God knows exactly. If I'm not back in a week…" Heinrich went out into the hall for a minute and came back with a small package in his hands. "Here are documents with the name of Greta Miller, a little money, and a blond wig because your face is too far from the Nordic type. But frankly speaking, there's only one chance of a hundred, taking into account that tattoo number on your hand. But it's also better than nothing. Nobody will come here while I'm gone," he repeated. "Under no circumstances, should you go to the front of the apartment. If you hear the doorbell, don't open the door. Did you understand everything, Rachel?"

"I did, *Herr Hauptman.*" Tears glistened in her eyes. Her heart was racing so fast that she thought she might faint.

For the first time during their conversation, their glances met. There was no hatred, no fear, and no indifference in Rachel's eyes. Heinrich saw only sadness that seemed bottomless.

"I'll see you later, Rachel," he said and took his suitcase. Without looking back, Heinrich closed the door behind him.

CHAPTER 16

―――――――――▼―――――――――

When Heinrich had arrived on the airport, a little transport *Luftwaffe* plane was ready to take off. A gray-haired *schturmban-fuhrer SS* met him near the top of the stairway and asked, omitting a formal greeting, "Heinrich Menke? I am Walter Zigler. Welcome on board, *Hauptman*."

The plane was so packed with large wooden boxes that they could hardly find two seats. The pilot came out of the cockpit and asked Heinrich, "Have you ever done a parachute jump, *Hauptman*?" He handed Heinrich a 'chute.'

Heinrich nodded. "Couple of times, in the Cadet School."

"Then you're experienced." The captain smiled. "If we're shot down, jump out, count to thirty, and pull the ring. Clear?"

"If until thirty, everything is okay." Heinrich smiled. "I can even count to a hundred."

"Fine." The pilot went back to his cabin.

"It would be better to just count to sixty, Heinrich, "Walter Zigler advised without a smile. "The freight is mined."

In spite of their fears, the flight was calm and, in less than three hours, they landed on a small airfield where three covered trucks waited for them. The SS soldiers took less than half an hour to empty the plane. Heinrich understood that they were in a hurry. When unloading was finished, Walter Zigler invited Heinrich to his car, an Opel Admiral.

On the first crossroad, the column of trucks moved aside and the car continued on the way to the center of the city.

"Is this the long way?" asked Heinrich.

"We've already arrived," Walter Zigler said. At that moment, in front of them, Heinrich saw a small town nestled between two mountains.

Life changed its costume like an actor—from war, with its horrible noise, blood, death and all the attributes of hell, to the peaceful silence of the white snow covered hills and mountains, a piece of paradise on Earth.

"It's the third time I've been here," Walter Zigler said matter-of-factly. "This is an unforgettable place, Heinrich. I'm sure that once you get to know it, you won't want to leave. For me, it's a punishment every time I fly back to Berlin. Do you ski?"

"Unfortunately not."

"Not a problem. You'll get an instructor, and in three days you'll forget walking."

The car passed picturesque hills, valleys, and a narrow, frozen river. At last they reached the center of town, with its threadlike streets, baroque churches with statues of martyrs suffering too theatrically, and taverns with huge signs. The car stopped near a gothic municipal building which held the commandant's office. Above the entrance, there was a huge flag featuring a red swastika. Opposite the building, there was a five-story hotel that obviously had been built recently, before the war began. Its plain architecture sharply and painfully contrasted with the gothic architecture of other buildings.

They went to the commandant's office. Zigler pointed to the hotel and said, "Most of the Germans live there. You can of course stay in one of the cottages, but they aren't as comfortable—there's no hot water."

"Lead me, Walter. I'm a first-time visitor to this charming place." Heinrich grinned.

"Willingly." Walter Zigler returned the smile.

Near the entrance, they passed a guard who saluted them and arrived at the commandant's office. The *oberschturmbanfuhrer SS* sitting at the desk greeted them by usual "*Heil Hitler!*"

He was ruddy of face and heavy of jowl, with a large, angry mouth and the yellow teeth of a heavy smoker.

Walter went to the desk to shake his hand, as he was an old friend, but managed to whisper, "*Hauptman* is the Fuhrer's godchild, be careful."

After those words a friendly smile already never left the *oberschturmbanfuhrer's* face as Walter Zigler introduced the men to each other.

"Heinrich Menke—Gunter Schwaab."

"First things go first. We have to have a drink, gentlemen," Schwaab said and took a bottle of Remy Martin cognac from his desk drawer. He proposed a toast, "To your pleasant stay here, gentlemen."

"*Prozit*"

After they drank, Walter remarked, "As always, Gunter, our stay here isn't to be recorded on paper."

"As always, Walter." The *oberschtumbanfuhrer* smiled and sipped his drink. "I do hope that you'll enjoy your stay here. A hotel is across the street; I'll call the manager."

"Thank you, Gunter," Heinrich said. "It was my pleasure to meet you. If you're ever in Berlin, I do hope that I'll be able to pay you back for your hospitality."

"It would be wonderful to visit Berlin," Gunter Schwaab said while he thought that Berlin was the last place he'd like to be now.

Heinrich and Walter crossed the small square and went into the hotel. The manager who wore the rogue face of a Gestapo secret informer was waiting for them; obviously *Oberschturmbanfuhrer* Schwaab had called him while Heinrich and Walter were crossing the square.

"I've prepared two suites on the second floor for you, gentlemen," he said, handing them the keys. "I'll personally take care of your luggage," he added, seeing the two suitcases being delivered by the Opel's driver.

"By the way," said Heinrich, "Does Frau Dornberger live here?" He turned to Walter and explained, "She is my aunt, the wife of *Schtandartenfuhrer SS* Otto Dornberger."

Walter Zigler nodded respectfully, hearing the high SS rank Heinrich mentioned.

"She's been here for almost two years, Captain; Frau Dornberger and her daughters. They have two adjacent rooms, numbers 417 and 418, on the forth floor."

"Does the telephone work?" Heinrich asked.

"In our hotel, everything works properly," the manager said proudly.

"Thank you. I'll give them a call later on."

Heinrich went to his room where he enjoyed a long, hot shower. Then he put a robe and sat in a chair. So far so good, he thought and crossed his fingers.

Then Heinrich dialed Katherine's number. But as he had supposed, no one answered—she wasn't in. Heinrich put on his civilian clothes. "I look funny," he muttered and grinned, glancing at the man in the suit who smiled back at him from the mirror.

He went downstairs and left a note for Katherine at the clerk's desk.

Walking along the narrow streets that sighed with a long forgotten air of silence and calmness, he came to a tavern and went in to have a tall glass of cold beer. His thoughts returned to Rachel waiting in Berlin, but he was sure she was in relative safety; the outside apartment door was locked and sealed with a Gestapo seal. Heinrich drank another beer and then returned to the hotel to ask the clerk if Frau Dornberger was back.

"She's in the restaurant, Herr Menke," the clerk answered although it was the first time that Heinrich had seen him. The clerk pointed to the door.

Standing at the door of the restaurant, Heinrich immediately saw Katherine and Martha sitting at a table near the window. As soon as he reached their table, Martha flung her arms around his neck. He kissed her, and then kissed Katherine's hand. She bent and returned his kiss.

"Aunt Katherine, you look wonderful!" he said. Then he corrected himself as he sat down. "You both look great."

"I cannot believe it, Heinrich, seeing you here!" Katherine smiled at him.

"And me too," Martha said, barely able to sit still due to her excitement.

After two years at this resort, Katherine has become ten years younger, Heinrich thought. Obviously it wasn't just a matter of the mountain air. "Uncle Otto asked me to see you." He looked down at the menu and gave his order to the waiter. As soon as the waiter stepped aside, Heinrich added, looking at Katherine's eyes, "And a small parcel." He sipped his water.

"Where's Eva?" Heinrich asked matter-of-factly.

Katherine turned her lazy eyes to him. "Oh, Heinrich, you don't know, she married almost a year ago. Otto doesn't know yet."

"It was a stormy love affair from the first glance," Martha added, toying with her folded napkin.

"He is a very good young man, a doctor's son from Zurich," Katherine said. "They would go on a honeymoon, but the war is everywhere. So they spent their honeymoon in Switzerland. I don't know if she will ever come back to visit us."

"I wouldn't come," Martha said. "It's too boring here—nothing but skiing as if I'm preparing for a world level competition."

Heinrich saw Walter Zigler came in the restaurant and waved to him. He wore a sports coat that made him look much younger than the black SS uniform did. When he reached the table, Heinrich introduced him to the ladies, "My friend Walter Zigler."

Walter kissed Katherine's and Martha's hands. Katherine asked him to share their table.

"Thank you," he thanked her politely. "Next time I would with great pleasure. But now I won't disturb you. You haven't seen each other for a long time." He bowed and kissed the ladies' hands again, holding Martha's a little longer than necessary.

"He's a very pleasant young man," said Katherine, looking at his back. "How long is he going to stay here?"

"I think, just as I am, for a week or so."

"How is Otto?" Katherine asked, at last. "I haven't seen him for ages, but he is still my husband." She smiled and settled back in her seat, her eyes betraying no interest.

"He is fine. You know he's a scientist, and all his life is in science."

"I know," Katherine agreed matter-of-factly. "Scientists devote their lives to science; that's why they have no time for a family." However Heinrich didn't hear any bitterness in her words.

After they finished lunch, Martha leaned toward Heinrich and whispered, "I am in the room # 417." But he pretended not to hear.

When they went out to the hall, Martha said, "See you later. I need to get manicure."

Heinrich and Katherine went up to his room where he gave her the parcel saying, "Uncle Otto asked me to hand this to you."

"It's about money," Katherine said, and carelessly put it in a pocket inside her sports bag. "My money is almost gone," she explained, and Heinrich understood that it wasn't the first package of money she had received from her husband. "What are you going to do with your free time here, Heinrich?" she asked without any real curiosity in her voice.

"Like everyone else, I'd like to ski. But I need a teacher."

"That's not a problem. We have several good instructors from Switzerland here. You know, the border's only in two kilometers away," she added. "We ski to the other side for shopping. But if you ski, it's so easy to lose your way..." She smiled. "But you're not a woman, you aren't interested in shopping. Ask Martha;

she'll give you the name of the instructor who taught her. Thank you again, Heinrich. I'll see you at supper." Katherine smiled coquettishly. "There's nothing else to be done. We only have one good restaurant. All the Germans living here gather under the one roof like a big family. "She grinned and stood up.

When Katherine left, Heinrich lay down on the sofa, thinking of how he would fulfill the second part of his mission. He had already guessed that the money for Katherine was only a pretext of his real mission—to move Dornberger's money from the Zurich bank to a separate account and to put the briefcase with his experimental records in the safety box. The more he thought about it the more he realized it wouldn't be easy.

Before supper, Heinrich went to the bar where he found Walter Zigler and Gunter Schwaab sitting at the bar.

"May I disturb you, gentlemen?" Heinrich asked.

"Who can disturb a conversation about women?" Schwaab grinned. "I heard Frau Dornberger is your aunt?"

"Are you surprised that such a young beautiful lady can be the aunt of such an old man as me?" Heinrich asked, and everybody laughed.

"Don't you object if I pay court to her, Heinrich?" Gunter Schwaab asked.

"I think she would be delighted," said Heinrich who already had guessed that Gunter was the reason for Katherine's late blossoming. "She's a woman. All her energy has been waiting for a necessary direction. Direct her, Gunter."

Later they all had supper together. They spent a nice evening talking about the latest movie with Greta Garbo and remembering 'gold' pre-war times when all of them were naïve and exalted.

Snuggled in her bed that night, and before she could fall asleep, Martha heard footsteps. Heinrich, she thought joyfully. The door opened and closed. She turned the lamp on and saw it was Walter Zigler materializing at her side. She screamed, "You're crazy, Walter!"

In response, he put his hand over her mouth and whispered, "Don't be silly, Martha, Heinrich's asleep." His voice was forced and rapid.

He put out the lamp, and Martha was quiet. She made love to him, slowly, gently as if she never wanted it to end. The obvious admiration in Walter's eyes was flattering to Martha.

When Walter left half an hour later, she lay on her back, still unable to understand what had happened. What insolence! Men become savages, she thought. Yet she felt good.

Zigler visited Martha every night until the end of his stay, and, to Heinrich's surprise, she didn't try to lure him into her bed.

CHAPTER 17

▼

When Martha introduced Heinrich her ski instructor, Johan, and called him "my brother, Heinrich," he understood that Johan was also a victim of the affectionate Martha. He was a man with a pleasant face, of approximately the same age as Heinrich. And it turned out that he was the former Switzerland slalom champion. Was he a Gestapo informer or not—it didn't matter.

"Johan, I only have a week vacation," Heinrich told him. "Can you put me on skis in one day?"

"I'll do my best if you spend the whole day with me."

"I definitely will."

While training, he told Heinrich that he had dreamed of opening a ski school for adults and children. But the war in Europe destroyed his plans. Only a few tourists who enjoyed life and paid no attention to the war ever came to that area. In order to earn a living, he had to work as a ski instructor. He lived with his parents who owned a small ski shop.

After the story, Johan talked to Heinrich about buying ski equipment. "If you need some really good skis and enjoy skiing, Heinrich, buy at my dad's shop. He sells the best items for a decent price because there aren't too many customers at the resort," Johan explained.

"But it's across the border, in Switzerland." Heinrich frowned.

Johan smiled and explained that the guards looked indulgently on people crossing the border, especially if they knew them. "They are suspicious only about those carrying luggage."

"It would be nice to visit your country. I've never been there. But frankly, when my aunt told me they go there for shopping, I didn't believe her." Heinrich's smile was innocent.

"Crossing isn't really a big deal," Johan said. "Even if guards stop anybody, he or she can pay to avoid trouble."

"If it's no problem, Johan, then I'd willingly buy my skis from your shop," Heinrich said and thought it wouldn't be possible to cross the border without Johan's help.

The following day he tried hard to follow Johan's instructions. By the end of the day, he felt rather comfortable on skis. The next day they made two trips down the mountain together, and then Heinrich went alone. Not too fast of course, but taking into account he was a novice, it wasn't bad at all.

"You are a good pupil, Heinrich," Johan praised him and offered to visit his father's shop the next day. "I think if we invite Fraulein Martha, it would be also amusing for her." He looked at Heinrich questioningly.

"That's a good idea," Heinrich agreed. It is a really good idea, he thought. I would be beyond suspicion.

"The whole round trip will take us no more than three or four hours," Johan explained matter-of-factly.

When he returned to the hotel, Heinrich asked Martha to join them. She agreed, but Heinrich didn't think that she was enthusiastic about the newly proposed experience. Without doubt, she had visited Johan's place before.

The next day Martha and Heinrich accompanied by Johan began skiing slowly so as not to put Heinrich in an awkward position. The skiing wasn't as difficult as he had imagined, and he thought the border was unsecured. The border patrol appeared in front of them unexpectedly. The officers seemed to know Johan and Martha because they saluted with a smile. One of them glanced at Heinrich questioningly. Johan said, "Hi, Basil. This is Heinrich, Martha's brother. We are going to my house. Heinrich intends to buy ski equipment. His rental skis are a piece of shit."

"Enjoy," said the officer, and all three continued on their way.

Several minutes later, they reached the small town of Dollenstrolle, as similar as two drops of water to Baaden; the same style municipal building, the same style cottages, all the same but smaller. Heinrich had to recall that the town of Baaden was on the German side of the border, but Dollenstrolle—on the Switzerland side.

"Here's my place," Johan said, as they reached one of tiny houses that sported a red-tiled roof. Inviting them for a snack, he introduced them to his father, a tall, lean, knotty athletic man of about fifty-five years old, with a horseshoe of gray hair around a freckled scalp. His wife was a colorless woman in a Tyrolean dress, wiry and gray, with permanent despair etched in her face. She didn't join them at the table. Her functions were limited to those of a maid. She set up the table and left the room. Heinrich didn't hear her say a word.

"The Germans have lost the war," said Johan's father, refer-ring to Heinrich, having unmistakably defined him as a German officer. Heinrich didn't want to support this conversa-tion and kept silent, drinking coffee. "Many people here sympathized with the German idea," Johan's father continued speaking as he had a rare chance to talk to a stranger. "It's not just the fact that many of us have German ancestors. Unfortunately a good idea was perverted into bad execution." He looked at Heinrich, but Heinrich avoided his glance.

"Our leaders were smart enough to keep neutral," said Johan. "That's why my generation is happier here than in Germany— we don't die on a war field."

"It didn't depend on what our leaders wanted," Johan's father said. "The Germans were smart enough to respect our neutrality. They needed us more than we needed them; we're the world's center of banking operations. Because of the war, our banks became richer, and that's good. But ordinary people lost ground, and that's bad. Here, in Dollenstrolle for instance, we were involved in the skiing industry for many years. But because of the war, that industry is dead. At least ten years will pass before Europeans return. My son Johan had dreamed that by his thirties, he would open an International Ski School. But now I think he will remain an instructor for his entire life although he is one the best ski sportsmen in the world."

"I think everything will be stabilized much sooner than you predict, sir," Heinrich said matter-of-factly. He had to say something because his silence had become awkward.

"Let's hope for the future then," Johan's father agreed. "Johan said you're going to support our small business and buy skis?" He changed the topic.

"I'll buy everything that Johan will tell me to because I hope to return again shortly," Heinrich said.

Martha did not take part in the conversation and yawned, visibly bored. Johan saw it. "Let's go over to the shop," he offered.

"While you choose skis, I'll be gadding about in the shops," Martha said as shopping had occupied her mind.

"Where shall we pick you up, sis?" Heinrich asked.

"In an hour, at the café across the bank."

"Do you have a bank in your town?" Heinrich mastered his surprise although he had noticed the building when they passed it.

"It's a local branch of the First Zurich Bank," Johan's father explained matter-of-factly.

"I do hope you provide a storage service to keep my skis until my next trip." Heinrich smiled.

"We definitely do, sir."

After Heinrich paid for the set of the most expensive skis in the shop, he left his old ones there; Johan promised to deliver them to the hotel the following day and return them to the rental office. "I'll do it all myself, Heinrich, don't worry," he promised.

Heinrich looked at his watch, and then glanced at Johan—it was the time to pick Martha up.

"You needn't a guide for the way home." Johan grinned. "Martha knows the way better than I do."

"Thank you, Johan," Heinrich said and they shook hands. "See you tomorrow."

At the café across from the bank, Heinrich sat down and ordered a cup of coffee. Then he looked around; Martha wasn't there yet. Looking at the bank building across the street, Heinrich thought that he must return here with Martha. His mind snapped into focus. But using what reason? Suddenly he slapped his forehead—in a month it would just happen to be her birthday. So all he had to tell her was that he'd like to give her a birthday gift before his departure for Berlin!

At that moment he looked up to see Martha, with her face tinged with red from the frost outside. He thought that at her age of twenty-six, she was every bit as lovely as she had been a decade earlier. She settled in the chair that he held out for her and told the waiter to bring a glass of Chablis. "It's one of the concessions of my advanced age." Martha smiled him seductively. "I cannot drink liquor anymore." She threw back her head in a laugh.

Heinrich thought that the day would move with seductive inevitability from a drink in this café to her room in the hotel.

Martha smiled as if reading his thoughts. "They say I too like men. One date, one goodnight kiss, and I'm in love." They both laughed. "But you are my true love, Heinrich. It's true." Her composure cracked, just for an instant.

Heinrich was slow in answering. "I didn't think I was capable of love then," he said thoughtfully. "One thing I am sure of those times—they are the fondest memories I have. But…it's just the past, Martha."

"If you remember the past, it means it's still in your heart, Heinrich. Why forget the charm of the past if we can repeat it in the present? Life is too short, especially during war time." Martha's glance was insistent. She didn't expect objections. What man could reject her love?

Heinrich thought that he must not disappoint her if he wanted to use her for the second trip to Dollenstrolle. He smiled but sensed his companion was holding onto some inner tension. "You are irresistible, Martha," he said and put his hand on hers. She pushed back a sprig of hair. "It's pretty fair." A slight smile flickered across her face. "This is the wrong time, the wrong place. Let's go home."

Heinrich waved at the waiter to pay for the coffee. They left and strapped on their skis. The darkness of the night surrounded them as they began their way home. But Johan was right; Martha knew the way not worse than he did.

When they reached the hotel, Martha invited him to come to her room. Heinrich understood that to refuse was an insult; in this case, he couldn't rely on her help for the completion of his mission. But to delay the inevitable sex, he asked her to come to the bar for a drink.

Sitting on bar stool, Heinrich ordered a whisky straight for himself and looked questionably at Martha.

"Today I'll make an exception and drink liquor." She smiled happily.

They were about to leave when Heinrich heard Walter Zigler's voice from behind his back. "Oh, here you are!"

Martha's eyes seemed to grow suddenly intent as though they harbored some secret she hoped Heinrich wouldn't guess. She silently finished her drink and ordered another one while Heinrich grinned at his thought. It obviously was a difficult decision for her—which of the two males to choose for the night.

Using the opportunity to make her choice easier, Heinrich said, "Sorry, guys, I'm dead tired today. Or else I'll be a rotten skier tomorrow." As he stood up, he kissed Martha on the cheek. "Good night, kid."

She arched her brows and returned the kiss on his lips. They were dry, then soft beneath hers. The liquor on her tongue had the aftertaste of fire. Heinrich shook Walter's hand and winked at him. He already knew that tonight Martha wouldn't be insulted.

The next day, as always having lunch together with Katherine and Martha, Heinrich said, "Several days from now, I'll be back in Berlin but before my departure, I'd like to buy you a birthday gift, Martha. Would you do me the favor of accompanying me to Dollenstrolle for shopping one more time?"

Martha was delighted. "Oh, Heinrich, you still remember my birthday! Of course, I'll go with you…right after lunch. It'll take us a couple of hours, and all the shops will be still open."

"It's very nice of you, Heinrich," Katherine said. "But you can buy something here, in Baaden."

"The shops here, as I saw, are very decent. I'd like to buy something special for Martha." Heinrich said. And then he added, "As a memory of our friendship."

"Heinrich, I'll be ready in an hour." Martha rose.

Heinrich followed her. "I'll see you at supper, Aunt."

He returned to his room. The only problem left was Dornberger's briefcase. There was no chance to take it with him as luggage; it would create suspicion as well as a lot of trouble in case the border patrol stopped them. Heinrich decided to attach all of Dornberger's records to his body, using bandages that he had purchased earlier in the pharmacy. In half an hour, he had succeeded in fixing them. He had grown a little thicker, but a wide sweater and a jacket concealed it.

This time they reached Dollensrolle without any trouble; Heinrich was sure that they were seen, but the patrol was invisible. Maybe the guards were accustomed to skiers without luggage frequently crossing the border; maybe they recognized Martha as Johan's girlfriend.

They came to the café to drink a cup of coffee, and left their skis there while they shopped.

"Wouldn't you like, Heinrich, to take your jacket off?" Martha glanced at him surprisingly. "I think it's hot here."

"I'm afraid of catching cold before I leave," he said in a monotone.

He hurried to finish his coffee and stood up. Martha intended to follow him but he stopped her. "Give me an hour. I want my gift to be a surprise."

"Oh, sure!"

"I'll meet you here later on." He sent her a smile and hurried to the door. He was sweating like he had just left a steam room.

Heinrich turned the corner and went into the first jewelry shop he saw. He quickly chose a gold Omega lady's wristwatch. "I'll pick it up in an hour," he said to the surprised salesman, and paid in full, not attempting to bargain.

Then he dashed out and, making sure that nobody was watching him, quickly crossed the street and went into the bank. Not counting two customers, the bank was empty. At the manager's desk, he bought the personal post box. It was easy. "Excuse me sir, where is the bathroom?" he asked the manager, and hurried there to remove Dornberger's journals from his body. The manager wasn't paying any attention when Heinrich returned from the bathroom with a plastic bag in hands. Maybe he did. But he was a professional—he took no notice.

Heinrich took his jacket off and wiped his sweating forehead. "It's too hot here," he explained casually. Then Heinrich told the manager the main purpose of his visit.

"Unfortunately sir, if you have an account at the main branch, you have to go to Zurich to open a separate account."

"Oh, no!" Heinrich shouted. He had not expected such complication. His drive to Zurich would not be unobserved; he would become a person of the Gestapo's interest. It was extremely undesirable.

"I'm too pressed for time, sir," Heinrich said. "There are only two or three days at my disposal. It would be greatly appreciated if you help me. I'll pay any expenses you incur."

The manager thought a short time, and then said, "Okay. I'll go tomorrow to my boss in Zurich and ask him to transfer your money to the Dollenstrolle's branch. But you have to come tomorrow to finish all the formalities."

"I'll come back before lunch tomorrow, sir." Heinrich drew a sign of relief. Walter Zigler had told him yesterday that they would fly back in three days.

Then Heinrich quickly stopped in the jewelry shop and picked up the watch. Handing him the box, the manager said, "It's a good bargain. Thank you, sir."

"I need also a diamond pendant for my aunt. But I'm too pressed for time today, sir. Will you show something for me tomorrow?" asked Heinrich as he decided to use the chance to buy a pendant for Katherine as the reason of another trip to Dollenstrolle.

"I'll do my best, sir." The manager bowed and thought he hadn't had such a profitable customer for a long time.

When Heinrich came back to the café, Martha was waiting him. "Where have you been, Heinrich?" she asked him with a shade of annoyance in her voice.

Instead of answering, he laid a box on the table in front of her.

"What is this, Heinrich?"

"Open it!"

When Martha saw a gold Omega watch nestled inside, she looked at him. Her eyes grew moist. "The watch is so nice," she said and put it on her wrist, putting the old one in her sport bag.

"Accept my congratulations with your upcoming birthday, my dear. Between you and me, I've also ordered a pendant for your mother, but it will be delivered only tomorrow. Will you come back with me?"

"I would accompany you to anywhere you want," Martha said and gave him an innocent smile. "Let's go home. It's getting dark."

When they reached the hotel, she kissed Heinrich and said, "It seems that you're avoiding me, Heinrich. But today I won't invite you to my room; I'm tired. Thank you again for the great gift."

Before going to his room, Heinrich went down to the ground floor bar. He needed a drink to diminish his inner tension. The bar was full, and he had trouble finding an empty stool. At last he sat and ordered vermouth with tonic. He was too tired for a strong drink. He sipped his drink, thinking over the trip tomorrow to Dollenstrolle to complete his mission.

"Where could you disappear to, Heinrich?" The voice came from behind Heinrich. "Here, where there are only a few places to go, and where it's impossible to not run into each other?" asked Gunter Schwaab.

Despite the mocking tone, Heinrich was suspicious about the question. As a senior SS officer in Baaden, he had to know everything about every officer who came there, even if the officer's arrival and departure had not been officially registered.

"I'm dead tired, Gunter." Heinrich smiled. "I promised Martha a birthday gift. And she forced me to accompany her to Dollenstrolle to the jewelry shop. I'm not too much of a skier, and it was punishment for me."

Gunter Schwaab sighed with relief—there was no mystery in Heinrich's behavior. Then he smiled. "I understand you quite clearly, Heinrich. For me too, women are a greater punishment than skis."

"But I couldn't buy a present for Martha and not buy one for Katherine. Unfortunately the pendant I bought for her can only be delivered tomorrow. And when I think that tomorrow I have to go to Dollenstrolle with Martha again, believe me I dream of going to Berlin as soon as possible."

"Walter Zigler told me that your plane will return the day after tomorrow," Gunter Schwaab remarked matter-of-factly.

"Good Lord!" Heinrich smiled. "If I didn't have relatives here, my stay would have been a vacation. With relatives, it has turned into devotion." He finished his vermouth and stood up. "I need to rest," he said. "Please Gunter if you see Katherine, don't tell her about my present; it will be a surprise for her before I leave."

"Make a quick trip, Heinrich. The weather forecast is no good for tomorrow—a heavy snow in the second part of the day."

Falling asleep, still analyzing his conversation to Gunter Schwaab, Heinrich thought he was still beyond local Gestapo suspicions.

The next morning, at breakfast, he saw Katherine sitting alone.

"Where is Martha?" he asked. "She promised me another ski tour."

"She is not well, Heinrich."

"Got the flu?" He was surprised.

"No." Katherine smiled. "She got her period; and wants to stay in bed half a day."

Maybe it's for the best, Heinrich thought.

Having no trouble crossing the border, Heinrich completed all the formalities at bank and opened a numbered account in the Dollenstrolle branch of Zurich's bank with $217,000 in it. The trading of Jews is a profitable business, he thought bitterly.

Then Heinrich stopped at the jewelry shop and bought the pendant for Katherine. Returning to the hotel by dinnertime, he was able to avoid the heavy snow that began after 4 p.m. If it had started two hours earlier, he would never have found his way home.

At the dinner table, he saw not only Katherine and Martha, but also Walter Zigler and Gunter Schwaab.

"As Herr Schwaab told me that you, Heinrich, and Herr Zigler will return to Berlin tomorrow, I thought it would be nice to have dinner together." Katherine smiled.

After everybody gave their order and the waiter left, Heinrich put a gift box on the table in front of Katherine.

"What is this?" she asked. Then she opened the box to see a diamond pendant. "Oh, Heinrich," Katherine exclaimed. "You are the best relative I have!"

"And you are the best aunt I have." Heinrich smiled. Then he turned to Gunter Schwaab, "Thank you for the precise forecast. If I spent in the shop an hour longer, you would find my frozen body out there."

CHAPTER 18

---▼---

The same *Luftwaffe* freight plane, with the same crew, took Heinrich and Walter on board. But this time, the plane was empty.

"Do you have the same parachute experience as last time, captain?" the pilot asked Heinrich, as they were old friends. Obviously he had had a good time in the Alps.

"Unfortunately. But my ski experience is beyond comparison," Heinrich said.

When they had almost reached Berlin, the plane was mistakenly shelled from the ground. But they avoided trouble, not counting the fact that pieces of broken window glass deeply cut Walter's cheek.

"Now I've got the chance to receive a second crest." Walter smiled, telling Heinrich good-bye. He was taken by ambulance to a hospital.

But Heinrich's thoughts were already far away. When he came to his apartment door, he drew a sigh of relief—the seal wasn't broken.

Heinrich opened the door and said, still on the threshold, "This is I, Heinrich." Nobody answered, and he went into the hall. "I'm back, Rachel," he repeated. But there was no answer from her or a sound of any kind. He walked on quickly toward

Rachel's bedroom. The door to Rachel's room was closed. Heinrich sat down on the sofa where he could watch it, waiting until she came out. But nobody did, and a vague worry penetrated in Heinrich's soul. He knocked on the door. "May I come in?"

Silence was the answer, and Heinrich opened the door. Rachel lay in the bed, unconscious. Her head hung helplessly; her face was crimson red.

Heinrich rushed over and grasped her hand. Then he opened his mouth to say something, but no words came except one, "Rachel!" He put his hand on her hot forehead; she had a high fever. Rachel opened her eyes but did not recognize him.

Heinrich was at a loss. In his bachelor's home, there were no drugs or medications. He remembered that there was a thermometer in the kitchen. So he rushed to the kitchen, found it and measured Rachel's temperature. He couldn't believe his eyes—the thermometer showed 41.3 degrees Centigrade.

Heinrich sat on the floor near the bed. He understood Rachel needed a doctor; otherwise she would die. But to call a doctor was just the same as calling the Gestapo; the number tattooed on her hand spoke for itself. He slowly rose and covered his face with his arms. "What can I do? What can I do?" he murmured desperately.

At last he decided to call his uncle. There are doctors in his laboratory, Heinrich thought desperately. They would help Rachel. He didn't think of how he would manage to transport her through the SS control point. He knew he would conceive of a plan. He couldn't even imagine suffering another setback.

Upon hearing a telephone operator's voice, he called the number and asked to be connected to *Schtandartenfuhrer SS*

Dornberger as soon as possible. "This is a matter of life and death!" he told the operator.

"Sorry, sir, the line went dead," the operator said in a minute. "But I'll try again."

After several minutes, Heinrich heard a buzz and picked up the receiver again to hear an unknown voice, "*Oberschturmfuhrer SS* Lichter's listening."

"This is Captain Heinrich Menke, *Schtandartenfuhrer* Dornberger's nephew. Connect me with him urgently!"

"That's impossible, *Herr Hauptman*. *Schtandartenfuhrer* is on a business trip. He will not be back for three days."

Heinrich hung up. This is the end, he thought hopelessly.

He went to the kitchen, boiled water and put several spoons of honey in a glass of tea—it was the only medicine he knew. He brought the tea to Rachel's room where she lay with closed eyes, in the same position. Heinrich tried to force her to drink the tea, but failed—she was too weak.

"This is the end," he muttered. "This is the end."

He measured Rachel's temperature. It increased to the point 41.6 C

And this moment, Heinrich was blessed; he remembered the Bavarian priest, Sebastian Knieppe. Otto Dornberger had mentioned him in his lab; the priest treated himself for pneumonia by jumping in the icy water of Dunabe River.

Heinrich rushed to the bathroom, opened the cold-water faucet and filled the bathtub. Then he undressed Rachel, picked up her light body and put her in the icy water. He held her in cold water until his hands turned bluish gray from cold. Then he briskly rubbed her lifeless body with a towel and carried her back to the bed. Her teeth chattered, so he covered her by two blankets. Then Heinrich sat on the floor near the bed.

"My Lord," he whispered, "please save my girl! Don't be angry with me for my ride to church on that St. Bernard dog. I did not intend to insult you. Please Lord, save my girl!" Heinrich felt like crying but his eyes were dry.

In her state of semi-consciousness, Rachel mumbled something incoherent. Senseless words from both mixed in the darkness, creating a weird atmosphere of pre-death craziness.

"I have to pull myself together." Heinrich regained at last his sense. "I have to persuade myself that everything is all right," he told himself, but in the next moment he began murmuring again. "Don't die, Rachel. Only God knows how I love you."

Heinrich took Rachel's hot hand in his and pressed it to his forehead. He sat on the floor near the bed until heavy sleep owned him.

Rachel's soft voice woke him up.

"Heinrich," she whispered weakly. "I need a drink."

He jumped up and brought Rachel a glass of water. After she drank, Heinrich measured her temperature. It was still about thirty-nine degrees, but the crisis had passed.

CHAPTER 19

▼

The division of coordination of scientific research for *Wehrmacht* stopped functioning long ago. After a reorganization of the research division of *Wehrmacht*, Heinrich and his boss Colonel Ollendorf, a heavy-set man in his late fifties, officially belonged to the staff of the Army's Weapons Department. Their duties were not too burdensome, and so when Heinrich saw his boss packing his personal things, he rolled his eyes in surprise.

"Sit down, Heinrich," ordered Ollendorf, answering Heinrich's silent question. "I've been reassigned to Field Marshal Klugge's headquarters. I had asked to be sent to the front where I would be more useful to the Fuhrer." The last words he said loudly, knowing there were many hidden microphones in the office. "There is little work here, and meteorologists predict a hot summer." Ollendorf looked at Heinrich attentively, and then continued, "I would willingly include you in my staff if you wish to be sent to the West front." He stressed the words 'West front.' Colonel Ollendorf had already made the decision to surrender to the Americans as soon as he could to get out of this inferno. He possessed valuable information about the FAU program and thought that it would essentially facilitate his after-war fate.

"Thank you, *Herr Oberst.*" Heinrich refused politely. "I have obligations here, in Berlin." He freed a cigarette from the pack in his pocket and stuck it in his mouth, with the words, "With your permission, sir."

Ollendorf looked at him with pity. He considered this young man cleverer. Silently, he extended his hand to Heinrich.

"Good luck, *Herr Oberst,*" Heinrich said and left the office.

Although the work at the Ministry wasn't too burdensome, it did require frequent short business trips to inspect the *Wehrmacht* arsenals. In the unoccupied parts of Germany, plants worked at full capacity, producing armament that exceeded the needs of the shrinking German army.

Realizing the approaching German defeat but looking toward the future, the Nazi leadership ordered the creation of a number of secret arsenals that wouldn't fall into the Allies' hands.

During one such inspection trip, Heinrich was taken to the field hospital with a shell splinter in his shoulder. The surgeon said, "It will heal in three weeks."

"Three weeks? That's impossible!" Heinrich exclaimed with impatience.

"What's the hurry?" The surgeon laughed. "Maybe in three weeks the war will be done and you'll stay alive." He was so tired that he was no longer afraid of Gestapo.

The next day, Heinrich left the hospital and, still pale from loss of blood, returned to Berlin. That same day he met Adolf Hitler in the corridor of the Reich Headquarters. Heinrich froze, raised his left hand instead of the bandaged right one. Recognizing him, Hitler stopped. Somebody from his retinue whispered him that Heinrich was wounded but had not remained at the hospital. Hitler took off the Night Crest from the neck of one of the officers who accompanied him, and hung it on Heinrich's neck. Heinrich saw that his hands were shaking.

"I'm proud of you, my boy," Hitler said, his voice trembling. Then Hitler moved on down the hall, forgetting about his god-child.

When Heinrich returned home, he found the table in the dining room set for supper, with two candles flickering in the darkened room. He looked at Rachel wondering what was going on.

"Today happens to be my 19th birthday," Rachel said, and a weak smile lit her face. She stood quietly for a moment, her face infinitely tender.

"My congratulations, Rachel," Heinrich said softly. "Sorry, I didn't know and didn't get a gift for you."

"You're with me, Heinrich," Rachel said quietly. "That's my gift." Her eyes became moist. She paused to calm her racing heart.

Heinrich poured wine in their glasses. "What can I wish for you, Rachel? I wish you a life, long and happy." He sipped his wine while Rachel took a gulp and coughed.

"Don't you like this wine?"

"It's the first wine in my life," she said. "I've never tasted wine. When we were arrested, I was thirteen years old."

Heinrich sighed heavily. "Soon this barbarity will be finished," he said firmly. "What did you do before the war?" Heinrich asked, trying to deflect her from her sad thoughts.

"I studied music since I was six, and dreamed of becoming a pianist."

"Then you will certainly be a pianist," Heinrich said convincingly.

He gestured toward the sofa in invitation for Rachel to sit, and put a Bach record on the gramophone. For a time both silently listened to the music.

"Music helped me survive," Rachel said thoughtfully. "When I'm sad or upset, I always listen to music. It lives inside me," she explained.

"Maybe because you, Rachel, are the music itself," Heinrich smiled and got up. "Thank you," he said, "you have presented me with an unforgettable evening."

Rachel also stood up and put her hands on his shoulder. "Kiss me, Heinrich," she whispered and closed her eyes. "Please, kiss me. Nobody has ever kissed me."

Heinrich held her brittle body in his embrace, and his heart felt into an abyss. His mouth touched her dry hot lips, and she, unskillfully, returned the kiss. He smelled her hair, her breath.

Then, unable to control himself, Heinrich began kissing her face, her eyes, and her cheeks. "I love you, Rachel," he whispered passionately. "Only Lord knows how I love you!"

"I love you too, Heinrich," she whispered. Tears coursed down her cheeks.

Heinrich sensed this and his eyes filled tears too. Tears of happiness mixed and turned into a stormy flood of passion. That flood carried them far away beyond reality where both were flung into the bottomless abyss of delight.

CHAPTER 20

▼

The next day Otto Dornberger called Heinrich.

"I have sad news for you, Heinrich," he said without preamble. "An hour ago *Oberschturmbanfuhrer SS* Kurt Schwartzenegger called me from Murnau to tell that your father was killed two days ago." Then he added, "There's nothing to be done. During war, people are killed."

"But he wasn't serving in *Wehrmaght*," Heinrich replied for some reason.

"He served the Fuhrer as we all do," Dornberger said, and Heinrich understood that his uncle wasn't alone in his office while talking to him.

Heinrich had not seen his father for more than two years. Despite the aloofness between them, he felt a heartfelt sadness. Although parents' departures were as regular as life itself, death ahead of time causes sadness. But what does 'ahead of time' mean? Who sets the schedule?

"How did it happen?" he asked.

"It was bad luck," Dornberger explained. "One of the Allies' bombers, on the way to Munich lost a bomb, and it hit the municipal building. Rupert has been already buried, but if you have a chance to visit Murnau, drop in at your home to take something valuable as a remembrance. Although the house is sealed, it can be vandalized. Accept my condolences, Heinrich. Your father was the Fuhrer's devoted servant." Dornberger added, and Heinrich was finally assured that Dornberger wasn't alone talking to him.

Within a week, Heinrich had the chance to get to Murnau. His new boss Colonel Messner, dry and emotionless like all engineers, included him in a group that had to make the decision about relocating a military arsenal in Munich suburb. That relocation could mean that the war was rapidly approaching its conclusion. Heinrich and all the other officers realized it.

After the inspection was over, Colonel Messner gave Heinrich two days to stay in Murnau and visit his father's grave. Heinrich drove to the Commendatory and handed his ID to the duty officer. "I'd like to speak to *Oberschturmbanfuhrer* Schwartzenegger."

Seeing Himmler's signature on the ID, the SS officer jumped from his chair, *"Yavol, Herr Hauptman."*

He made a quick call. Another officer came and silently showed Heinrich to the Schwartzenegger's office. When Heinrich arrived, Schwartzenegger stood to greet him. He was a short, unpleasant type with yellow, smoke-stained teeth and a mustache '*a'la Hitler.*'

"Take a seat, captain." He pointed Heinrich to one of the armchairs near his desk. "Will you have anything to drink?"

"No, thank you, sir," Heinrich refused. "I want to take a bath and rest a little. There are only two days at my disposal."

"Tomorrow, one of my officers will show you to the cemetery. Your father was buried behind the chapel."

"Thank you, sir." Heinrich stood up and raised his right hand.

"By the way," Schwartzenegger stopped him, "Don't be surprised if you find evidence of a search in your house. Your father wasn't an ordinary citizen. He belonged to our elite; so the SS removed and sealed any papers having a state clearance." He looked at Heinrich's face attentively.

What an unpleasant type, Heinrich thought again. "I understand, sir," he said. "I haven't been in the house for close to ten years. I left Murnau as a teenager, and since then I've lived with my uncle, *Schtandartenfuhrer SS* Dornberger." Heinrich said. After a short pause, he added, "Regarding the papers…I think now they are more secure."

"I am glad we understand each other, captain. Believe me, I am entirely at your disposal…And my best regards to your uncle," Schwartzenegger added.

Heinrich went out of the Commendatory and walked along the familiar street. He left this silent town as a naïve, inexperienced teenager just entering life. He has now returned as an experienced man who dove into human mud, blood and suffering, psychologically much older than his physical age.

Heinrich looked around. The war almost had not touch Murnau. None of the houses were destroyed. The only bomb that had touched the town had fallen on City Hall and destroyed one of its wings. And killed Rupert Menke, he thought and pinched himself that he called his father not father but Rupert Menke. He remembered that it was worth saying only good things about the dead or nothing at all.

Heinrich walked for three blocks more, turned around the corner, and saw the familiar house where he had lived for the first fifteen years of his life. He broke the seal on the door and went in. He stood on the threshold for a moment and entered the hall. Nothing had changed—neither color of walls or furniture. He sat on the familiar black leather sofa and closed his eyes.

The nostalgia of childhood usually painted with colors of unforgettable charm. We remember the heat of the fireplace, Mother's tenderness, and Father's back defending us from all winds and troubles. What could be more remarkable than childhood remembrances?

Heinrich thought that the heat of this home had never warmed his soul. Alas, everything that remained in his memory was his mother's hysterics and his father's eternal ill nature. He tried to remember whether he had ever heard a kind word from Father; but he could not. Unfortunately he felt nothing but a light sadness about the childhood that had passed in that house.

Pushing away his recollections, Heinrich lit a cigarette and inhaled deeply. He wanted to drink something. The charm of the past was in the fact that the past had already passed; he remembered reading that phrase somewhere. Was there a charm in his past?

Heinrich rose, took his uniform off and went to the bathroom. When he turned on the hot water faucet, there was no water. He sighed and turned off the faucet. It's worth a drink, he thought automatically.

Searching for alcohol, Heinrich saw the open safe door in Father's study. He remembered that the SS had expropriated all papers having state interest. Heinrich grinned and thought that obviously the only papers that had had interest were money. At last he succeeded in his search and found a bottle of schnapps.

Then Heinrich had only one wish—to fall asleep and not to think.

In the morning, he was forced to shave with cold water. Hearing the doorbell, he went to the entrance and opened the door.

"*Heil* Hitler!" A young, tall but rather hard-faced *unterscharfuhrer SS* greeted him from the threshold. "*Unterschturmbanfuhrer SS* Schwartzenegger sent me to drive you to the cemetery, *Herr Hauptman*. I'll show you your father's grave. Take your time, sir. I'll wait you in the car."

"Thank you, *unterscharfuhrer*. Give me another ten minutes."

Heinrich finished shaving, put on his uniform and went out to the car waiting for him near the entrance. Soon they reached the church, with a small cemetery behind it.

The officer showed Heinrich a fresh grave decorated with a wooden crest. There was a sign on it, RUPERT MENKE, 1895–1945. He was only forty-nine, Heinrich thought absent-mindedly.

"I suspect that you will want to stay here alone for a while, sir, and you do not need my assistance anymore. I'll wait you in the car," the officer offered delicately.

"Thank you," Heinrich said. "Take your time. I'll return home by myself."

Heinrich stood by his father's grave for several minutes and thought that Rupert Menke, like hundreds of thousands of others, could have been killed somewhere at the front. But in any case, he wouldn't stay there pricking himself for the absence of a son's feelings.

"Forgive me, my Lord," he said aloud and left, without a glance back.

He walked home, submerged in thoughts, but they were far from Murnau. He returned home, closed the door behind him and looked around as if the house was unfamiliar.

Did he want to take something to remember his childhood? He walked slowly around the house. His glance stopped on the photo with his favorite St. Bernard dog, the one that was his mount into the church. Heinrich put the photo into his pocket and went into his mother's bedroom. He looked around: empty walls, a crucifixion above the bed. Did Menke sleep with other women on the same bed? Heinrich sighed. He rushed out of that room into his father's study, almost hitting the massive writing desk, with a large photo of the Fuhrer on the wall behind it. The wall safe was broken, its door hung open…

Suddenly Heinrich felt blessed, remembering that there was another safe in this house, in the kitchen, in the wall behind the big freezer.

In the seventh or eighth grade, he had planned a party for his schoolmates while his parents were out of town. When the beer supply ran out, Heinrich remembered that he had seen a supply down in the kitchen fridge. It was locked, but Heinrich knew where the key was kept. But when he stood on tiptoe and tried to get it on top of the refrigerator, the key fell between the freezer and the wall. Frustrated, Heinrich pulled the freezer away from the wall. To his surprise, behind it he saw the small metal door of a wall safe. Paying no attention to it, he got the key, moved the freezer back before opening it, and took the beer out. When he returned to the hall with all the beer in his hands, the guys greeted him by a loud "Hurrah!"

Now, remembering that safe, Heinrich went to the kitchen. The freezer, with its door ajar, stood in the same place; the SS men hadn't moved it away from the wall. Heinrich strained as he had in his childhood, trying to move it out from the wall. At last he succeeded and saw the metal wall safe.

Heinrich understood it would be a waste of time to try to find the lock combination. He sat at table, thinking over the situation. He had only one day at his disposal. What could he do without help? But help was beyond consideration. Heinrich remembered his father was a thrifty man who kept various tools in the basement. So he went to the basement, and among all the useless and useful tools, found what he searched; it was an electric drill.

Heinrich worked for almost six hours without a break, and finally managed to open the safe's door. Lining up everything in front of him, he had for his viewing an old newspaper, with time-yellowed pages, an envelope, and a pack of money. Dollars, he thought automatically. They interested him the least of all, and he put them aside.

Then Heinrich opened the envelope and…couldn't believe his eyes to see thirty years old porno photos, in which Rupert Menke was compromised with Adolf Hitler and several unknown young men.

Heinrich understood that the reason for the unsuccessful SS searches lay in front of him. Large drops of sweat fell on the top photo; these pictures could cost the life of any one who held them in hands. His first reaction was to destroy them immediately, but then he put them back in the envelope.

Laying it to the side, Heinrich opened the newspaper to find an article from the "Chronics" section marked by the red pencil.

Heinrich read it carefully. The article was about an auto accident with two casualties; it seemed Heinrich the usual police chronic. But why did Rupert Menke keep it in the safe, with those explosive photos, for more than twenty-five years? He reread the article again. '*A baby is still missing and hasn't been found. It is conjectured that the baby has become a victim of wild animals in the forest.*' An awful case, Heinrich thought matter-of-factly.

Suddenly his heart jumped. He looked at the date: June 1920. No, it had no relationship to him—he was born three months later. But why had Rupert Menke marked the article and kept it in the safe for twenty-five years? Maybe he was the cause of that accident and felt the pricks of conscience? Heinrich thought. No. He rejected that thought. Rupert Menke and pricks of conscience—it was nonsense! But something was wrong. He proceeded to read again, slowly repeating every word aloud. Unexpectedly, with all the fibers of his soul, Heinrich realized that he was the missing baby. He made a weak attempt to persuade himself that he was born three months later and had no relation to the baby. But he already knew the truth. They had simply changed the date of his birth. For the first time in his thoughts, Heinrich called parents "they."

Heinrich stood up. His dissipated glance stayed on the bottle of schnapps he drank the day before. He poured the alcohol in the glass and drank in one big gulp. But it did not bring comfort; he only felt nausea. Suddenly his legs failed him; he realized that the people who had perished in the car accident, the lieutenant and his wife, were Jews. A shiver passed through his body. Heinrich pressed his head with both hands. "No, no, no," he whispered desperately. But every "no" that he whispered sounded in his head with a painful "yes." Yes, yes, yes...

He crashed down in the chair. It meant that he, Heinrich Menke, a captain in the German Army, the Fuhrer's godchild, the nephew of the *schtandartenfuhrer SS* was a Jew. My Lord! He couldn't stand with this thought in his head. Heinrich felt that the sweat dampened hairs on his head stood on end.

Motionless, with closed eyes, Heinrich sat at the kitchen table for a long time. He felt more dead than alive. Then, almost automatically, he took his gun from its holster and laid it in front of him. He looked at it with wild eyes.

"This is the only exit for me," Heinrich decided finally, and took the gun in his hand.

But when Heinrich was ready to pull the trigger, he remembered Rachel. My Lord, my shot would kill her too, he thought desperately. No, he could not kill Rachel; she had to live. Heinrich sighed heavily and put the gun back in the holster.

CHAPTER 21

▼

When Heinrich entered the front door at his home, Rachel ran to greet him. Upon seeing his dark face, her heart fell. She caught his hand. "What happened, Heinrich?" She asked with a worried frown. "Your face looks odd. Is everything all right?"

Silently, he laid the old newspaper in front of her. Rachel read the red-penciled article but failed to understand how it related to him. She looked at Heinrich questioningly.

"The missing child is me," he said hoarsely. "I am a Jew, Rachel. I'm a Jew," he repeated, his gaze on the outspread paper.

Suddenly Rachel cried out. Her tears grew into a nerve wrenching sobbing. She embraced his head with both hands and began to kiss his eyes, cheeks and lips passionately. "My Lord," she whispered through her tears, "I always knew You existed." Then, getting calmer, she said, "I always knew you, Heinrich, were God's miracle sent to me." She took a gulp of cold water from the glass in front of her. "Since that day when you tried to stop your sobbing with Bach's music," she explained. "I heard it."

She tenderly pressed Heinrich's hair. "Everything is from God. I haven't told you that in the concentration camp, I tried to commit suicide by hanging myself after my parents and two brothers were killed in the gas chamber. An old rabbi saved me and took off the loop. When I recovered consciousness, the rabbi said, 'my girl, to kill yourself is a sin because life is given to us by God; only He can take it back. Here, on the Earth, we live only for a short time; there—we will live forever. Remember, that life is God's miracle.' What could I have understood, a naïve kid who had lost all my relatives in one moment? I understood what it meant, only when I met you, Heinrich. I understood that life is a miracle. I could have died many times, but I live—this is a miracle. You could have perished in that car crash with your parents, but you are alive—and this is a miracle. We are together, Heinrich, and this is also the miracle."

"I am a captain of the German army, Rachel. I am German. I have been German for twenty-five years. Now I must hate the people among whom I had lived for all my life. But I don't feel hatred toward them in my soul. I feel only tired and indifferent. And contempt for myself because I will never be able to look my people in the eyes." Heinrich's hands were trembling, and he shook his head miserably.

"It's not your fault, Heinrich. You could live your whole life and never have exposed your past, never known that you were a Jew. God opened your eyes, Heinrich. As the rabbi said, 'we all were sent to this world to accomplish our mission.' I already know my own mission." Rachel smiled. "My mission is to love you, to give births your children, and to make you happy."

Rachel embraced his head and pressed it to her breasts. Feeling the heat of her skin, Heinrich closed his eyes, and gradually the inhuman tension of the last days left him. Let the world around me die, let Germany go to the abyss of crimes, he thought; let the punishment reach everyone who deserves it. He, Heinrich Menke, no longer belongs to their world.

Heinrich Menke died with the world in which he had lived. He still wears the military uniform, but he already lives in another world. This is Rachel's world, magic and sparkling world, one in which he had just made his first awkward steps. But he'll learn about that world and will be able to look people in eyes without shame.

Heinrich did not show Rachel the Fuhrer's photos—she was too pure for such mud.

The next day, sitting at the desk in his office, Heinrich tried to decide what he could do with the Fuhrer's photographs. Of course the Fuhrer was a holy man for the German nation, and his morality could not be the subject of discussion. Only an idiot, who wished to go through all the Gestapo circles of hell before receiving a bullet in his temple, could doubt it.

Finally Heinrich decided to give the photos to Otto Dornberger. He was seeking chances to save his life and tried to find something of interest to the Allies if they captured him. Maybe if these photos got to the Allies, Heinrich thought, it would help them overthrow the Fuhrer from his pedestal and show the Germans what they had worshipped all those years.

Heinrich still had mixed strange feelings about Otto Dornberger, the culprit of killing of hundreds of Jews who had become victims of his experiments. As a fanatical adherent of science, professor Dornberger inspired Heinrich's respect. But as a pathological anti-Semite, *schtandartenfuhrer* SS Dornberger inspired his aversion.

If Heinrich had no feelings about Rupert Menke, he did continue to feel a kind of gratitude to Otto Dornberger for the warmth of the family hearth, the warmth that had melted his frozen teenage heart. If Heinrich had found himself among judges who were deciding Otto Dornberger's fate, he was not sure that he would have been able to sentence him to death.

Upon meeting his uncle, Heinrich gave him the envelope, saying, "I found them at the house." He couldn't say 'in my father's house.' "My first reaction was to destroy them. But then I thought that only you, Uncle, must make the final decision about what to do with them."

Otto Dornberger opened the envelope and looked at the photos. Finally! He had wanted to have something like this since the day Rupert Menke was arrested. He felt Rupert was bound to have kept something from his past to save his life. Now he knew exactly what Rupert Menke had kept. Silently, Dornberger put photos into the wall safe. Then he returned to his chair. His face was twisted and utterly tragic. After a long silence, he spoke. "It's the right decision, Heinrich." He smiled with the corners of his lips, his voice perfectly controlled and casual.

But Heinrich couldn't have imagined that having given Otto Dornberger that envelope he had signed his uncle's death sentence.

During one of Dornberger's business trips, his aide-de-camp *Oberscharfuhrer SS* Dietrich Reckmann was searching for money and opened the safe in Dornberger's office. He had learned the combination long ago but thought that the professor kept in the safe nothing excepting the medical records of his research. All the previous times that he'd opened the safe, he had found nothing. And this time Reckman's search was vain as well—he did not find money. The Russian front tank divisions were already observed only a few kilometers from the lab, and Dietrich Reckman hadn't the slightest wish to be captured by the Russians or to be blown up with the lab. The complex was mined.

Although not finding any money, Reckmann was surprised to see an envelope in the back of the safe. He decided that luck had at last winked at him and he had finally found money. Opening the envelope, he saw…the Fuhrer's photos. Reckmann froze. He was so scared that he himself called the Gestapo.

"This is a matter of national security!" Reckmann shouted in the receiver. The voice on the other side trailed off, and he waited. Then he quickly explained that he had found very important papers in Professor Dornberger's safe.

In less than an hour, two large, black cars stopped near the entrance gate where *Oberscharfuhrer* Reckmann waited for the SS people, frozen in a *"Heil* Hitler."

The *Schtandartenfuhrer SS* who got out the car waved his hand and asked to be shown to Dornberger's office.

Reckmann placed the envelope in front of the *schtandarten-fuhrer.*

"Where did you find them?"

"I took them from Herr Professor's safe," Reckmann asked, with a visible pulse pounding at his temple.

"Who told you the combination? If you saw the photos before this, why did you call us only now?" His colorless eyes drilled Reckmann.

"I spied on Professor Dornberger when he put documents in there, and I remembered the combination." Reckmann was thin-lipped with fear.

"When?"

"Several week ago."

"Why didn't you call us then?" *Schtandartenfuhrer's* face sported a suspicious frown.

"There was no envelope there when I opened the safe a month ago," Reckmann said, his voice trembling.

"Why did you look inside?"

"I thought Professor Dornberger kept money in the safe," Reckmann confessed.

"Who saw photos except you?"

"I think, only Herr Professor."

"Thank you, *Oberscharfuhrer.* I'll consider your promotion later on. But now, you'll go with us to my office to sign official papers as a witness to the search and extraction."

"*Yavol, Herr Schtandartenfuhrer!* Reckmann bawled joyfully.

"Close the safe." *Schtandartenfuhrer* put the envelope in the pocket of his uniform and went to the door.

Oberscharfuhrer SS Reckman rushed to follow him, and both jumped inside one of the cars. But when the vehicle suddenly stopped on the dark road, Dietrich Reckmann guessed that he was a dead man.

"Please!" he whispered, his voice frightened, pleading.

Shot on the way to Berlin, his corpse was thrown on the road.

Professor Otto Dornberger did not return to his office; his body was never found.

CHAPTER 22

Inevitably approaching the end, the war had marked on the calendar the day of the Allies' victory and the German defeat—May 9th, 1945. That day Field Marshal Kietel signed the Act of Capitulation.

Heinrich and Rachel pulled the heavy curtain aside at the window. The day was breaking. The stillness was strange—the stillness of the first hours of a new day. They couldn't speak. They didn't look at each other; they stood side by side, with Rachel's hand nestled in Heinrich's. They gazed at the bright sky; or perhaps, they did not look, only listened to the stillness of early morning.

The situation for Rachel and Heinrich now changed to the opposite side. He had managed to avoid surrendering, but found himself in the position of a man without documents, hiding from justice. To go through denazification, he had to surrender. If he surrendered to the Russians, he would be sent to one of the camps for the war captives. If he surrendered to the Americans, he would be sent in one of the denazification camps. In either case it meant many months, if not years, of separation from Rachel. Perhaps he would lose her forever.

Heinrich sat in the apartment, every day losing more and more hope of finding an exit from the dead end. What he definitely knew—he had to avoid being captured by the Russians; an officer from Hitler's headquarters would be imprisoned for a long time.

"We have to decide where you'll live, Rachel," he said. "Only in that case can I keep the hope that one day I will find you and see you again."

"I don't have any relatives, in Berlin or outside," Rachel said quietly. "When I go out and look at the faces of people on the street, I'm afraid of them although now these people are themselves dying from fear. I hate them, Heinrich! I hate all of the Germans though I try to persuade myself that I am wrong. But I won't be able to live in Germany, not in Berlin or anywhere else. I want to leave this country."

"But where can we go? I know only German and French, a little bit, from a course at school. But France isn't far from Germany in her anti-Semitism. Where can we live, Rachel, except in Germany?"

"When I was a little girl, my father's friends who used to come to our house, said that all Jews had to go to our motherland, Palestine. But my dad considered us German Jews and used to say that our motherland was Germany. Some of them have left, and they are alive; my dad stayed here, and they burned him." Her eyes were full of tears.

Heavy silence filled the room. At last Heinrich said, "To go to Palestine, we have to have British papers. And that's a big problem." Enthusiasm evaporated from his voice.

"It means we have to get them." Rachel took Heinrich's hand and pressed it to her lips. "We don't have another way."

"This section of Berlin is under Russian control." Heinrich sighed. "I don't have any idea how we can leave."

"We have to go during the daytime," Rachel said. "During the day, there's a chance that they won't stop us."

"I think you are right. We don't have the documents, but we have money. It's a lot—$19,000. I took it from Rupert Menke's safe, with the newspaper," he explained. "We can give all of them for documents. You have to hide it all on your body because there are fewer chances you'll be searched. Even if our chances are negligible, we have to try." Heinrich gave a firm nod.

"I know, Heinrich, that everything will be all right," Rachel said softly. "If God has saved us up until today, He will help us this time, too. I know it. I feel it by my heart," Rachel said with persuasion.

CHAPTER 23

▼

Captain Leo Berkowitz, the duty officer of the 22nd Infantry Unit, was sitting at his desk, dreaming about the future demobilization when a MP Sergeant reported that a German couple wished to talk to him.

Captain Berkowitz had spent three years at the East Front, since he voluntarily joined the US Army in 1942. From the day of his birth, he had flat feet and could easily have avoided the draft. Since he was a young, beginning screenwriter in Hollywood, he had dreamed of writing something extraordinary that would shake up Hollywood by its roots. But until he created that "something," he wrote scripts in the style of old westerns, and one movie studio after another rejected them. Leo Berkowitz was a smart Jewish man, and he realized one day that only his fresh impressions of the war could help him create that "something." He had joined the Army despite all his mother's tears and his father's attempts to dissuade him from the decision.

Besides English, Leo Berkowitz was fluent in German, and that fact had defined his fate. After finishing officers' school, he was promoted to the rank of first lieutenant and sent to the Army Intelligence Division of the 22nd Infantry Unit where he had led the way from Normandy to Berlin. During that time, he was wounded twice, awarded two Purple Hearts and promoted to the rank of captain. By the end of the war, he had collected in the attic of his head such an amount of fresh war impressions that he had more than enough for that script to shake up Hollywood. Now Leo Berkowitz dreamt of the demobilization so he could start his life's main work.

Berkowitz looked out the window of his office, still dreaming about the demobilization. The day promised to be warm and strangely sultry for spring in Berlin. As he dragged his thoughts back to the present, the MP Sergeant led a German couple into his office.

"Take a seat, please," Berkowitz said in German as he pointed to two chairs in front of his desk.

"We came for help, Herr Officer." Rachel took the initiative and looked deeply into Leo's eyes. Then she told him the history of their lives.

Berkowitz listened without interrupting her. The amazingly beautiful eyes of the woman sitting in front of him held him captive. He had no doubt that she told him the truth.

When Rachel stopped talking, she handed Leo the newspaper with the article about the car accident circled and said quietly, "We are Jews, Herr Officer, I and my fiancé. My name is Rachel Gecht," she said and looked at Leo Berkowitz with a slow, deliberate, graceful gesture that she made out of the simple turning of her head. "My fiancé's name is Heinrich Ginsberg."

After three years in the field, Leo thought that he had seen everything; blood and death, suffering and hopes, broken fates, but what he heard now could not be compared with anything. In front of him sat Hitler's godchild reincarnated in his Judaism as a Phoenix from the ashes.

Why did he believe in this fairy tale? Leo could not say. But he had believed, even before Rachel rolled up the sleeve of her blouse and showed him Buchenwald's number on her hand.

"How can I be of use to you?" Leo asked sincerely.

"We need papers, Herr Captain," Heinrich said frankly. "Everything that I know is my parents' last name from that article—Ginsberg. It's the truth," Heinrich declared defensively as if he expected the officer to distrust them.

"I'll give you a pass valid for the American zone." Leo Berkowitz said after a long pause. He leaned forward in his chair. "But it's a temporary document. You have to address your request for permanent papers to one of the local magistrates. What else can I do for you?" There was no fake interest in Berkowitz's voice.

Looking at the young people sitting in front of him, he realized that the story of their lives would be a great plot for a script, the writing of which he had dreamt for all his life.

"I don't know if I can ask you for another favor, Herr Officer," Rachel said hesitantly. "None of my relatives are alive, but I remember one of my late father's friends. His name was Baruch Silverman. He was a high-ranked person in some International Jewish Organization. I don't remember the name of the organization…maybe it was the World Jewish Congress. I was a little girl, but he was a close friend of my father. If you would let him know I am alive…"

"I'll try, Miss Gecht," Leo Berkowitz said although he was not sure he would be able to do it.

He couldn't say why, but he would do anything this young lady asked him. He signed and sealed the passes for Rachel and

Heinrich. Handing them over, he asked, "How can I find you if I locate this gentleman?"

"We'll rent a room somewhere nearby, sir" Heinrich said. "If you allow it, we'll give you a call and leave our phone number."

After Rachel and Heinrich thanked him heartily and left, Leo closed his eyes and thought about how unpredictable fate was. *"Who can predict tomorrow, and what tomorrow is? Tomorrow's hope, and dream, and sorrow—is only destiny."* He remembered the verses that he had read before the war, but couldn't recollect the poet's name. "That's right." He sighed. "Every Jewish life is destiny."

He went to the office of his superior officer, Lt. Colonel Thomas Grithings, and asked his permission to call Los Angeles. He did not explain why, and Grithings did not ask any questions. He was a typical South Carolina man who grew up in an atmosphere of anti-Jewish prejudices. Captain Leo Berkowitz had changed his superior's attitude about Jews, and Lt. Colonel Grithings respected him.

After several unsuccessful attempts, Leo telephoned his old friend, the playwright Barry Nyman. He heard Barry's voice distorted by distance.

"This is Leo Berkowitz, Barry."

"Who?"

"Leo Berkowitz, you dopey fuck! Are you already so famous that you've forgotten an old friend's name?"

"Are you alive, Leo?" His surprise was sincere.

"Yes, you idiot, I am. And I need your help. I want you to find a man, Baruch Silverman by name. Before the war, he was a big *balabos* in the World Jewish Organization."

"Why do you need him?"

"Barry, try to understand what time we live in. If I call you, I need your help."

"Where are you calling from, Leo? The connection is bad."

"From Germany. You may have heard that we won the war. Write down my number."

Nyman wrote down Leo's phone number and said, "Okay, I'll do my best and talk to a rabbi in my synagogue. If a man you talked about was a *balabos*, the rabbi had to know him."

"Okay. But do not forget, Barry, it's urgent." He hung up.

Barry really did his best. After his best friend Leo joined the Army, he felt guilty that he was a weak-willed man who couldn't follow Leo's example. During that period of his life, he shared the mentality of most American Jews thinking that European problems were of no interest to Americans. Who could imagine the scale of the developing Jewish tragedy? Barry Nyman was only an ordinary Jew, nothing more. But why the 'big wigs' of Jewish leadership did nothing?

In our entire history, he thought, the unfortunate Jewish tendency to take an excessively optimistic view, to mistake temporary improvements for permanent ones, had never had such devastating consequences. Even after the most extreme measures had been taken against the German Jews and their persecution was in full force, Jewish minorities in other countries, not directly affected, refused to believe that the same could happen to them.

Even after the first two million European Jews were killed and American Jews received information about that tragedy, The *New York Times* only published a small article about that tragedy on the page seventeen, among all the other nonsense and advertisements. American Jews were afraid that by standing up for their people in Europe, they would be blamed for the absence of patriotism; it could create a wave of anti-Semitism that would affect their secure lives in America. He, Barry Nyman, was among those who silently closed their eyes about everything. But by silently accepting evil, had he not become a participant of the crimes, Barry wondered bitterly.

Why didn't their leaders try to mobilize the Jews and persuade them to fight Nazism with political means? If, in the first few years, they had succeeded in organizing an effective anti-Nazi boycott, mobilizing the Jewish influence, especially in America and England, against the Nazi regime while it was still weak, and if millions of Gentiles had joined them, they might have produced a suspension of the Nuremberg Laws and possibly made arrangements where German Jews could emigrate. But unfortunately, influential American Jews fiercely rejected that idea, refusing to believe that the same could happen to them.

"Stupid idiots! We're all stupid idiots who always try to find a non-Jewish scapegoat to be blamed for our tragedies," Barry muttered. He was irritated with himself for feeling like he was part of the Jewish herd. "We all can be blamed for what happened." Barry Nyman felt like a piece of shit, and went to the nearest café for a drink.

On Saturday, Barry went to the synagogue to talk to Rabbi Wassel, an influential member of the American Jewish community, an Old Testament Jew who never forgave or forgot, and who possessed no trace of a talent for keeping personal and political affairs separate. Once he had adopted a movement or an idea, he served it with the utmost devotion. He was a loyal friend to all those who shared his views, and only his views.

Rabbi Wassel was among the few American rabbis who took the warnings seriously. Even in June of 1940, he made the gloomy forecast that the prolongation of the war might mean the annihilation of half the European Jewry. But he was violently attacked by the press as a prophet of disaster and indignantly asked how anyone could bring himself to speak of such things. He had sharply criticized the American Jewish leadership for its position during the war. Hence, he had few friends in the American Jewry.

"Baruch Silverman?" Rabbi Wassel had asked repeatedly when Barry Nyman requested that he find the man. After a short silence he added, "Yes, I know him. He's one of few Jews who predicted this catastrophe and who supported my position about it. Unfortunately, we were the minority. I think he's somewhere in Europe now. I'll get in touch with High Commission for Refugees. Baruch Silverman was our representative in it. Anyway, we'll find him, Barry," Rabbi summarized. "I'll be in touch with you."

"It's urgent, Dr. Wassel," Barry reminded him, his voice sharp as the edge of a finely honed knife. "Let's save at least one Jewish life if we couldn't save millions." He sighed as he rose to his feet.

"One life is the whole world." Rabbi Wassel nodded.

Less than a week later, Leo picked up the telephone and heard a strange, unhurried voice, with a strong British accent. "May I talk to Captain Berkowitz, please?"

"Speaking."

"My name is Baruch Silverman. An old friend of mine, Rabbi Wassel of Los Angeles, gave me your phone number and urgently asked that I get in touch to you," he said in a very quiet voice.

"Yes, Mr. Silverman, I'd like to ask you a question, sir," said Leo, getting right to the point. "Is the name Gecht familiar to you?"

"You said, Gecht?" After the short silence, Silverman verified, "Yes, I knew a man named Albert Gecht. He was a Vice Chairman of the German Zionist Council. He was arrested, with all the members of his family, in 1939. As far as I know, they all died in the concentration camp."

"Did Mr. Gecht have a daughter?" Leo Berkowitz asked, with a palpable feeling of eagerness.

"Yes, a girl about thirteen, but I don't recollect her name."

"Rachel."

"Yes, sir, you are right, Rachel. Now I remembered her name."

"She survived, Mr. Silverman, and needs your help. You're the only man who can help her regain her life," Leo Berkowitz said quietly as if the words he spoke were the most natural thing in the world—an appeal for a help for an unknown girl.

"Is she seriously ill?"

"No, sir, she is quite well for a girl who has spent six years in the concentration camps." Leo Berkowitz calmed him.

Within two weeks, Baruch Silverman arrived in Germany as an official representative of the World Jewish Congress for his controversial meeting in Bonn with the future German

Chancellor Conrad Adenauer. After the meeting, he went to Berlin to see Rachel.

Using his political connections, he helped Rachel and Heinrich to get passports and all the necessary papers giving them permission to go to Palestine, which still remained under the British Protectorate.

PART III

▼

THE PROMISED LAND

"Isn't my help inside me?"

—Ketuvim, Iov, 5-6

CHAPTER 24

▼

With the end of the war, the Palestine problem entered an acute phase. Relations between the Jewish Agency and the British had been strained during the last year of war, but as long as the war lasted, the Jewish Agency avoided open conflict with Britain at any price.

The "White Paper Policy" formulated in 1939, which kept a stranglehold on immigration, was rigorously not enforced by the British government. This put the Jewish Agency in the difficult position of cooperating with Britain while rejecting the White Paper at the same time. A peculiar situation had taken place—the Palestinian Jewry fought on the British side of war as if there were no White Paper, and fought against the White Paper when there was no war.

After the defeat of the Nazis, when the number of Jews surviving in occupied countries could be estimated, it was immediately obvious that the maintenance of the status quo in Palestine was bound to lead to bitter conflict. There were more than half a million Jewish survivors in concentration camps in Germany, Austria and Italy. It was quite clear that the only possible solution to the refugee problem was a large-scale immigration to Palestine. There was simply no other country ready to accept them, and the great majority ardently wished to go to Palestine.

The British government, which had allowed it to be forced into adopting a policy in consideration of the Arabs, was unwilling to recognize that elementary fact. It continued to restrict immigration, so that the Jewish Agency found it compelled to agree to a plan for taking these refugees without Britain's permission.

Tension increased steadily. In Palestine something resembling a state of war existed between the Jewish population and British authorities while the Jewish Agency's relationship with London grew ever more distant and strained. The whole process reached a climax with London's decision to arrest the leading members of the Jewish Agency in Jerusalem, intern them and, in effect, impose a state of siege on Palestine.

Such was the situation in Palestine when Rachel and Heinrich arrived in Tel Aviv. They had avoided the usual problems that thousands of refugees had as Baruch Silverman had provided all the necessary papers to give them permission to enter Palestine. As a representative of the World Jewish Congress, he had dealt with British authorities for a long time, and was such an extraordinary diplomat that he maintained friendly relations even with Ernst Bevin, a man considered by most of Baruch Silverman's colleagues to be an anti-Semite.

From their first step on Palestinian soil, the East impressed Henry and Rachel. On the passport that Heinrich had obtained with Baruch Silverman's help, he took his father's name, and now he was Henry Ginsberg. After the all terror of the last years, gloomy and frightened faces, dead bodies, hatred, desperation, and destroyed buildings, they found themselves in the epicenter of an unreal, colorful world of such beauty that they could never have imagined.

Tel Aviv attracted them more strongly every day. They so admired the street pavement—now a grayish-blue, and now violet, washed by rains and reflecting a swarm of restless lights, a profusion of flowers, a picturesque crowd on the streets. They fell in love with ordinary, but extraordinary Tel Aviv.

People's smiles on the street were wide and friendly. They were smiles of the chosen people—chosen to survive the awful past and to look forward to a happy future. On the buses, people emotionally discussed the latest political news as well as the most intimate events of their family's lives: parents' health, children's weddings, and love affairs. And everything was so natural, so informal, so friendly, and full of the true wish to help, to ease pain, to share joy, that Rachel and Heinrich could not express precisely what captured reconciliation.

But the level was different for each of them. For Rachel, it was the feeling of a Jewish girl stepping on her native soil. For Heinrich, it was still the sensation of a newborn. He was no longer German, but he had not yet become a Jew. The Jew that was born inside him had only just taken its first, unsteady steps on Jewish land.

They had no communication problems—most Jews who immigrated during this period were European Jews, *Ashkenazi.* Most of them knew German or Yiddish that was close to German. More difficult was communication with *Sabra* whose parents were from Asian and African countries. In that case, they communicated mostly using body language because *Sabra* knew only Hebrew and Arabic; and they looked more like Arabs than Jews. It seemed strange but all understood each other. To expand their knowledge, Rachel and Henry began studying Ivrit at classes in the local synagogue. The language was not as difficult as they had imagined, and soon they made great progress.

Although the future was still foggy for them, fate or God made the first move. Rachel found work as a kindergarten music teacher, and she was delighted to start working. More and more, Henry was inclined to enter the university to continue his education. But his knowledge of various subjects needed to be regained, and he worked hard to improve it. While Rachel was at work, he read everything he could find in the local library in German, not only preparing him for the entrance exams, but also widening his knowledge of historical subjects.

On one of those days, after breakfast, Henry sat in his chair and opened the first history book he laid his hands on:

> 'Fleeing Mesopotamia, the first wandering Hebrew tribes had barely set foot in that land before history condemned them to ten centuries of warfare, migration and slavery. Finally, fleeing Egypt under Moses, they began their forty years trek back to the hills of Judea to found their first sovereign state.
>
> Its apogee, under David and Solomon, lasted barely a century. Living at the crossroads of the caravan routes to Europe, Asia and Africa, installed on land that was already a beaconing temptation to every nearby civilization, the Hebrews endured a millennium of unremitting assaults. Assyria, Babylonia, Egypt, Greece, Rome, each in

turn sent its cohorts to conquer their land. Twice, in 587 B.C. and in A.D. 70, their conquerors inflicted a supreme ordeal of exile and destruction of the Temple they had built on Jerusalem's Mount Mariah for Yahweh, their one and universal deity. From all that desperation and the suffering accompanying it grew their tenacious attachment to their ancient land.'

Henry took his glance from the pages. Who could have thought a year ago that he would be sitting near a window in a Tel Aviv apartment, reading a book about the history of Jewish people, his people? Why was he given such a fate? What was his fate, he wondered. To become a Jew? That would be more than enough. But he felt his destiny wasn't restricted to that. He must do something for his people. But what could he do, a man who didn't even have a useful profession?

He has to enter the university and become a biologist. That destiny was clear for him. Why a biologist? Because since the day he treated Rachel with cold water, following Pastor Knieppe's example, his dream was to save the lives of people who were doomed to die. Would it be interfering with God's will? Henry tried to discard the heretic thought and again opened the book.

'Reinforcing its appeal, giving it a continual contemporary urgency, was the curse of persecution, which followed the Jews into every haven in which they had taken shelter during their dispersal. The roots of Jewish suffering grew out of the rise of another religion dedicated, paradoxically, to the love of man for man. Burning in the ardor of their new

faith to convert the pagan masses, the early fathers of the Christian Church strove to emphasize the differences between their religion and its theological predecessor by forcing a kind of spiritual apartheid upon the Jews. The Emperor Theodosius II gave those aspirations legal force in his code, condemning Judaism and, for the first time, legally branding the Jews as a people apart.'

Henry stopped reading and closed his eyes. Why did people always complicate life, creating new gods? Wasn't the creation of Christianity a strict violation of the First Commandment—the God is One? Weren't all tragedies in the world punishment for that violation? Who knew the answer?

He continued reading.

'Dagobert, King of Franks, drove the Jews from Gaul, Spain's Visigoths seized their children as converts; the Byzantine Emperor Heraclius forbade Jewish worship. With the Crusades, spiritual apartheid became systematic slaughter. Shrieking their cry "God's with us," the Crusaders fell on every hapless Jewish community on their rout to Jerusalem.

Most countries barred Jews from owning land. The religiously organized medieval craft and commerce guilds were closed to them. The Church forbade Jews employing Christians, and Christians living among Jews. Most loathsome of all was the decision of the Fourth Lutheran Council in 1215 to stamp out the Jews as a race by forcing them to wear a distinguishing badge. In England, it was a replica of the tablets on which Moses received the Ten

Commandments. In France and Germany, it was a yellow 'O,' a forerunner of the yellow stars that the Third Reich would use one day to mark the victims of its gas chambers.'

There was nothing new under the sun, thought Henry. Why didn't people take history lessons?

Edward I of England and later Philip the Fair of France expelled the Jews from their nations, seizing their property before evicting them. Even the Black Death was blamed on the Jews accused of poisoning Christian wells with a powder made of spiders, frog's legs, Christian entrails and consecrated hosts. Over two hundred Jewish communities were exterminated in the slaughters stirred by that wild fantasy.

In Germany, Jews were forbidden to ride in carriages and were made to pay a special toll as they entered the city. The Republic of Venice enriched the vocabulary with the word "ghetto." In Poland, the Cossack Revolt, with a ferocity and devotion to torturing unparalleled in Jewish experience, wiped out over 100,000 Jews in less than a decade. When Russian czars pushed their frontier westward across Poland, an era of darkness set in for almost half the world's Jewish population. In 1880, after the assassination of Alexander II, the mobs aided by the czar's soldiers, burned and butchered their way through one Jewish community after another, leaving a new word in their wake— "pogrom."

Henry felt a pain in his stomach. The sufferings of his people for millennia made him sick. He couldn't read any more. He put down the book and closed his eyes. "Why were we always so passive, not struggling for our dignity?" he muttered bitterly. "Why did we always accept what had happened 'as is,' considering it our destiny and not trying to change it? Why?" Henry felt nauseated and went to the kitchen to have a drink.

Imperceptibly, he began thinking "we" instead of "they." He thought about what he had already decided to be done; he finally decided to be circumcised.

Several days later, upon returning home from the work, Rachel spied Henry's pale face and ran to him. "Are you okay, Henry? Are you well?"

"I'm fine," he assured her. "But I won't be able to sleep with you for several weeks, honey."

Rachel raised her brow in surprise.

"I was circumcised," he explained. "It's not a big deal, a little bit extra skin gone." He smiled.

Rachel hid her face in his chest. "My Lord," she whispered. "Why did you give me such happiness?"

"I had two reasons for it," Henry explained softly. "First of all, I don't want being separated from my people in my future life. And secondly, how could I marry you without it?"

CHAPTER 25

—————————▼—————————

Soon after the Basel Congress, the attempt to reach understanding with the British government was recognized as hopeless. Perhaps the Jews had to thank fate or Ernst Bevin for being so intransigent: if the British government had been more accommodating, it was doubtful that 1948 would have seen the founding of the Jewish state. Bent on avoiding an open conflict, the Jewish Agency was, in fact, ready to make extensive compromises. However, all the concessions were frustrated by a rigid British position on Arab acceptance.

Due to this situation, Baruch Silverman's visits to Tel Aviv became more frequent; the Jewish Agency tried to use his political experience for secret diplomacy.

Brilliantly educated, he was a diplomat of the old school, whose motto was "the way of truth is the way of compromises." He was a liberal Zionist who believed in the possibility of a peaceful life with Jews and Arabs together. He was too good for the time in which he lived. But he saw much deeper into things than his colleagues, and so his position was not always congruent with the positions of the most Jewish leaders.

Baruch Silverman always stayed at the house that he had given to Rachel and Henry. It was really an apartment complex, a huge romantic attic with a balcony; one of three bedrooms was always free for him.

During one of his stays, his old friend Ben-Gurion visited him and asked if Baruch could attempt to persuade Albert Einstein to become the first president of the future Jewish State. Ben-Gurion had no doubt the state would be created.

"The Jewish Agency Executive would be very interested in it, Baruch," he said. "Einstein's name would bring recognition of our state to the highest international level."

"I'll try, David, but frankly, I doubt he'll accept the offer," Silverman remarked thoughtfully.

"Why? It's an honorable offer, isn't it?"

"It is. But I think, as a man, Albert Einstein is too equal-minded for both sides—Jews and Arabs. He is too human."

"You know him quite well, Baruch. Everybody knows he is a scientific genius; but who is he as a man? Very often the genius and the man are different persons."

"You are right David, very often, but not in this case. We live in a time of great demoralization, during which the worst times in all human history were perpetrated. But even in that world, he remains a great, innocent child. He is unbelievably trusting, and people often succeeded in fooling him because he can't imagine that anyone would deliberately abuse his trust. I think he understands nothing of political reality, but takes it for granted that politics must rest on moral principles. He hates war, aggressive nationalism and reaction. But I'll try to talk to him, David."

Baruch Silverman met Einstein in Boston where the scientist was delivering a lecture at MIT; he had been invited to present on the theory of relativity for the Boston political elite. The auditorium, including Baruch, didn't contain experts, and soon most of listeners couldn't follow the lecturer.

Not trying to catch the idea of the lecture, Baruch thought that Albert Einstein was the personification of every great quality a man could have—goodness of heart, honesty and boundless love for all living creatures. It would have been almost impossible to discover a character defect in him; but perhaps, his most amazing quality was the simplicity and modesty of all truly great men.

After the lecture, Baruch walked along the night-darkened streets of Boston with Einstein and asked him if he would be interested in Ben-Gurion's offer.

Einstein stopped, smoked a cigar and, for some times, kept silent. Then he said thoughtfully, "You know, Baruch, I think my Zionism is an impulsive type. I don't have a Jewish education, I've been very briefly acknowledged by Judaism."

For Baruch, Einstein began to sound as if he were trying to persuade himself. But then he returned to the point again. "I am a scientist, Baruch. Let's leave political positions for the politicians. I think a friend of mine Dr. Weizman would be the proper man for such work. And please, Baruch, tell Mr. Ben-Gurion I was very grateful for the great honor he has offered me."

CHAPTER 26

▼

Rabbi Myron Boxter sat at the desk in his tiny office, preparing for the Sabbath. He always used the service for short discussions with members of his small congregation about general questions of Judaism, as well as the current situation in Palestine. His discussions were based on examples from the Torah. In the upcoming service, he intended to speak about the purpose of creation. He wrote:

> *"Why did God create the world?*
>
> *There is a limit to how deeply we can probe, but our sages give us some insight into this question. To the best of our understanding, God created the world as an act of love. It was an act of love so immense that the human mind cannot begin to fathom it. God created the entire world as a vehicle upon which He could bestow His good.*
>
> *But God's love is so great that any good He bestows must be the greatest good possible. Anything less would simply be not enough.*
>
> *But what is the greatest good? What is the ultimate good that God can bestow on His creation? If you think about it for a moment, the answer should be obvious. The ultimate*

good is God himself. There is no greater good than achieving a degree of unity with the Creator Himself.

It's for this, that God gave man the ability to resemble Himself."

Hearing a knock at the door, Rabbi Boxter stopped writing.

"Come in," he said and, at seeing Henry, smiled openly. He knew the extraordinary fate of this young man. What is fate, he thought, if everything is foretold from Above? Maybe fate was something what we could still change in our life, something that still depended on us?

From a distance, a visitor might think Rabbi Myron Boxter was a man about sixty years old. Up close, he would realize that the rabbi was probably ten years younger than that. All the predecessors in his father's line were rabbis. And he continued the family tradition. But he became a rabbi not because of the family tradition; but rather because he had found his own way to God. First, he graduated from medical school and became a doctor. Since childhood, he had dreamed of treating people, and he did it with love and dignity. What Jewish doctor was not a liberal? Winston Churchill was right when he said, "if you are twenty and you are not liberal, you don't have a heart." How many people realized he was also right when he said, "If you are thirty, and you are still a liberal, you don't have brains"?

If you facilitate human pain, you cannot avoid coming to the dream of creating a happy society where pain doesn't exist. So, logistically, Dr. Boxter found himself among anti-Fascist volunteers in Spain. But there, struggling in the International Brigade against General Franco's troops, Dr. Boxter realized, unlike his comrades, that the Communists, in the case of their success, would not be any different from the fascists. This shocking thought came to his mind when he saw a young Falangist soldier shot in cold blood, without need. The captured soldier looked like a boy of sixteen; he was frightened and crying like a baby. But the unit commander, a Soviet instructor, calmly shot the boy in the head.

"He was the enemy," he said. "Every Franco's soldier is an enemy. You have to understand it; otherwise you'll lose the battle."

Leaving left the International Brigade, Myron returned to Palestine where his family had lived since the beginning of the century, after they left anti-Semitic Poland. For two years he had practiced medicine in Tel Aviv, but then he finished the Rabbinical School and made his old father happy. He became a rabbi. If before that day he had treated people's bodies, now he began treating their souls, directing them not to the way of tolerance and meekness, but to the way of struggle for their dignity.

Myron Boxter continued the family tradition, but he did not become a traditional rabbi who lived in the world of the soul, not connecting that world with reality. Instead, he became a rabbi-warrior who realized that the way of the God's truth was not the nice, peaceful way of resistance to evil. Vice versa, based on the Torah, he showed people that Jews had to fulfill God's will, even if that way seemed to be the way of annihilating Israel's enemies.

"Would you find a couple of minutes for me, Rabbi?" Henry asked him.

"Any time, Henry." Rabbi showed him to a chair.

Henry sat. "As a matter of fact, I'd like to make arrangements for my wedding ceremony."

"That's wonderful!"

Like his words, his deep dark eyes were direct, challenging under their line of dark brows. Wiry haired, gray despite his age, with the force of will and intellect etched in his face, Rabbi Boxter was a man proud of his family long past as rabbis who helped his people keep the faith. But now, in the middle of the twentieth century, he felt it was time for him to fulfill another mission—public servitude to the Jewish people.

"I think it will be a small ceremony, Rabbi," Henry said. "My fiancé and I have neither relatives nor friends."

"Friendship is the unity of souls. If you're a member of my congregation, you have many friends."

After they fixed the date for the ceremony, Henry thanked him and stood up.

"Don't be in such a hurry, Henry." Rabbi Boxter smiled, and then he took a small velvet bag with an embroidered crown on its surface from his desk. He handed the bag Henry and said, "This is my wedding gift to you, Henry."

Henry stared at him.

"This is a *tefilin*. When you put it on, you'll feel as if you are another man because your energy would be connected directly to God. Take it, Henry, you are the chosen one." Then Rabbi Boxter went to the bookshelf and took one of the books. He opened it and read:

> *"Hear O Israel, the Lord is our God,*
> *the Lord is One.*
> *And you shall love the Lord your God*

with all your heart,
with all your soul,
and with all your might.
And these words that I give you today
shall be on your heart.
You shall teach them to your children
and speak of them
when you are on the way
and when you are at home,
when you lie down,
and when you wake up.
And you shall bind them for a sign
upon your hand
and for a tefilin
between your eyes.
And you shall write them on the Mezuzah
of your doors and your gates." (Deuteronomy 6, 4-9)

"This is the *Sh'ma*," Rabbi Boxter said. "It's the most important part of our prayer service. It is the first thing a Jew learns as a child and his last words before he dies."

Henry took the small box and the thin book. "I cannot find words to express my gratitude, Rabbi," he said with excitement.

On his way out, Henry stopped on the threshold and glanced back. Rabbi Boxter was looking at him, his lips moving slightly as though he were memorizing Henry's face or praying.

CHAPTER 27

▼

When the day of their marriage arrived, Henry saw how many friends he and Rachel had. The whole congregation came to congratulate them.

Then, there was the *huppa* ceremony. They repeated the words of prayer after Rabbi Boxter.

Then, there was the broken glass under Rachel's foot.

Then, there was the lavish dinner. Women brought meat pies, fish, salmon of that virginal tint suitable for a wedding party, a wedding cake so pink that even salmon paled before it, several kinds of wines.

Then, there was the Jewish music. The fiddler began to play such a sad melody that his violin cried about all who never reached a wedding day, about all the innocent victims who were perished for the sake of their faith. The Jewish violin cried as if she wanted to say that crying facilitates suffering. Jewish souls need facilitation because they carry the heavy burden of generations' memory. The violin cried about broken dreams and frustrated hopes, cried as if she'd like to say that after those tears all the dreams would be regained, and the heavy burden of the Jewish soul would again turn into a light dream resting on the wings of hope.

And then, there was the dance of hope, an explosion of joy and happiness, *"hava nagila,"* with its whirlpool of happiness. Now the violin said that we, the Jewish people, remember the past, but we also see the future. We are already in the future where there is no pain and suffering; we are already in the future where God has forgiven our sins and again made us His beloved people.

And at the epicenter of that whirlpool of happiness, there were Rachel and Henry, two halves who became that day, in front of God, one.

CHAPTER 28

———————▼———————

God had intervened. Israel was born in circumstances that were truly unique. For two thousand years, the revival of the Jewish state in Palestine had been the passion and dream of a scattered people. For fifty years, it had been a political program. And toward the end of 1947, it became, at least, a certainty.

The publication of Herzl's *The State of the Jews* in 1897 was the beginning. Then there was the *Balfour Declaration* in 1917, and nearly thirty years of British mandatory rule that inevitably was coming to its end.

Events moved quickly. By 1946 the validity of the League of Nations British mandate was undermined by the League's disappearance; the whole problem was referred to the United Nations, which had taken the League's place as the supreme international organization.

The United Nations acted with self-confidence and dispatch. The Secretary-General summoned a special session of the General Assembly, which met in April 1947.

By a decisive majority, UNSCOP—the United Nations Special Committee on Palestine consisting of representatives of Australia, Canada, Czechoslovakia, Guatemala, India, Iran, the Netherlands, Peru, Sweden, Uruguay and Yugoslavia—recommended the partition of Palestine and its division between two new independent states, one Jewish and the other Arab.

But the Arabs rejected the UN plan because they could not tolerate the idea of a Jewish state in even a part of Palestine. The Jewish leadership realized quite clearly that as Arabs had rejected all plans to resolve the problem before, they would reject it again. And this time, in the case of having a Jewish state, its settlers could not avoid a military confrontation with the Arabs.

Realizing the inevitability of the future conflict, David Ben-Gurion sent Israel's secret emissaries to the world arsenals to begin Zionist arm procurement immediately as the Arabs rejected the first recommendation.

Perhaps it was enough, until British transferred their military arsenals to the Arabs. By that time, almost all channels of weapons delivery to Israel were shut off by British troops. In case of a future military conflict, it could cause a disaster.

Given this situation, a call from Baruch Silverman to discuss "a problem of mutual understanding" was more than timely for Ben-Gurion. Silverman hinted about the arms procurement, so Ben-Gurion immediately scheduled a meeting with him.

Sitting in a car driven by Ehud Avriel, who had vast experience in illegal weapons delivery to the Jewish settlers, Ben-Gurion refreshed his memory of all the main Jewish weaponry arsenals; a large-scale military conflict with the Arabs would have catastrophic sequences.

When Rachel opened the door, Ben-Gurion wasn't surprised; he already knew the unique history of the two young people living here. But wasn't the history of every Jew who survived the Holocaust unique?

After Rachel prepared coffee, she discreetly departed. Baruch Silverman turned to Ben-Gurion. "As I hinted, David, our meeting is about weapons for a future confrontation with Arabs. I think we won't be able to avoid it." He took a considerable pause.

"If a diplomat, such as you Baruch, thinks so," Ben-Gurion went on elaborating his statement, "it means the confrontation is inevitable."

"Several days ago Henry and I had a discussion about the situation in Palestine, and he unexpectedly made a confidential offer which, from my point of view, could be considered very seriously. That's why I asked you, David, for a meeting. You know, Henry and Rachel are like my own children," Silverman said, turning to Ben-Gurion. "But I think it would be better if he explained everything himself."

Henry seemed flustered. "You obviously know, gentlemen, that before my wife Rachel and I moved here, I was an officer of the German *Wehrmacht.* I was involved in operations to hide military arsenals from the Allies forces so we could use them later for future resistance. The Nazi leadership was assured that soon the German Phoenix would rise from the ashes; they accepted the decision to relocate those arsenals to remote areas. I took part in the inspections. Despite the fact that I am assured that most of arsenals are now under Allies control, perhaps some remained hidden. But even if all of them were under their control, I'll definitely be able to contact people who can be useful to us and sell us weapons."

"But that would be a large-scale, expensive operation, Henry," Ben-Gurion interrupted him. "Unfortunately, we don't have the money." He thought he has come here in vain to discuss an unrealistic project.

"I do have the money, sir," Henry said forcefully. Half musing, he shook his head. "In the last few months of the war, *Schtandartenfuhrer SS* Dornberger asked me to perform a delicate mission and put the significant amount of $217,000 in his numbered Swiss bank account. I am the only person who knows of the account number, since Otto Dornberger didn't survive the war." Henry paused and gulped his cold coffee.

Then he continued, "This is dirty money, gentlemen. *Schtandartenfuhrer* was involved in secret ransom operations. With several other high-ranked SS officers, he liberated several dozens rich Jews whose relatives could pay a lavish ransom. Rachel and I thought about what could be done with this money to bring the maximum good to our people. And now, I am assured it couldn't be more useful than buying weapons to defend ourselves in the inevitable future war."

The usually reserved Ben-Gurion jumped from his chair and embraced Henry. "Do it, my boy, and God will help you!" Then he turned to Ehud Avriel who was listening quietly, and asked no questions. "Discuss all the details together. Nobody can understand them better than you, Ehud."

When Ehud and Henry left for the adjacent room, Ben-Gurion said, "You have to be proud of this man, Baruch. If he succeeds in bringing the weapons, I would sleep much better when the war begins."

"Me too," Baruch agreed.

In the adjacent room, Ehud and Henry sat and looked at each other. The men were sympathetic to each other from the first glance.

Ehud was only thirty-four, but looked much older. His hair failed to conceal his boldness. He had come to Palestine at the end of thirties from the Hungarian capital of Budapest, against the will of his parents who considered Hungary their motherland. They survived in the concentration camps. After the war Ehud found his parents through the Red Cross. They were on their way to Palestine when a British patrol ship sank their boat near the shore.

At twenty-seven, Henry was a very good-looking man who possessed the charm of naturalness and individuality, but also was exacting and distrustful. His hair was already streaked with gray.

"It will be an extremely dangerous operation, Henry," Ehud said. "The British are blocking Palestine from the air and the sea to prevent the large-scale immigration." When he talked about the British, his face moved from one color to another, a kaleidoscope of hues.

"Things are not as desperate as they may seem, Ehud." Henry sighed, understanding Ehud's emotions.

"Not desperate. But bleak. Depressing."

"I know." Henry nodded.

"Do you have any ideas how to reach our goal?" Ehud's question was direct.

"I think we have to talk about two phases—buying the weapons, and its delivery. Buying is easier." Henry said.

"Why?"

"I'll fly to Germany and try to find the people who were involved with me in the arsenals relocations. I think everything can be bought, especially now, when the Nazi idea has collapsed and most of the former officers are without work or money. I am more than assured of success in this first phase."

"It will be extremely dangerous, Henry. Feeling the smell of big money, the Nazis will try to simply rob and kill you. You said the Nazi idea collapsed. I think you're wrong. Nazi Germany collapsed, but the idea remained alive. It's like German anti-Semitism. It will never vanish."

"Nobody wins without risk. But I'll be very careful. As you saw, my wife is pregnant and soon will give birth to our child. I still dream of being a papa." Henry smiled. "Regarding to the second phase of the operation, weapons delivery, I haven't the slightest idea."

"I'll discuss the delivery first with the people in my group, and then we'll provide the detailed plan to the Old Man to be approved. But I think we have to discard the airlift from the beginning. We had two pilots who served with the British Air Force during the war, but both of them are now out of service: one guy was killed by the Arabs; the other is still recovering from an air crash. Besides, I think air space is more closely guarded than the sea. In case of the plane getting shot down, we would definitely lose everything; in case of a sea delivery, there's still a good chance of reaching our destination. The British ships patrol the bounder of the neutral waters. But at night, we have a good chance to penetrate them. Soon they are going to leave Palestine, so they aren't in a hurry to equip their ships with modern radars. I'm inclined toward sea delivery."

"Germany had no harbors except on the Baltic." Henry tapped the side of his cheek in deep thought.

"That's why I think you have to deliver the cargo to one of the French ports. I understand, Henry, that it complicates the task. In reality, it will consist of three phases: buying weapons in Germany, transferring them from Germany to France, and delivery to Palestine. We need a team of at least ten to twelve men. I'll think about whom I'll be able to recommend for that work. Then we'll discuss all the details and the final schedule. When will you be able to fly to Germany?"

"As soon as I receive the documents," Henry said. "I spoke briefly to Baruch about it. Diplomatic coverage would be the best because it would give me a chance to go through all the occupied zones in Berlin and France if we decide to deliver the cargo to a French port." Henry struck his forehead with his hand. "Ehud, an idea has come to my mind! It has to be a passport from one of the Latin American countries, a trade attaché or something like that. That would be a plausible explanation for the Germans about why I would be interested in buying weapons. Let's say, General Eugenio Trujilio, in Dominican Republic, needs it to support General Stressner's revolt in Paraguay. It would be understandable, wouldn't it?"

"That's a good idea, Henry. I'll discuss the detailed plan with the Old Man as soon as it is done. Let's meet again with my team in Jerusalem in several days. I'll let you know, okay? And now, let's go back down the hall. I wouldn't mind another cup of coffee."

When they returned the room, Ben-Gurion said, "Looking at your faces, men, I thought about how wonderful it would be to be thirty years younger and join your team!" He smiled. "You know, Baruch and I came to the conclusion that in a situation where the United States had already imposed an embargo on all arm shipments to the Middle East, and with Britain still freely selling arms to the Arab states, we are free to do everything necessary to defend ourselves. But it wasn't so easy to persuade such a liberal diplomat as Mr. Baruch Silverman that our operation wouldn't be considered illegal." Ben-Gurion laughed, being on top of his spirits.

Within a week, David Ben-Gurion had approved the detailed plan of the operation and asked Baruch Silverman to help with diplomatic coverage for Henry.

CHAPTER 29

Baruch Silverman was the only man who could help with Henry's documents. Among his friends, he numbered Vatslav Gust, a brilliantly educated, former Prague University professor who had served in British Army Intelligence and who sympathized with the Zionist idea.

They had become friends when Baruch was an observer for the League of Nations, and Vatslav Gust was the Czechoslovakian representative for the same agency. When he studied Arabic and read the *Koran* with its hateful ideology, Vatslav had become sympathetic to Zionism. After the Nazis occupied Czechoslovakia, he joined the British Army and served with the rank of Lt. Colonel in the Army Intelligence.

Baruch met Vatslav in London and asked for help. They walked down a broad, quiet boulevard to find an empty bench that looked as if it were waiting for them. They sat, and Baruch frankly told him that the Israelis hoped to buy weapons in Germany in order to be prepared for a future war with the Arabs. He did not play games. They both knew that war was inevitable.

"Do you remember, Baruch, our conversation with my brother, Eduard Benes, at the Hotel Beau Rouge, on the eve of the war? We tried to persuade you of the necessity for real action after the Nuremberg Laws if you wanted to achieve your goal." Vazslav asked.

Baruch nodded. "I never felt so ashamed as if it were my personal fault." He sighed, recollecting that meeting.

At Hotel Beau Rouge, Vatslav had introduced him to Eduard Benes, Czechoslovakia's Foreign Minister. Benes was one of the gentile leaders who couldn't accept the world Jewry's passive reaction to the promulgation of the Nuremberg Laws.

When Baruch went to his room, he found Benes shouting, pacing back and forth across his corner room. For almost two hours, he reproachfully demanded to know why Jews had not reacted on a grand scale and immediately called an International Jewish Congress to declare all out war on the Nazi regime. He assured Baruch that he and many other non-Jewish statesmen would have given them their full support.

"Don't you understand," he shouted, "that by reacting with nothing but half-hearted gestures, by failing to arouse world public opinion and taking vigorous action against the Germans, that the Jews are endangered their future and their human rights all over the world? If you go on like this, Hitler's example will be contagious and encourage all the anti-Semites throughout the world!"

Uncomfortable and ashamed, Baruch tried to defend the Jewry's attitude by pointing out the difficulties in politically organizing a dispersed, homeless people, and the reluctance of many Jewish spokesmen to take a hostile position toward Germany as long as governments maintained friendly relations.

None of Baruch's arguments had any effect, and the conversation plunged Baruch into gloom.

Differing from his emotional brother, Vatslav was reserved. But in response to Baruch's explanations, he remarked, "Mr. Silverman, you have to realize that by reacting in such an indifferent manner, Jews will lose the respect of many well-meaning friends who expected a united, deeply perturbed Jewry to proclaim a moral and political crusade against the Nazi regime."

Baruch's recollections were rapid and painful.

"I'm glad that after the war, the psychology of the Palestinian Jews changed," Vatslav said, returning Baruch to reality.

"I think the war changed the psychology of all Jews," Baruch agreed, still looking preoccupied.

Vatslav smiled. "I think you have remained the same idealist I knew you to be before the war, if you believe in that. The Nazi beast is dead, and Jews are happy that everything is over. But it's over only in Europe. In Palestine, it's just the beginning. If you, Jews, don't take radical action, I am afraid that the scale of possible Jewish extermination by the Arabs would be comparable with the Nazi's. I'm happy that you have discarded your philosophy of tolerance. If you knew Arabic and read the *Koran*, you would understand the real danger of the Arab world to Western civilization. As always, Jews will be the first. Unfortunately we, in the West, underestimate it in favor of the moment of today's situation. We need their oil, and think our favoritism will help us in future.

But we're wrong. Muslims are intolerant of the whole Judeo-Christianity world. Thousands years ago we had stopped their attempt to spread their faith all over the world only because we killed hundreds of thousands Muslims. Now they will make another attempt, and the number of victims will be much more because we Westerners have become too benign after the war that we won."

The pale sun sunk below the horizon and the air turned suddenly cold.

"It's beginning to drizzle," Vatslav said, rising. "London's weather hasn't changed. Let's go for a walk, Baruch."

They went along the boulevard leading to the river. For some time both kept silent, submerged in their thoughts. At last they reached the edge of the riverbank where the smell of water wafted up on a breeze.

"What about a drink, Baruch?" Vatslav pointed to a small café several steps from them.

"Good idea." Baruch agreed and they went in.

The café was almost empty. They sat at a table, and a swollen-faced waitress walked up, looking questioningly. "What would you like to drink?"

"Vermouth with tonic would be nice." Baruch smiled her.

"We have the same taste." Vatslav joined him.

When the waitress brought their drinks, Vatslav took two gulps, and then continued, "I'm a British officer, Baruch, but I consider the British position on Palestine short-sighted and unbalanced. By the way, many officers share my point of view. Alas, our official policy leads us in the opposite direction because Mr. Bevin is blinded by his anti-Zionism. He is not an anti-Semite, and his anti-Judaism concerns only Palestine. But he's a slave of the British Crown." Vatslav took another gulp, and then reached for his cigarettes. Baruch did not interrupt him, and he continued, "I think that one day our politicians will realize the danger to our existence. Unfortunately," Vatslav took another gulp and continued, "politicians never take history's lessons into account. That's why every time we are punished more and more severely." Vatslav emptied his glass and then said; "I think that if I help one Jew to receive a Latin-American diplomatic passport, I won't contradict my duties as a British officer." His sharply chiseled face expressed a strong will.

Ten days later, Baruch put a diplomatic passport issued in the name of Heinrich Menke, a Trade Attaché of the Dominican Republic, on the table in front of Henry.

"The passport is clean," he said. "You are a newly appointed attaché in Zurich. I think you have to book a ticket on one of the British ships going to sail to Europe. But let me give you, Henry, a piece of advice; don't pay cash if possible, because it would be a joke to rob you. And please, be as much careful as you can. Don't forget that what you are going to do is risky business, maybe more risky than anything that you were involved in before."

"I will, Baruch. We still have to discuss all the nuances of the operation with Ehud and his men in Jerusalem. We can't predict every possible situation, but I rely on God. He's helped me many times before, and I want to hope that He will help me again when the results of my mission are so necessary for my people." Henry paused and looked openly to Baruch. "But of course anything can happen to me. And I want to ask you…If I die, Baruch, take care of Rachel. She has been gone through all the circles of hell and deserves a happy life. She will soon give a birth to our child," he added.

Baruch silently embraced Henry. Then, after a long pause, with tears in his eyes, he said, "You are both a part of my family, Henry. I want you to know it."

CHAPTER 30

$\blacktriangledown$

When Ehud called Henry and invited him to Jerusalem to take part in the final discussion of the coming operation, Rachel wanted to go with him, but he persuaded her to stay home. "It's not a tourist trip, Rachel, especially in your state." He tenderly touched her belly.

It wasn't his first visit here. During an earlier trip, he and Rachel spent a few days in Jerusalem before going to Tel Aviv. Their first steps on their new land had not allowed a chance to enjoy sightseeing or walking along the streets. That time, the picturesque atmosphere of the capital remained behind their backs. When they were there the second time, the city impressed them both; they would like to have much more time to enjoy it.

But a tourist couldn't see that in Jerusalem antagonism between Jews and Arabs has reached the highest level; a tourist didn't see that inner tension when Jews could expect pogroms every day. Jerusalem remained a picturesque, unique city, in which the past and the present were mixed in a picture for the future.

A tourist saw life there that looked like a merry-go-round of a county fair, curling, flickering and glittering until one's eyes hurt. The city shone like a house where people were celebrating a wedding, unaware that death was lurking outside their windows. Had Jerusalem forgotten to wind the clock? Had Jerusalem failed to tear off the leaves of the calendar for a long time?

Henry walked to the meeting and looked around. He saw people with friendly faces, but also foreign to him, and hostile. He discerned, beneath the happy-go-lucky surface, a touch of mournfulness. The atmosphere of the city suggested preparations for a journey, to only God knew where.

When Ehud's group gathered in a small apartment that belonged to the sister of one of the group's member, Ehud introduced Henry to everybody. They greeted him in a friendly way. Then Ehud said, "Men, let's finalize the details. The Old Man has already approved the plan; I brought you to coordinate the details and to answer any questions you might have." He looked at his people, but everybody remained silent.

"The operation consists of two parts. Both are equally dangerous and equally important. They are independent from each other and, at the same time, are two parts of one whole. But there is a big difference between the two. By doing his job, Henry risks only his life; the second phase puts all our lives in jeopardy as well as the safety of our people in Palestine." Ehud paused but nobody interrupted him.

"Henry has to deliver the cargo to the French port of Toulon. It's relatively small, and doesn't have a navy base nearby. Toulon was chosen because we have our people working in the harbor. As I said, the first phase is a one-man operation. But dealing with former Nazis is extremely dangerous; Uri Vecksler would cover him in Germany. He is the best," Ehud said, turning to Henry. "On his shoulders are more than three years of military service in the Jewish Legion inside the British army. You even won't be aware of his presence." Ehud lit a cigarette, blew out smoke and continued, "If the first part is successfully completed, Henry will send a telegram to Toulon: 'Dear Jaclyn, I am on my way. Kiss you, Henry.'

We think that the first phase should be completed within ten to twelve days. During that time we have to prepare two ships for departure, about one hundred tons capacity each. One of them has to be packed with old machinery, and will be used to deflect the British Navy's attention. It has to be discovered by a patrol ship and captured. Of course the ship's crew will be arrested for violation of trade embargo and imprisoned. I think not for very long because the British troops soon leave Palestine."

"Why do you think the British will intercept the first ship, Ehud?" asked one of the silent men with a skeptical look.

"They will receive a tip from the Arabs with information about the ship's route," Ehud explained. "The arrest of the first ship must narcotize their vigilance. They wouldn't expect another ship at almost the same time; it'll increase the chance that the second ship will reach its destination."

"Crew members will be our men?" Henry asked, still weighing his last words.

"Only our men," Ehud verified. "Every ship will be operated by a crew of five, who are all experienced sailors." Ehud pointed to the silent people.

"But arresting the first ship cannot guarantee success," Dan Bonar said thoughtfully.

Ehud smiled. "Yes, Dan, nobody but God can give you a guarantee. They say if you want to make God laugh, tell Him about your plans for the future. We can only ask Him for help." Then he said seriously, "This is the best-case scenario, but we have to be ready for the worst when the second ship is intercepted."

"What can we do against a patrol ship with its large-scale automatic guns? If discovered, the game would be over; they can sink our ship. And they will definitely do it because they are on the Arab's side." One of the sailors remarked gloomily.

"We have to forget our Jewish defensive mentality," Henry remarked. "In this situation, we have to attack first."

"A civilian ship against a military boat? "One of the sailors asked, with his lip curled in a sneer.

"Let's turn our ship into a military one," Henry said thoughtfully. "If I succeed in my mission, I'll also deliver two large-caliber guns, the same type the British use on their ships. We'll put them on the front and rear decks and camouflage them as ordinary cargo."

"Good idea!" Ehud agreed. "In case of interception, we'll fire first, before the British realize what has happened. We'll win a moment and the situation. I think every one must understand quite clearly that the British boat must be sunk. Unfortunately we cannot afford to take captives; it would cause huge diplomatic complications." A blush stole over Ehud's face, but he quickly regained his self-control.

Silence fell as the Jewish men pondered the thought that they would have to kill British sailors, even if they would surrender.

Ehud felt the gloomy atmosphere. "Let's hope we can manage to avoid it," he said. "If not," he added firmly, "you have to realize that the price of our failure is too high. That price is not only our own lives, but that of our State and its future."

"It's quite clear, Ehud," said finally one of the team members. "Don't talk so much."

Several days later, the Trade Attaché of the Dominican Republic in Zurich, Heinrich Menke, left Palestine for Liverpool on board a British ship. At sea, he wrote Rachel a letter, which he mailed from England.

> *"Honey,*
> *You won't believe it, but I have become a diplomat! I smile when I want to punch a man on a jaw, and I drink to the health of those who deserves to be hung…"*

CHAPTER 31

▼

After sunny Tel Aviv, Berlin met Henry with a downpour, and to him, it seemed to be a part of hell: destroyed buildings, gloomy faced people on the streets, dark clouds in the sky—everything depressed him deeply. But he marked that the atmosphere surrounding him was quite different from that of the first days after capitulation. Many pubs and restaurants were open; there were almost no beggars on the streets. The stupid Americans had already implemented the Marshall Plan to rebuild the destroyed German economy, and many of Germans asked the question; wasn't it stupid to struggle with these men who were ready to sell everything for money?

Berlin stirred up an entire gamut of feelings, sensations that Henry considered buried in the depth of his soul. My Lord, he thought, I could remain a part of the gloomy past; empty windows of destroyed buildings stirred his soul. If he hadn't opened the wall safe in Rupert Menke's kitchen and hadn't found that article about his long dead parents, he would have remained Heinrich Menke, a captain of the *Wehrmacht* who, if he hadn't killed anybody, at least had done nothing to prevent the killings. But who could prevent that global human tragedy that supernumerary he'd turned out? Naïve idealists like Baruch Silverman and others Jewish leaders?

Now he returned to the world that it seemed that he'd left forever. But Henry had returned as another man, with a new mission. It was time to discard everything from the past that still lived in his soul as a painful wound. It was high time to stop feeling like an innocent victim who was set free of his guilt. If there hadn't been his aimless past, there wouldn't be his present.

The only decent hotel remaining from the pre-war era was *Kaiser*, now it was called *Uhland*. Luckily it had not suffered from bombardments and was fully functional.

Henry handed the clerk his diplomatic passport and, without having to answer any questions, received a fifth floor large single room, with a private bathroom.

Upstairs, in his room, he prepared a bath. Soaking in the hot water, still pushing out thoughts about his strange fate, he realized that, unlike Rachel, he couldn't say he hated the people around him. But he also couldn't say they were totally indifferent him. He had the feeling of a traveler who visited a familiar but foreign country. Would he be able to live again among these people? Probably not, Henry decided finally. If the whole nation was criminal, how could you find a scapegoat? Hitler was no more or less a criminal than Rupert Menke or Otto Dornberger. But maybe, if criminality was the norm, no criminal had to be charged and found guilty because the silent majority was no fewer criminals than the shouting minority.

After the hot bath and its following cold shower, Henry stared into the mirror before him and, for a moment, studied the outlines of his face. It was a strong, commanding face, with a prominent nose and sorrowful, brooding eyes hinting at tragedies that had marked his life. Then he dressed and went downstairs where he met the clerk who wore the face of a gigolo and *schturmfuhrer SS* simultaneously.

"Hi," Henry said. "Where's the night life here?"

"Just as everywhere else." The clerk shrugged. His face betrayed no emotion. "If you are still alive, you live," he said, with a blank face and sighed.

"But it's better to live well," Henry responded in the same manner. "Listen guy, where can I meet old friends? I haven't been in Berlin for almost two years."

The clerk looked at Henry indifferently and shrugged again. "SS men usually visit *Berlin*—it's a pub around the corner. *Wehrmacht* officers usually go to *Progress*. It's the former *Faterland,* if you remember the restaurant on *Kaizerschtrasse.*"

"I know." Henry nodded.

He had a late lunch in the hotel buffet, enjoying the fragrant, strong coffee. Then he walked along the streets, looking at Berlin with the eyes of an outsider. He had a strange feeling that he had only recently learned the history of the city that was the capital of the country that he had considered his motherland for twenty-five years. Why had Jews lived here since 1247, for more than seven centuries, remaining second-class citizens and serving the country that had betrayed their trust so many times?

By seven o'clock, Henry had found *Progress*. He remembered the restaurant under the old name *Faterland,* as it was a favorite place for off duty officers. From his first glance, it seemed that time had stopped. Then he noticed that while the interior was the same, the visitors were different. Most of them were American or British officers, some of them accompanied by local ladies. Two unescorted women were sitting at the bar; they would not have been allowed in the 'Fatherland.'

Henry went to the bar and sat on a high stool. He ordered a drink, and then turned to the side of the room. But nobody attracted his attention. The bartender put a glass on the counter in front of him. His face was obliging and squeamish. Why most bartenders remind me of gigolos, Henry thought. It's like their trademark.

One of the women sitting at the bar tried to talk to him, but she felt her words submerge in a vast, empty space. When she saw that he remained indifferent, she wasn't insistent. Henry had another drink, and then he took his glass to sit at an empty table.

Half an hour later, a duet appeared on the stage—a pianist and a violinist. The violinist was an old man, with long gray hair falling on his shoulders. When he finished playing on the stage, he walked around the tables, playing mostly classical music; but sometimes his melodies were mindful of Jewish motifs. Henry wondered whether the violinist was a Jew.

At the break, Henry invited the old man to his table. The man sat and put the violin on his knees, looking at Henry questioningly.

"Are you Jewish?" Henry asked offhandedly. He couldn't explain why he asked a direct question.

The man lowered his eyes. "Yes, I am," he said quietly, a tremor in his voice. His fingers trembled.

"Why are you here?" Henry asked.

The old man's eyebrows rose in surprise. "I was born here," he said dismally. "In Berlin, there was my house." Then he sighed. "I have returned home," he repeated. "I was lucky to survive, sir." He rolled up a sleeve, showing Henry the Auschwitz number on his hand.

Henry offered him a drink but the old man refused politely. "Thank you, sir, but I do not drink when I play." He sniggered.

"Your house isn't here," Henry repeated thoughtfully, fighting down the urge to say more.

The man did not understand him. "Strictly speaking, sir, my house was destroyed during the war. I live in an apartment, with my pianist companion." He waved to the side of the stage. "Mr. Herbert von Karajan promised us a work as soon as he organizes his Berlin Philharmonic Orchestra. But now we have to earn a living here," he said as he tried to excuse himself.

"Go home, old man," Henry said in a different tone of voice. He opened his wallet and gave the man $100. "Go home," he repeated.

"Thank you so much, sir," the old man said gratefully. "What music do you want me to play?"

"Thank you. I prefer Bach, but it's not for a restaurant," Henry said coldly, and the old man left, murmuring to himself, "What a strange man!"

Henry felt his calmness oozing away, and his mood plummeted. He thought that eventually this old man would willingly perform Richard Wagner's music in front of an audience consisting of former Nazis. Was there a limit to Jewish tolerance? He thought bitterly.

He ordered another drink, gulped it and again looked around. The restaurant was full, but Henry did not see anybody in whom he could be interested.

MP patrol came into to check documents. A sergeant looked carefully at his Dominican passport. "Okay, sir," he said and saluted Henry, returning the papers. Henry made no reply. The violinist began playing a Tyrolean waltz. Henry finished his drink and left.

For the next several days, Henry spent all his evenings in the restaurant but met none of his former acquaintances. He already became nervous that he could jeopardize the whole operation that rested on a casual meeting.

"Are you waiting for anybody in particular, sir?" the bartender asked him politely one evening after he ordered his usual drink. This officer, the bartender had no doubt that Henry had been an officer, had obviously no money shortage and always left lavish tips. "I can offer you the best of our girls," he said confidently. He nodded to a woman approaching the bar.

Before Henry could refuse his offer, he heard, "My God, Heinrich, is that you?" Then he felt a kiss on his cheek.

"Emma?" He remembered her name. Not because he remembered her face, but because of her deep, husky voice. She used to be one of the telephone girls at headquarters, and he had spent couple of weeks with her. She was neither beautiful nor ugly. When her rather ordinary face was changed by a vague, barely participle smile, she looked rather attractive. But excepting her voice, Emma was a typical German girl—stupid, submissive and frigid. They have parted quickly but kept friendly relations.

"I cannot believe I see you, Heinrich!" A happy smile brightened her face that was heavily made up. Emma sat on the stool near him.

"What will you have to drink, Emma?"

"Any red wine would be nice. I haven't seen you in ages, Heinrich. Where have you been? Are you all right? I see you are all right!" Emma rarely took a breath between each sentence.

"There have been some changes in my life, Emma. Now I am a citizen of the Dominican Republic."

"What Republic?" Confusion reflected on her face.

"It's in Caribbean Islands." Henry smiled.

"Really? You are kidding me! And what are you doing here?" She couldn't stop asking questions.

"I am a Trade Attaché of the Dominican Republic," Henry said and laughed at the significance of his words.

"Unbelievable!" Emma threw out her arms. "Not. Nothing is unbelievable. You were always the best, Heinrich. And now, you have become a diplomat." She was still trying to comprehend the news.

"I am in Berlin for several days, but haven't met any of my old comrades." Henry had changed the topic. "Where are they?" he asked, his voice indifferent.

"That's not a surprise. This place is too expensive for the most of them. Only a few men who are lucky enough to work with Americans can afford it here. And most of them are still in the denazification camps."

Henry pondered that for a moment. It's not good, he thought and then asked, "Did you meet any one the last time?"

"No." Emma shook her head. "Maybe Willy met somebody," she remarked thoughtfully.

"Willy?" Henry rolled his eyes but his face betrayed no emotion.

"You know him, Heinrich, Major Ehrenkrantz. Wilhelm Ehrenkrantz. I live with him."

Emma intercepted Henry's glance and blushed. "Without my work here, we wouldn't survive."

"I understand." Henry opened his wallet and put $200 in front of her. "Tell him that I'd like to talk to him. He'll find me here."

"Oh, Heinrich!" Emma drew in a sharp, short breath. Then she took the bills. "I've never held such a large amount of money." Tears sparkled in her eyes. "You were always the best, Heinrich, and you still are." She kissed him on the cheek and silently went away.

For some time Henry tried to collect his thoughts. Before leaving the bar, he looked back at the stage where the old man played violin. The old man of forty.

CHAPTER 32

The next evening, when Henry came to the restaurant, former Major Willy Ehrenkrantz was waiting for him sitting at the bar. Henry recognized him. He was a rather short man, with a clipped mustache. His flabby face betrayed his weak point—a bottle of schnapps. He had lost his left hand in Russia, in the Kursk battle, but had not wanted to be demobilized. Not because of strong feelings of German patriotism, but rather being afraid of staying alone an invalid, since his wife had abandoned him before the war began. He was a distant relative of Colonel Ramm, Field Marshal Keitel's aide-de-camp, and the colonel had recommended that he be responsible for the officers' buffet at the headquarters. At last Willy Ehrenkrantz had received the work that was mockingly called by the officers "a dream of an idiot." Unfortunately his dream job collapsed with the collapse of Germany. If not for Emma who pitied him, Willy Ehzenkrantz would probably have died of starvation or drinking.

"Heinrich!" Willy briskly interjected. His joy of the meeting was sincere. "What will you drink? We have to drink for our meeting. Schnapps?"

"Today I'd prefer Scotch. It's my treat, Willy," Henry said as he remembered Emma's words about this restaurant being very expensive. "Make your choice, old chap."

"In that case, I'll also drink Scotch," Willy tersely replied.

The bartender put drinks in front of them and they drank. Then Henry said, "Let's take a table. It's too noisy here."

Once settled at a table, they ordered dinner and the waiter quickly served them appetizers.

"Emma told me she couldn't believe her eyes when she saw you. I still cannot believe my eyes either. I see you are okay," Willy said and smiled thinly. Then he sighed and began eating as if starving.

"I'm in Berlin for several days but have met no one of the people I knew. Where they are?" Henry asked.

"Most men who were lucky enough to surrender to the Yankees are still in denazification camps. Staying there is like having a vacation." Willy grinned. "Those who surrendered to the Russians are done. They were sent to Russia, and if they are ever come back, I think it will take many years." He took a big gulp of his Scotch. "The luckiest of our men joined General Gellen's Agency—the Abver's heir which is under the CIA. They took the men who knew some Reich's secrets. I could have gotten a job there only in one case—if they would be interested in the secrets of officers' kitchen." Willy laughed, his mouth quirked wryly. "Unfortunately, I'm not lucky," he added seriously. "That's why I am dying here like a piece of shit." He sighed heavily and filled his glass again.

"Maybe I'll help you survive, Willy," Henry said thoughtfully. He paused. "I wonder if you are able to contact some people who could be useful to my business." He eyed Willy intensely.

"I'm all ears, Heinrich." Willy leaned forward.

"I do not know if Emma told you, but I'm a diplomat, a Trade Attaché of Dominican Republic."

"Dominican Republic? Where is that? In the Caribbean?"

"You were good in geography at school, Willy." Henry smiled. For some time, he smoked the cigarette he had just lit. "Strictly speaking, I've got dual citizenship," he explained. "I'll be quite frank with you, Willy; here, in Germany, I need to buy weapons for the government I represent there."

"Who's interested in weapons when the war is over?" Willy shrugged.

"Here—nobody, in the Caribbean—many people. Most of the Caribbean countries' regimes are dictatorships, and they are under the UN embargo. My new Fuhrer, General Eugenio Trujilio, needs weapons. It's my speculation that the weaponry I have to deliver is not for the Dominican army. He wants to help his protégé in Paraguay, a young man, Stressner by name. Remember his name, Willy; he is pro-Nazi, and soon he'll give jobs to many of our people."

"How can I be of use to you, Heinrich? I'll do everything I can."

"First of all, put me in contact with Gellen's people who can assist me in buying. I am talking about a large deal. Your commission, Willy, will be no less than $10,000. I think no one will be unhappy with this deal, trust me."

"If anybody in this world still remains to be trusted, it's you, Heinrich. You gave me hope of regaining my life, and I'll try not to miss this chance. I know a couple of men who could be useful and who won't refuse to earn some money. I'll bring them to you." Willy swallowed hard, then forced a wan smile, seizing the opportunity presented him.

Henry waved to a waiter. "It's time to have dinner, isn't it?"

The dinner was lavish—meat pies, crab salad, steaks. They talked about the good old times when they, the Germans, were winners. At last Willy wiped his mouth and leaned back. Henry offered him a cigar.

"You know, Heinrich," Willy said, "I think war is a gamble, and no gambler can win constantly. The clever gambler must stop on time. We thought we could conquer the world, and it was a mistake. If after taking Europe, we had stopped, wouldn't it have been enough for us to enjoy life?"

"I am not a gambler." Henry smiled.

A violinist stopped near the table and looked at Henry questioningly, expecting an invitation to play something. But Henry did not pay attention to him, and the man returned to the stage. His humped back carried eternal guilt.

After a cup of coffee and another cigar, they left the restaurant. The weather had sharply changed. The wind, swirling about with frigid blasts, chilled them to the marrow of their bones and they hurriedly wished each other good night. Luckily, the hotel was around the corner.

Willy kept his promise. In a day he introduced Henry to two men. Despite the fact that they wore civilian suits, their bearing betrayed their status as professional officers.

"Let me introduce you to each other, gentlemen," Willy said. "Captain Heinrich Menke, the Fuhrer's godchild." The officers introduced themselves as Captain Schemmer and Major

Gankerdt. The captain was a faceless man, short and panther lean, far away from the Aryan type; the major was older than his companion, a knotty man with a horseshoe of gray hair around a sun-freckled scalp. Then they showed Henry their IDs.

Before they sat at the table and ordered drinks, Henry asked to be excused. He had a short chat with the bartender and returned to the table. Beverages were delivered in no time. As soon as a waiter left, Henry said, "My friend Willy has obviously explained in general the purpose of my stay here, in Berlin. I am the official Trade Attaché of the Dominican Republic, but my mission in Berlin is specific. You know about the strict UN embargo on weapon shipments to Latin American dictatorships. My second motherland, the Dominican Republic, is one of them. General Trujilio is a long time German friend, and our duty is to help him. He has enough weapons for his own army, but he needs more to help one of his people in Paraguay, General Stressner, to obtain power. In case of Stressner's success, it will be another pro-German regime which will provide jobs and shelter for many of our men." Henry paused and checked himself slightly.

Then he continued. "I'll be quite frank with you, gentlemen. Before the war ended, as an officer at the headquarters, I was involved in the creation of secret arsenals for a future partisan war against the Allies forces. Unfortunately, my godfather was wrong about the resistance—we Germans, were defeated not only physically but, most of all, psychologically," he said bitterly and sipped his drink. Then Heinrich continued, "I think some arsenals still exist. But maybe I'm mistaken and all them are already under the US Army control. It's my recollection that one of them was not too far from the French border. I'd like to ask you, gentlemen, to figure out if there is any chance of buying what I need. I think General Gellen's office keeps such information.

I am a buyer. Connect me with a seller. I'll pay you a good commission—$5,000 for each of you. If we continue our cooperation and you are able to provide a shipment to the French port of Toulon, for instance, I'll double your commission. Of course, payment for the shipment is separate. I am not talking about other expenses. I think it's a good idea to secure your future now, gentlemen," Henry said, his mouth tightening in a resolute smile. He paused and looked at the officers.

The unexpected offer left them speechless for some seconds. At last Major Gankerdt, as senior officer, swallowed and gave a simple, heartfelt reply, "Herr Menke, we would be happy to help you in your mission. How can we reach you?"

"I'm staying at the Bavaria Hotel, but I spend every evening here." Henry waved at the waiter and ordered a bottle of cognac. As soon as it arrived, he poured it in the glasses and proposed a toast. "Let's drink for our trust in the future, gentlemen!"

After they drank, Henry said, "Let me make you a small present to mark our meeting, gentlemen." The officers saw three ladies approaching the table. The bartender knew his job, Henry grinned to himself. The ladies were nice, fresh and still good-looking for their occupation.

"They are yours, gentlemen. And please, excuse my leaving as I still have a lot of work to be done." Henry shot the men a furtive glance and wished them a good night.

At the end of the next day, Captain Schemmer came to the Major Gankerdt's desk.

"I've found his file in our archive, Herbert. Everything is true." He read from a paper he held in hands. "Heinrich Menke. Born in Murnau in 1920. Captain. Awarded by the Night Crest in 1945. No details. Fuhrer was really his godfather."

"Learning how he had arrived to Germany would at least give something solid to proceed from." Major Gankerdt's voice was dry, professional. He couldn't resist laughing at his own cold wit.

Captain Schemmer looked at him with surprise. "I've checked it out. He's clean."

"The dual citizenship is also plausible?"

"Having the Fuhrer for a godfather, he could even receive a triple citizenship if he'd like to." Schemmer put the paper back to the file. "It looks like we pulled out a winning lottery ticket, Herbert."

"I agree Hence," Major Gankerdt said. "It would be stupidity to lose our chance. He mentioned secret arsenals. What about them?"

"I've checked that too. He was right; there were several of them. The closest arsenal to the French border is in Burhaussen. But that area is still under the US jurisdiction."

"Okay. Now let's do our job. We have to contact the American man who is in charge there, in Burhaussen. This Menke offers big money. Only an idiot could refuse. Yankees are also business people. I think we'll find mutual understanding. Tomorrow I'll be in touch with Menke and ask him to clarify what exactly he wants to buy. Your immediate task is to find

an American and collect all the information about him. Okay?"
A stricken expression twisted Major Gankerdt's face.

"I will, boss." Captain Schemmer smiled, displaying the yellow teeth of a hard smoker.

CHAPTER 33

———————▼———————

Without any problem, Henry took a train to Dollenstrolle. He found an empty seat near the window, sat and closed his eyes.

Have you heard the war was over? Really? What war? We live in Swiss; the last time we were at war, it was a war with Russia, almost 300 years ago, under the King Karl XII. Ah, Germans! They always start wars, and always lose. They don't have brains for peace because they don't know how to make money in peacetime. We know. Bring your money at our banks. Did you steal? Okay. Did you rob? Okay. Did you kill? Okay. No questions. We are a highly moral people. Do you want Jewish money back? Alas, it already belongs to our State; nobody survived to withdraw it. Do you tell us that the people were perished in gas chambers? Who cares? We cannot violate our rules: no heir—no money.

Being submerged in his thoughts, Henry heard a conductor's voice, "Destination!"

"*Wo sind wir?*" asked an old lady having a nap in the front seat of the compartment.

"Dollenstrolle." Henry smiled and picked up his suitcase. "It's the last stop."

In the street, Henry looked around. He saw the same red-tale houses, the same calm life style, and even the same indifferent expressions on people's faces. In almost two years since he had been here, nothing had changed.

Henry hired a taxi and after a ten-minute ride was in the hotel. Henry had booked a room in the hotel beforehand, from Berlin.

"I only want the room number fifty," he said firmly as he came to the clerk's desk.

"Why only number fifty, sir?" Surprised, the clerk allowed asking a question.

Henry explained to the clerk that it was his lucky number.

"No problem, sir," the clerk said. "The room number fifty will be prepared for you."

Henry needed to meet Uri Vecksler, the man responsible for his cover. Henry hadn't seen Uri since his departure from Palestine, but physically felt that Uri was permanently around; he was a professional, in the proper sense of the word. In order to contact him, Henry had only a Berlin telephone number. After withdrawing money from the Dollenstrolle bank, Henry had to give it Uri; it would be stupid to keep them in the hotel's safe.

When Henry dialed the number, he heard in the receiver the trembling voice of an old woman. "Frau Richter listening."

"Can I talk to Irvin Magen, please?"

"He is out. Leave a message."

"Tell him the watch will cost 1250 or 1255."

"1250 or 1255?"

"That's right."

"I will." She hung up.

Numbers meant Henry would be in Dollenstrolle, October 12, in room fifty and would wait for Uri at 5:50 p.m.

Today was October 11th. Henry had almost a day at his disposal. To kill time, he decided to visit Johan's house. Why did he decide to visit his former ski instructor? It was an impulsive decision—simply to kill time.

Henry left the hotel and went along the street. Several times he checked to see whether anybody followed him, but couldn't discover a tail. Then it turned out that he had forgotten where Johan lived—all houses were too alike. He dropped in at a small café, ordered a cup of coffee and asked the woman at the counter, "Excuse me, do you know where the ski instructor, Johan by name, lives?"

The woman looked at Henry but kept silent. Obviously the question wasn't enough for her to give an answer, and Henry added, "He was my instructor and I was at his house, but I forgot the house number."

"Johan?" she repeated. "Of course, I know him. Everybody does. His house is just around the corner."

Henry thanked her, sipped his coffee and left. When he turned the corner, he recognized the house. He knocked, and in a second saw on the threshold an old woman. She looked at him questioningly. Henry guesses she was Johan's mother.

"Excuse me, ma'am. Can I see Johan?"

The woman continued looking at him silently, and he added, "Johan was my ski instructor two years ago."

"Come in," she said in neutral voice. "He is not here, but will be back shortly."

Henry remembered the sitting room where he and Martha had a chat with Johan's father. To continue a conversation, he was about to ask the woman about her husband when Johan came into the room. Seeing a stranger, he also looked at Henry questioningly.

"Hi, Johan," Henry said. "Perhaps you don't remember me. My name is Heinrich Menke. You were my ski instructor for a short time almost two years ago."

"I remembered you, Herr Menke," Johan said.

"Since I'm in Dollenstrolle, I decided to see you. What about a couple of beers outside?"

"Willingly."

They went to the pub, and a rosy-cheeked waitress brought their beers.

"How is your father? I remember him, he had a fresh mind."

"He died," Johan said neutrally.

"I am sorry. When?" Surprise widened Henry's eyes.

"More than a year ago. A heart attack."

"My condolences, Johan," Henry said amiably.

"Thank you."

They drank their beer and kept silent for some time. Understanding the reasons behind the extended silence, Henry sighed. Then he asked, "How about you?"

"I'm okay."

"I remember that you had dreamt of opening a ski school for children."

Johan grinned. "Dream and you'll be happy as the British people say."

Henry ordered more beer, and then asked, "Have you heard about my cousin Martha and her mother Katherine? I've lost track of them."

"They said that Katherine moved to South America, with Herr Schwaab." Johan said matter-of-factly.

"With whom?"

"With Herr Schwaab, the former chief of the Baaden Gestapo."

"And is Martha with them?"

"I'm not sure. I heard she returned to Berlin." Johan paused with his beer halfway to his mouth. In his eyes pleasant remembrances flashed for a second.

Henry looked at his watch. "I was glad to see you, Johan," he said amiably. "Good luck. Life goes on. I'm sure that you will open a school for children." He shook Johan's hand and quickly headed toward the exit.

On the way to the hotel, he again checked to see if there was a tail on him, but couldn't find any one suspicious around.

The next day Henry withdrew the money and also took Otto Dornberger's journals from the post box. Putting everything in a big dark brown briefcase that he had purchased in Berlin, he returned to the hotel.

At 5 p.m. sharp, he heard a knock at the door. Henry opened the door and embraced Uri Vecksler who looked like a typical Swiss businessman wearing a dark-gray suit and glasses with an oversized frame.

"I am clean, Henry," Uri said with perfect calm.

They talked for almost an hour, and then Uri rose. "I'm afraid I'll miss my train." He sighed.

"Uri," Henry said, "in this briefcase, there is not only money but also the scientific journals. If something happens to me, please give them to my wife Rachel. She knows what to do with them."

"I will," Uri assured him and went out as silently as he came in.

CHAPTER 34

Full Lieutenant Wilfred Patterson was not happy to receive the new appointment as the commanding officer of a recently founded arsenal in a small city of Schofthaussen. This arrangement was the harbinger of the future demobilization, but Lieutenant Patterson was not in a hurry to leave Germany.

Born and raised in one of the small towns of South Tennessee, before the war he was a small clerk in a warehouse. He considered his life boring and uninteresting; the salary he earned hardly allowed him to pay his debts, not to speak of the zero chance of promotion; the unemployment rate was so high that he was more afraid of losing his job.

When he was called to the Army, of course it was a chance to die. But the Army had given him another chance too—to avoid thinking about tomorrow. Because Wilfred Patterson had a high school diploma, he was sent to short-term cadet school, and then received an appointment in one of the Army units under General Bradley. With a lieutenant's rank, he took part in many military operations but was lucky enough to avoid death or even being seriously wounded; three light wounds brought him two Purple Hearts and a promotion to a full lieutenant rank. Now, at age thirty-seven, he was an athletic man, broad-shouldered, tall and dark-haired.

Wilfred Patterson had survived the end of the war in Berlin and thought about staying in the Army to continue his career. The thought of returning to his native town in Tennessee made him sick.

He was not married. But while serving in Berlin, he had no sexual problems. After the capitulation, Berlin streets were full of prostitutes ready to sell themselves for as little as a chocolate bar.

So the appointment to Schofthaussen made Wilfred Patterson unhappy. Perhaps one of the Army human resource idiots had read in his file that he had worked in a warehouse, and decided to send him to that forgotten-by-God arsenal. The arsenal was discovered only recently, after one of the informers had given them a tip. But because the German army did not exist any more, the Americans hadn't yet decided what to do with the weapons they had found.

So when a silent German wearing a civilian suit came to his office, Wilfred Patterson was surprised. He wasn't in the position to do any favors for civilians; he was sent there only for technical work—to count and register what the hidden arsenal had in stock.

But the visitor turned out to be a former officer who was serving currently at Gellen's Agency. He showed Wilfred Patterson his ID that featured the name Herbert Gankerdt.

"This is not an official visit, Mr. Patterson," Herbert Gankerdt said in perfect English. "I'd like to discuss with you, sir, one item which, I do hope, will be a point of our mutual understanding. But your office isn't the proper place for it. What about having lunch with me, let's say tomorrow at two o'clock? There's only one decent restaurant in this small town— Dietrich's Place. It will be my treat," he added politely.

While Herbert Gankerdt was talking, Wilfred Patterson watched him, his gaze steady and thoughtful. Curiosity for a moment overcame his discipline.

"Why not, Mr. Gankerdt?" A slow smile grew over Patterson's face. "By the way, where did you learn English so well?

"In the NYU." Gankerdt returned the smile. "I graduated in 1933. I am half-American; my mother was German. My parents divorced when I was fifteen. After graduation, my mother insisted that I came back to Germany. To satisfy your curiosity totally, sir, during the war I served in Mr. Walter Schellenberg's office."

Patterson narrowed his gaze. He scanned the face of the man sitting in front of him intently, his mouth tightening in deep consideration. This man was sympathetic to him.

"If you tell me, sir, that you were born in the States, and carry American citizenship, your information would be enough to apply for a job in the US army."

"Alas, my mother had the huge mistake of giving birth to me in Germany." Gankerdt's smile disappeared.

"Okay, Mr. Gankerdt, it would be my pleasure to continue our conversation tomorrow," Wilfred Patterson said, standing up and ending the talk.

When his visitor left his office, Wilfred tried to speculate what kind of mutual understanding could be found between an officer of the US army occupying Germany, and a former intelligence officer of the defeated German Army; even taking into account that the Gellen's Agency was created by the US intelligence office. How could he, Lieutenant Wilfred Patterson, be useful in that cooperation? Let's postpone the answer until tomorrow, he decided finally. Wilfred Patterson rubbed his forehead, feeling a headache coming on.

CHAPTER 35

─────────────▼─────────────

Wilfred Patterson had come to the final conclusion that to reject the offer Mr. Gankerdt had given him would be unforgivably stupid. At any rate, his Army career was finished; demobilization was a matter of several months away. What could he expect at home except warehouse work with a top salary of $100 per month? Yesterday Gankerdt's offer was breathtaking. It wouldn't be too difficult to sell weapons to a Dominican man. Nobody knew exactly what was in the arsenal's stock. If he reduced the total amount of weapons in his report, nobody would even pay attention to it. Who counted rifles when the war was over?

In the worst-case scenario, if the bargain revealed, he would be dishonorably discharged. That wasn't a big deal; if he had about $100,000 in his pocket, he could start a new life.

Lieutenant Patterson discarded his last doubts. Show me the money, he grinned at his thoughts, and I would sell my arsenal to the devil himself.

"You can give your protégé my phone number," he advised Mr. Gankerdt, "and we'll discuss the details of the bargain."

Henry and Lieutenant Patterson met each other in a city park. Patterson looked attentively at the man in front of him, studying the angles of Henry's face. The buyer turned out to be much younger than he expected, with an open, trustful face. In dealing with people, Wilfred Patterson had gotten accustomed to relying on the first impression. He remained satisfied.

"Major Gankerdt recommended you, sir, as a person who can help me in my mission," Henry said. "My name is Heinrich Menke, and I am a Trade Attaché of the Dominican Republic." He handed Lieutenant Patterson his passport.

Patterson looked at the photo and returned the passport. He was slow in answering. "Depends..."

"Depends on price," Henry clarified.

"Depends on a reasonable price," Patterson agreed.

Henry handed him a piece of paper.

Patterson looked at it and whistled. "You are kidding me."

"We are talking about big money." Henry said calmly.

"We are talking a big shipment, sir. You want to buy half of my arsenal."

Henry smiled. "I think not more than ten percent."

Then he described his needs in detail. When he finished, Patterson pondered his words for long moments before he broke the silence.

"It'll cost you $120,000." Patterson said after hesitation. It was one of the oldest games in the world, and he was afraid to ask a low price. Meanwhile, his unrealistic request could kill the bargain.

"$90,000; and the shipment itself is not your headache," Henry offered.

"Deal." Patterson agreed. The price seemed to satisfy him.

"I'll pay $100,000 if you add five light cannons and five large-scale machine guns to the list." Henry leaned forward.

"I'm not sure about light cannons. I haven't seen them in my arsenal. If I don't have them, I would add ten large-scale machine guns."

"Okay. When will you prepare the shipment?"

"I think in a week. How will you take them out?"

"I'll discuss this matter with Major Gankerdt and let you know. How many trucks do I need?"

"I think at least five Studebackers. In what currency will you pay me?" Patterson watched Henry, his silver-blue eyes glittering and waiting.

"In the US dollars."

"Fine." Patterson dragged in a steadying breath.

They shook hands and Henry rose.

"I'll see you later," he said by a way of good night. "It was a pleasure to deal with you, lieutenant." As he exited, he shot a surreptitious glance backward.

The next day Henry discussed with Major Gankerdt how to transport the cargo to the French harbor. He decided not to be stingy—safe cargo transportation was the most important phase of the operation.

"Listen, Herbert," Henry said as they drank their brandy in the bar. "I totally rely on your organizational skill. I would pay you $30,000 more for safe cargo transportation. It would be up to you to allocate the money and arrange how many people will be involved. It's big money. And of course, $5,000 commission for each of you."

"Okay, Heinrich, we'll do it," Gankerdt said, satisfaction in his voice. He quickly estimated that at least $10,000 would stay in his pocket.

Within a week, Henry sent a telegram to Paris. '*Dear Jaclyn, I am on my way. Kiss you, Henry.*'

CHAPTER 36

───────────▼───────────

When Henry and Lt. Patterson met the second time, everything was prepared for shipment. Henry checked some boxes at random—all familiar labels.

"Sorry, I couldn't find cannons, but as I promised, I've added even twelve more large-scale machine guns." Patterson said.

"That's fine." Henry smiled in gentle understanding.

"When are your people ready to take everything out?" Patterson wondered.

They scheduled the day.

"You told me, Mr. Menke, that the shipment isn't my headache and you don't need my help for loading," Patterson reminded him.

"That's right, sir."

"In that case, when will I be able to get my money?" The question was direct.

"My man will deliver it to your office on the eve of the shipment. Does that suit you?"

"Fine."

Three days later, five large Studebakers with Major Gankerdt's crew moved to the arsenal's gate. It didn't take his people much time to load the cars. When the task was done,

Lieutenant Patterson handed Captain Schimmer the necessary papers that were good enough for the American Zone. But close to the French border, two French Intelligence officers would sit in the head car and follow the column. Henry was right when he decided to rely on Major Gankerdt's organizational skill. The column reached the harbor without any problems from the military police.

Responsible for the second phase of the operation, Ehud Avriel met Henry at the harbor. On a distant pier Henry saw two hundred-ton trawlers. One of them, carrying the name San Domingo, was freshly painted and looked brand new. The ship was already full with junk machinery, and it was to be sacrificed to the British for the success of the second ship, the San Juan. That ship looked like old garbage but had a newly installed diesel engine.

When all boxes were loaded on the San Juan, Captain Schimmer came to Henry. The captain of one of the ships saw it. Turning to his sailor, he said loudly in Spanish "I think we are overloaded, Federico, and will sink before we leave the harbor."

"You are too pessimistic, Jose." Another man laughed.

Captain Shimmer smiled. "Your men aren't happy with the big shipment," he said. Then he changed the topic. "We have finished our agreement, Henry."

"It was my pleasure to deal with you and your people, Hence." Henry said.

He waved, and one of the silent men standing nearby gave him a briefcase. Henry handed it to Captain Schimmer who opened it and saw packs of US dollars. He thought it was worth recounting them, but Henry, as he read those thoughts, said,

"Don't doubt it, Hence. This is an exact amount we talked about." He smiled and added, "Just like in the bank."

Captain Schimmer returned the smile and gave Henry his hand. "Good luck, Henry. It was our pleasure to deal with you. If, in the future, we can be useful, don't hesitate to contact us."

As soon as empty trucks were gone, Ehud's crew rapidly installed two large automatic guns on the San Juan's deck. They camouflaged them as big boxes but, in case of necessity, the camouflage could be removed in seconds. When all the preparations were done, Ehud conducted a last minute meeting to check the final readiness of his crew to the operation.

"Men, I won't mention how important it is for our country to have these weapons delivered safely. Let's do what we can, and let's God help us," he said, summarizing his short speech.

The military weather forecast they received was correct. Heavy clouds already covered the sky; tomorrow the sea would be very rough. It wouldn't be too pleasant to find themselves in the middle of the sea on the board of a hundred-ton displacement old ship. But the rough weather meant less chance of meeting any British patrol Navy boats.

Ehud looked at his watch. The first ship had left the French harbor exactly on time—it was ten p.m. She had to be intercepted by the British around two a.m., before the stormy weather began.

At approximately the same time, Vachid Abbas, an Israeli Arab-Christian whose whole family had been slaughtered by Muslim fanatics, came to the British authorities with information about the shipment. "I heard two Jewish men talked about it, sir," he told the British officer and explained, "I know Hebrew."

The British officer assured Vachid Abbas that the shipment would be intercepted.

"When we take the ship, the cargo will be yours," he smiled wryly.

The San Jose was intercepted as soon as she crossed the neutral water border. As soon as the ship stopped, three British sailors jumped on board to check the navigation journal and papers. The cargo was identified as "machinery," but who could check what was inside the big wooden boxes in the hold? The British detained the ship until the cargo was checked, and then convoyed her to the harbor. Three hours later, the second ship, San Domingo, also crossed the neutral water. It was already four a.m. Heavy rain minimized visibility. Pitching and rolling was so strong that Ehud, who was standing near the captain in the cockpit, was afraid the crew would be seasick.

"An hour more, and we'll be at home," said the captain. Suddenly his voice changed. "Ehud, the British! They got us!"

Ehud vainly tried to see something through the curtain of heavy rain. "Are you sure?"

"Positive."

"How far are they?"

"In five minutes they will be close to us."

Then Ehud saw the flashing light. "What do they say?"

"They request we stop."

Ehud ran from the cockpit, threw the camouflage from the gun on the deck and gave an alarm signal for the crew. In two minutes everyone was ready for an assault.

The captain was not mistaken. They all heard the sound of a siren and saw a British naval boat approaching them. And at the same moment Ehud shot.

The British sailors did not expect armed resistance, and it cost them their lives. They managed to make only three shots in response. But one of them was deadly for Ehud. He was killed instantly.

When the short battle was over, Henry sailed to the British ship and fixed a small package of explosives in her hold. But it was enough to make a big hole; in less than half an hour, the British ship vanished in the dark waves of the sea.

Ehud's death depressed the crew. Gloomy silence accompanied the San Juan until the ship had reached a small harbor in Fishery kibbutz where kibutzniks rapidly unloaded it.

Then the San Juan was re-fitted and again became a fishing trawler.

CHAPTER 37

After Henry succeeded in weapons delivery, he concentrated on his family life. The unforgettable event highlighted his existence; Rachel gave birth to their son. In memory of her father, he was called Moshe.

Several days after Henry returned home, he received a call from Ben-Gurion.

"I am proud of you, Henry," he said. "Since you succeeded, I sleep much better." He sighed in the receiver. "And I share your pain about Ehud's death. He was one of my best men." He paused. "I'd like you to replace him."

"Thank you, sir," Henry said without enthusiasm. "But I'd like to concentrate on entering the university."

Ben-Gurion laughed. "Soon all of us will be concentrating on war with the Arabs, and after that on something else. Think over my offer, son." He hung up.

Henry sighed. His conscience was pure—he had spent dirty Dornberger's money on buying weapons for the Jewish settlers, and transferred the rest of it to the Haganah. He was blessed with a son. He wanted to concentrate on family life.

But in his analyses of the situation, Ben-Gurion was right; it wasn't the right time to be concentrating on family life. It was the time to concentrate on fighting that inevitably was approaching.

The UNSCOP proposal was for the partition of Palestine into a Jewish and an Arab state. It allotted less territory to the Jews than the plan submitted by the Jewish Agency in 1946. The chief disadvantage of the plan was its checkerboard arrangement. Nevertheless, the Zionist leadership was inclined to favor the proposal while the Palestinian Arab leadership opposed it. On November 29, 1947, the partition proposal went before the UN General Assembly.

By this time, Palestine had become the focus of a growing cold war conflict; the Soviet Union rushed in to rival the United States in currying favor with Palestine Jewry. With the support of those two great powers, the partition proposal managed to obtain the necessary two-thirds majority in the General Assembly. A Jewish state as the final outcome of Zionist endeavors in Palestine had now been officially recognized by the world.

The next day, severe Arab rioting broke out in various parts of Palestine. In effect, the Arab-Israeli war had begun. As soon as he heard the news, Henry called Ben-Gurion's office. He was immediately sent to the Seventh Brigade, which was fighting in Jerusalem where the heaviest battle between Jews and Arabs took place.

To his horror, Henry saw that the Seventh Brigade suffered severely from a lack of ammunition. He desperately needed the weapons that he had delivered from Germany. There wasn't even effective medical service; the Brigade had no doctors, nor enough stretchers. If only he had a medical diploma! Talking to himself, Henry considered the struggle with the Arabs who were equipped with the latest British weapons a suicide mission.

But he became a good commander, carefully preparing every operation and infusing his own courage into his men. After one of his men was killed, and another one wounded, a new man came to their unit, Abel Riss. He was a young man, with the chubby face of a child and bright, wondering eyes. He swore and spat, or rather pretended to spit—his mouth was absolutely dry. He was frightened but wanted to sound brave.

"We'll fall into the devil's pants," he said with a deep breath.

"Are you afraid?" Henry asked.

"I am," Abel confessed.

"It's always like that at first. You'll get used to it. Even now, I'm frightened every time we go out; but I've grown up with it."

"How can you be afraid if you are used to it?" Abel flashed a surprised expression.

"That's just it. I've gotten used to be afraid." Henry replied as he went toward the staff.

The offensive continued without interruption, now on one front and now on another. Everybody knew it but not every one, like Henry, felt they weren't properly prepared for battle.

A message from the battalion commander pushed Henry to start offensive, "You should execute your task at all costs. Unfortunately this is the brigade commander's order."

"Idiots!" Henry grumbled to himself. "Don't they understand what it means 'at all costs'?"

Henry realized that his first battle as an Israeli officer was lost before it really began. His forces were much too weak for a day frontal attack. After several attempts, he understood that the only thing left was to minimize his men's losses by organizing a rapid retreat. But vicious Arab fire and an Arab Legion counter-attack thwarted his attempt.

The field telephone buzzed again, and Henry jumped up.

"You have to take Latrum, Henry," he heard the nervous voice of the battalion commander. "A large convoy of weapons is waiting on the highway. Without your success, they cannot reach Jerusalem." When Henry kept a gloomy silence, he added, unafraid about being heard by Arabs, "I have no doubt that we shall win, but the present heavy casualties could be avoided. Sorry, Henry. The young have something to learn from the old." He sighed heavily and said in irritation, "This is a stupid order. But an order is an order."

Henry rose to lead his people for a new assault. Suddenly a sharp pain burnt his chest, and he fell down. Henry made an attempt to get up, but failed. His lips still moved but nobody could hear what he tried to say. He felt no pain. Lying on his back, he saw the sky that grew darker and darker. Was it night already or had he simply closed his eyes?

When Henry opened his eyes and regained consciousness, he saw a smiling face of a female doctor.

"Welcome back, Henry" she said. "You've lost a great deal of blood, but now everything is okay."

Henry looked up at the doctor's face as if he couldn't quite believe what he was hearing. From behind the doctor's back, Henry saw Rachel's face. She pressed his hand to her lips. In her eyes, there were tears, but Henry read in them that he would live.

"The doctor says you will be released in two weeks, sweetheart," she said softly. "Now you have to rest. I'll come again tomorrow." Rachel kissed him and smiled, her smile was reassuring. She kissed him again and went to the door.

"Rachel," Henry said quietly. She turned to him. "Bring me my *tefilin*, please," Henry smiled weakly as a myriad of emotions flashed across his face. "Two weeks at the hospital is a long term," he muttered half to himself.

The doctor hadn't made a mistake in her forecast. After two weeks, Henry was released from the hospital. His war was over. Now he could concentrate on his family and his plans for the future.

At the end of the year, Rachel gave birth to their second child. It was a girl. In memory of Henry's mother, they called her Esther.

PART IV

▼

ADVANCING IN YEARS

"Here is the road. Go along it. If you want to the left, go to the left. If you want to the right, go to the right."

—Prophets, Ieshaia 30.21

CHAPTER 38

After the Independence War was over, Henry received several insistent offers to continue his military career. But he had firmly rejected them in favor of continuing his education.

One day he came home grinning. "Rachel, I'm a student again! This is the third time, so this time I do hope to receive my university degree."

Rachel smiled in answer. "If you firmly decided to become a doctor, you will be a doctor, sweetheart. I know you."

At twenty-nine years old, Henry turned out to be the eldest student in his group. The rest were mostly young boys and girls, children of people who had recently immigrated to Palestine and survived the Holocaust.

The atmosphere at the university was quite different from the prudish atmosphere of European universities. Henry breathed the air of freedom, independence and happiness. The light sparkling in the eyes of the young people around him was the light of hope. Hope for the future.

It wasn't the hope to continue a family tradition or to join "the intelligence cast." It was the hope to become useful to their people, to find a well-deserved place among them.

The professor's staff was also unique. World-famous scientists from all over Europe who had survived the Holocaust created a unique atmosphere of spiritual Renaissance. Every lecture was so brilliant that students enjoyed not only the lectures, but also post-lecture discussions which quickly turned into exchanges of opinions about life in general—from personal experiences to divine philosophical aspects of Israel's existence.

Among the most brilliant professors who delivered a course on general physics was Dr. Emile Feingold. Slender and tall, with the high forehead of a thinker on a curly haired head, Dr. Feingold was a world-famous physicist who had taught at Berlin University before World War II. Unlike his liberal Jewish colleagues, he understood the nature of Nazism earlier than others and left Germany for Palestine in 1934. His family did not share his views and stayed in Germany. All of them perished later in concentration camps, except for his sister Miriam who survived. He found her later with the help of the Red Cross, and she joined her brother in 1946. Since then, Miriam dedicated her life to her brother and became both sister and mother for him. Dr. Feingold had never been married and now, at fifty-five, had no intention of changing his life style, dedicating his life to science.

In one of his lectures, when referring to his work at Berlin University, Dr. Feingold mentioned Professor Otto Dornberger's name. "He was a very talented scientist, but unfortunately a pathological anti-Semite. Dr. Dornberger was one of the initiators of the 'Open Letter to the World Common Opinion,' with an appeal to understand Nazi ideology. More than 300 university professors signed the letter, and it's an enigma for me how such a talented scientist could be a pathological anti-Semite. I could never find the answer to that question." Dr. Feingold said.

After the lecture, Henry went to Professor Feingold. "You know, Professor, I also knew Dr. Dornberger in Berlin."

Dr. Feingold looked at Henry with surprise.

"I attended Berlin University before the war," he explained, "but I was there only for one semester."

Dr. Feingold looked at the young man; the gray hair on his head and his deep eyes told him that the young man knew the price of suffering and joy, desperation and hope. Dr. Feingold liked Henry—he reminded him of his younger brother who had died when he was ten years old. But now, looking at Henry's face, he had such a feeling that his brother was reincarnated and now stood in front of him.

Dr. Feingold did not ask Henry any questions in the auditorium, but invited him to have a cup of coffee. A reserved man, Dr. Feingold needed to talk to someone who could understand, who sympathized and offered a different point of view. Henry was such a man.

Emile Feingold and Henry Ginsberg became friends despite the twenty-five year difference in their ages. If they say that friendship is a more profound feeling than love, they both were blessed.

When Henry invited Emile and his sister Miriam to his house for dinner the first time, little Moshe, at seeing them on the threshold, asked, "Are you my grandparents?"

Emile embraced the boy and answered, "Yes, my son, we are."

"But why didn't you come before?" Esther asked.

"We were far away, children.'

"Now you'll live with us?"

"No, children must live with their parents. But we'll live quite near you."

"And you'll come to our house often, okay?'

"Okay."

The children took the toys that Emile and Miriam brought them and ran away to their room to play.

The Ginsbergs and the Feingolds had become one family. When Henry and Rachel went on a short vacation, or she accompanied Henry to the numerous scientific conferences, Miriam always stayed with the children. Not to speak of the holidays when all of them gathered together. The life of all four gained another sense; they tried as much as possible to be together. If before their becoming friends, each of them could have considered him or her happy, now the level of their happiness had increased four times.

The system of higher education in Israel had just been created. There was no time to organize before starting work. Many things were still wholly outside the experience of anyone in the staff. Educated in Egypt, Britain, Poland, Italy, the US, Germany and a dozen other countries, the instructors and professors had been accustomed to thinking and expressing themselves in a variety of ways. But diversity had also had its compensation. United in a common case, teachers and professors enriched one another by the variety of their experiences and outlooks.

His university years remained forever in Henry's memory as a wonderful period of scientific brotherhood that had passed all too rapidly, like a fairy tale. But suddenly, the fairy tale turned into reality; Henry graduated and began working at Professor Chaim Geldorf's laboratory.

Medicine was a wonderful and mysterious world. The deeper Henry penetrated it the more he was assured that he had not made a mistake in the choosing of his profession. Sometimes Henry opened Dornberger's journals and read them. He couldn't stop admiring Dornberger's ability to see a light at the end of a tunnel, and tried not to think about the moral price of results. Thoughts bitterly dashed through Henry's mind when he read about one unique case. While a prisoner was fixed in the camera for research on the influence of high technological coolants, he unexpectedly received a 380-volt shock wave. When the prisoner was taken out, the insignificant being was dead and delivered to the morgue to cremate. But the patient had unexpectedly come back from his short, deep coma. Coming through with a deadly headache, he developed the unique ability to see human internal organs. It turned out that this man could see with his eyes, and also his brain, and even his hands. His palms generated electro-magnetic hesitations in a millimeter diapason. Dr. Dornberger supposed this frequency was favorable for human interim organs and, "if a generator of that frequency is created, it could be used for treatment of many diseases."

Henry's work at Professor Geldorf's laboratory turned out to be very fruitful—he quickly became a professor's closest associate. At seventy, a pre-War Nobel Prize winner in biology, Professor Chaim Geldorf had reached the peak of his scientific productivity long ago; for many years he had not created any fresh ideas. Henry became that idea generator that Professor Geldorf desperately needed. But Professor Geldorf remained a decent man and a true scientist; happiness for such people was to grow a scientific pupil more gifted than the teacher himself. Working with Henry, Professor Geldorf could be happy watching Henry turns into a large-scale scientist.

When Henry told Professor Geldorf about his idea—to treat sick internal human organs with the help of a special coolant agent, Geldorf was one of the first who supported Henry's concept although most of his colleagues considered it utopia.

The idea was simple—inject through a vein a special pilot carrying a cooling agent with a temperature close to absolute zero (-273 K) Reaching the bad tissue, the pilot would be exploded and freeze the tissue's perimeter, turning it into a fragile icicle. And then, because of the difference in temperature from adjacent tissues, the bad tissue would be broken like a shattered icicle into many micro-pieces. Melted, they would be taken out of the body in the urine. The success of that research would be revolutionary for medicine—the age of traditional surgery would be over.

But the research included a wide complex of not only medical but also physical, chemical, bioengineering and technological problems. It was a huge step forward in developing of science in the second part of the twentieth century.

Professor Geldorf spent the rest of his energy on obtaining government funds for Henry's research. Despite his age, he even flew to New York and met with many influential Jews; he succeeded in persuading them to make multi-million donations for his lab. When Professor Geldorf at last retired, naturally Henry occupied his chair as the director of the laboratory.

Although the work in the laboratory took almost all his time, Henry couldn't refuse an offer to become a university professor. He taught two courses—one in medicine, another in biology. Young students accumulated the energy in his soul that was necessary for his work. For Henry, teaching was the same artwork as a sculptor's. The difference was in the final result; a sculptor tried to reach perfection in dead clay while a professor tried to create a perfect human being. Was there a bigger reward for a teacher?

CHAPTER 39

▼

Time. Who invented time? Only the day before yesterday, he arrived in Palestine. Only yesterday, he graduated from the university. But today, his colleagues call him a 'metre,' and his children were grown. What did time mean?

Thousands of years ago there were no hours or minutes. Time was only measured by sunsets and sunrises. Happy time! In the third millennia B.C. Egyptian priests introduced the first sun-moon calendar. It wasn't very accurate. For five years, there were twelve months a year, but for the next three—there were thirteen. Gaius Julius Caesar resolved the problem and modernized the calendar in 46 B.C. The sun calendar became the official calendar for the Roman Empire; people knew they became a year older every 365 days. Did it make them happy? Maybe they would have been happy if they knew they were younger in reality. Roman astronomers considered a year to consist of 365 days and 6 hours. But in reality, a year was eleven minutes and fourteen seconds shorter. Pope Gregory XIII reformed the system—it was said that after the 4th of October followed the 15th. Thanks to Pope Gregory, Catholic people could pray at the same day. But not at the same time, because in winter and in bad weather, sun watches read different time.

Who made people happy? It was a British monk who has invented mechanical watches. Then people could control their lives with the accuracy of minutes and seconds.

Did it make people happy? Perhaps not, that could be why history did not keep the monk's name. What does time mean? It's only a human invention. But without this invention, life turns into total chaos. On the other hand, if time is only an invention, it means it doesn't exist in reality.

Despite of all the scientific achievements, people perceived time not through watches, but through our feelings. When we wait for an important call, even a few minutes may seem the eternity. But while involved in our favorite business, we don't pay attention that the day has already passed. What does time mean? This is what we have in our brain, and it makes photos with a three-second frequency.

The event which took place three seconds ago has already become our past; it has gone. Only our memory kept it. What does time mean? Perhaps tomorrow we'll know it didn't exist at all.

Henry grinned at his thoughts and recalled them to the present. Today it was unusual that the family gathered on Sabbath eve—Rachel, Moshe, Esther and him. Unfortunately Emile and Miriam couldn't come. Since Emile began working at the Dimona center, he had no free time.

While Rachel set the table, Henry looked at his grown children. Only yesterday they were small children, he sighed. Only yesterday I was young. Again time! What's the source of our unhappiness? Does our life only consist of yesterday and today? We can remember and analyze them. But what is the future if not a volatile hope? You cannot analyze the future because God hasn't yet given it to you.

Moshe already wears a military uniform. A tender smile touched Henry's lips as he glanced at his son. He is a handsome, tall, lean, blond, blue-eyed man. Not the usual type of Jew. He could be a warrior of King David's time, Henry thought. The military uniform suits him, but doesn't make him seem older. His face is young and handsome. Perhaps Israeli soldiers are the most handsome men in the world. In several months, he'll finish his IDF service, but he remained as hectic in his emotions as he had been in his childhood.

Henry transferred his glance to the daughter. Unlike her brother, Esther was a brittle brunette, with beautiful black hair and green eyes. Her brother had an impulsive, choleric temperament while she seemed to be reserved. Henry could not remember whether he had ever seen his daughter's tears since her childhood. She also had not changed much—now she was an emotionally reserved young lady, just as she was an emotionally reserved child; she doesn't like to expose her feelings.

It was strange that none of them were inspired by his medical career. They had chosen their own ways. Both, since their adolescence, were not inclined to exact sciences; Moshe chose the Juridical Faculty, Esther—the Faculty of Foreign Languages. She specialized in Spanish, but was already fluent in Hebrew, German and French.

"You know, Dad, several days ago my friend Ariel showed me *Haaretz* where I read a long article about you. I didn't know you saved the lives of so many sick people."

Henry smiled. "It's not just my achievement, son. Many doctors have used the results of my research. Strictly speaking, they are the men who saved lives, not me."

"Frankly, it's too complicated for me. Physics, chemistry—it's not for my poor brain. I remember that you always told me, "Don't babble baloney, Moshe, you have to study. But to bubble baloney was the thing I could do. That's why, considering the circumstances, I have no other choice but to enter Law School after the Army."

"That will be the right way for you, brother," Esther said without a smile. "You always wanted to invent the easy way to make money." Her gaze narrowed.

"That's right, sis," Moshe agreed conciliatory. "Since I read that in the US most of lawyers are millionaires, especially divorce lawyers in Hollywood, I was strengthened in my decision." He addressed her with the spirit in which her words were given.

"Okay, guys!" Rachel smiled. "Following the US tradition, one child in the family had to be a lawyer, another one—an accountant. Will we follow that tradition?" She glanced at her daughter.

"Definitely not, Ma. I have already made my choice—languages. I want to be a translator." Esther said firmly, a haunted expression in her eyes.

"It looks like I've failed to interest my own children in medicine." Henry shook his head with a smile. "But there's nothing to be done; we live in a democratic country where the right of choice is one of our liberties. I've already put up with it."

As in her childhood, Esther lit the candles and Henry read a short prayer, "*Baruch ata adonay elogheiny melech aolam asher*

kidshanu bemitzvotav vetzivanu leadlik ner shel shabat kodesh!"
Then they sat at the table. After supper, Esther and Moshe went
to their rooms, and Henry sat on the sofa watching Rachel
removing the plates.

Twenty years have past in a flash, he thought. Only yesterday,
she was a nineteen years old girl. And she still remains a girl;
time has not put a print on her face; it's as beautiful as it was
twenty years ago. Only the color white strokes her thick hair,
but it only reinforces her charm. She sacrificed her pianist career
for him. Perhaps she would have been an outstanding pianist. Is
she sorry about it? Many times Henry wanted to ask her, but
who would tell the truth? Was Rachel still happy with him now,
when the children were grown and would soon leave their parents' aerie?

Maybe he needn't ask the questions. She always read his
mind. The bond between them was undeniable. It was as if an
invisible cord ran from his head to hers, and they could telephone each other: the one sensing the other's thoughts. If he
always knew before she spoke what she was going to ask him,
there was the same connection in reverse.

He and Rachel did not know if Moshe had a girlfriend, or if
Esther had a boyfriend. If they lived in their parents'
house...But Moshe served in the Army; Esther lived in the university dormitory. It was natural. If children don't live with their
parents, they mature earlier. Rachel and he were still young, but
they didn't understand the modern language of the new generation. What does "boyfriend" mean if an old lady talks about the
old gentleman with whom she lives to avoid loneliness? Or what
does "girlfriend" of a young man mean if he sleeps with the girl
and has no intentions to marry? Time passes too quickly—a

new language, new fashions, and new views…How rapidly time goes…

Tomorrow we'll go to the synagogue, Henry thought. Perhaps Moshe and Esther go to the synagogue only on High Holydays—Rosh Hashanah and Yom Kippur. They belong to the new generation. Israeli society is getting more and more secular. Is it possible to have a secular society in God's State? Isn't it unnatural that the State itself killed the faith?

Rachel and he had never pressed their children about religion. Everybody must come to the faith by himself or herself. This is the Jewish faith; it's different from all others. Everyone must make his or her choice voluntarily. But why, in such case, do the media try more and more to kill the faith? Don't they realize that by killing the faith, they would kill Israel?

Henry discarded his thoughts. Today there was the eve of Shabbat. God gave them the happiness of life, the happiness of love, and the happiness of being together.

Rachel finished washing the plates and sank in the coach near Henry. He silently embraced her. They did not need words; souls speak quietly. She touched his hair with her soft palm.

"Do you remember, honey, we took Moshe and Esther to the Nature Museum?" Rachel asked.

"Why did you recall it?" He arched a brow.

"I don't know. I simply thought since that time, they both have not liked biology."

"They both were already at the age to inoculate their interests." He shot her a thoughtful glance in acknowledgment of this comment.

"But that visit caused the opposite reaction, honey." Rachel sighed.

Henry raked his memory for the time. He remembered that among the other exhibits was a baby in a bottle. It made Moshe mad; he hit the bottle with his hand and ran away. Esther followed him.

"Such things should not be exhibited for children. It would make them have nightmares," Rachel said after a pause.

She was always right, his Rachel. Since then, his children had lost all interest in medicine.

"Maybe our grandchildren will follow in your steps. With God's help, it will happen soon." She again touched his hair.

Henry closed his eyes. Her touch was as tender as his Mother's touch would have been. Still with closed eyes, Henry saw a strange sight—the women's figure gleaming in the moonlight. Then, silently, she made her way until she reached a big tree where she stood for a time. It seemed Henry that it was as she was waiting for him to speak. Mother!

Henry shuddered and opened his eyes. "It's late, sweetheart," he said. "It's time to sleep."

CHAPTER 40

The sad news came from New York—Baruch Silverman had died unexpectedly from a heart attack in his Long Island house. He was seventy-nine years old, and died in his sleep.

Receiving the call from Baruch's son, Henry took no time to book two seats on an El Al flight to New York; Rachel and he had to give Baruch their last respects. They hadn't too much time. According to Jewish law, Baruch Silverman had to be buried as soon as possible. Henry called the university to cancel two lectures, and the same day he and Rachel were onboard a plane.

The flight was calm and the plane arrived on time. Within forty minutes, they were at the hotel room, taking time to only take a shower.

The coffin was installed inside the largest New York Park West synagogue. The hall was full of people. Despite the fact that Baruch had not occupied an official position for many years, among the people who came to give him their last respect were diplomats, businessmen, clergymen, city and governmental officials.

Henry went to the table and signed on the line of those who wanted to give a short speech. When the rabbi called his name, 'Professor Henry Ginsberg of Israel,' he went to the podium.

"Ladies and gentlemen! On this sad day, giving our last respects to Baruch Silverman, many called him a unique human being.

Sharing all those warm words, I cannot agree that Baruch was a unique human. He was a particular Jew as God wanted to see all of us—a moral example for others. Who was he for my wife and me? It's difficult to find the proper words. If our parents gave us physical life, he had given us spiritual life, pointing the way out from the dead end where we found ourselves after the war. That's why he will always remain more than a close relative for us."

After the formal part of the ceremony in the synagogue was over, the cortege of cars moved to the cemetery. There were at least a hundred cars, and police had to stop traffic along the street.

"Who is being buried?" indifferently asked one of the passers-by.

"No idea. Another rich Jew, I suppose," replied another.

At the cemetery, the process was repeated but Henry did not talk. At last the rabbi read a prayer, and the coffin was lowered into the grave.

After the last ceremony, close relatives and friends drove to Silverman's home. He was survived by three sons, a daughter and nine grandchildren; his wife had died six years before.

"Good Lord, he did not suffer," Rachel said quietly.

Henry nodded pensively. "Death is death."

Henry found himself sitting near the gentlemen over sixty years old, with the face of a former professional boxer.

"I'm familiar with your works, Professor Ginsberg," the man said. Then he introduced himself, extending his hand, "I'm

Professor Millman. Nahum Millman, Dean of Harvard Medical Faculty.'

"My pleasure," Henry said, shaking his hand.

"The pleasure is mine." Millman smiled. "I'm impressed with your research, Dr. Ginsberg."

"Thank you, sir."

"Have you ever thought about moving to the United States? Here, there are many more opportunities for you. Perhaps you can't avoid a budget deficit because the most of money in Israel is being allocated to military items. Am I right?" His chin lifted.

"Israel had her own specifics, sir." Henry said matter-of-factly.

"Yes, you live on a volcano in expectation of an eruption."

"After every eruption, the soil is more fruitful." Henry smiled.

He apologized and, without even putting the glass to his lips, went out to the deck to smoke a cigarette. While he was smoking, he heard the door behind him open. He turned around and saw a teenage girl, Baruch Silverman's granddaughter.

"Hi," she said, "I'm Deborah."

"Hi, Deborah." Henry couldn't understand what impressed him about the girl's appearance. "I'm Henry Ginsberg."

"I know," she said expansively, without a smile.

"Yes, you know my name," he agreed. "The rabbi introduced me at the synagogue."

"I've known you for two years," the girl said, with a strange look in her eyes.

"That's impossible, Deborah. I've never been in New York before."

"I've known you since the day when my grandpa asked me to edit the manuscript of his memoirs. He described your unique fate in it," she explained.

"Now I see!" Henry exclaimed. "You said 'unique fate.' Every fate is unique, Deborah. Your fate is no less unique than mine although you are only entering life. Believe me."

Now Henry realized what impressed him about the girl's appearance—her eyes. She had crystal blue eyes, not typical for a Jewish face.

"It's getting chilly outside," he said. "You can catch cold."

They returned to the room, and Henry sat back at the table near Dr. Millman.

"Let's return to our sheep, Dr. Ginsberg." He smiled with the corners of his mouth. "What if I offer you a tenured position at Harvard, in addition to the director's position in the Lab of Perspective Research? It'll bring you more than a $100,000 per year, not counting the consulting fees from private companies."

"It's a tempting offer, Dr. Millman. Sorry, but I have to reject it. My home is Israel. Under different circumstances, I could very well understand why some Jews would choose to live here, but I want to go home. I need to go home." Henry attempted another smile.

"But we're scientists, Dr. Ginsberg! We work not only for our country, but also for mankind. Science cannot be imprisoned within borders." Dr. Millman raised his eyebrows.

"That's one point of view. In many aspects, globalization can be useful for science, I agree with you. But I am not an anti-globalist; I am a nationalist." Henry's answer was very calming. "In science," he added.

"Nationalism leads to the dead end," Dr. Millman objected bitterly. "Take, for example, the Soviet Union. They lost more than they gained in not exchanging scientific information with the Free World."

"It's a matter of survival for them." Henry remarked matter-of-factly.

"But we are doctors, not military experts," Dr. Millman objected emotionally.

"But we still remain citizens." Henry looked at Dr. Millman carefully, summing up the conversation.

Dr. Milman smiled. "We are, Dr. Ginsberg," he agreed and changed the topic. He rolled the wine around his tongue and his face flushed with pleasure.

When Rachel and Henry returned to the hotel, she asked him, "Shall we stay in New York for couple of days to sightsee, honey?"

"Sorry, darling. I have to go back. But before our flight, you have time for a bus tour. The city is beautiful. I promise you that we'll spend our next vacation here."

"Do you remember when we last had a vacation?" Rachel kissed him on the cheek. "Okay. They say *dream and you'll be happy*. I'll dream!"

CHAPTER 41

Moshe and his friend Ariel Blum sat in a café, sipping espresso. They served together in the same unit but seldom received leave at the same time. Ariel was rushed, waiting for a bus to get back to the unit while Moshe had just received his forty-eight hour pass. Their service would be finished in a few months; they both were eager to attend college then. They talked about their plans for the near future when Ariel said, "What a beautiful *shiksa*! Unfortunately my bus is coming, I have to go." They shook hands, and Ariel ran to the bus stop.

Moshe turned. At a distant table, he saw a charming girl who wrote something in a notebook. The tender oval of a slightly sunburned face and long, curly blond hair attracted his glance like a magnet. For some minutes, he looked at the girl, then took his cup of coffee and went to her table.

"Excuse me, is this seat vacant?"

The girl glanced at his military uniform and the Uzi machine gun on the shoulder. "No, it's not." She shrugged. Her smile was welcoming.

He sat. "I'm Moshe," he introduced himself, extending his hand.

"I am Peggy." She put aside the notebook, put it into her bag and looked at Moshe absently.

"Are you a tourist?" Moshe asked. "You don't look like a local girl."

"No, I attend lectures at the university as a member of the Student Exchange Program," she explained. "I study at Harvard Medical School in the USA, but for a whole semester I'll be attending lectures at the Medical Faculty here."

"In several months, I'll be attending Law School," Moshe said, intercepted her glance at his military uniform. "My service will be over then," he explained. "Anyway, you decided to become a doctor. Is it the family business?"

Peggy smiled. "No, my father is a politician. But I want to be a biologist. That's why I came here to listen lectures by Professor Ginsberg; he is a world-famous biologist," she said, her voice rich.

Moshe laughed, and Peggy looked at him with surprise.

"He is my father," Moshe explained. "Peggy, this is fate. You came to Israel to listen to lectures by a famous professor, and casually meet his son in a small café. It supports the idea that there are no accidents; as my dad likes to say, every accident is a forecasted by God regularity."

Peggy smiled. The smile brightened her face and created two small dimples on her cheeks.

"Peggy," Moshe said, looking directly to her eyes, "I'd like to see you again."

"But you serve in the Army."

"Every week or two, I have a leave." Moshe said. "And now it's peace time."

Peggy nodded her head quickly without speaking. Then she wrote a telephone number and the address on a napkin. She gave it to Moshe. "I'm going to stay here for at least three more months. I'd also be glad to see you, Moshe."

"I'll call you, Peggy. You are beautiful." He stood up and extended his hand. But then he said, "Will you allow me to take you out?"

She nodded 'yes.'

Peggy and Moshe roamed through the outskirts of the city in streets so narrow that they looked like crevices went to the fair. "Let your heart be appeased; the object of your love will not desert you," Moshe said, remembering a phrase he has read somewhere. She loved the words 'object of your love,' they soothed her.

Perhaps for this reason or perhaps because the whole evening had been so translucent, she hadn't even asked Moshe whether he was leaving soon. And now he was leaving.

Since that day, he used every moment of every leave to see Peggy; even when he was with the unit, he tried to call her just to hear her voice. He had often pondered his feelings about Peggy, but the riddle remained unsolved. All he knew was that life, which before had been full to the brim, seemed empty when he did not see her.

He had never once thought of the possibility of introducing Peggy to his parents. First of all, he tried to persuade himself that she was attracted to him only because he was Professor Ginsberg's son. "She is good-looking and intelligent; it cannot be denied, but aren't there others no less good-looking and intelligent? If there's anything original about her—she is eccentric. Such girls become heartless women who ruin their husbands or neurasthenic capable of taking up a revolver."

But Moshe continued persistently, gloomily, and passionately to think about Peggy. For two weeks he even stopped meeting her to prove to himself that he could live without her. Why think of her all the time? That girl, without the rights that long friendship gives, without heart-to-heart talks, without ardent embraces, a foreigner that had entered his life, a *shiksa* had become dear to him.

He called her. "Hi, Peggy. It's Moshe."

"Hi, Moshe. Where did you vanish to?"

"I had vanished in my thoughts."

"In thoughts?"

"In my thoughts about you," he said seriously. "Meet me. Perhaps I'll be able to say to you what I want to say."

"Sure. When?"

"I'll wait for you at eight this evening near the monument." Moshe hung up before she could answer.

When he met Peggy, they walked along, now very slowly, now rapidly. The rain had driven the usual strollers away, so they walked down a deserted avenue. They had managed to tell each other everything it seemed, but not a word had they uttered about what filled their hearts.

Peggy stopped, looked at Moshe. Then she suddenly shrank away as if she saw something in his eyes, and then just as suddenly embraced him. He remembered nothing; he only kept repeating softly, "Peggy…Peggy."

Rain pelted down on them, but they didn't have an umbrella. Thinking fast, Moshe ran to the road and waved down a taxi. The Arab driver had already finished his shift, but the address Moshe gave him was quite near the taxi garage, so he took the passengers. Moshe couldn't stop kissing Peggy until the driver announced, "Guys, you have arrived."

They got out, and Moshe showed her to the tiny one-bedroom apartment that he and Ariel shared. This was the first time that Peggy had visited his lodgings. Moshe turned on the tape recorder, and sounds of Charles Azanavour's voice filled the room. Peggy moved to the bookshelf and was surprised to see books of Eastern poetry. She opened one written by Amir Dechlevi almost a thousand years ago, and read, "*True love doesn't wish power. Offering—this is its balm, self-sacrifice—this is its happiness. Law of passion—is only a game of love, not more...*"

Moshe took the book from her hands and put it back on the shelf. He opened another and read, "*You are my hope, but there is grief in my eyes; I cannot satisfy my thirst only by seeing a spring...*"

After Moshe's kisses and a glass of wine, Peggy lost her senses. She recovered them only when she found herself on the couch, with Moshe attempting to unbutton her dress.

"No, Moshe, no. For God's sake," she whispered.

"Why not?" Moshe asked. His fingers trembled as he tried to light a cigarette. "Aren't we going to be married?"

"For God's sake," she whispered again. "I cannot. Not today, please." She put her clothes in order and went to the door. Then she returned and kissed Moshe gently. "Don't be angry with me, sweetheart. I love you very much."

Before he could answer, Peggy ran away. When she returned to her apartment and lay in the bed, she couldn't sleep remembering every minute of the evening. Why hadn't she remained with Moshe? She could not answer the question. It would change nothing although she was still a virgin. But something stopped her from making that last step that most of her girls-friends had passed long ago.

Her virginity wasn't a burden for her—until that evening her flesh was indifferent to those who tried to seduce her. But she thought that sex would lose its magic mystery if she indulged. She knew everybody would kid her if she confessed her thoughts. And she hadn't the slightest wish to share them with anybody. The longer she listened to her girlfriends' chatter about their sex lives, the less she wanted to be in their shoes.

She understood that her male peers only played the role of sexual lions. She turned them off even before they tried to kiss her. None seemed to be the one to guide her into the mysterious world of love and sex.

When she had met Moshe, she opened her heart to him. He did not try to rush things; he seemed to be the man she'd been waiting for.

I hurt him when I left so abruptly, she suddenly thought, and her dismay seemed to grow. He wanted me to prove my love, but I didn't give in him. Now he'll think I don't love him. And everything was so nice—music and a fire burning in the electrical fireplace…What a fool I am! Carol McCormic told me that she gave in the first time somewhere in a basement on a pile of garbage bags, Peggy remembered.

At last, exhausted by her thoughts, Peggy fell asleep.

CHAPTER 42

———————▼———————

Moshe did not respond to her calls, but Peggy tried to calm herself by saying that he hadn't received any leave. Army was Army, there was nothing to be done; she had to wait. She called several more times until she heard the man's voice in the receiver. Her heart vibrated.

"Well," she said with a barely audible breath. "Moshe?"

"No, this is Ariel. Who is this?"

"My name is Peggy."

"I know you," Ariel said. "You're the beauty I've seen in a café near the bus stop."

"That's right." Peggy smiled in the receiver. "When can I get hold of Moshe?"

"I am happy to give you a straight answer; tomorrow he'll be here."

"Thank you!" she said joyfully and hung up.

Maybe he doesn't love me any more, she thought. Did she love him? What a foolish question! How could she not love him if she fell asleep and woke up with his name on her lips? How could she not love him if she still felt the touch of his fingers? If it's not love, what was it? Peggy felt her cheeks burning and pressed them with her hands. Ice cold hands. She stood up and looked at the mirror. "How awful I look!" she muttered to her reflection.

The next day, Peggy did not go to the university and spent most of the day in bed. She felt bad. Several times she wanted to call Moshe and already had the receiver in her hand, but at the last moment hung up. She didn't want to look at her face in the mirror. First she wanted to put make-up on but instead, she stepped outside.

She inhaled a fortifying breath. It was drizzling. She had forgotten to bring an umbrella with her, but decided not to go back. She pulled her coat collar up to her ears and slowly walked along the street.

The world around her was damp. Drenched passers-by covered by umbrellas were faceless human beings. Shop windows were wet with tears; even cars were wet with an eagerness to move their owners from their everyday lives to the world of illusion.

Peggy moved automatically; she stopped if she saw a red light, continued on green. She saw nothing but diffused cars' headlights reflected from the wet road. Pools of light on the sidewalk appeared and vanished as her shade extinguished them. Peggy thought about nothing. When the street lights suddenly vanished, she looked up from the road and found herself in front of Moshe's building. How she could come here if she'd gone to the opposite direction, she wondered absently.

Looking around as if she still hoped to see saving light spots again, ones that would lead her further, Peggy only observed that it was dark and wet around her. The rain stopped drizzling and began pouring from the sky. The wind howled. The night suddenly grew black as the depth of perdition. The wind whirled around her, soaking her to the skin.

Peggy suddenly felt cold and feverish. Slowly, stopping on every step, she went up to Moshe's apartment and stood in front of the door. Several times she extended her hand to the door-bell, but lowered it each time. At last she rang the bell and leaned against the wall. Obviously he hadn't yet gotten his leave yet, she thought, and then the door opened.

"My Lord, Peggy!" Moshe's eyes flew open in surprise. "You are wet to the bones. Come in." He helped her to take off her wet coat.

Ariel's sleepy face appeared behind Moshe's back. At seeing Peggy, he quickly dressed and went to the door saying, "Sorry, guys, I have to visit my uncle." He winked at Moshe and closed the door behind him.

Moshe tugged Peggy closer to the fireplace. "What hap-pened?" he asked, but only heard the sound of Peggy's teeth chattering in reply. "I'll fix you a cup of hot coffee and you'll feel better," Moshe said, his voice distinctly soft.

The warmth of the fire weakened Peggy, and she dozed on the couch. She again saw spots of light, but this time they played on Moshe's face. They did not vanish; they danced a waltz of warmth and love.

"Drink this, Peggy, otherwise you'll catch cold," she heard Moshe's voice. "The best medicine for a cold is coffee with cognac. So I prepared it for you."

Peggy drained the warm liquid and looked at Moshe. What a nice face he wears, she thought while pleasant warmth spread over her. How handsome he is!

Taking her heart in hand, she dared words she never thought she'd utter to a man, "I love you. Kiss me, Moshe," she said and closed her eyes.

His hands, so soft and tender, touched her breast that strained in expectation of the caress. My Lord, what happiness is to be loved! She smiled through her tears at her thought, and even the sharp pain that pierced her body didn't force her to weaken the embrace as their love strove to accomplish great heights.

CHAPTER 43

▼

In the vicinity of Aqaba, which sits at the head of a narrow tongue of water, Saudi Arabia massed 20,000 troops along with Egyptian and Jordanian troops. Egypt announced that any ships attempting to carry oil or strategic material to the port would be shelled and sunk.

The port of Aqaba was the only Israeli outlet to the Red Sea and the Asian oceans beyond. Israel informed President Lyndon B. Johnson that he had "a week or two" to use any diplomatic pressures he could muster to open the port again. It was quite clear that very soon Israel would launch attacks on the neighboring Muslim states if the matter were not resolved.

Receiving that information, the US State Department 'strictly recommended' the American citizens to leave Israel as soon as possible. The same evening, Peggy received a call from her father who demanded that she come home immediately.

"I called our Embassy," he said, "Get in touch with our Consul Jack Smith, and he'll reserve a ticket for you."

"But I haven't finished my work!" Peggy tried to object. "It's quite calm here, Dad."

"It only seems that way to you. War will start in several days. You must be crazy to stay there. You can continue your studies at any university you want—from Harvard to Princeton. I think their professors are no less qualified than in Israel," he said venomously.

The next day Peggy still waited for a call from Moshe although she understood that evidently, in expectation of war, his military unit could be relocated and he had had no chance to contact her. Only after a third, insistent and angry parental call, she contacted the American Embassy. The next day she left for New York.

Ten days after that, after months of escalating border skirmishes and general military mayhem between Muslim and Israeli troops along the borders, war broke out.

It was the first time when Moshe took part in a real large-scale military operation. For the first time, he saw a dead enemy soldier. But before the Arab died, Moshe saw him dying. The man's face was upturned, his hands suspended as if he were praying; then his body dropped clean away leaving only his hands on the metal of M-60 tank. Moshe loathed it.

"Take it easy," the lieutenant said. "We defend ourselves against annihilation."

The battle was short and victorious. But after, for the first time in his life, Moshe thought if Arabs are so anxious to kills us, we must destroy and kill them to save our homes and our land. But wasn't this land their land, too? A short thought suddenly visited him, but he discarded the positive answer. It cannot be their land if God gave it to us. And now we're struggling and dying only because many generations of our predecessors violated God's request to kill all our enemies. Today we pay for the liberalism of previous generations.

In a blitzkrieg of troop thrust, aerial sorties and mechanized sweeps, the Israeli military moved simultaneously on all fronts, smashing the Muslim armies massed on the borders, then rolling onward to seize the Sinai peninsula and the Gaza Strip from Egypt in the south, the Old City of Jerusalem and the broad Western banks of the Jordan River and the Golan Height from Syria in the north.

Virtually overnight, Israel tripled the size of the territory it controlled.

CHAPTER 44

▼

After the war, Moshe served two more months until he was demobilized and sent home. His life returned to the usual circle—it was time to think about the future. He finally decided to continue his education in law.

If wartime had deflected his thoughts from Peggy, they now returned to her. He called her. Nobody responded. He tried several times later, but the result was the same. The next day Moshe decided to stop off into her place, but the door was locked. Moshe was an insistent man, and he found a landlord, an old Greek woman.

"Excuse me, ma'am," he said. "I'm trying to get hold of a young lady from apartment B, but no one answers my calls. Does she still live here?"

The old woman looked at him attentively, and then said, "Alas, young man. She has moved out. On the eve of the last war," she clarified, and then explained, "She was American, and they were told by the Embassy to leave the country." Then at seeing Moshe's distraught face, the old woman added, "She paid in advance for half a year, so I haven't yet found a new tenant. The apartment is still hers, and if you want, you can get in. Maybe you'll find her American address or a telephone number." She gave Moshe the key. "It's difficult for me to go upstairs. Please bring the key back." She smiled him.

Moshe thanked her, took the key and went into the apartment. He looked around. It was a tiny studio apartment with a recliner-sofa, a small bureau, an armchair, a crucifix on the wall, and an unsigned lithograph on another wall. He sat on the sofa. He closed his eyes and memories attacked him as he physically felt the heat of Peggy's body. Then he opened his eyes. She left nothing—no books or papers. Moshe returned a key and left the building.

Day by day passed, and Peggy's image was becoming more and more blurred. Everyday life attacked Moshe with its routine.

Unexpectedly, three months later, the phone in his apartment rang. Moshe picked up the receiver. "Hello."

Silence came as an answer.

"Hello," he repeated.

Then he heard a voice, "It's me, Peggy."

"Peggy? Where are you?"

"I am in New York."

"I'm so glad to hear your voice. How are you?"

"Lousy." She paused. "I am pregnant."

"Pregnant?" Moshe repeated, not quite under his breath, as he did not know what to say.

Long silence came. He did not know what to say, she waited for his response. At last she said hoarsely, "Please, Moshe, come to me. Please," she repeated. "Put down the phone. I live alone. Let me know when you will get here."

"Okay, I'll fly there," he said although he hadn't the slightest idea of how he could fly to New York.

"Please," Peggy repeated and hung up after giving him her phone number.

Moshe looked at the paper where he had written that number. "Yeah." He rubbed his forehead, thinking, trying to get rid of an unexpected complicated subject. He hadn't yet realized what had happened. What he did realize was that his youth was over. Submerged in his thoughts, he sat for a long time and did not hear the door open. Ariel came in and switched the light on.

"Why are you sitting here in the dark, Moshe? What happened?"

Moshe told him the story. Ariel was his devoted friend, the only man who could understand him. Ariel whistled. "The thing that you can do is to invite her here. She'll make *giur*, and you'll marry her."

"It would be the best way," Moshe agreed. "But to persuade her, I have to fly to New York. It's not a telephone business. And there are two 'but'—I don't have money for a ticket, and I don't know how to explain the need to fly to New York to my parents. Very ticklish situation, isn't it?"

"From every situation, there must be at least two exits," Ariel smiled. "Do you remember what we taught in the Army?" He fell into deep thought, and then said, "It seems to me, I've found one of them. In a month, my second cousin in America is going to be married. She invited me, but frankly I had no intention of going. I haven't yet given her the answer. We'll fly to the US together, and it would be a plausible reason for your parents."

Moshe embraced his friend. "Arik, what would I do without you?"

CHAPTER 45

▼

The El Al plane landed exactly on time. Moshe called Peggy in advance, and she met him and Ariel in the airport. Her round belly was already very visible when she came to them. Her face was pale, and today he wouldn't call it a beautiful face—without make-up, she looked like a typical British girl—fresh but colorless.

He kissed her on the cheek. "Remember my friend, Ariel?" He asked.

"I remember. Hi, Ariel." She gave Ariel a soft smile. "You can stay in my apartment, too," she offered.

"That's very nice of you, Peggy," Ariel said, "but I have to go to my relatives' house. They're waiting for me, so I'll see you later." Turning to Moshe, he added, "We'll be in touch."

"Definitely," Moshe said, and Ariel went to the line of people waiting for a taxi.

"Where are we going?" Moshe asked Peggy at a loss.

"To my place. I left the car on the parking lot." Peggy moved forward. Moshe picked up his bag and followed her.

She found her Toyota among the other cars, and he climbed in. Silently, she started up the engine and drove away. There was no traffic until they reached Manhattan. It was Moshe's first visit to New York. He looked out of the window at skyscrapers, myriads of cars, colorful crowds on the streets, policemen on horses. After his calm Israeli life, everything around him looked like shots for a futuristic movie.

They kept silent. Moshe did not know what to say, but felt silence was getting uncomfortable. Peggy's face was motionless, pale.

"I'm glad to see you, Peggy. Your pregnancy makes you even more beautiful," Moshe said, a little awkwardly.

"Do you think so? But when I look at the mirror, I see an ugly face." Peggy breathed with relief.

They reached a high-rise building where Peggy had rented a small apartment. She managed to park the car not too far from the building. After them going inside and taking the elevator, she opened her purse, took out a bunch of keys, and let Moshe in.

"It's a cozy place," he said, looking around and seeking a spot to put his traveling bag.

"Make yourself comfortable. The bathroom is over there." She pointed to the door near the entrance. Then she smiled. "When the front door is open, you can't see it. Here, in Manhattan, everything is tiny. If you want space, you have to pay a huge amount of money."

Moshe took a hot shower, and then opened the cold-water faucet. The cold water refreshed him and he put back in. When he came out, Peggy embraced him. "Do you still love me, Moshe?"

"More than you can imagine, Peggy," he said and kissed her. Her lips were dry. "Does he really love this woman or does he try to persuade himself of it? She's carrying my baby," he thought. "Of course, I love her."

"I don't have anything special in the fridge. I'm not much of a cook." She pointed to the corner of the room where a stove was. "I've never used it."

Then Peggy prepared two sandwiches, with mayonnaise and ham. But he refused softly, "Sorry Peggy, but I don't eat pork. It doesn't mean I eat only kosher, but I never eat pork."

She cried.

"That's okay," he said. "I'll make toast."

They ate without appetite. Moshe asked Peggy about the university, her friends, and about her plans for the future. But he carefully avoided the main item. It was already late when he said, "We have to be married, honey." Moshe declared encouragingly.

"Yes, we have to get married," she repeated silently, as an echo, but with satisfaction.

"I think we should fly back to Israel, and I'll introduce you to my parents. I am more than assured that they will be happy for us. You'll make *giur*, and we'll marry."

"What is *giur*?" she asked sourly.

Moshe smiled. "Not everybody is perfect; you have to become Jewish."

"I cannot, Moshe." She cried again and slumped in a chair. Her head jerked up. She cast a desperate pair of eyes on him.

"Why?" His tone was cold. "Don't you love me?"

"I do love you, sweetheart, but I cannot do it. My parents would curse me." Her voice sounded awash with desperation.

"Why? Who are they? What are they? You never told me about your parents." A great time to ask, he thought as his words came out.

"They're rich," Peggy said evasively.

Moshe grinned. "I'm not asking you about their bank account. What do they do?"

Peggy sighed heavily. "My father is the co-chairman of the Christian Coalition of the USA," she said very softy. "His name is John Witherspoon IV. You have to understand what it means. My mother, Carol, is a socialite. She collects donations for the Republican Party, and dreams of one day being appointed as the US Ambassador to France, like Pamela Harrison was."

"If your father is Witherspoon IV, he considers himself royalty?" Moshe asked caustically.

Peggy missed the sarcasm of his remark. "His predecessors were among the people who came here on the board of 'Mayflower,'" she explained matter-of-factly.

Moshe ran his hand through his hair and kept gloomy silence. At last he said pensively, "Tomorrow we'll go to the City Hall to fill out the marriage application. Our marriage will only be a civil ceremony, nothing more. And now, let's go to bed. I'm tired." Then, with sudden relief, he pushed his chair back and stood up.

He had never had sex with pregnant women. It turned out not to be as difficult as he had imagined. Tired but satisfied, Moshe reclined on the pillow and thought that his future didn't seem too bright. Is everything forecast from Above? He pondered the thought, falling asleep.

CHAPTER 46

▼

The day to fly back to Israel was approaching, and Moshe called Ariel. "Arik, I have to cancel my flight."

"Postpone?" Ariel did not understand.

"No, cancel," Moshe repeated. "Let's meet tomorrow at eleven o'clock, at Central Park."

The next day, Moshe sat on a bench, deep in thought. Was Peggy the woman who had been insinuated into his heart or was it just a phantom, someone unreal, except in his own imagination?

Seeing Ariel, Moshe waved at him and rose from his bench. They embraced, and then they silently started walking along the alley. At last Moshe said thoughtfully, "I have to stay here, Arik." He sounded somewhat mollified.

"Didn't you offer her to fly with you to Israel?" Ariel's brows drew together.

"I did." Moshe sighed miserably, his voice crooning.

"Is she silly or stubborn?" Ariel bristled at Moshe's tone, and then seemed to realize the direction of his thoughts.

"Neither. Her father is the chairman of the Christian Coalition, and she's afraid of being cursed." Moshe smiled weakly. "Sometimes things are really quite ridiculous, Arik."

Ariel whistled. "Jewish happiness," he said. "Couldn't you find another *shiksa,* with ordinary parents?" Then he became serious. "Are you going to marry her without your parents' blessing? You have to call them and explain the situation."

"It's too late, Arik. When you return home, go to my parents and tell them I love them. Ask them to forgive me. I think one day I'll say it myself. But now I cannot," he said in a very quiet voice.

"What are you going to do here?"

"I'll find a job." Moshe tried to sound serene.

"A job? What about studying?"

"Another day another nickel," Moshe smiled weakly.

Ariel stopped walking. They sat on the bench and smoked. Moshe inhaled deeply. "I cannot fly home, Arik," he said nervously. "Peggy's going to give birth to my baby. If I run away, my father will be the first who stops respecting me. There is nothing to be done, it's my destiny."

"It's your destiny," Ariel agreed.

He stood up. They embraced, and Moshe quickly went to the exit. In the end of the alley, he stopped and turned back; Ariel was looking at his back, waving. Moshe quickly turned around the corner; his eyes were wet.

Several days later, at breakfast, Peggy told Moshe, "My parents have invited us for dinner next Sunday."

"We cannot avoid it." Moshe sighed. "Where do they live?"

"In Pennsylvania. It'll take us about four hours to reach their place."

"It's rather far, but you are a good driver," Moshe said encouragingly.

On Sunday, after a rather long trip that took them not four but more than five hours, Peggy stopped the car near a massive brick colonial house surrounded by several acres of meticulously landscaped land. The front door was open, and they went into the hall.

"Good day, Ms. Peggy." The black maid, with a snow-white apron, greeted her. She looked with curiosity at Moshe. "I'll let Mr. Witherspoon know that you have arrived. Come in, please."

Peggy's parents were sitting on the sofa. Her father, a man about sixty, with a bourbon complexion, did not stand up, and Peggy went to kiss him on the cheek. Then she embraced her mother, a slender lady with a wrinkled face. From a distance, she looked younger.

"This is my husband, Moshe," Peggy said. It was visible that she was nervous. Her mother felt it and invited Peggy to help her in the kitchen. Both left and the men remained alone. Moshe sat in an armchair. He felt uncomfortable in this rich home.

"At last I see my daughter's choice," John Witherspoon said, with a shade of bitterness in his voice. "I'll call you Michael, okay? Living in Rome, do as the Romans do, remember? Moshe is a name for a narrow circle of people," he added. He did not say Jewish people, but Moshe understood him quite clearly. "What are you, Michael? Tell me about yourself."

Moshe sighed. "Not too much to be told, sir," he said. "Before I married Peggy, I'd just entered Tel Aviv University Law School. Before that, I had served in the Army for three years. Before that? I was still a child," he smiled. "Not too impressive a biography for an interview."

"Did you take part in the Six Days war? It was a very impressive victory."

"Yes, sir, I did. On the Egyptian front."

"And what did you do as a soldier, Michael?"

"I drove an M-60."

"Now you are in the US. What can you do here?"

Moshe sighed again. "I can be a truck driver, sir. They say drivers earn good money. I have to pay for Peggy's medical school. Then I would think about my law school."

John Witherspoon laughed. "It's not a bad idea, if your wife, Michael, wasn't Peggy Witherspoon." He looked at Moshe carefully. "We belong to a society where all would laugh at me if my daughter married a truck driver. Do you understand me?" Sneer sparkled in corners of his eyes.

"What can I say, sir? I cannot jump over my head. I don't see another way for me here. I only began my life, but I want to begin it properly."

"From the height of my age, I see another way for you, Michael. Why not take out a loan?"

"A loan?" Moshe repeated. "No one will give me a loan; I even don't have a green card yet."

John Witherspoon laughed, beginning to like this man. "I'll give you a loan, Michael."

"Sorry, sir, I cannot take your money. I still want to my self-respect. Sorry," Moshe said firmly.

"I'm not talking about giving you money, Michael. I am talking about a loan you need for a decent life in America until you find your place in the American society. I am talking about a loan, with 10% interest. What can I lose?"

Peggy's mother called them to the dinner table. There the conversation focused mainly on the latest Hollywood rumors, and Moshe took little part in it. He hadn't the slightest idea about the people of which they spoke. He tried to think over his father-in-law's offer. Could he accept the offer or would it make him too dependent on the man? But how could he reject it? Without money, he wouldn't be able to take care of his family that in a few weeks would consist of three people.

In Israel, he had the solid support of his own family behind him; here he was a foreigner in a foreign land. He had to survive.

Although Peggy's father did not seem as dry and rational as she had described him, Moshe had not felt a wave of warmth between them, even after her father had made his kind offer.

At last the dinner was over. Moshe thanked his parents-in-law for hospitality, and they left.

Closing the door behind them, John Witherspoon turned to his wife. "That man is reliable. But you both must convert him, Carol. My daughter's husband cannot be a Jew—it'll jeopardize my position as a chairman of the Christian Coalition."

The next day John Witherspoon put $100,000 in Peggy and Moshe's joint bank account.

CHAPTER 47

▼

Returning home, Ariel could not pluck the courage to call Moshe's parents for several days. At last he did.

"Dr. Ginsberg, this is Ariel, Moshe's friend," he said in a sort of neutral way.

"Hi, Ariel. Isn't Moshe with you?" Henry was worried and felt his throat grow dry. "Where is he? What happened?" He could hardly talk.

"Don't worry, sir. He's in good health, and everything's all right with him. But he remained in New York," Ariel said, his voice slow.

"Why did he do that?" Henry did not understand. "Weren't you together at your cousin's wedding?"

Ariel held the receiver silently for a few more heartbeats. Then he said, "Moshe is married, sir."

"Who married?"

"Moshe, sir."

"Listen, Ariel, can you come to our place and tell us what's happened? Please," Henry added. "Otherwise I won't understand anything. But is he really okay?"

"Yes, sir, he is fine." Ariel sighed as he realized that he wouldn't be able to avoid a frank talk with Moshe's parents. "I'll come to your place in two hours."

Two hours later, he arrived at the Ginsbergs home where Rachel and Henry were anxiously waiting for him. Ariel saw that Moshe's parents were very nervous and concerned.

"Tell us the truth, Ariel. Is he healthy?" It was the first question Rachel asked, and she was sweating harder than seemed necessary.

Ariel assured them that Moshe was in good health, and nothing had happened to him except he had married an American girl and stayed with her in the United States. Then Ariel told them all the details of Moshe's situation, but he saw a spark of distrust showing in Rachel's eyes as she stared at him. She was dry-eyed, but on the edge of nervous explosion.

"Moshe asked me to tell you the truth. He is very upset that he didn't ask your blessing," Ariel said. "He loves you very much." After a pause he said again, "He loves you very much."

Only then did Rachel realize what had happened. She sobbed.

"I am sorry," Ariel said silently. "I need to go, but I'll be in touch with you." He left, carefully closing the door behind him. Only then he took a handkerchief and wiped his forehead.

Rachel's sobbing became so loud that her whole body shuddered convulsively. Henry embraced Rachel, trying to calm her. "Why did he do it to us? Why did he spit on us, Henry?" She had an odd look on her face.

"He couldn't avoid marrying that girl, Rachel. She is pregnant." Henry sighed.

Rachel looked at Henry attentively. "Don't try to defend him. If he loved us, he would come home and confessed to everything. Who is closer in our world than parents? We know it better than anybody else." Rachel's sobbing developed into a silent cry. She croaked as though she were losing her voice.

What could Henry object to? He was shocked at Moshe's decision. For all his life, he tried to be his son's best friend. He was even more frank with Moshe talking about life than most fathers were with their children. He had no secrets from Moshe, and expected the same attitude from his son. Moshe had betrayed their friendship.

"You have to go to bed, honey." Henry breathed. "Lie down and take some aspirin or, even better, sleeping pills. There is nothing to be done; children become adults." He helped Rachel go upstairs, put her to bed, and covered her with a blanket.

"I will never forgive him, Henry," Rachel whispered.

Henry nodded with a shrug, aware that it was useless to argue with Rachel now. Henry brought her the pills and a glass of water. "Take them, darling." He sat on her bed and pressed her hair softly. "Don't try to formulate a judgment now. Let your mind settle on the situation." Then he kissed Rachel and headed for the door. On the threshold, Henry turned back. "We'll forgive him, honey, as soon as he returns. He is our son." Henry paused, his eyes narrowing pensively. Then he silently closed the door behind him.

CHAPTER 48

▼

Esther walked along the university hall, thinking over the theme of her diploma '*King David—a Poet*'. It would be a pleasure to work on it. She had already begun reading the *Teghilim,* the book of psalms written by King David; each psalm was a perfect poem. Had anyone analyzed its poetical perfection before? She wondered. Full of thoughts, she crashed into a man carrying a big brown portfolio.

"I am sorry!" Esther said and peered at the man.

He didn't look like a student, more like a young professor, and she was confused. They squatted, gathering the dropped books. Their palms touched. "I'm sorry, professor," she repeated, managing a half-smile.

"Don't mention it, miss." He smiled in answer.

Like his callused palm, his strength, his nearly gold eyes, and his voice were unusual. Combined with his thick, sleek pelt of black hair and the mustache that contrasted with the curve of his occasional smile, he was a definite change from the usual white-haired university professors. They gathered their books and stood up.

"What's your name, miss?" he asked good-naturally. His eyes narrowed, and he fixed them on her.

"Esther Ginsberg."

"What are you studying?"

"English Literature."

"Have a nice day, Ms. Ginsberg." The man smiled again and left.

Mark Levine was not a university professor. He was a Mossad operative who came to the university to visit his former curator, Abe Barenboim, who really was a professor of English Literature. Abe Barenboim worked for the Mossad, and was a talent spotter who would recommend selects students for future work with his organization.

Esther Ginsberg's green eyes did not make Mark Levine indifferent. He wasn't the usual type of slim-hipped, vaguely male women's curators. He was a serious man, with a serious job; moreover, he had a wife and two children. But for days after that accidental meeting, Mark could not forget Esther's face. He tried to dismiss thoughts of her, but failed. Tired of struggling with himself, he went again to Professor Barenboim.

"Abe," he said as much professionally as he could, "the Agency has eyes on one of your students. What can you tell me about Esther Ginsberg?"

A tiny smile curved Abe Barenboim's lips. "I thought I was the first who saw the makings of a perfect field officer in this charming girl—she has beauty, intelligence, leadership, charisma, attitude and the ability to speak several languages." His voice was definitive and positive.

"Thank you, Abe. You read my thoughts." Mark Levine shook his hand and left.

After the second "accidental" encounter on the street, their meetings became frequent. Esther liked the fact that Mark was older than she was. He was a handsome man, and she caught the envious glances of other girls when she was with him. But despite Mark being more than ten years older, when he was with Esther, he behaved like a youngster. For almost six months, he couldn't decide on a desperate course of action such as a kiss.

Such status might have lasted forever if Esther had not taken the initiative in her hands. One day she invited Mark to her room where Mark quickly lost his head and could no longer control himself. His control had always been his greatest vulnerability, but the sight of her small breasts did nothing to help. Esther did not play games. With a broken sigh, she turned toward him. Suddenly fire burst within him spreading up from their embraced bodies.

Mark hesitated before uttering his next words. Finally he whispered, "I love you, Esther."

Esther smiled. "I know." She looked at him for a long minute.

Then Esther extinguished candles and made love to him drawing his body into her long arms and legs.

"Oh, Lord," Mark groaned. "You're a virgin!"

"I was." Esther said it quietly, with a brave nod although she was quite nervous. Her mouth curled into a slight smile. She opened her mouth to speak, but no sound came out.

But Mark Levine did not wake Esther's sexuality. She loved him, his touches, his kisses, but she remained almost indifferent to the sexual act itself.

When Esther learned that Mark was a Mossad operative, it increased her respect for him, but she firmly rejected his offer to join that staff.

"My way goes in the other direction." She smiled. "I'm not Mata-Hari."

"You would be better," Mark returned the smile, but did not insist. He decided that time would work for him.

Their secret relationship lasted for almost a year, until Professor Barenboim told her that Mark had perished in the line of duty. He had gone to meet in Syria with an Arab who was a Mossad agent. But the Arab was exposed and killed; then Mark Levine was ambushed and captured.

"But he managed to avoid tortures," Professor Barenboim said, looking strictly in Esther's eyes. "He hung himself in the cell."

Esther fell into depression after Mark's death. She felt alone ever more than before, and when the Mossad came for her the second time, she didn't turn them down. Six months before, Mark had introduced her to his boss, the Mossad Deputy Director of Operations, and now Esther told him 'okay.' There was another reason for her decision; she didn't want to ask her father to help her get a position after graduation. She wanted to reach her achievements by herself. From whom did she inherit her genes for independence?

After Esther graduated, she was sent to the Mossad training facility. There she learned how to recruit and run agents. She learned the art of clandestine communication. She learned martial arts and defensive driving.

After a year of training, she was supplied with a cover identity and a Mossad pseudonym. She joined the group that had a simple assignment—to find and deliver Dr. Fritz Bekkenbauer, the former Chief Medical Officer of Maidanek to Israel. He had worked at a concentration camp, and was blamed for the inhuman experiments on thousands of Jews.

The Israelis decided to bring him to justice, even after Adolph Eichman was sentenced to death and hanged. It would be a symbolic act—to show the world that many Nazi doctors and scientists managed to avoid justice for their crimes.

They would prefer to bring in Dr. Joseph Mengele, the Chief Medical Officer of Oswiecien concentration camp. He had been found to be a Nazi criminal at the Nuremberg Trials but managed to avoid justice by escaping to South America. Before the Mossad found his tracks in Brasilia, he allegedly had drowned on one of the Brazilian beaches.

In reality, Dr. Mengele and Dr. Bekkenbauer were only executors of tasks given them by their superiors at Max-Plunck-Gesellschaft. One of their scientific gurus was Dr. Adolph Butenandt, a Nobel Prize Winner for his research on sex cells and hormones. During WW II he actively cooperated with Luftwaffe, creating *demopitin*—a drug compound that could improve the ability of pilot's blood to survive in cold water or in severe climate. He also researched the influence of mold on liver cells. Dr. Butenandt knew perfectly well that Dr. Mengele and Dr. Bekkenbauer provided him with liver cells, cells cut without anesthesia from Jewish children; but it didn't bother him at all.

Another of Dr. Bekkenbauer's gurus was Dr. Ottmar von Wershhauer, a world authority on the study of twins. Out of nine hundred twins in Oswiecien, less than fifty survived, but he believed that they died happily helping the progress of science.

None of these doctors were punished after the war. Adolph Butenandt kept, as before, his position of president of Max-

Plunck-Gesselschaft; Ottmar von Werschhauer became the chairman of the German Anthropological Society. Colleagues pretended they did not know about their criminal Nazi pasts; both even consulted for *The New York Times,* and published their articles on its pages.

Why they remained without punishment?

The Mossad made a final decision to bring Dr. Fritz Bekkenbauer to justice. Taking into account that he, like most of Nazi criminals, was hiding in Latin America, and Esther was fluent in Spanish, she was given one of the leading roles in the upcoming game.

CHAPTER 49

▼

A plain building on the King Saul Boulevard in Tel Aviv does not attract tourists' attention. The building is like many others in the vicinity. And the name of the office inside sounds inoffensive *The Institute of Intelligence and Special Tasks* or *Mossad Le-Tafki Me Unadim.*

Strictly speaking, the Mossad is only one of five Israeli intelligence services. But it became the symbol of the secret war of the time. In comparison to its two big brothers, the CIA and the KGB, the Mossad is a small organization; its total staff doesn't exceed 1500 employees, among them there were no more than fifty to one hundred special agents.

One of them became Esther. Today she took part in a meeting conducted by Bernard Lau, the Deputy Director of Operations.

"Except for Dr. Mengele and Dr. Bekkenbauer, we think that Dr. Otto Dornberger also should be brought to justice. But he was killed at the end of the war. So we concentrated our attention on Dr. Bekkenbauer. We did not know much about him until the autumn of 1957 when Gessen County of the German Republic Attorney General, Mr. France Bower, provided us with the information that he lived in Paraguay under the name Alfred Fruchtman. First of all, we have to be certain in that it's him. So we shall assign two people that main task. Then, after their report, we'll discuss the operation in details."

These two people were Esther and Aaron Shalom, a recent graduate from Barcelona. Like Esther, he was fluent in Spanish—his parents had immigrated to Israel from Macao.

They succeeded in identification of Dr. Arnold Bekkenbauer. He was successfully captured and brought to the Israeli court where he tried to persuade the judges that he only fulfilled the orders of his superiors. But he was found guilty and hanged in the Ramle jail.

During the trial, Dr. Bekkenbauer strictly pointed to his superiors from Max-Plunck-Gesselschaft, the Nobel Prize Winner Dr. Adolph Butenandt and his colleague Dr. Ottmar von Wershauen. But they've never been indicted in Germany.

Still during the Paraguay operation, Esther felt she was not indifferent to Aaron. After they returned home, they met often. Aaron turned out to be a soft, intelligent and devoted friend. And a handsome man. His eyes were green, flecked with yellow, like wild summer grass. He had a long, straight nose, and several times she had to restrain herself from reaching out and touching his perfect lips. Was she falling in love or had her time to be married come?

One day Aaron invited her to go sailing with him on a small boat. It was a sweltering day in late July, with very little wind. As the boat drifted over the still water, Esther and Aaron lay in the shade of the limp sails, drinking icy beer and talking about nothing. Suddenly Aaron stopped speaking and looked at her eyes. "Will you marry me, Esther?" he asked her seriously.

His voice faded into the slap of the water below them and the steady rush of the breeze. Watching her face, he saw a glint in the corner of Esther's eyes; welling tears that she blinked away quickly. Then she closed her eyes.

"I will," she said silently, and felt the taste of his hot lips on hers.

CHAPTER 50

▼

Seventeen weeks later, Peggy gave birth to twin girls. She insisted on calling them Barbara and Christina, and they were baptized at the Church of St. Luke. Moshe did not attend the ceremony, and it caused their first big fight.

"Can't you understand, Peggy, I am a Jew? I cannot attend a Christian ceremony." Moshe's reply was sincere.

"So what? They are your children. Why do you always emphasize your religion? Judaism was the base of Christianity. The difference is not big enough to spoil our life. We trust in the same God." Peggy said coldly.

"In general," he agreed.

'If you weren't so stubborn, everything would be much easier. My dad said that Senator Stromhold promised to take you on his staff. You would receive a unique opportunity, don't you understand?" Peggy's voice was full of irritation.

"Why didn't he do it, if he promised?" Moshe asked mockingly.

"Don't be stupid. He can't have Jews in his staff," Peggy said as if this was a commonly accepted fact.

"I haven't the slightest wish to join the anti-Semitic staff." Ice could have formed on Moshe's words.

"He is not an anti-Semite, but he is a righteous Christian. He has to go by the rules of the Christian Coalition."

"Let's change the topic, Peggy," Moshe was so tired. "This conversation will only lead us to the dead end."

Peggy cried. "You are an egoist, Moshe. You don't consider your family, you don't think about your daughters' future. You think about nothing."

Moshe tried to calm her down, but Peggy slammed the door behind her as she ran to her room.

On the pretext of Peggy needing to complete her medical training, the children were moved to her parents' house. How could he object? As soon as he took John Witherspoon's money, he had no right of speech or opinion. The only way for him to become independent was to finish law school as soon as possible. He had to concentrate on his studies, Moshe decided with a deep breath.

But Peggy did not stop her attempts to influence Moshe to change his position about conversion. More and more his family life turned into punishment. He understood that she was under a strong influence from her parents, but what could he do? He loved Peggy, but was it enough for their family happiness?

One evening she told him, "Dad called. My cousin Willy has won the gubernatorial race in Pennsylvania, and they want us also to join the inaugural party."

`"Frankly, I'd be there like 'a white crow.' But if you want, we'll drive over."

"We have to attend the party," she said in irritation. "You will always be 'a white crow' until you become man enough to pluck up the courage to discard your Judaism. It makes you weak and inferior. If I had known how weak you are, I would never have married you."

Moshe did not want to wait until Peggy became hysterical. He left the room. His mood plummeted.

On the way to Pennsylvania, the next day, he was driving his new Lincoln Mark VII. He liked the car, its powerful engine, its unique body, and its leather interior. The car gave him the feeling of freedom that he didn't have in everyday life. The road was deserted. Tall trees on either side twisted in the gusty wind, and a bright sun shone through broken clouds. He pressed the accelerator and the speedometer showed seventy-five. The Lincoln rose and fell over the gentle landscape.

Peggy, in big sunglasses, sat in the passenger's seat silently. They still hadn't spoken since the big fight the previous day. Moshe also silently looked at the road.

"Maybe you'll talk to me now?" Peggy turned her face to him.

Her question remained without an answer.

"Shit!" Peggy suddenly cried hysterically. "You are shit, and always will be a shit."

The twitching muscles on Moshe's cheeks, dancing a hectic dance, suddenly stopped. He sharply pressed the brakes, and the car jerked to a stop. Moshe slowly turned his pale face to Peggy and awkwardly slapped her cheek.

"Bitch!" he said through clenched teeth and opened the passenger's door. "Get out of here!"

Peggy jumped out to the road, the door slammed shut, and the car turned the corner. She stood there for some time at a loss, then closed her eyes and sat on the edge of the road. Inside, she felt nothing but self-pity. This feeling has spread through her body wrapping her inch by inch.

"Hi, beauty!" someone called from a car, but she did not move.

The car drove away, and Peggy again submerged in the abyss of herself. The tired sun hid behind clouds, and she felt a chill. She stood up and walked slowly along the road. The left shoe pinches, she thought automatically. Another car stopped.

"Can I give you a lift, miss?" An open door invited her in. Peggy sat, not looking at the driver.

"It's muggy today," the driver tried to maintain a conversation. "I see you aren't a local woman."

"No."

"My name is Jeff Brown." The man introduced himself. "I was born here. A shitty town."

Peggy lowered her window. The flow of fresh air stroked her face, and she remembered Moshe's slap.

"Where do you want me to drop you off?"

"Just anywhere, "Peggy said indifferently.

Jeff Brown looked at her attentively and turned to the right. "This is the only decent hotel in this town," he said. He stopped the car in front of a dirty-gray building. "What about a drink?" His glance was long and questioning.

Peggy shrugged indifferently, and he accepted her gesture as consent. Brown got out the car hurriedly, offering Peggy his hand.

The hotel was old-fashioned and gloomy, like an out-of-fashioned suit made of expensive fabric. They went to the bar on the ground floor and sat at a table. Several customers looked at them indifferently. One of the girls in the bar nodded at Brown.

"What will you drink?" Brown waved to a waitress. His bold head shined in the lamplight.

Peggy drank one drink after another. She didn't listen to Brown's chatter and his old, trite jokes. A wave of self-pity covered her and it grew bigger and bigger with every gulp.

...Peggy recovered consciousness only when she felt Brown's thankful kisses on her body. He dressed hurriedly, took out his wallet and put $50 on the bedside table. Then he thought a little, and added $20 more.

Peggy looked at the money in terror. Her teeth trembled so loudly that she did not hear the sound of the door closing behind the man. She lay in the bed motionless for almost half an hour. Then she ran a shower and stood under the hot water for a long time. Putting her clothes on, she slowly like a somnambulist, headed for the door.

In front of the hotel door, she saw Moshe's Lincoln.

"Good Lord!" he sighed nervously. "I've been looking for you all over the city." He helped Peggy into the car.

The lump standing in Peggy's throat suddenly melted. She sighed convulsively, and then, became engrossed in the car's dash, crying silently heavy, bitter tears.

"That's all right, honey, that's all right." Moshe patted her head tenderly and switched the engine on. "It's a long way ahead."

"Ma'am!" Peggy suddenly heard. "Ma'am!" Peggy saw a bellboy running to the car. "Sorry, Ma'am," he said, "You forgot the money."

"Drive, Moshe," she whispered. "For the God's sake, drive." Then she added, "Drive me home, please."

"What about your cousin's inauguration?"

Peggy didn't answer. She had always tried to never let her emotions get the better of her. But now, sitting in the car, her hair plastered to the side of her face, composure deserted her. She slowly fell forward until her head rested on the dashboard. Then the tears came and she wept.

"Please, drive me home," she repeated in a weak voice.

Silently, Moshe turned the car in the opposite direction.

PART V

▼

TO FIND YOURSELF

"Let people know that they are only people, forever!"

—Teghilim 15, 11.

CHAPTER 51

▼

Henry was sitting at the desk in his lab, writing an article summarizing the results of his latest research. When he cut his glance off the paper, it stopped on a calendar page. It's already June, he thought absently, and suddenly realized that in two months it would be his silver wedding anniversary. Twenty-five years have passed like a second, he thought.

It seemed to him that it was only yesterday that Rabbi Boxter had performed their wedding ceremony, and he was afraid that no one would attend it because he and Rachel had neither friends nor relatives. Twenty-five years! Now he was not afraid anybody would attend his anniversary. Then Henry thought it wouldn't be quite a happy day for Rachel if she doesn't see their children at the table. But Esther, with her husband Aaron, was somewhere abroad. He remembered that Rachel was so happy when Esther brought the news she was going to marry. But their work required frequent business trips; there was nothing to be done. Moshe…the fact that his son had cut off connections with the family was a painful, open wound for Rachel and for him. Finally Henry decided to spend the evening only with Rachel.

What could he give Rachel for an anniversary gift? For twenty-five years, he had not bought her jewelry. He knew she was indifferent to decorations. Her lovely pianist fingers were beautiful without any decorations. But today, Henry decided to buy her a diamond ring.

He couldn't concentrate on the article any more. Closing the office, he went out to the street. He intended to hire a taxi but then changed his mind and sauntered along the street. Henry rarely walked, and now looked at the buildings and shops with a curiosity as if he was seeing them for the first time.

Among the others, Henry saw a jewelry shop. The counters were full of sparkling rings, pendants, colliers and watches.

The salesman at the counter looked at Henry professionally and asked politely, "Can I be of any service to you, sir?" His Ivrit language was too perfect and told the customer he wasn't born there; he only did his business here.

"DuBaeur has served you for 150 years." Henry read the big sign above the counter, and guessed that the shop belonged to the famous South African company.

"What would you buy for a silver wedding anniversary?" Henry asked the salesman.

The salesman smiled. "I've just recently celebrated forty-five years, sir. But if I were as young man as you are…" He paused, and then went to the safe. He removed a little box and put it on the counter in front of Henry. "'VS1' clarity, 'A' color, 2.3 carats," he explained professionally. "What size does your wife wear?"

"I suppose her size is 6," Henry said hesitantly. He hadn't the slightest idea what 'VS1' clarity or 'A' color meant.

"That's the exact size of this ring, sir," the salesman said, measuring the ring.

Henry took the ring in hands and felt it generated mysterious warmth. "I'll take it," he said without hesitation.

The salesman looked at him with surprise because he hadn't yet named the price. When he did, he expected the customer to ask for a discount; he was ready to give a 20% discount. But Henry didn't ask for one. "I'll take it," he repeated.

He gave the happy salesman a deposit and said he would pick the ring up in a day, as he needed to withdraw the rest of money from his bank account.

On their anniversary evening, Henry brought Rachel a twenty-five rose bouquet. "My congratulations, honey," he said when she opened the door.

She embraced him and whispered happily, "I thought you forgot, Henry."

Henry kissed her and went to the hall. "Don't you object if we spend the evening at home?"

"It would be wonderful, dear." Rachel went to the kitchen and soon set the table. They sat and Henry poured champagne in two glasses. "Before I propose a toast, honey, I have a gift for you." He took a small box from his pocket and put it on the table.

Rachel opened it and, impressed by the clarity of the stone, was speechless for a moment. Then she said, "Only God knows how happy I am, Henry!" Then she added softly, "Because you are God's gift for me." Tears of happiness sparkled in her eyes. Rachel stood up, came to Henry and took his head in her hands.

"Thank you, darling," she said.

Henry was about to lift his glass of champagne when they heard the bell ring.

"Who is it?" Henry asked with surprise.

"No idea," she said and went to the door.

When she opened it, she saw the smiling faces of Emile Feingold and his sister Miriam.

"Although nobody invited us, we decided to come and congratulate you." Emile handed Rachel a bouquet of flowers; Miriam kissed her.

"They say an uninvited guest is worse than an Arab," Emile said entering the room. "But we are Jews, aren't we?" Emile handed Henry a book. "Here is my present for you and Rachel."

Rachel read the title *My Life In Another World*. "Did you sign it, Emile?" she asked.

"Sure."

"Guys, it's a real present for us that you've come," Henry said with an amiable smile while Rachel put two more plates on the table. When they sat, Henry said, "Let me propose a toast."

But at that moment they heard another doorbell.

"This is getting annoying." Henry smiled and went to the door.

As Henry opened the door, he saw Rabbi Boxter standing on the threshold.

"Can I come in? I think if I had performed your wedding ceremony twenty-five years ago, I can perform a silver anniversary too."

At age eighty-five, Rabbi Boxter was still straight and lean. He walked without a stick, and only his gray beard spoke to the fact that he was over seventy. How far over, you could only guess.

Rabbi kissed Rachel, and Henry introduced him to his friends.

"I know you, Rabbi, quite well," Emile Feingold said.

Rabbi peered at him. "Have we met before? Are you a member of my congregation?"

Emile Feingold smiled. "No. But Henry often told me about you; so I am happy to see you."

At last all sat at the table. "I do hope there won't be any more unexpected visitors whom I love." Henry smiled. "Let me propose a toast."

"Let's start with a prayer." Rabbi Boxter interrupted him, with a light smile. "Proper praying is like a man who wanders through a field, gathering flowers one by one, until they make a beautiful bouquet." Then he became serious.

"Our God and God of our ancestors! Let your presence be manifest to us in all Your works, so that reverence to You fills the hearts of all your creatures. May we bow before You in humility and unite to do Your will with one heart, that all may acknowledge that Yours are power, dominion and majesty and that Your name is exalted above all. Amen."

Finished the pray, he added with a smile, "Now it's your turn, Henry."

"What can I say? I am a happy man. God gave me my wife, and she brightened the world. Before I met Rachel, the world was colored only in two paints—black and white. For the last twenty-five yours, I see a many-colored world. I love you, Rachel and, with God's help, I'd like to live with you another twenty-five years." He drank his glass of champagne, and everybody followed his example.

Rabbi Boxter paid attention to the book Emile presented to Henry.

"It's an intriguing title," he remarked. "What's the book about?"

"It's a memoir. Remembrances about my meetings with the pacifist Niels Bohr, the communist Enrice Fermi, the fascist Werner von Braun...I am trying to understand why all of us, scientists, serve the system but not pure science."

"Was there such an individual in the whole history of science?" Rabbi Boxter asked.

"Maybe one—Lord Cavendish," Emile answered thoughtfully.

"I heard the name somewhere," Rabbi said.

"Ernst Rutherford named his research laboratory after him—now it's the Cavendish Lab," Emile explained.

Henry looked at his friend. Since Dr. Feingold had joined the team of scientists working on the Israeli atomic project, their meetings had become rare—he worked in the Dimona Center. Henry never asked his friend about his work, although he guessed of course, in which research Emile was involved in Dimona—an isolated site in the Negev Desert.

Now Emile had a short vacation; to be exact, he took several days off to come and congratulate Esther and Henry on their wedding anniversary. To see Henry meant to exchange opinions with him. Their conversations could be specific, could be general. They could discuss the latest art exhibition of Marc Chagall or the problems of the First Allyah—the first wave of Zionist immigration since 1882 to 1904; they could discuss militant ideological commitments of kibutznicks or rumors about the coming resignation of Ben-Gurion who was already getting old.

Today they didn't talk too much; they mostly enjoyed silence, because silence between friends is the highest level of spiritual understanding. Today Rabbi Boxter also shared that understanding.

Henry poured champagne in their glasses. "I've missed you, Emile," he said. "I needed your advice, your expertise."

"My expertise in medicine?" Emile was surprised.

"I need if not your expertise, but your intuition. I've got a dilemma of two ways in my research."

"What way did you choose?"

"Because you weren't around, I've chosen the way God hinted me."

Rabbi Boxter smiled. "You've definitely chosen the best way, Henry. The Lord blesses you and keeps you. The Lord makes his face to shine upon you and be gracious to you. The Lord lifts up His countenance upon you and gives you peace."

"But in research, the best way often leads to the dead end," Henry remarked thoughtfully. "If we could forecast the future, how many mistakes we could avoid!"

"Maybe our future mistakes are only the repetition of mistakes of the past, and to avoid them we have to know the past?" Emile asked with a strange look.

"Unfortunately, Emile, nobody can know either the future or the past. In the distant past, maybe thousands of years ago, an ancient doctor had already resolved today's scientific problems, but the results of his research hadn't come to us," Henry said thoughtfully.

"One cannot understand the present unless one understands the past." Rabbi Boxter agreed with him.

Emile again looked at him strangely. Then he took a gulp of champagne from his glass and glanced at the candles on the table. Their flames had almost vanished.

"People can see the past," he said matter-of-factly, his voice unnaturally neutral. But then he clarified his words emotionally. "God has given us a chance to see the past."

Rabbi Boxter looked at him with arched brow but did not interfere with what he said.

"Sorry, Emile, I did not catch your thought," Henry said. "What did you have in mind?"

Emile sighed heavily, and then said, "I have never told you about it. Now I will." He went to the candles and extinguished the flames. Then he sunk back in the armchair. "In fantastic fiction movies, people call such appliances "time machines." From the scientific point of view, this is a chrono-vision device; people consider this device a fantasy. But in their fantasies, writers have created modern science much before its creation. For example, the underground train, robots, and so on." Emile paused and looked attentively at Henry and Rabbi Boxter. Then he continued, "Any fantasy becomes reality, sooner or later. It's only a matter of time." He paused again. "A machine of time has been created," he said firmly.

Henry and Rabbi Boxter kept silent, trying to realize the sense of Emile's words as he continued, "The inventor who created that device was a Catholic priest named Pellegrino Ernetti. But he was not only a priest. In the scientific world, he was known as a specialist in the field of quantum physics. Later on, when we became if not friends but very close acquaintances, he told me that he had brought forth the idea of the device more than forty years ago. Then he was teaching theology, and a point of his special theological interests was exorcism." Emile paused to take a gulp of champagne. It was visible he was a little nervous.

"Why do weak spirits never live in Jewish bodies?" asked Rabbi Boxter. "I have never read about such cases in our books."

"This is a good question, rabbi," Emile said without a smile. "I think it's because Judaism is the only true religion given by God. All the rest are inventions of people. Weak spirits are part of God's punishment, I suppose. But I'm not a specialist in religious questions; I am only a scientist although I know very good scientists and doctors who are rabbis, too."

"Emile, please continue your story," Rachel said. "I'm eager to know what happened with Father Ernetti's device."

"I had a common passion with Father Ernetti. It was polyphonic melodies or pre-polyphony—the ancient music written and performed since the XIV century B.C. to X century of A.C.

Ernetti was one of the best, if not the best, researchers in the world who specialized in the history of this music. He was the head of the faculty of Pre-Polyphony at Venedetto Marchello Conservatory on the island St. Giorgio.

The idea of the machine, which could penetrate through time, came to his mind as a result of his passion for ancient music. He dreamed of knowing how the ancient music instruments sounded on the performance of the opera *Thiest* by composer Kwintius Annius Kalaber. The first performance of the opera took place in 169 B.C. The opera was in great demand, but the upper class rejected it because of its revolutionary ideas.

Kwintius Annius Kalaber perished soon after the first performance; the opera was officially prohibited for performances, and its score vanished; only fragments of the opera came to our days.

But even in fragments, the opera impressed Pellegrino Ernetti. To hear the opera in the original performance, he tried to reconstruct it. But the reconstructed opera did not impress the listeners. And to listen to the original opera, Pellegrino Ernetti decided to create a machine that would help him to penetrate through time.

Pellegrino Ernetti was befriended many world-famous scientists who often visited him on the island where he lived. I also visited him several times. There were twelve of us who Pellegrino Ernetti considered his friends. Among them, there were Enrico Fermi, the creator of the first nuclear reactor and a 1938 Nobel Prize Winner, and Werner von Braun, the creator of Hitler's FAU. Frankly, I did not feel comfortable shaking his hand. But there, in Pellegrino Ernetti's house, we were not communists like Enrico Fermi, not fascists like von Braun, and not Zionists like me. We even were not Catholic, Protestant or Jewish. We were members of one *scientific architectonia*, the brotherhood of scientists. We talked about the reality of creating a time machine.

"I do not know whether the creation of such time penetration device is benevolence or damnation," Pellegrino Ernetti remarked one day.

I remember I asked him to clarify his thoughts, and he said, "The device can be used for the extraction of any information from any historical period, but it's dangerous for mankind."

"'Did you find a conception of such device?' I asked him directly.

"'The conception itself is not too complicated, Emile," he said. "It comes out from the knowledge of ancient music. Still Pythagoras, in 350 B.C., told that the sounds of music going out from musical instruments to space transfer into atom-like particles. They keep different energetic poles. Extracting those particles from space, you can extract and restore ancient music; and that means we can re-create audio-visual pictures of the past."

"Here Ernetti sharply stopped and changed the topic," Emile said. "He did not want any information about his time machine to become public, and I, frankly speaking, was very skeptical about his work."

"Emile, why do you think he succeeded?" Henry asked.

"He did. I was invited to see the testing of his device."

Deep silence came after Emile's words. Henry saw Emile's hands trembling.

Emile took a gulp of water, and then continued his story after a long pause. "Firstly, we wanted to check whether the scenes we saw were real. We began from a scene that occurred not too long ago, and there were a lot of documents that supported the reality of those events. We adjusted the device to direct it to Benito Mussolini who was giving one of his speeches. Then we went deeper into the past, much deeper, directing it at Napoleon. If I understood quite well, he spoke about the abolition of the Venetian Republic and the declaration instead the Italian Republic. Then we went to ancient Rome, and we saw a scene at the vegetable market, in Emperor Trojan's rule. It was simply magnificent." Emile made a pause and then said, "Pellegrino Ernetti's dream became true. He had listened to the antic tragedy *Thiest* by Kwintius Kalaber in its original performance."

"What did he get? Sound? Picture?" Henry asked, still being under impression of Emile's story.

"Both. Not like a movie, but like a hologram, in volume. Images weren't too big, but with movement and sound."

"Could he choose what he wanted to see, or did the device work randomly?'

"We could focus it on a definite place and time," Emile said.

"Why has no one ever heard of it?" Rabbi Boxter asked thoughtfully.

"Because everyone who saw the device in action quickly realized it would be dangerous; it would change our picture of the world. There wouldn't be any more scientific, political, or diplomatic mysteries. What was the most dangerous in that machine, it would eliminate religious mysteries. One Italian journalist, Vinchenzo Maddaloni, I remembered his name, said that he had seen, with the help of Pellegrino Ernetti's machine, the real face of Christ, and heard his sermon. The sermon was taped and shown to the Pope Pius XII, to members of the Catholic Academy and the President of the Italian Republic. And after that—a deep silence. I think the church is afraid of the truth about Christ's life, because if Christ is not God, Christianity is a type of idolatry. It could create a world tragedy because it would break the status quo of modern morality and religion. Obviously the time machine vanished in the Vatican. And soon after that, Pellegrino Ernetti also mysteriously perished. Such a sad story," Emile finished his story and made a deep breath.

"I think one day somebody would re-invent that device," Rachel said. "In our time, it's simply impossible to hide such a discovery for a long time."

"Maybe Pastor Ernetti was blessed by the creation of his device to fulfill God's mission?" Rabbi Boxter asked thoughtfully.

"What mission?" Henry asked.

"His mission was to destroy the false trust. If he could show that Christ was an ordinary man, not God's son, as Christians believe, can you imagine the consequences of such a discovery for more than a billion of His followers all over the world? Personally I am sure Ernetti realized it after he had heard Christ's sermon. But that discovery turned out to be too heavy burden for him as a human being."

"Why was a Catholic priest chosen for that mission?" Emile asked the rabbi.

"Logistically I can understand it," Rabbi Boxter said. "It had to be one of the worshipers of Christianity. It couldn't be a Jew because God gave us our religion. We never tried to revise our faith or to create false gods. It couldn't be a Muslim either. What we call the Muslim religion, it's not a religion; it is a faith. Mohammed himself did not consider himself the creator of a new religion. He created a compilation of existing monotheistic religions to be adapted to Arab conditions. And, as a matter of fact, this is the only religion of hatred, not love. If some Muslim saw, with the help of the time penetrating device, that Mohammed had been a criminal, terrorist and pedophile, would it change the Muslim attitude to Mohammed and their religion? These people still live in the seventh century. Yes, it had to be a Christian priest. And he was a genius scientist."

"You told us, Emile, that your friend vanished under strange circumstances. What does 'vanished' mean? Was he killed by Vatican agents?" Rachel asked.

Emile asked Rachel to bring him a glass of water, and emptied it in several big gulps; his lips were dry. Henry seemed Emile's story was a long awaited confession. Then Emile said in neutral voice, "No, he was burnt."

"Burnt?" All three re-asked almost simultaneously. Their eyes widened.

"Pellegrino Ernetti's carbonic cadaver was found in his office. But his clothes did not suffer; neither the furniture in the office nor the chair on which he sat."

"It's impossible," Rachel said softly. "It's mystical."

"No, honey, science today can explain this phenomenon," Henry remarked thoughtfully. "Such cases had a place in the past, as well. I read that in ancient Phives an archeologist found a papyrus describing the turning of an ancient priest into a torch going to the sky. Charles Dickens wrote a book *About a Self-Burning of a Human Body*, published in 1857 by a famous chemist von Libitch."

"Yes," Emile agreed. "Science calls it 'pyrochinez.' It explains that self-burning occurs because chemical elements of the body contacting each other or the air can generate fire creating pure phosphorus; then this phosphorus reacts with oxygen, creating an explosion." Nobody interrupted him, and Emile continued, "But…a human body is two thirds water and non-combustible material. To burn it, we have to create very specific conditions: several thousand degrees temperature and a long duration time. Even a straight lightning's strike cannot burn a human. Burning is a chemical reaction of oxidation; this reaction differs from the flame of a bonfire only by the speed of the reaction." Emile again paused as if being deeply submerged into his thoughts.

Then he gulped half a glass of water that Rachel had refilled, and continued his story.

"After Pellegrino Ernetti's death, I tried to create a physical model of the self-burning conditions. I realized that the only way was to change the temperature of real time. Fantastic? I don't think so, though I've failed. I think that in the cells of our body, some unknown energy processes go on. These processes equal in their capacity to cold thermo-nuclear reactions. I think a cell is a real nuclear reactor, and the cell's energy is created by such reactions. It means our bodies are capable of creating chemical elements that are necessary for it. What will happen in case of a malfunction? The uncontrolled nuclear reaction will have place. If it becomes a chain reaction, it will be accompanied by the huge splash of energy; and this energy can burn, turn the cells of tissue of our body into ash.

But this is only my attempt to give a scientific explanation of Pellegrino Ernetti's death. The more I study the physics of this phenomenon the more I doubt that a human can control it," Emile finished his confession with visible relief.

"Do you have in mind, Emile, that only God can control it?" Rachel asked, but Emile left her question without answer.

"Just to be is a blessing, just to live is holy," Rabbi Boxter remarked thoughtfully.

Henry took another bottle of champagne and poured it in their glasses. "Let's drink for all of us," he said. "Let's drink for fulfilling missions God gave us in this world. If we do it, we'll be happy. Be happy!"

CHAPTER 52

In his fifty-fourth years, Professor Henry Ginsberg created a large scientific school. Hundreds of doctors and researchers proudly considered themselves his scientific pupils.

Since the time when he began delivering his lectures at the university, every year he used to take seven to ten doctors who had shown ability for scientific work to his doctorate course. In their turn, each of his aspirants was a scientific leader of three or five capable senior students; and every senior student led one or two junior students who expressed their desire to participate in research after regular student hours.

While participating in research, all of them published their results in scientific journals. There was no seniority in such publications; very often among three co-authors, Professor Ginsberg put his name in third place while the two in front of him were names of unknown students. To attend his class or to be taken to his doctorate course was a great honor and the dream of many.

As always, at the beginning of the semester, Henry went to the auditorium for the meeting with his new aspirants. There were nine of them—six men and three young ladies.

He held in his hand a sheet of paper with their names. He called a name, and then gave the new aspirant several minutes for a presentation—in a few words to tell about him or her, and about their experience. They also reported in which direction they'd like to continue their research.

In front of him, Henry saw young but self-assured in their vocation people. Henry liked teaching because by giving students his knowledge, he absorbed from them the admiration of youth; he saturated his soul with their hopes, and became a participant of their future. In those moments, he felt like a sculptor whom God gave the rare ability to create his masterpiece.

The turn of one of the young ladies came. She stood up. "Deborah Levine," she introduced herself. "Graduated from the NYU Medical School," she said and looked at Henry.

When their eyes met each other, Henry suddenly felt uncomfortable. He read in Deborah's eyes more than he'd like to see as a teacher. Her eyes cried about love fulfilled her heart.

Henry was accustomed to admiration in the eyes of his students. Almost all the girls fell in love with him. At fifty-four, he was slim and had the face of a man of forty. Even the thick gray color in his hair did not make him appear older; he was as handsome as a middle-aged man could be.

He was always delicate about the admiration that female students expressed toward him, and never allowed adultery with even one of them. Not only because he was a teacher, but also because he loved Rachel. She never doubted he was faithful to her although beautiful young girls-students permanently surrounded him.

For many years, Henry got accustomed to reading students' admiration in eyes. But he always knew it was the amorousness of the youth into the experience and knowledge of the teacher. In Deborah Levine's eyes he read love. "It's impossible," he calmed himself. "We have never even met before." But looking in Deborah's eyes, he felt uncomfortable.

Strictly speaking, Deborah could not be called beautiful. Her facial features were slightly irregular. She had thick chestnut hair above a high forehead, blue eyes as crystal pure as a mountain stream, and red, plump lips, not colorless from frequent using of lipstick, and not totally covering her white teeth. She was far from the Biblical type of beauty.

Henry could hardly wait until the presentation was over and hurriedly left the auditorium. Why did he feel so uncomfortable?

For almost three months, Henry tried not to be alone with Deborah. He even discussed her dissertation work with other aspirants' presence. He tried not to think about her, but the harder he tried to discard her image, her face stood in front of his eyes like a daydream.

Once she stopped him in the hall. Henry had finished his lectures for the day and was hurrying to the lab when he heard somebody called his name, "Excuse me, Professor Ginsberg." Henry turned and saw Deborah Levine. "I want to ask you for a great favor," she continued in German. Henry raised his brows. "I think it wouldn't be impertinent to invite you to my birthday party. It happens to be my 28th," she explained. "Students of our group would be happy to see you." At seeing Henry hesitating, Deborah added, "Please, Professor."

"Okay, Deborah." Henry smiled.

A joy splashed in her eyes, and she handed him a note with the restaurant's name and address. Then she hurriedly headed to the exit. Henry glanced at the paper. It wasn't a place for student parties; it was a fashionable restaurant.

There was a tradition he had created at his school long ago—participating in student parties. On one hand, an invitation was a sign of the students' respect; from another, invitations emphasized that they were not teachers and students, but allies and like-minded persons. Debra knew about that tradition, and that he could not refuse her.

A table for ten was set up in the corner of the room. Among young people, Henry never felt older than they were. He told them jokes from his medical practice, and they laughed until tears appeared in their eyes.

Then the conversation touched on Israeli politics, and they began to discuss seriously how many years remained until the Arabs unleash a new war.

"It will be an endless process until we realize that Meir Kahane is right; Arabs have to be expelled from Israel if we want to exist. Only our weakness is the reason for wars. If they realize that the new 'status quo' is forever, they would stop their attempts to change the map," said a quiet young man with big glasses on a thin face.

The other people at the table were mostly leftists who considered Arabs if not brothers but distant relatives. As most of Jews, they wanted to live in peace with everybody.

Henry didn't take part in polemics. First of all because science was beyond politics; secondly, he had not forgotten he was a teacher whose position had to be fair and balanced.

A small orchestra appeared on the stage, and they played *Argentine Tango*.

"Would you give me a birthday gift, Professor? Please invite me to dance." Deborah smiled him.

Henry could not refuse her. He lightly embraced Deborah's body. Keeping her close to him, Henry felt dizzy. He felt his own body began slowly to dissolve in air. It seemed him he was losing his equilibrium, and to avoid falling, he had to embrace Deborah closer.

In heels, she was almost as tall as he was, and their faces were close to each other. Not to fall in the abyss of her eyes, Henry closed eyes and hardly moved his legs as if under hypnosis.

Suddenly he felt her wet lips on his, and heard her hot whisper, "I love you, Henry. Only God knows how I love you…"

He opened his eyes for a moment but quickly closed them again. "It's impossible," he also whispered in answer. "You don't know me, we never met each other."

Argentine Tango finished, and the next selection was a rock-'n'roll tune. But they stayed in the middle of the floor, embracing each other, motionless as if the world around them didn't exist.

"We have met each other," Deborah said loudly, trying to shout the music. He looked at her with surprise. "Thirteen years ago you attended my grandfather's funeral. I am Deborah Silverman."

Henry shuddered. Baruch Silverman's burying ceremony highlighted his memory, but he couldn't remember the face of Baruch's small granddaughter.

The music stopped. Henry offered to escort Deborah back to the table. When they sat, all of Deborah's fellows had left already. They remained alone.

For the first time, Henry looked at her face with an open glance. She smiled at him in answer. Her smile brightened all the corners of her face; the minor irregularities of her face vanished. Now it was the face of a Goddess. He looked at her eyes and suddenly remembered…

After the funeral, friends and close relatives of Baruch Silverman's family had returned home. While he was smoking outside, a sliding door opened. He turned around and saw a teenager girl on the threshold.

"Hi," she said, "I am Deborah."

"Hi, Deborah," Henry said. They talked a little, and then he extinguished the cigarette, took the girl's hand, and they returned inside.

"I remembered you," Henry said. "You were a little girl; now you're a princess. But I am too old for a young princess."

"Love isn't a matter of age," Deborah said thoughtfully. "It's from God. He either gives us love or not. I think most people who talk about love don't know what it is. They call "love" a feel of gratitude, satisfaction, tenderness, and understanding, even a habit. But it's not love. I know that I love you, Henry; I had loved you since the first day I saw you when I was a girl. Then, when I was sixteen, my grandfather asked me to edit his memoirs. Many pages were dedicated to you; that's why I can say I know you for a long time.

I love you, Henry. I tried to kill my feeling. I tried to persuade myself it was only childish amorousness. I was even married to a very good man who loved me. But we divorced within three months because I couldn't feel anybody near me. What can I do, Henry? I graduated from medical school because it was my only chance to enter your doctorate course and see you." She took a nervous pause, and then gulped her wine. "I know you are married, and I should never forgive myself for breaking up your family. What I need, Henry, what I beg of you, Henry,—is only to be near me. Allow me to see you some-times. Allow me to be close to you, sometimes. Allow me to kiss your face, sometimes." Deborah's eyes were full of tears.

Henry tried to bubble something about Deborah's broken future but in his soul, he had already stopped resisting. Nothing depended on him. Nothing depended on Deborah. Everything was forecast. How could he resist a feeling sent him from Above? Sent as a blessing? Sent as a punishment?

Henry closed his eyes. Only silly people call events and meet-ings casual. There is nothing casual in our life. Life is a chain of objective regularities understandable only to God. But who can understand His logic?

Henry opened his eyes and looked at the beautiful blue eyes opposite him. If dark eyes reflect an abyss of passion, in the blue eyes you see only the way. Where does it lead?

Henry's foolish thoughts existed beyond him. It seemed to him that he observed himself from the side; he took Deborah's hand, carried it to his lips and kissed it. Then he said, "I've loved you since the first moment I saw you in the auditorium." Then he touched her cheeks with his fingers. Fingers became wet from her tears. He tasted her tears. They were not bitter. Why do people say "bitter tears? The second man who observed them from the side wondered how the tears of happiness could be bitter.

Then, as if Henry were hypnotized, he waved to a waiter and paid the bill. They left the restaurant and stopped on the street waiting for a taxi. As if for the first time in his life, Henry saw the street where they stood: the whitewash brick exteriors of houses, the brightly painted window frames, the flowers spilling from pots on the front steps. "A perfect place to walk a dog," Henry said automatically.

A taxi stopped nearby though he did not call for it. He held the door for her as she climbed in, and gave a driver his address. Rachel was still at Esther's house, helping her after she had given birth to her daughter, Rebecca. Henry did not think about whether anybody could see him entering the house after midnight with a woman. He thought about nothing. He couldn't think. He did not exist in time and space. The taxi stopped near his house. He paid and got out, still not feeling any reality of the events.

As soon as the front door closed behind them, he pressed Deborah's body to his. Two trembling forms stood, embraced each other, lost their sense of time; two bright human souls among myriads of others…

CHAPTER 53

───────────▼───────────

For his age, Rabbi Boxter had kept a clear mind. He retired from the position of the synagogue's chief rabbi but went to his office every day. With the years, he became an unofficial part of the institution that, during those same years, had grown from a small synagogue into a large-scale Jewish center.

For the members of congregation, Rabbi Boxter was a *tzadik*, and many people used to come to see him every day; some of them—to receive his blessing, others—a piece of advice.

Henry came and glanced quickly around the office, noting both the old-fashion, comfortable furniture and the obligatory framed photos on the wall, showing Rabbi Boxter shaking hands with Chaim Weitzman, Ben-Gurion, Golda Meir, and with the man who was hated by any mere politician—Rabbi Meir Kahane.

Seeing Henry, Rabbi Boxter smiled. "I'm always glad to see you, my boy. How is your beautiful wife, Rachel? I haven't seen you both since the day of your anniversary."

It wasn't because of their generous donation to the synagogue that Rabbi remembered Rachel and Henry. He loved them since the day that he had performed their wedding ceremony. Henry was the only Jew-neophyte in his congregation. Rabbi pointed to the chair, and Henry sat. Rabbi put his glasses on and looked into Henry's face attentively.

"I see something worries you, Henry," he said.

Henry sighed deeply. He didn't know how to start. Silence came, and Rabbi did not interrupt it. At last Henry said, "I'd like to ask you a question."

"I'm all ears."

"Can love be punishment?"

"I don't think so, Henry. Love is the Lord's award."

"Can the Lord award a family man?"

Rabbi Boxter took his glasses off and looked at Henry from beneath his eyebrows. He saw something gnawed at Henry inwardly.

"Tell me what happened, Henry," he said.

Henry confessed.

"It's beyond me, Rabbi," he said. "The Lord is my witness, I tried to stop. But love for Deborah filled my heart. How could I reject her love if she sacrificed her life for the sake of love for me, if she had loved me for years, since she read my name in her grandfather's memoirs? I love her, Rabbi. But the terror of this situation is that I have not stopped loving Rachel. She was half of my soul, and she is; but the other part of my soul, which belonged to me, doesn't belong to me anymore. It belongs to Deborah. What can I do if I love them both? I would never leave Rachel, I would never bring her harm and pain, but now I feel that if I break it off with Deborah, I would also die. What is going on, it's beyond me. I did nothing to get involved in adultery. But it's not adultery, Rabbi! It's not." Henry paused and sighed bitterly.

"Deborah is much younger than you," Rabbi said thought-fully. "Perhaps...perhaps your mind needs to relax by contemplating other beautiful objects."

"Yes, she is only twenty-eight. But her age doesn't play a role."

"Are you no longer attracted to Rachel?"

"No, she's beautiful, and in her forty-six years, she's still in blossom. When she accompanies me, I catch signs of other men's admiration when they look at her. She is still perfect and beautiful, maybe even more beautiful than Deborah. But I cannot live without both. I tried to find an answer in the Torah, but I failed. So I came to you; you're a *tzadik*. Please, tell me what can I do? I am at a dead end, and do not know how to get out. Help me!"

Rabbi Boxter sighed deeply. For some time he said nothing for the simple reason that there was little he could say. He was an old man who, many years ago, had buried his own wife, but this moment reminded him all too painfully of the woman he had married in the full flush of hopeful youth.

"Mishnah teaches that the world stands upon three things; upon law, upon worship, and upon showing kindness. Not upon love," Rabbi Boxter said after a long pause. "Mankind is imperfect. To be perfect, a Jew had to comply with 613 commandments. I'm not sure any *tzadik* could do it in his lifetime. During the first part of his life," he corrected himself. "What does love mean? Only God knows because only God gives it. A *tzadik* is not God, and is not even God's messenger. What advice can I give you, Henry? I don't know. What I do know, love cannot be a punishment; love is a blessing." Rabbi paused, being submerged in his thoughts. Then he continued. "A short-time passion leads to adultery; adultery leads to the dissolution of flesh. This sin is punishable because a short-time passion is the check of true love. If a man breaks his obligation given in front of God, he is sinful.

What can a man do if God blessed him twice in his life? I'll be frank with you, Henry. I do not know. Our predecessors were blessed with love more than once. If you lived in time of Moshe or King David, it wouldn't be a problem. God's laws remained constant for millennia; but man's laws have changed—now he can be married to only one woman at time. Nobody would understand your life with two women, even if you love both and they both love you. Is it immoral from the point of view of God's law? I am not sure. Is it immoral from the point of view of modern society? I am sure.

This is not a rabbi's position, Henry. This is the position of an old man who tries to understand a young man. What advice can I give you? I do not know. It's your choice, and let God bless you in your decision."

Henry rocked back in his chair and gave Rabbi Boxter a long look. He was grateful to the old man for his sincerity, but he grimly wondered if he was going to redeem the mistakes of his past at the cost of his future.

"Thank you, Rabbi," Henry said softly and headed to the exit, feeling the rabbi's glance on his back.

Henry strode through the streets that were glistering with the remnants of a recent rain. Everything was mixed up in his head. He adhered to his own rules of life, which enabled him to remain self-possessed under all circumstances, but now his usual world was broken forever; he felt like an old man who had lived a long and sinful life.

Henry stopped at a small café with the inevitable fat, hairy-lipped hostess and two cranks ready to argue half a night with everybody about everything. But he wasn't in the mood to talk. He ordered a cognac and drained it in one gulp. The two cranks argued about the future. Henry laughed bitterly and loudly at their words. One of the cranks silently nodded toward his side and twisted a finger near his temple.

Does the future exist? Henry thought absently and ordered another drink.

CHAPTER 54

Deborah was sitting in a cozy Jerusalem café, reading a paper and waiting for her close friend, Rivka Macher. For the last six months, studying together in Professor Ginsberg's classes they had become close friends.

With her fair complexion, reddish hair and gray eyes, her good looks were German rather than Jewish. She wasn't too socially outgoing, even reserved, and it took Deborah time to realize that Rivka was a sincere, frank and devoted creature.

Now she had decided to sacrifice her research career in favor of a medical practice in the new settlement Gush Katif. Her husband, also a doctor, had accepted an offer to become the head of a small hospital recently opened in the new settlement, and Rivka decided to follow him.

Entering the café, she waved Deborah and sat down at her table. "I'm so glad to see you, dear," she said as she kissed Deborah on the cheek. The table Deborah occupied was near the entrance, and Rivka said matter-of-factly, "This isn't the most convenient table for conversation."

Deborah nodded. "All others are busy. It's lunch time."

"Okay, we won't pay attention to the crowd," Rivka agreed and ordered a cup of coffee and a tuna salad.

"Anyway, you have finally decided to drop out?" Deborah asked.

"Finally. I think I'll be more useful for my people working in the settlement than in the research lab." She smiled. "I think the level of my ability for research is lower than Professor Ginsberg's."

"He evaluates your ability very high, as I know." Deborah smiled.

"Every once in our life, we must make our own main decision," Rivka said without a smile. "This is mine. I regret only one thing—not being able to see you." Rivka took a sip of coffee and continued, "But you have to know that my house is always your house."

"I know, my friend," Deborah said softly and put her hand on Rivka's.

"Seriously," Rivka said, "I think you have to come to Gush Katif as well. Not now, maybe later. When you give birth to a baby, it would be much easier for you to raise a child there than here."

Deborah looked at Rivka sadly. "I won't be able to live, not seeing Henry," she said. "It's beyond me."

"Poor girl!" Rivka smiled. "I think everything will be…"

She did not have the opportunity to finish her phrase.

A sudden explosion deafened Deborah. Then she felt a piercing pain in her head and fell down losing consciousness. Surprisingly, she recovered it in several minutes and heard somebody's voice, "Easy, this girl is alive."

Deborah tried to open her eyes and made several attempts to open her eyelids. But she couldn't because a sticky, heavy liquid covered her face. "Who poured wine on my face?" She then guessed it wasn't wine but blood. Then the wild pain in her head lashed at her and she fell into a black abyss.

Deborah recovered consciousness again, lying on a hospital bed after surgery. Her bandaged face was linen-white, but the headache gone. Her first question to the doctor standing near her bed was, "Where's my baby?"

The doctor smiled. "You're a lucky girl," he said. "You were wounded in your head, but your body wasn't damaged. I think you'll give birth on time."

"Thank you, doctor," Deborah whispered. Then she suddenly caught the surgeon's hand. "What's my friend Rivka Macher?"

The doctor didn't answer. "You'll be okay," he repeated and made an attempt to release his hand. But Deborah pressed it as strong as she could with her weak fingers. "Rivka Macher?" she repeated.

Doctor sighed heavily. "She's dead."

Deborah's fingers became suddenly weak. She cried silently as the doctor left the chamber. A nurse remained sitting near her bed, not trying to calm Deborah. The more a girl cries the easier for her to heal, she thought. Dry eyes only increase pain.

Suddenly Deborah stopped crying. "I have to make a call," she said. "Please."

"Give me the number, and I'll call your family," the nurse offered.

"Please let Professor Ginsberg know that I'm here." Deborah gave her the phone number, and the nurse went to the nursing station to make the call.

After receiving the call, Henry reached the hospital after two-hour drive.

Emergency Room Director Dr. Malka Hafazi greeted him with a neutral, "Shalom, Dr. Ginsberg." She was an ascetic, middle-aged woman, with short-cut hair 'a'la Golda Meir' style. Henry studied her face for news, but she was impassive.

"She's better than one might have expected," Malka Hafazi said. "A lot tougher than she looks."

"What happened?" How did it happen?"

"Crap came at her from the blast."

"From the blast?'

"They can be nasty, the Arabs. But what nearly killed her was bleeding. I'll show you to her room, Dr. Ginsberg."

Henry rushed over to Deborah and grasped her hand. Then he opened his mouth to say something but no words came, and he broke down and cried. He quietly pulled himself together.

"A tear of two doesn't do any harm," Deborah said softly. Then she smiled weakly. "They did not split my head; my head's in one piece, I think. I'm so happy to see you, Henry. When I see you, I know that now everything will be okay."

"It will definitely be, sweetheart." Henry took her weak hand and pressed it to his lips.

He stayed with Deborah for the better part of a week, and was delighted to see her making progress.

"I'll leave you darling for couple of days and be back on Friday to take you home. Dr. Hafazi assured me that on Friday you would be ready to depart."

"That would be wonderful." Deborah's smile was happy. "By Friday, I promise to look much better."

But the next day Deborah unexpectedly went into a coma. When the nurse called, Dr. Malka Hafazi rushed into the room accompanied by Dr. Max Yakub, the surgeon. They talked in hushed voices.

"The impact of the blow had perhaps caused some clotting under her skull," Dr. Hafazi said speculatively.

"And it appears that the clot has been growing and may continue to grow. We shall operate as soon as we can," Dr. Yakub agreed.

The operation began at dawn and continued for most of the morning. At about noon Dr. Yakub came out to say, "We've saved the baby, but it's too early to say if we've done more than that."

"I have to call Dr. Ginsberg," Dr. Hafazi sighed tiredly. But then she decided to postpone the call. Let's hope for a miracle, she thought.

The miracle hasn't happened; the next day, Thursday evening, Deborah died.

CHAPTER 55

▼

Henry was in the lab, talking to his assistant, Dr. Veksler, when he received a call from a hospital.

"Dr. Ginsberg? Unfortunately I have to bring you sad news; Ms. Debora Levine died an hour ago." The voice of a woman was metallic and indifferent.

"Who died?" Henry repeated. The sense of words hadn't yet reached him. When it did, he felt the earth dissolved under his feet. To avoid falling, he caught Dr. Veksler's elbow.

"Are you all right, Professor?" Dr. Veksler asked.

Not answering, Henry rushed out of the lab to hire a taxi. "Hospital! As quick as possible!"

Less than an hour later, he rushed into the ICU Administration. Having seen his mad glance, the nurse understood who he was. "Room three," she said and sighed. She saw too many human tragedies. To observe them was a part of her job.

Henry opened the door and saw the bed. Deborah's body was covered with a white linen sheet. He pulled it aside. The skin of her face hadn't yet become gray, and it seemed that she was sleeping. Somebody had joked with him. It was a cruel joke. "Wake up, darling," he said softly. "I'm here. I'll take you home."

She did not answer.

"Wake up," he repeated insistently and leaned to kiss her. Her lips were cold. Suddenly he had realized it was not a joke; Deborah had died. Henry felt as if somebody kicked him as hard as he could beneath the belt, so strongly that he could not breathe. Henry convulsively tried to gulp fresh air; then his legs became like cotton wool, and he fell on the floor near the bed, repeating like a parrot only one phrase, "Wake up, darling; wake up, darling. Please, wake up."

Then on the same level as his eyes, he saw Deborah's hand hanging from the bed. He took it and pressed it to his lips. Only now the spasm in his throat left and he produced a cry. It wasn't a human cry; it was an animal's cry, so long that all medical personal at the nursing station shuddered. It was a cry of loses, a cry of pain, a cry of a dead love.

Henry did not know for how long he had spent near Deborah's bed. Respecting his suffering, nobody came in the room. At last Henry recovered his senses and stood up. He again kissed her dead lips. "I love you, Deborah. I'll always love you," he whispered, and carefully put the white linen back over her body. He left the room to go to the nursing station where Dr. Hafazi was writing in a medical chart.

"I'm so sorry, Dr. Ginsberg," she said, her eyes red. "The impact of the blow had caused an unexpected clot." She tried to explain him what happened and that the baby had survived, but he did not hear her.

"A baby?" Henry asked nervously.

"Ms. Levine gave birth to a healthy boy," another doctor calmed him. "A little premature, but everything will be okay.

The baby needs some more attention for several weeks. The healthy baby," she repeated and smiled that sad smile of hers.

"Give me the baby," Henry requested nervously.

The head nurse looked at Dr. Hafazi, and then said, "The baby needs to spend a week or so in a medical institution, Professor Ginsberg."

"Give me the baby," Henry demanded in a sharp tone. "This is my baby." His hands were trembling.

Dr. Hafazi nodded. "Okay, Professor. Please sit down and wait until we prepare the baby. He needs special treatment at a medical institution, and please do not forget that he has to be under observation at least two or three times a week. But if you insist…please, sign the papers documenting that the baby was released at your request, against medical advice." She gave him the papers.

Henry signed, not looking at what he signed, and sat in the chair to wait. He did not hear what the doctor told him. He observed himself as from the side, as he had several months previously at Deborah's birthday party. It was very strange to see himself that way. The man from the side thought it was a pity that he wasn't a psychiatrist. Why was it a pity not to be a psychiatrist?

At last the door opened and the nurse handed him a baby covered in a blanket. Henry took the baby and left, forgetting to say thank you or following the tradition of giving the nurse a tip. The baby was sleeping.

The man from the side waved down a taxi and Henry got in, said the address. Finally he looked at the baby's face. It was a beautiful baby face. All baby faces are nice, he thought, but the man from the side told him he was wrong—the face of the baby he held in his hands was the most beautiful in the world. Because his son was a child of God's love. "You are right," Henry said aloud, and the man from the side vanished.

The taxi stopped near the entrance of his house. Perhaps he paid too much automatically because the driver tried to return most of money. But he said, "Keep the change."

He took up the baby who was still sleeping calmly, and came to the door. He rang the bell. Rachel opened the door and Henry stepped in.

"This is my baby," he said and licked his dry lips. Then he sat on the sofa, still pressing the baby to his chest.

He looked at Rachel's face. Suffering was briefly reflected on it and vanished. Only her eyes began to fill with tears. They dropped uncontrollably, and she did not make an attempt to wipe them.

"This is my baby," Henry repeated hopelessly.

"I know." At last she took a napkin to wipe her eyes, but her tears did not stop; the drops grew larger.

Henry said, "Forgive me, Rachel, I loved her. She died."

"I'm very sorry she died," Rachel said quietly, her voice sincere.

"Are you sorry?" Henry looked at Rachel with surprise, but felt the sincerity of her words. Then he said, "But I never stopped loving you, Rachel." Tenderness appeared in his face like a blush.

"I knew it. I knew everything, Henry."

"How could you know?'

"When a woman loves, she feels everything." She wiped her eyes.

"Will you forgive me, Rachel? I am a bad man." Henry swallowed the saliva in the back of his throat.

"What do I have to forgive you for? Love is God's present. You could not reject it. Nobody can." She sighed heavily, and Henry felt a lump in his throat.

The baby moved and cried. Rachel took him in her hands, rocking him, and he became silent.

"This is my baby," Henry said again as though he tried to persuade himself that he was a father of the baby.

"This is our baby, Henry," Rachel said, still rocking the baby. Then she sat near him on the sofa and stroked Henry's hair. "This is our baby," she repeated. Then she added, "But we have to give him to Esther for a while. She recently gave birth to our granddaughter and still has a woman's milk in her breasts."

Henry looked at Rachel suspiciously, and she intercepted his glance.

"No more than for three or four months," she explained. "Then we'll take him back. But first of all, you have to make arrangements for his circumcision now." Rachel put the baby between two pillows and returned to the sofa.

"We have to give him a name," she said after a pause.

"I think it would be fair if he wears the name Baruch. Baruch Silverman deserved this honor, didn't he?" Henry said thoughtfully.

Henry lowered his head to Rachel's knees and closed his eyes. They were dry, but he felt the drops of Rachel's tears falling to his cheeks. "I love you, Rachel," he whispered. "I never stopped loving you."

After they buried Deborah, Henry put a marble plate on her grave with a simple sign: **Deborah Levine-Ginsberg, 1945–1973.**

What more could he do except giving Deborah his name?

CHAPTER 56

▼

A call from the Israeli Consulate with a request to urgently join his military unit broke the fetters of Moshe's family life.

He had already watched the TV breaking news; the new Middle East war had begun. Peggy was in the medical school, but within three hours he had to be onboard a special plane reserved for Israeli citizens. He did not even have time to go to his parents-in-law's house to give a good-bye kiss to his daughters. First Moshe wanted to write a note to Peggy, but then changed his mind and called John Witherspoon, his father-in-law.

"John, I have to leave quickly to join the Israeli army. We are at war," he said.

John laughed in the receiver. "We are not in war, son, but you have to go," he said calmly. "I respect your decision although I have always been against the dual citizenship."

"Peggy is at school, and I couldn't get hold of her. Tell her I love her."

"I will," John Witherspoon said in neutral voice. "Although Middle East wars don't last long, take care of yourself." He hung up.

Within three hours, Moshe was onboard one of the planes full of reservists who temporarily or permanently had lived in the US. All conversations were about the war; optimistic speeches of people who were accustomed to Israeli military superiority.

Soon Moshe could embrace his friend Ariel. Israeli military always tried to gather reservists in the same units where they had already served before; it created almost a family atmosphere and increased responsibility for every soldier.

"Hi, American!" Ariel embraced Moshe. "You look great. Have you forgotten the Ivrit language? Otherwise we risk driving backward when the order is forward." He laughed. He hadn't lost his sense of humor.

Moshe saluted Lieutenant Abe Shub, his unit commander who always used their M-60 as a head tank.

'Hi, American!' Abe Shub echoed Ariel's words. "Welcome to your native soil."

But the cheerful atmosphere quickly changed as soon as they took part in the attempted assault. After a one-day attack, they have lost four Centurions and two M-60 tanks, not counting fourteen soldiers dead and more then twenty men wounded. They hadn't gotten accustomed to such losses. The mood plummeted.

A month passed by. The bloodiest and the most terrible month. The days stood like angels, incomprehensible above the ring of annihilation. Every man in the unit knew they were loosing the war. Not much was said about it. Moshe and Ariel tried to avoid talking about it too.

Tanks, anti-tanks aircraft, bombardment—words, words, words, but they held the horror of the world.

"Tomorrow we'll have to try a night attack. If we fail, we'll have to retreat," Abe Shub said gloomy as he returned from a meeting at headquarters.

Another wave of the counter attack had just come up at four a.m., but it wasn't unexpected for the Arabs. Heavy bombardment with anti-tank missiles brought a crushing force to bear on Moshe's unit.

What idiot gave the order for the attack, Lieutenant Shub thought as he shouted as loud as he could, "Forward, forward, follow!"

Soldiers' faces are encrusted; their thoughts are devastated; they are weary to death. How long had it been? Months, weeks, days? Only hours.

The blast in front so deafened Moshe that he did not realize immediately that his M-60 tank was crippled. They managed to get out through the bottom access door and dove into the dugout. Breathless, they were laying one beside other, waiting for the charge. They suddenly ran into another man from his unit; Moshe did not remember his name, a Centurion's driver. He was sitting on the bottom of the trench; his face looked sullen, he was panicked.

"Get out of here!" Lieutenant Shub commanded, "It's too dangerous to stay."

But the man showed his teeth like a cur. He did not stir. "Fuck you," he said indifferently as if it did not concern him.

Ariel seized him by the arm and tried to pull him up. Then he grabbed him by the neck and shoved him like a sack. His head jerked from side to side, but he returned back to reality.

Shells whistled around them, and suddenly Lieutenant Shub gurgled and turned green and yellow. Moshe jumped up; he was eager to help him. Shub's throat was parched; everything danced red and black before his eyes.

"Are you okay, Abe?"

He did not answer. Still on his legs, he was already dead. Then he fell down, not like a dead man, like a wounded one; first he dropped down on his knees, and then his body fell in the dirt face down.

Moshe still tried to shake him but Ariel said, "He's dead; get out of here, Moshe! Quicker! It would be worse if Arabs capture us. We can't shelter ourselves properly for the explosions!"

Another shell whistled by. This time Ariel fell. "Shit!" he said. "My shoulder…" Moshe bound his wound and comforted him, but the wound began to bleed profusely. Moshe gathered him up and started off at a run, at last reaching the first aid station. Not only did his legs and hands tremble, but lips as well. But on his lips, there was a happy smile—his friend Ariel was saved.

Then Moshe went to the local headquarters to report that they had lost their tank. The headquarters was a disorderly movement of people shouting for arms, ammunition or help; it gave the building an atmosphere of despairing hysteria. A wounded brigade commander had to give his orders from the stretcher.

Hearing Moshe's report, a lieutenant with a tired, worn-out face asked him in condemnation, "How could you leave without helping your commanding officer? I'll send you to a court marshal." His voice was threadlike, quavering.

Moshe looked up at him in wonder as if he couldn't quite believe what he was hearing; a second ago he had explained that Lieutenant Shub was dead. He got pissed and refused to answer any other stupid questions.

Happily for him, the lieutenant was called to another room. Another officer came and asked Moshe what he was doing here. He explained, and the officer sent him to another unit. "They've just lost a driver," he explained casually.

The war went on.

CHAPTER 57

▼

Again a war…In two previous wars, in 1956 and in 1967, the Middle East wars began with massive multi-pronged Israeli air and ground invasions into Muslim lands. The Israeli Air Force devastated the airfields and planes of the Arab countries with their surprised attacks.

In the two previous wars the Israelis then pushed out in their M-60, M-48 and Centurion tanks to crash through the defensive formations of the miserably equipped Arab armies.

For twenty-five years Israel was the invincible military power of the Middle East. This, plus a sense of national vigilance, made a successful Arab attack close to impossible.

The Arab attack in 1973 was different. It was the first time that the Arabs fielded forces drilled in the disciplines of modern battle tactics; they were equipped with up-to-date integrated weapons systems for coordinated ground, air and water operations.

With the help of Soviet supplies, the Arabs had the advantage of numerical superiority and complete surprise with which they launched their attacks into Israeli territory. During the first day of the battle, fifty-one Israeli planes—more than 10% of Israeli Air Force—were ripped from the sky by Muslim missilery. In the month of October 1973, the Israelis lost over 49% of the entire tank corps, one third of those occurred within the first seventy-two hours of war. The Israeli occupational garrisons had been pushed back off the Suez. The Arab armies were consolidating to continue their push outward across the occupied Sinai.

Of course, Henry Ginsberg, a colonel of Military Medical Services, couldn't know that at the same time when he was desperately trying to provide proper treatment for hundreds of wounded Israeli soldiers, Defense Minister Moshe Dyan delivered his report to PM Golda Meir.

"This is the end of the Third Temple," he finished gloomily.

When he left, Golda Meir closed the door behind him, and paying no attention to the aide, still in the room, wept openly. Tears streamed down Golda Meir's face.

"What's the matter?" the aide asked.

She looked at him with unseeing eyes. "Dyan wants to talk about the conditions of our surrender." She sobbed, brushing away her tears. "But I would rather commit suicide than agree to it."

Golda Meir ordered Israel to prepare for a nuclear Massada— an atomic holocaust that would consume Israel as well as the surrounding Islamic capitals and oil fields.

Israeli's thirteen atomic bombs were barely assembled in a secret underground tunnel during a seventy-eight hour period at the start of the war.

At that time the Egyptians had repulsed the first Israeli counter-attack.

Along the Suez Canal, causing heavy casualties, the Israeli forces on the Golan Heights were retreating in the face of a massive Syrian tank assault.

The central army hospital near Al-Kuneitra was under permanent bombardment for several days. It was clear to everyone that the situation was getting worse and worse with every day; the common mood was gloomy.

As the 2nd Army Chief Doctor, Colonel Ginsberg was invited to the extraordinary meeting conducted by Brigade General Nahum Brill. With his thirty-two years, he was the youngest Israeli general, a 1968 war hero. Trying to remain calm, he read Moshe Dyan's order to retrieve Al-Kuneitra within twenty-four hours in expectation of a massive Syrian assault.

Looking at General Brill's face, Henry thought that the man could be his son in age; he was too young to be a general. The people around him asked stupid questions, but Henry didn't hear answers. Henry thought he was doomed to retreat. He never took part in victorious operations: WW II, the battle for Lantum, and now—Al-Kuneitra. Even the victorious war of 1967 had not touched him—it was finished before he took part in it.

Somebody must take responsibility for what's going on, he thought bitterly. This is a disaster, a total intelligence failure. If Lantum's casualties can be referred to as a lack of experienced intelligence, when underground intelligence hadn't yet turned into State intelligence, now military failure has no excuses.

"Do something, goddamnit!" Henry said in irritation. "Are you Army officers or a piece of shit? You've got nukes; use them! Otherwise the Muslims would slaughter all of us." He left, slammed the door, and gave orders for the immediate evacuation of the hospital.

He walked through the ward, accompanied by only the head nurse. All 150 beds were occupied, the hospital was over-full;

wounded soldiers lay in all the halls. Henry did not remember such casualties ever in his practice. He looked at the faces of young, wounded men. They were as gloomy as the faces of doctors and nurses around them. The sound of permanent bombardment told for itself.

The face of one of the sleeping wounded soldiers seemed familiar to Henry. And at the same moment, he felt his legs become cotton wool. Not to fall down, he had to catch the elbow of the nurse who looked at him with surprise.

"Who is this man?" Henry asked her, instead of reading the chart with the patient's name on it, hanging on the bed.

"Moshe Ginsberg," she read, "a sergeant of the 3rd Division." Only then she guessed that she was talking about Colonel Ginsberg's son. "Is he your son?" She licked her dry lips. Henry had already come to himself. Not answering, he took the chart and read the diagnosis; left below the knee amputation.

At that moment, the wounded soldier woke up. He looked at Henry, still not understanding the reality around him. He closed his eyes again, but then rapidly opened them wide again. "Daddy?" Moshe's eyes were full of tears. "Forgive me, Daddy." He took Henry's hand and pressed it to his cheek.

"That's all right, my boy, that's all right," Henry said hoarsely, feeling his eyes also filling with tears. "Everything will be okay. You have only lost a part of your leg, luckily beneath the knee. After a war we'll make you such an artificial limb that nobody will recognize it; you won't be even limp."

"I'm so happy to see you, Daddy," Moshe whispered. "Now, when I see you, I know everything will be okay."

The next day General Brill's brigade stopped the Syrian assault, creating a springboard to retake Mount Hermon and Golan Heights. But the casualties were severe; among them, there was General Brill himself.

When Henry heard about Nahum Brill's death, he felt a prick of conscience. "My Lord, forgive me," he whispered.

Golda Meir notified President Richard Nixon about Israel's possibly using the A-bombs. The White House was making a choice between two awesome threads: an Arab oil cut off, which would devastate industrial America, or an atomic war launched by defeated Israel. Richard Nixon did not respond to a message from Saudi King Faisal, and began the largest in the history of America airlift of military weapons, supplies and support equipment for Israel to compensate for the Israeli military loss.

At the same time, God intervened and the Israeli armies began to turn the tide of battle against the Muslim forces.

With the US supplied weapons, the Israelis were effectively cutting into the Arab missile thickets. Breaking a corridor through to one section on the Suez Canal, they began pouring M-60 tanks across into Egypt for counter-attacks behind the Muslim lines. To the north, in similar actions, the Israelis began a counter-attack that would ultimately retake Mount Hermon and the Golan Heights.

In the field the war continued, and it went increasingly badly for the Muslim forces. The Israelis, now on the offensive, had begun further invasions of Egypt, surrounding the Egyptian Third Army and attempting to seize both the town of Suez and the main Egyptian oil port Adabiya.

Under the enormous international political pressure created by the nuclear emergency, the Israeli advances into Egypt stopped. A 7,000 men UN peacekeeping forces arrived to separate the combatants, and a solid cease-fire finally took effect.

Israel emerged as a clear military victor. The Arabs had not liberated Jerusalem or even held on to any substantial part of the occupied territories, and the Muslim armies were in tatters. Israel had regained the whole of the Sinai and controlled territory thirty miles deep inside Egypt proper.

CHAPTER 58

▼

Still in the hospital, Moshe began writing a letter to his wife Peggy.

> *"Dear Peggy,*
>
> *I wanted to write this letter to you, still in the U.S. Now I have enough time for it. I am at the hospital. I was wounded and lost the lower part of my left leg. Doctors say I am a lucky man, and an artificial limb wouldn't be recognizable after I'll be trained to walk.*
>
> *War is war. In the U.S., after the Vietnam War was over, people had already forgotten that war is a game with death. It seems to me here, in Israel, that this game became so habitual that it's been turned into gambling.*
>
> *Lying here, in this hospital room, I remembered every minute of our family life and came to the final conclusion to put a period to it. I think you understand I am right.*
>
> *I loved you. My love was like a splash of lightning; I could do nothing to resist my feelings. I followed you like a young sacrificial bull. I forgot about my family, my parents; I wanted only one thing—to be with you.*

Looking back, I cannot forgive my stupidity. How could I not to invite my parents to our wedding? How could I not ask their consent to our marriage? At any rate, they loved me too much to say "no," and I knew it. But I didn't do it, because you, Peggy, did not like it.

I do not blame you. It was your family who wanted to cut me off my roots. And you were too much under your parents' influence. You were a good Catholic girl too much.

Only later did I realize how deep, almost on a genetic level, was their anti-Semitism. They were so proud by their predecessors who sailed to the United States on board the Mayflower, but you broke the purity of their race and married a Jew!

But they knew their influence on you and still dreamed of cutting me off my family, (you have succeeded in it) and from my faith as well.

We lived together under one roof, we loved each other, we slept in one bed, but spiritually we lived in different galaxies. It was a wild situation; I went to synagogue to celebrate Jewish holidays; you went to church to celebrate Christian ones. On the door of my house, a garland hung, the garland that hung in Calvin's time to mark Christian houses in case of anti-Jewish pogroms.

You did everything to lead me to understand the necessity of my conversion to Christianity. And I have to confess, I was close to it. Only one more step, and in front of me would be the open doors of elite families; only one step, and in front of me, taking into account the business con-

nections of your father, there was the career of Casper Wineberger or Barry Goldwater. Only one step…

I was on the edge to make you and all your family happy. But…I couldn't take this last step. It was beyond me. Maybe it was on a genetic level. I couldn't betray the faith in which I was born; I couldn't betray my parents, even for the sake of my love to you, Peggy.

When you had given birth to our beautiful daughters, I was the happiest man in the world. Not for long, however. You baptized them and you didn't even ask my opinion. I understand that logistically they had to be Christian, if their mother is Christian. I had to put up with it although I understood there would be little in common between us in the future. You have sent them to Sunday school, and I had to put up with it.

Several months ago, before I left to take part in this war as an Israeli citizen, I heard that your parents talking to each other and they called me 'a kike.' Perhaps I was a weak man. I should have taken this step earlier, but I couldn't pluck up the courage for it. If I had not left the United States, I obviously would stay near you and continue to put up with everything.

I am happy the war was broken. My war. And I've made my decision.

I don't think, Peggy, I have to ask you for your forgiveness. I was a faithful husband and, I think, not a bad father.

With this letter, I am sending you all the legal papers for a divorce. I don't have too much to give you, but everything that we have—is yours: the house, the car and every poor

*penny on our joint account. Later on, when I find my place
here, in Israel, I'll send you 50% of all my regular income.
This is not a matter of money, but my obligations before
my daughters. Here, in Israel, there is a different system of
jurisprudence, but I hope, after my recovery, to find my
own place in Israeli's society and pass the bar.*

*I beg you, Peggy, for only one thing. Please, don't deprive
me of my fatherhood and don't bring our daughters up to
hate me. I did not deserve it. I know my daughters will
always be Christian, but let them know they are half-
Jewish. If you trust in God, He would bless you for that
step.*

*Always yours, your former husband and the father of your
children,*

Moshe."

Moshe put a period at the end of the sentence and put the
papers in the envelope. He sealed it, not bothering to re-read
anything. Then he called for a nurse.

"Do me the favor of mailing it to the USA," he asked her.

Within three months, Moshe received official court divorce
papers, but he had never received Peggy's answer to his letter.

Almost three years later, one evening, Moshe came to the parents' house with a girl.

"This is my fiancée, Leah," he said, introducing her to Rachel
and Henry.

Leah was a young widow, with a boy of three. Her husband had been killed on the Egyptian front, and her child had never seen his father.

"Welcome to our family Leah." Henry smiled. "I do hope you're not a doctor."

"Alas, sir." Leah returned the smile. "I'm 'a dry warm.' I work with numbers; I am an accountant."

"That's fine." Henry turned to Rachel. "Having a family accountant, maybe we'll at last get rich?"

"Aren't we rich, Henry?" In Rachel's eyes, there was happiness.

CHAPTER 59

―――――――▼―――――――

For the first time after the 1973 War, Henry thought that something was deeply wrong in Israeli society. Nobody took responsibility for the deep intelligence failure; nobody was punished for the severe casualties Israel suffered in the last war; no one of leadership rank was even forced to retire. Moreover, most of generals responsible for the defeats of the first phase of the war were promoted and transferred to the Ministry of Defense. Victorious fanfares deafened cries of sorrow. Everything returned to square one.

But Henry's views had sharply changed. It was the first time he looked at the Israeli political landscape as an outsider. How could he be a member of MAPAI? It had always been a liberal leftist party called the Labor Party, but in reality it was a Trotzkist Communist Party. Socialism had the advantage of dictatorship, and Ben-Gurion's time had proven its necessity for the Jewish State. But Ben-Gurion's time had passed. Henry left the MAPAI and joined the LIKUD. When the MAPAI leadership knew about his decision, they were shocked that the world-famous scientist, who had been a party member for more than twenty-five years, had left them. But after he rejected their seductive offer to become a Knesset member after the next elections, they quickly forgot about Henry. Now he did not receive any attention from the media, which was consolidated in the leftists' hands.

But his membership in the LIKUD party also turned out short-lived. He realized that, in many aspects, both parties were twins; it was LIKUD who made the biggest concessions to the Arab, not the Labor party.

When did Israeli pseudo-democracy turned into a caricature? Bitter thoughts visited Henry more and more often. No country in the world had dozens of registered parties representing nobody but its own leaders: religious and anti-religious, leftists and rightists, communist and socialist. And of course, all parties defended only the interests of their members: Sabra, Ashkenazi, Russian, Euphiopean, Arab…And of course, all of them ultra-liberal, all of them preach friendship, brotherhood, love and peace. Peace now. Peace at any price.

As a scientist, Henry tried to understand what processes were happening in Israeli society. His brief historical research gave him the answer.

The malaise, from his point of view, was not just an Israeli one, but also a Jewish one, typical of both Diaspora and Zionist history in the modern era.

It was strikingly evident among pre-Holocaust German Jewry, many of whom attempted to win the favor of surrounding anti-Semitic society via self-reform, and among American Jewry during the Holocaust, many of whom did not seek to aid their European brethren out of fear that such "nationalism" would offend Americans.

Jewish pathology, in Henry's views, resembled the pathology of abused children who seek to appease the abuser by becoming good, and purging themselves of the supposed failings. The syndrome often entails a delusional grandiosity—the idea that one can control one's environment by appeasing the aggressor.

Surveying the history of pre-modern Jewish Diaspora to find out why it was immune to this self-abasing syndrome, Henry found the answer in the strong communal institutions that reinforced identity and pride despite hostile environments. Even among the parts of Spanish Jewry that had secular education and relatively high access to their surrounding society, sturdy communal scaffolding prevented wide-scale defection.

Similarly, much of Eastern European Jewry showed resilience in the modern era, even when religious institutions eroded, by replacing these with secular ones like Jewish labor unions and political parties.

Among the Jews who led the Zionist movement, however, there were many who were seized by Diaspora anti-Semitism and for whom Zionism meant, in part, purifying Jews of their alleged defects. A wide circle of German Jewish *"intelligencia"* fervently opposed statehood and insisted that Judaism was strictly an ethical, universalizing mission that would win the Arab's affection if so it were prevented.

The countervailing force was David Ben-Gurion, an energetic realist who was able to synthesize modern secularism with healthy pride in the Jewish souls, land and tradition.

In this affirmative Ben-Gurionist nationalism that basically prevailed in the first three decades of Israeli existence, there were two factors, as Henry contended, that partially unraveled it.

One was the persistence of the Arab siege, even after the victory of the 1967 Six Day War. The other was the triumph of the Menachem Begin's Likud party in the 1977 elections that finally gave much of the Labor and the Left a Jewish *"bete noure*"—in the shape of Begin's largely religious and traditional constituency.

But the self-blaming mentality quickly gathered steam among the offspring of Zionist pioneers whose own Jewishness was wounded and ambivalent and who lacked the inner resources to cope with persistent Arab hatred. They projected the bewildered self-indictment that the Arab siege induced in them.

Loosing its political influence, the Left reinvented Zionist history to show Jews as colonialist aggressors, and the Arabs as passive victims suing for peace.

Writers and artists expressed alienation, even loathing toward the Jewish state. Post-Zionist "educators" stripped their curriculum of Jewish content in hopes of producing a de-racinated "universalistic" Israeli that no one perceived as objectionable.

Most significantly, and unlike other democracies, the anti-nationalism of the elites found a wide resonance in the populace, depraved by the media. Many Israelis, worn out by the siege, were eager to believe the peace camp's promises of an end to conflicts achieved via self reform, meaning, in this case, the relinquishment of all territorial claims, the suppression of specific Jewish-Zionist values, and a creation of a Palestinian state in whatever borders were demanded. They were enticed by the view that Arab hostility was a function of Israeli misbehavior, and thus within Israel's power to palliate.

Had no one seen that it was suicidal for the nation? Was the whole nation in the pose of an ostrich hiding its head in the sand in order not to be seen? Was Rabbi Meir Kahane the only one who tried to save the nation from self-destruction? Alas, there are no prophets in one's own motherland—he became the national enemy # 1 in his own country.

History is painful and familiar, Henry thought. Violation of God's commandants is always punishable. It was. It is. It'll always be.

Finally, Henry left the LIKUD to become an independent conservative. Politics are not for me, he decided. I have to concentrate on science only.

CHAPTER 60

▼

Moshe rushed into Henry's office with a newspaper in his hands. "Dad, you are a Nobel Prize winner in Medicine!" He handed Henry a fresh copy of the *Jerusalem Post* morning edition folded to the editorial.

Henry had known he was one of the contenders. For the last several years, his name always circulated among the projected winners, but he was accustomed to not being named. When he saw somebody's name in lieu of his own, he wasn't upset. What is a Nobel Prize? It's only the satisfaction of self-esteem, nothing more, he thought. For the last few years, awards had turned into a political process, rather than appreciation of outstanding achievements in science. The choice was always subjective if humans made it. Were there objective criteria of achievements? Certainly not. Maybe winners in science deserved their awards more. Awards in Peace and Literature were totally political. Among the winners are mediocre writers and terrorists. It was a shame.

Now he'd joined the club. Did he feel happiness? No, he felt nothing but emptiness. Why?

These thoughts flashed through his mind as he asked Moshe, "What for?"

"It is said for your pandemic-determinant theory," Moshe read in the paper. "For me, that's a dark forest, Dad."

Henry smiled. "One day I'll try to explain it to you, son."

"Even don't try. It would be wasted time." He extended his hands.

After Moshe left, Henry was flooded with telephone congratulations, official and unofficial, friendly and envious, At last he felt his mouth grow dry, and asked the secretary not to connect him with anybody. But several minutes later she came into his office. "This is the prime minister, professor."

Henry sighed and picked up the receiver. He didn't like the PM, as the man was too ambitious to be sincere.

"My congratulations, Dr. Ginsberg; personal and official. Your award is a great honor for Israel and Jews all over the world. Although the number of Jewish Nobel Prize winners exceeds all others, you are the first Israeli scientist who has been awarded. This is recognition of our state."

"Thank you, sir." Henry wanted to add that science had no bounds and can be considered international, but changed his mind. "Thank you, sir," he repeated.

"We'll arrange an official ceremony in your honor, Dr. Ginsberg, in my residency as soon as you return from Stockholm, if you don't object."

Henry did not object. He hung up and closed his eyes. Then he left home. He wanted to see Rachel. Today it was her day.

As he opened the door, Rachel embraced him. "I'm so happy for you, Henry! I always knew this day would come." She kissed him.

Henry smiled and sat on the sofa. "You know sweetheart, I feel nothing but tiredness."

"You'll feel satisfaction later. You aren't yet accustomed to the thought that you have become a part of history."

"History is the past. I don't want to get out of the present yet, darling."

"You are too much in the present, Henry." Rachel smiled.

"Talking to the PM, I had such a feeling that my award was politically motivated."

"Every award is politically motivated, but you are a world-recognized scientist."

"Thank you for the compliment, darling." Henry laughed. Then he said, "I do feel tired. I'm going to have a nap for half an hour."

He went to the study and lay on the sofa. But when he closed his eyes, he felt somebody sits on the sofa near him.

"Hi, nephew!" In his ears, Henry heard Otto Dornberger's cheerful voice. "At last we were awarded with the Nobel Prize. Better late than never. I have dreamt about it since the day I became a scientist. Now we've shared the Prize."

"You cannot share the Nobel Prize with me, Dr. Dornberger. I was not awarded it for the continuation of your research, but for my own pandemic-determinant theory."

"It doesn't matter, Heinrich. As a researcher, you are my creation. You would never reach your brilliant scientific achievements if, at the beginning of your career, you hadn't used the results of my work. You deserve the Prize not for your doubtful theory, but for your methods of treating malignant tumors with coolants. You've saved thousands of lives, and this is the main achievement of your scientific life, Heinrich. Even if you don't want to admit it, I am a full partner of your success." Otto Dornberger laughed loudly.

Henry felt a piercing headache. He kept silent, trying to find words to object. But when he found them, Otto Dornberger had already vanished. Henry stood up and went downstairs.

Seeing his face, Rachel frowned. "What's happened, darling?"

Henry had a preoccupied look on his face and didn't answer immediately. "I cannot accept the Nobel Prize," he said tiredly. "I still feel that I'm Otto Dornberger's assistant. I have no moral right to accept the Prize."

Rachel looked at him attentively. "If you have made a decision, Henry, it means you have made the right decision." She sighed, and then added, "It's pity of course, I won't be able to feel like a millionaire's wife, but I think I'll live through it. There's nothing to be done." She smiled him through her tears.

"Thank you, sweetheart." Henry kissed Rachel on the cheek and returned to his study.

He sat at the desk and began to write a letter to the Nobel Committee.

"Dear Mr. Chairman,

I was deeply impressed by the high recognition of my modest service to science.

To receive the Nobel Prize and come into the history of science is the fate of chosen people who put the moral purity of science higher than temptations of the surrounding world. Therefore, estimating my work from the moral point of view, I cannot accept the high award of the Nobel Committee.

Let me explain my position. Considered to be the progenitor of many directions of thermo-medicine, I, as a matter of fact, hadn't been that man. I have continued (although I managed to achieve many extremely useful results that saved thousands of lives) research begun by the Nazi professor Dr. Otto Dornberger who, from 1935 until 1945, held the rank of schtandartenfuhrer SS and experimented on the prisoners of fascists concentration camps. As a result of his experiments, hundreds of prisoners died, forced to put their lives on the altar of science.

For almost half a century, I have suffered, trying to answer the question whether I had to continue using data received on the blood of innocent people. If I destroyed Dr. Dornberger's scientific journals, I would never have been achieved the results that today helped to save the lives of thousands of people all over the world. Can a scientist be the cause of death, even for the sake of life?

Looking back, I am in torment, but I don't repent of my misdeeds. If to save even one life means to save the whole world, I have saved thousands of worlds, and it brings me moral satisfaction as a scientist. But moral satisfaction of a scientist is not the equivalent of his moral purity.

These thoughts do not give me the right to accept the high award of the Nobel Committee. I think the members of the Committee, and you personally, Mr. Chairman, would understand the reasons forcing me to refuse the Nobel Prize, and won't consider my refuse as disrespect.

Sincerely,

Dr. Henry Ginsberg."

At last Henry sighed with relief. He has made his choice. Now his conscience is calm.

The next day, after he refused the Prize and published his 'Open Letter to the Nobel Committee,' the leading newspapers came off the press with headlines "Israeli Scientist Continued Nazi Research," "Moral Collapse of Israeli Science," and "Who Are You, Dr. Ginsberg?"

Gloomy Moshe brought the papers to the father's office. "You have to sue them, Dad," he said. "They perverted the truth."

"That's a typical example of 'yellow press,' son," Henry said calmly. "They always pervert the truth, publishing lies in large scale. When they are caught, they always publish an apology in the small scale."

"You have to sue them, "Moshe repeated. "Why do they want to crucify you?"

"Son, you have your liberal friends, and you ask me this question?" Henry smoked a cigarette although he smoked seldom until recently. Then he continued, "Because I publicly supported those who were against giving the Arabs our land. They can't forgive me for it. Liberalism, son, is a mental disorder. I tell you it as a doctor. Analyzing our nation's behavior, I have found the reason for it. This is a syndrome of people who are under siege for a long time; and I call it 'besieging syndrome.'"

"Everybody can have his or her point of view; we live in democratic society. But such behavior is a shame!" Moshe sighed heavily.

"I'm glad you opened your eyes, son." Henry smiled. "If you want to sue your friends, I give you my authorization. But can you remind me when, in our democratic country, a citizen won a case against the liberal media?"

When Moshe left, Henry tried to concentrate on his work, but couldn't. He left the lab, trying to avoid his colleagues.

In several days Henry received a letter from Stockholm. In the letter, the King's Academy of Science and the Nobel Prize Committee supported the Award.

> *"We appreciate, Dr. Ginsberg, the high moral criterion with which you judge yourself and your work. You were awarded the Prize for the creation of unique pandemic— determinant theory although in equal estimation you could be awarded it for outstanding achievements in the field of malignant tumor treatment, which extended the opportunity to defend us totally against this disease in the nearest future.*
>
> *The King's Academy of Science would expect your participation in the Award Ceremony on March 30, 1988.*
>
> *Sincerely,*
>
> *Professor Leonard Bucholtz,*
>
> *Academy Secretary."*

When Henry read the letter, he called Rachel. "Darling," he said. "I am afraid you have to go to a dressmaker to order a new evening gown. I will need a tuxedo too. We have to go to Stockholm."

He didn't hear Rachel's response in the receiver for a long time and repeated, "Are you with me, darling?"

"Henry, I'm so happy!" He heard at last.

CHAPTER 61

───────────▼───────────

After the unforgettable ceremony in the King's palace, Rachel and Henry were sitting in the king's box at the theater, watching a performance of Russian Ballet. They shared the box with another Nobel Prize Winner, Dr. Jack Halloway of Massachusetts Institute of Technology and his wife Carol.

After many nervous months saturated with vanity, sickness and apathy, Henry was happy to dive into the atmosphere of theater, with its soundless flashes of crystal lamps and motley audience. What Rachel and he really needed—to forget reality.

Sitting in the box in expectation of the performance's beginning, Henry thought that all theaters were built in the same manner. It was a closed space inside of which a spectator had a chance to find an outlet for his or her emotions. Can an enclosed space create such an outlet? Maybe only the open theaters of ancient Rome used to give such an opportunity? Inside them, everything was natural—tears, pain, suffering, death…Why were theaters built open? Maybe architects understood that the souls of murdered gladiators had to have an outlet to the sky?

When an actor studied how to play, the audience studied how to assist. With the years, a real death changed to a fake one. The actor created a falsity, and the spectator went to the theater to assist him in it.

The false death needn't an outlet to the sky; and theaters became a closed space, a place of entertainment, acquaintances and adulteries.

A modern man or woman cannot live without a theater like a drug addict cannot live without drugs—a theater gives them the illusion of love, suffering and death.

Time, spectators, and artistic criteria—everything had changed, but what always remained was the necessity for spectators to leave reality because the more awful reality was the more a spectator dreamt of leaving it.

Of all the muses, Henry loved ballet most of all, and Rachel shared his love. They loved it for the sincerity created by the silence of dance. Today's performance consisted from fragments of the Seventh Symphony by Schostakovich.

Barbarian horned hard hats that reminded them of fascists' hats filled the stage, creating a weird impression. Applause broke the silence.

"Look, Henry," Rachel said, pointing to one of the boxes. "Germans."

The people in the box sat with stone faces. They did not applaud despite the brilliant performance.

"They look like Germans," Henry agreed. He took Rachel's binoculars and looked at the box she pointed to.

The face of one of the women in the box seemed Henry familiar. He pushed the binoculars closer to his eyes. Martha! No, it's impossible! He continued to examine the woman's face. No gray hair. But they could be dyed of course. Make-up could hide years. Maybe she had a facelift. It's getting routine now for a woman over fifty.

Martha had a birthmark between her breasts, he remembered, but what could he see through theatrical binoculars?

"Of course they're Germans." Jack Halloway said. "If I were in their shoes, I wouldn't applaud either. Our awful past was a great one for the Germans."

"For them it was just a normal war." Carol shrugged.

Her words hung in the air for a moment.

"Normal? Concentration camps, gas chambers..." Rachel was shocked.

"They did not think so. For Germans, Hitler only terminated enemies of the state," Jack Halloway remarked and then, as it was the intermission, he offered to go to the bar.

"I don't mind," Rachel said. "I'm thirsty."

"I'd rather stay here," Henry said matter-of-factly.

As soon as they left the box, he picked up the binoculars. The German's box had also emptied. Only the woman Henry considered might be Martha was sitting there, reading the program.

Throwing caution to the wind, Henry went directly to her box. He couldn't explain why. Was it simple curiosity?

He opened the door to the box and went in. Seeing a strange man, the woman lifted her brow with surprise.

"I beg your pardon, madam," Henry said in German. "Are you Frau Martha Dornberger?"

The woman smiled. "You are mistaken, sir. "My name is Frau Beckman." Her eyes were cold.

Henry was ready to apologize when he saw a familiar birthmark on her breast. "Martha, I am Heinrich Menke," he said quietly.

"Sorry." The woman looked at him, and Henry saw irritation in her glance. "Sorry," she repeated. "I do not recollect."

A buzzer sounded; the break was over. A tall, gray-haired man came into the box. Seen Henry, he also looked at him questioningly.

"Hence," the woman said, "this is Herr Menke. He says he knew us in Germany, but I cannot recollect him."

"Me neither," the man said in a husky voice.

The second buzzer sounded and the theater lights began dimming slowly.

"I beg your pardon," Henry repeated. "I was mistaken."

On the way to his box, Henry smiled. Why did I want to see my past? To be assured that nothing had changed in German mentality? Or it was a simple curiosity to see the first woman with whom I had had sex in my life?

He went to the bathroom and washed his hands as if he wanted to be cleansed from the past. Yes, the charm of the past is in the fact it had already passed, he thought returning to his box.

"Where were you, Henry? "Rachel whispered as he returned to the box. "Are you okay?"

"I am more than fine, darling."

The second act of the performance was fragments from Cinderella by Chaikovsky. He looked at the stage; Cinderella reminded him of his granddaughter Deborah. Remembered her face, he smiled.

…She lightly flew in the dance, surrounded by nymphs. But suddenly the circle of nymphs vanished and changed into the black hands of a clock. With every strike, one hand fell on

Cinderella's legs; and she wasn't a princess any more, she was a plain girl...

...Midnight approached. The prince and Cinderella must leave, and at that moment a nymph appeared between them. With every clock's strike, she shook like a pendulum; time was inevitable.

"Wonderful performance," Henry said loudly. "Time is inevitable, isn't it?"

"Who can object that statement?" Dr. Halloway smiled.

PART VI

▼

THE DAY OF JUDGEMENT

"People walking in darkness, have seen a great light."

—Prophets, Isaiah, 9.1

CHAPTER 62

Henry woke up in the middle of the night. Again those frequent dreams…

To discard them, he went to the bathroom to splash cold water on his face. Then he returned to the bedroom, lay down and closed his eyes. But sleep had already left.

Why, for the last time, did he feel lonely? Near him was his wonderful, devoted wife. Without Rachel, he wouldn't live. He always needed her support, even in his professional work. She could listen and understand him, even if not understanding the scientific sense of what he was talking about. To listen and to understand is a rare feature—an art given by God. She was getting old, though never complained of pain. He felt it. What was the sense of complaining if nobody could help?

He'd like to have a little bit more warmth from his children. Maybe he wanted too much? The distance between parents and children was getting bigger with the years if they weren't involved in the same activities. This was the law of life; there was nothing to be done. Unfortunately, his children were not. He always felt that gap; sometimes bigger, sometimes smaller, but the gap between him and his children always existed.

After her fieldwork for the Mossad was over, Esther became one of the administrators. The work put its print on her—she was too dry. It would be nice to see her more feminine, Henry thought.

She was a good daughter, called frequently although didn't visit the parents' house too often. What were her dreams, her intentions and her hopes? He didn't know. Not more than an old father can know about a grown daughter. Did she love? It seemed to him, her marriage was not equal. Did she have lovers? What did she think about Israeli politics? He would never know. She was the product of Israeli society. She served society; it meant she never doubted. What was the sense of doubting if doubts could change nothing? Maybe she thinks our society needn't change. A happy woman!

Her husband, Aaron, was polite and indifferent like a clerk in a hotel. Henry hadn't the slightest idea about Aaron's inner world. He was a typical leftist, always overly optimistic because he believed that all the issues could be solved easily, and that the Palestinians were forthcoming, and willing, and just waiting to conclude an agreement. Aaron was a distant relative, 'in-law.'

But Esther and Aaron had given him one of the most valuable gifts of his life—his granddaughter Deborah. When he knew Esther was going to give birth, he asked her if it is a girl, to name her Deborah.

Esther looked at him and said, "Certainly, Dad, if you love this name more than others." She said "love," not "like;" he remembered. Did she know about his love of Deborah then? Or simply guessed that he kept some sentimental remembrances of his past?

How rapidly time passed! Now little Deborah is already eighteen. He is a happy grandfather. Sometimes it seemed to him that little Deborah was his own reproduction, only in girl's body. She even looked like his daughter, not a granddaughter; she had the same oval face, the same long eyelashes, and the same color eyes. And she was the only member of the family who connected her future with medicine. Deborah was his continuation. How could he find words to glorify God for His miracle to him? Tears of happiness…he again knew its taste…

His son Moshe…Good Lord, he had found his place in life after that injury. He became a prominent member of Israeli society, a successful lawyer and a legal consultant for numerous corporations.

For some time he and Moshe had become closer. Tears of happiness always made people closer. He was happy for his son's achievements. What was in his soul? Alas, he became too liberal. Didn't his children become victims of society, depraved by the media?

Henry recollected one of their conversations, which kept unpleasant sediment in his soul. At little Baruch's birthday party, they talked about the new Israeli immigrants, and Moshe shocked him with his views. "They should shake the blood-soaked dust of Europe from their feet and adapt to their new environment in lieu of trying to keep little bit of Russia, Poland or Germany," Moshe said emotionally. "We've got Muslim Arabs here, and Christian Arabs; unless Jews here are prepared to become Jewish Arabs, they have no future in this part of the world."

"That's not a particularly pretty sight, son. You mean if Jews assimilate, they'll live in peace with Arabs? But that sort of peace they could have even in Europe. For two thousand years, we've struggled against all odds to stay Jewish, and now you are saying that once we get back to our own land, we should give up the ghost? We tried to assimilate in Europe and couldn't. Torquemada wouldn't let us; Hitler wouldn't let us. By the way, son, the first Jews that Hitler exterminated were not the Hassidim; they were assimilated Jews."

"Okay, Dad. Don't call him an Arab Jew here. Call him a Palestinian, but we must stop being Europeans."

"These crazy views I heard from Shimon Peres. For a long time, he's called for Israeli participation in the Arab League. When did he become your political guru?"

"He is not my political guru, but this is my sincere point of view."

"And you think, Moshe, that'll bring peace?"

"Nothing can bring peace. But the existing situation will get worse and lead to a terrible slaughter. We still can avoid it."

"But there is another way, Moshe—Arab expulsion from our land. It's labor pain, but no nation was ever born without it."

The last time they stopped speaking without reaching a mutual understanding. Unfortunately, Henry thought, and sighed deeply. Liberalism is a mental sickness; it strikes people who reached achievements even more often than failures. When did Moshe begin worshipping success and money? Was this his fault as a father because he worked too much and did not pay proper attention to what had been in Moshe's head? Yes, he knew he could be blamed for everything, even for Moshe's failure with his first marriage. His former wife, Peggy, had never responded Moshe's letters. But even if this stupid woman responded, what would he find in common with his grown daughters? They were of course brought up as anti-Semites. It is sad, but human stupidity is unrestricted.

How could the media deprave society so easily? Pragmatism became the norm of life. At Moshe's last birthday party, Henry asked his son if the rumors about the PM's corruption had a base of fact, and the PM had received a $3,000,000 bribe from the Jericho Casino that was under Palestinian control.

Moshe laughed. "From legal point of view, Dad, it could hardly be called a bribe. He received that money as profit from a joint enterprise."

"Son, how do we call 'a joint enterprise with the enemy'? I know only one word—treachery." Henry rolled up his eyes questioningly.

"You carry the mentality of the last century, Dad." Moshe smiled. "By the way, do you know that most of the casino customers are Jews? Do you think they don't know where their money goes?"

Henry sighed. "It's a wonderland, son. We ourselves cut off the branch of the tree where we sit. If I understood your explanation correctly, the rumors are not baseless?"

Moshe laughed again. "Of course, they aren't. All the prosecutors who investigated that case came to the conclusion that he, and both his sons, had to be indicted. Naturally, his strongest desire was to avoid indictment for his role in corruption scandals."

"What forced the prosecutors to change their minds?"

"To avert indictment, the PM had to take the bold initiative of changing the public agenda away from the media's focus on investigation. And he did it brilliantly. Still under investigation, the PM made a move to head off the indictment by the new left-wing Attorney General. As the media bleated daily, the new appointee's first order of business upon taking office was to decide whether or not to indict the PM and his sons in what had become known as 'The Greek Island Affair.'

The day after Attorney General came to office, the PM invited the radical left-wing, and I would call him a Communist, columnist Yoel Marcus from *Haaretz* for a visit at his residence in Jerusalem. He outlined for Marcus his plan to withdraw from Gaza. As expected, Marcus embraced the PM's plan, and thus the radical Left was brought on board the PM bandwagon. Shortly thereafter, Attorney General closed the investigation on the PM and his sons. When at the press conference Yoel Marcus was asked about his own opinion, he said cynically, 'We know the PM is corrupt, but we must protect him because he has placed the legal establishment on the horns of a dilemma.' They had to decide what moves them more, their love of the law or their hatred toward the settlers. It was an easy decision, Dad,—they chose hatred."

"I don't want to spoil your birthday party, son. Let's talk about something more pleasant than Israeli politics." Henry changed the topic.

Henry looked at his watch. It's still 3:30 a.m.—too late to take sleep pills. He tried to discard his sad thoughts and again closed his eyes. At last he fell asleep, but his sleep was not deep.

…Henry saw in front of his eyes a young man wearing a nightgown and sleepers. He was messing around in a clothes closet. "What are you looking for, Dad?" Henry asked him.

"I am looking for my military uniform, son. Have you seen it?"

"A Nazi military uniform?" Henry was surprised.

"A German military uniform," the man said in irritation. "I didn't serve in the Nazi Army; I am a German Jew, and I've served Germany."

"Why did you serve Germany, Dad?" Henry's curiosity was sincere.

"Because it's my motherland, son!"

"It's not your motherland. You are a Jew." Henry said in the form of a strict statement.

"So what? I am a German Jew. Judaism is a religion. I've always considered myself a German and wanted my son to become a respectable member of German society. Whom did you become, son?"

"A member of Israeli society."

"Did you forget your motherland, son?"

"I have found my motherland, Dad."

"Did you so easily leave my grave in Germany?"

"You don't have a grave, Dad. Germany has killed you." Henry answered, so tired.

"Why do you call me, Dad, old man?

Trying to find a proper explanation, Henry fell asleep at last.

CHAPTER 63

———————▼———————

"Dr. Ginsberg?" The soft, deep woman's voice in the receiver seemed familiar.

"Speaking."

"This is Giula Hess from Channel 4. Do you remember me?" She introduced herself, and at the same moment her voice materialized in Henry's eyes as belonging to the charming young woman who had interviewed him after receiving the Nobel Prize.

Giula Hess was the niece of the late General Avraham Deri, former Deputy Chief of General Staff of the Israeli Army. He was popular in the IDF, not only as one of the most decorated Israeli officers, but also for his intolerable position concerning the Palestinians. Because of it, he was forced to resign.

His niece, Giula Hess, was one of the first open lesbians who supported the rights of sexual minorities, and one of the vocal supporters of the leftist organization 'Peace Now.'

"I couldn't forget one of the most beautiful women I've ever met in my life," Henry said, his compliment sincere.

"You are also one of the most attractive men I've ever interviewed," Giula Hess returned the compliment. Then she said, "I am calling you, Dr. Ginsberg, to invite you to take part in the TV program 'Our Nation.'"

"What caused such an unexpected interest in my modest person?" Henry smiled in the receiver.

"Oh, Dr. Ginsberg," she sang on the other end of the line, "you are the Nobel Prize winner, you aren't a modest citizen."

Henry missed her adulation. "'Our Nation' is a very eclectic program," he remarked matter-of-factly. "You discuss a wide specter of problems—from politics to sex. What are you going to discuss with my participation, Giula?"

"The most actual for our nation problem—the disengagement plan." Giula said. Her tone couldn't be softer if she had been talking about love.

"Who will discuss this problem?" Henry was interested.

"You will be in a good company, Dr. Ginsberg; the PM, Shimon Perez, Rabbi Brook of Religion Party, the playwright Dan Horowitz…"

"And when have you scheduled this program?" Henry asked although he already began guessing the reason of Giula's call.

"On Sunday, at 2:30 p.m."

Henry kept silent, pondering the opportunities; the PM would be promoting his unpopular plan; it was supported however by the Labor opposition leaders and *intelligencia*. His participation would only show that he represented nobody but himself, a crazy scientist. At the same time, on Sunday, he had agreed to deliver a speech at the anti-disengagement meeting near the PM's residence.

Giula Hess didn't interrupt the silence, expecting Henry's okay, but he said, "Sorry, Giula. I've just checked my schedule on Sunday. I'll be very busy. Why not invite Rabbi Meir Kahane instead of me? He's a political figure; I'm only a scientist."

Giula Hess almost choked on his heretic offer. Henry repeated his 'sorry' and hung up. He closed his eyes, feeling a definite satisfaction from his refusal.

...Israeli Media. Another game they wanted to play with him. It had always been in leftist's hands because they always understood the force of propaganda and brainwashing. When Gebbels said that the most repeated lie is the truth, he didn't invent the formula; he took it from the arsenal of Soviet Communist propaganda.

The more Henry thought about unbelievable Israeli politics the more unbelievable for him was the media game. The media tried, and succeeded, to persuade the public that a mass armed uprising of Jews against Jews was impossible because it was simply impossible. The PM was corrupt? Who cared! He was going to sell the Biblical Land? Who cared! We are democracy. We can't struggle with each other; we have to accept the governmental decisions even if the whole government was totally morally corrupt.

Did the acceptance of the inevitability of events really live in the Jewish soul?

Maybe something was mentally wrong with Jewish people? Maybe something was mentally wrong with the nation if anyone couldn't pluck up the courage to sacrifice a single life for the sake of the nation's survival? Or maybe it concerned only the Right, but the Left had no obligations at all?

Didn't it lead to the conclusion that there was something about this nation that periodically drives it into fits of mendacity, incapable of resisting the fever that burns the marrow of its bones?

It was the fever of this land, of Eretz Israel. Did the past, in which the Hagana troops shelled the rival Irgun arms ship 'Altalena,' become painful lesson for the future? Not at all, Henry thought, history repeats itself, only with more mockery.

"I heard you talking to somebody," Rachel said, entering to his study and bringing him pills he took for his high blood pressure.

"I had a chat with a charming lady from Channel 4, Giula Hess." Henry smiled. "She tried to seduce me to meet her in the studio of 'Our Nation.'"

"She is really charming, but she is the only one that I feel no jealousy about, darling." Rachel laughed.

CHAPTER 64

Time of inevitable losses came.

Rabbi Boxter died after a stroke; he never recovered consciousness. After his death did Henry realize how many people loved and respected him—the narrow street around the synagogue was packed full; people passed by the coffin for more than an hour to express their last respects for the rabbi.

Who could better share about Rabbi Boxter than his old friend, the plain doctor from the Gush Katif settlement? He said, "A man comes into the world with pressed palms as if he wants to say that the whole world belongs to him; but then leaves the world with open palms as if to say, 'Look, I'm not taking anything with me.' Rabbi Boxter was a rare man who came into our world with palms already open."

Then Henry's dear friend Emile Feingold died. Only after his death, papers called him "the father of the Israeli atomic bomb." Emile was an idealist dreaming of contributing to the creation of the man-operated nuclear reaction that would serve Israel in peaceful purposes, creating Israel energy independence from other countries. But even if he didn't reach that goal, his contribution into Israeli physics was difficult to overestimate. Emile Feingold was an honored member of many European academies of science, and many world-recognized physicists came to Israel to take part in the funeral ceremony.

Emile Feingold was a dreamer and a poet. In his personal journal that his sister Miriam gave Henry in accordance with Emile's will, Henry wrote verses written by Emile in his youth, in Germany.

> *"I have a dream.*
> *We'll come to our native land*
> *In the lights of sunset,*
> *And inside the holy walls of Jerusalem,*
> *Still in dusty cloths,*
> *We, staying on knees silently,*
> *Would bless the Lord for that day."*

Miriam died less than a month after her brother's death; she couldn't live without her brother. Long ago they became not a brother and a sister, but one whole.

After all these deaths, Henry felt depressed. He suddenly realized he was not a young man, and the best part of his life had gone. What was ahead? Will be the rest of his life only a preparation for his own departure? God gave him a good life, his dreams became true, love lit his life, his children found their places on the Earth; even his grandchildren were already grown. He had found his vocation, and reached the highest of professional achievements. God gave him everything that made a man happy.

Death? It's as natural as life. A part of God's succession of life and death; a person's life was like a blow of the wind; his days were a passing shade. Rabbi Boxter, Emile, Miriam…Only their bodies died, but their souls went to another world. He would keep them in his heart—they were and always would be a part of his own heart.

After Henry buried Miriam, he finally decided to resign from his position of director of the research laboratory. He felt his scientific productivity lessening, and it was high time to open the way for a new generation of researchers full of fresh ideas.

Henry hadn't yet decided which of his assistants he would recommend for that position. As always, he decided to discuss it with Rachel.

CHAPTER 65

▼

Sitting at the desk of his study, Henry continued working, analyzing data received from his assistant Dr. Lazaris. They strictly supported his pandemic-determinant theory; he was right in his scientific intuition.

At last tiredness pressed him. He stood up and lay on the sofa, still thinking over Dr. Lazaris' results. But his eyes seemed glued together. As soon as Henry reached that state, he saw Dr. Otto Dornberger sitting in the chair in front of him. A white lab coat hardly covered his SS uniform.

"Hi, nephew. Haven't seen you for a long time."

"Hi, Dr. Dornberger," Henry said in a tone of pure ice.

"Aren't you glad to see me, Heinrich?" Otto Dornberger laughed. "I remember you called me 'uncle.'"

"Until I knew you weren't my relative, sir." Henry said dryly.

"I was more than your relative, Heinrich. I was like a father to you. Your father gave you life, I—saved it."

Henry looked at Otto Dornberger with wide eyes. "Why do you think you saved my life, sir?"

"When I took you in my house, I've already known you were a Jew, Heinrich," Otto Dornberger said matter-of-factly.

"But you were a Jew-hater, Dr. Dornberger! Why did you save my life?" Henry's surprise was sincere.

"Why? First of all, I studied you, Heinrich. I asked myself the question whether a Jew could be a German? And I came to the conclusion—never, on a genetic level. Particular people call it 'Jewish blood.' But when I realized it, I had already felt you would be my spiritual son in science. Do you know, Heinrich, why you could not destroy my scientific journals though many times you were close to it? You have lived on its pages as my patient. Didn't you guess it? Start at page 253, and re-read it. All my patients were identified with names; Aaron, Sarah, Meir…Only one was 'patient X,' that was you, Heinrich. These pages are dedicated to psychiatry and psychology although that field had never been the focus of my scientific interests."

"So you've saved my life only to observe 'patient X'?"

"No, Heinrich. Human being is a more complicated creature, even the simplest of us. Do you remember the words 'to save even one life means to save the world?' By saving you, I saved the world. That's why I wasn't punished severely in the world where I live."

"Where do you live, Dr. Dornberger?"

Dornberger laughed. "In another world, nephew. Since you killed me, I live in another world."

"I did not kill you, you know it. I only heard rumors you were killed at the end of the war."

"You did it, Heinrich. When you brought me the envelope with the Fuhrer's photos, you've killed me. Since then, I have lived in another world and observed you from Above. I was your scientific guru, Heinrich; I remain your scientific guru."

"And you weren't punished for your crimes, Dr. Dornberger?"

Otto Dornberger grinned sadly. "It turned out that there was no hell in another world; Christian imagination is totally wrong; Dante Alighieri was a visionary." He grinned wryly.

"And there is no punishment for sins?" Henry lifted his brown in surprise.

"Punishment exists, but it's beyond human imagination. Man cannot penetrate God's intentions," Otto Dornberger said. Then he explained his thought. "No physical punishment exists, but punishment of soul."

"I didn't quite catch your words, Dr. Dornberger," Henry said thoughtfully.

"It's quite clear, Heinrich. In committing crimes and sins on the Earth, we punish many generations who would live after us. Have you seen around you crippled people, people with corrugated bodies, people born without legs or hands? Souls like mine are placed in such bodies for purification through physical suffering. My soul is in one of them, but I think my purification would not be as long as Dr. Mengele's or Adolph Eichman's souls." Then Otto Dornberger sharply changed the topic. "I am glad I didn't make the mistake of forecasting your scientific future, Heinrich; your achievements are very impressive.

The good teacher is always happy when his pupil surpasses his own achievements. You've received the Nobel Prize; I only dreamed about it."

"Awards are being given by people. They are not essential for a scientist." Henry shrugged.

"What's essential?"

"The results of your work; their implications."

"I'm glad you said it! Now you understood the main stimulus of my activity—I thought about the future and did not pay attention to the present. As you did."

The short nap almost gone and Heinrich opened his eyes. Otto Dornberger vanished. Henry lay for several minutes with open eyes, fighting the rest of sleep. Again these dreams, he thought. Last time they come to my head too frequently. He sighed. I am getting old.

Henry felt headache begins, so he got up and took two aspirins. Then he went downstairs and sat on a couch near Rachel watching TV.

"You look weary, sweetheart," she said, looking at him. "You work too much."

"I saw Otto Dornberger in my sleep again," he said in an expressionless voice.

"We cannot totally discard our past," Rachel remarked thoughtfully. "Fifty years have passed," she added. "I don't feel hatred in my heart any more."

Henry looked at his wife. "Me neither," he said silently. Then he changed the point. "Tomorrow Dr. Lazaris will conduct his general experiment which will either support or reject my pandemic-determinant theory. He asked me to be present, and I cannot refuse him; he is a very emotional person, you know."

"I know," Rachel agreed.

"What is your opinion if I recommend him for the director's position in lieu of me? I think it's time for me to resign."

Rachel looked at him carefully. "Do you have any particular reasons for resigning, darling?"

"No. I have nothing except my age. Unfortunately the age of scientific productivity is shorter than a man's age."

"As I know, everybody considers your productivity extraordinary."

"I feel it diminished, and significantly. Nothing wrong with me, but only youth generates revolutionary ideas in science." Henry smiled. "Old age only summarizes achievements. And, in most cases, prevents achievements of the new generation. By the way, what is your opinion about Dr. Lazaris, sweetheart?"

"I don't know his professionalism as you do, but you always separated him from the others. I met him several times on different occasions and he seemed me a pleasant and modest man."

"I am glad, darling, that our impressions coincide." Henry smiled at Rachel as he rose from the couch. "So don't worry if I come home late tomorrow."

CHAPTER 66

⯆

"Hi, Daddy!" Esther's voice in the receiver sounded more cheerful than usual. "Deborah and I wanted to come to your place on Sabbath eve, okay?"

"Have you begun celebrating Sabbath, sweetheart?"

Esther couldn't see her father's smile on the other end of the line, but she felt the irony in his voice. She has missed it. "Deborah likes to light candles in your house," she said friendly. "But frankly speaking, I'd like to talk to you about her. You know, she took part in the student meeting in support of Igal Amin's right to be married in jail..."

"What's so awful about that? He had to have the same rights as all other prisoners, I suppose."

"But he is not an ordinary prisoner—he is Itzhak Rabin's killer," Esther objected.

"So what? Would it be okay to give him permission to marry if he had killed not a Labor PM but a Likud one?" Henry grinned in the receiver.

Esther again missed his question. "I'd like you, Dad, to talk to her; she loves you even more than us, her parents."

"I must confess that I also love her more than anybody else," Henry smiled in the receiver.

"Dad, you are the best," Esther said matter-of-factly.

Henry was about to hang up, when Esther said, "By the way, one of my colleagues asked me to introduce him to you."

"Is he from your Agency?"

"Strictly speaking, not. He is from the Shabak, but we were university pals." Esther explained with a bland tone.

"Sorry, sweetheart, I haven't the slightest wish to see a KGB man in my house. But if you have already promised to arrange a meeting, let's do it in one of the restaurants."

"Okay." She sighed. "I will."

In a week, Henry sat at table in a small, quiet restaurant. In front of him, there sat a man about fifty, with a plain but pleasant face, who looked more like a computer analyst than an Israeli KGB officer.

"Thank you, Dr. Ginsberg, for agreeing to meet me," he said after greeting Henry. His voice was quiet and monotonous. "My name is Shlomo Pleaner. I am a Deputy Director of Shabak Agency."

"Do you have an ID?" Henry asked with a shade of mockery, but the man didn't catch it.

"Sure." Shlomo Pleaner showed Henry his ID that confirmed his identity.

A waitress came and they gave their orders. When she brought a pitcher of water, Henry poured some in his glass, took a gulp, and remarked matter-of-factly, "I didn't know that Shabak was interested in biology."

"Shabak is interested in politics, Dr. Ginsberg," Shlomo answered without a smile.

"Sorry, Mr. Pleaner, but we have different points of view because I am not interested in politics."

"Nobody can avoid taking part in politics, sir, if he isn't an ordinary citizen. I would have never been allowed to worry you if your political activity, sir, had not brought harm to the PM."

"I am afraid we talk in different languages, Mr. Pleaner. I am a scientist, and am far from politics. Ten years ago I left Mapai, several years later—Likud. I am a registered independent conservative, so I have no obligations to the current PM or somebody else."

"But you are the leading Israeli scientist, Dr. Ginsberg, a Nobel Prize winner; even if you don't belong to the party, your every step has a national resonance. Our leadership considers that participating in students' meetings against the disengagement plan, you would bring harm to our national interests; many people consider you an advocate of violence." Shlomo Pleaner made a long pause. Then he added, "Possible violence."

Henry began to get angry. "And you want me to support the PM who violated all possible moral norms?" His question was icy cold.

"He is a democratically elected head of the government, Dr. Ginsberg," Shlomo Pleaner said, without enthusiasm in his voice. "We live in the Jewish State; it's different from all others."

"Really? Sorry old man, but I consider all democracies subject to the same laws. But maybe you're right, and ours is quite different; the PM's totally abandoned the platform on which he was elected. He betrayed his own party that rejected his policy. In each democracy, in such a situation the PM must resign, but not in our country. Do you call that democracy, Mr. Pleaner? You are a clever man; you cannot fail to understand that we have the most corrupted government in modern Israeli history.

This government represents nobody, and you want me to support its legitimacy?

Thank God, I am a scientist, not a politician. I don't struggle with the PM; I only express my views. It's totally legitimate in the democratic society, isn't it?"

"I cannot share your point of view, Dr. Ginsberg. In a democratic society, citizens must fulfill their obligation to support the elected leader," Shlomo Pleaner said as he pronounced the phrase that sounded as if he had learnt it by heart in advance.

The waitress brought their orders. Henry ate a small piece of a veal cutlet, but it seemed tasteless and he pushed the plate away.

"You have to realize the consequences, Dr. Ginsberg," Shlomo Pleaner said softly, avoiding Henry's eyes.

Henry laughed. "Are you trying to frighten me, Mr. Pleaner? Maybe you want to remind me of General Rafael Eitan's fate? In our democratic state everything is possible. A seventy-six years old man, the former Chief of General Staff, a member of Knesset and the leader of the main opposition to the PM party, simply fell from the pier after the midnight and drowned. Funny, isn't it? In any country it would be called a dirty job. Do you have a fresher idea in my case?" Henry did not try to disguise his anger.

Shlomo Pleaner kept a gloomy silence, and Henry's face grew more crimson with anger. "I had no intention of bringing harm to anyone, Mr. Pleaner, but I advise you to think about what would be a real harm for the PM if a Nobel Prize winner applies for political asylum in the U.S. because Israel is turning into a dictatorship?"

Henry waved to the waitress for a bill.

"The joint bill, sir?" she asked as she came to the table.

"No, separate."

Henry paid his bill and left the restaurant, without saying good-bye.

CHAPTER 67

It happened, what the whole world thought would never happen in Israel. A commanding officer of the 5th tank brigade, Colonel Uri Barrel, left five dead government securities officers and two of his own men behind him, had taken power.

The whole operation lasted less than twenty minutes. His tanks surrounded the Knesset building during a government session, and after a small amount of shooting arrested the cabinet ministers headed by the PM. Knesset was dismissed, its members put under home arrest. All political parties were declared unlawful. The Israel borders were closed and marshal law declared on the whole territory of Israel. The shocked country frozen near their TV screens, listened to Colonel Barrel's appeal to the nation.

> *"Citizens of Israel, brothers-Jews!*
> *The corrupt government that led the country to self-destruction has been overthrown. The dictatorship that wore the cloth of a pseudo-democracy doesn't exist any more. The Army took power not to usurp the power, but to restore Independence, Law and Dignity of the Jewish State.*
> *We ask you to keep calm and avoid any disorder.*

During the next year, we are going to introduce for the nation's approval the First Israeli Constitution and transmit the power to a democratically elected President.

We also appeal to our Arab neighbors to avoid any acts of terror; they will be punished severely, without so-called 'adequacy of response.'

"Unbelievable!" Rachel said, turning to Henry. "I could never imagine such a thing happened in Israel."

"Time changes people, darling." Henry remarked philosophically.

"Is it for the best?"

Henry smiled. "But definitely not for the worst. We have already reached the bottom of moral corruption. This colonel sounded like a sincere man who loves Israel. So let's live and see…"

"Said the blind man?" Rachel returned him smile.

In two days, when Rachel had just hung up the phone after talking to Esther, she heard another buzz and thought Esther had forgotten to tell her something. She picked up the receiver again. "Yes, darling." But she heard an unknown voice. "May I talk to Dr. Ginsberg, please?"

"It's for you, Henry," Rachel said and gave him the receiver.

"Listening," he said.

"Dr. Ginsberg? This is Colonel Uri Barrel. Sorry for taking your time, sir. It wouldn't be impertinent to ask you about a favor? Allot me half an hour of your time for a conversation with me."

"I am at your disposal, colonel."

"Thank you, sir. I'll send a car for you."

Henry hung up. "Colonel Barrel wants to talk to me," he said, answering Rachel's mute question.

"What about?"

"No idea. But I think it would be good talking to the new leader to have the imagination about who's who."

Less than an hour later, accompanied by a polite lieutenant aide-de-camp, Henry came to the colonel's study in the building of the Ministry of Defense.

Colonel Barrel stood up and offered Henry his hand. He showed him to an armchair and sat in the opposite one. "Thank you, Dr. Ginsberg, you have agreed to talk to me."

Colonel Barrel was not a husky soldier, with a machine gunner's massive neck and shoulder muscles; his sensuous features were pleasant and intelligent. If not for the military uniform, he would be taken for an assistant professor at the university rather than an Army officer. Henry liked Colonel Barrel.

"First of all I'd like to make my position clear, Dr. Ginsberg; we do not wish to keep a military rule for a long time. We'd like to transfer the power to a civilian government as soon as possible although the military rule in this historic phase seems to me more constructive than a pseudo-democracy. This is only my personal point of view, and I understand it's disputed. But I think it's much better to have a strong Jewish State, which is being disdained by the world but survives, than the continuation of the terror and distraction that had already begun, with the blessing of the world. The only guarantee of Israel's survival is trust in God, and the strong Israeli Army. That's why I think we must not be afraid of the future."

"In this point, I totally agree with you, colonel. But I'd like to ask you a strict question; what's your intention regarding to the PM's fate, and the fate of the leading members of his cabinet?"

"I'll give you a strict answer, Dr. Ginsberg," Colonel Barrel said. "I don't want Jewish blood to be poured, even for sake of justice; no one will be sentenced to death. I think they have to be brought to the court and indicted for the national treasury; the court will decide their fate. But I think the most awful punishment for the Jew would be stripping away his Israeli citizenship and banishment from the country for life. Of course, all old regime politicians have to be banned from political life in the future.

But first of all, we have to look forward and construct the base of our new state—constitutional democracy. And I want to ask you, Dr. Ginsberg, to help us to regain Israel, to make it not a permanent subject of mockery in the international arena, but a proud and strong state respected by our friends and our enemies also."

"In what form do you see my helping, colonel?"

"I'd like to offer you the position of Interim Israeli President until the next general election takes place. Take the real power, Dr. Ginsberg. You are a world-recognized scientist; you will be a world-recognized President."

"I have to confess, it's an unexpected offer, colonel," Henry said frankly. "I'm afraid I am not ready for such responsibility. I carry the mentality of the last century, with its old-fashioned conservatism."

"It's exactly what we need, sir, that old-fashioned conservatism on the government level," Colonel Barrel said, looking fiercely into Henry's eyes.

"The main problem of our society is its relation with the Palestinian Arabs." Henry sighed. "What's the Army position on this item?"

Colonel Barrel stood up, came to the desk and took a book in his hands. He opened it and read:

> *"And if you do not listen to the voice of your God to perform all His commandments and statues, you will be cursed, and a newcomer living in your land will tower over you, higher and higher, and you will be lower and lower, until he is the head, and you are a tail…"*

Colonel Barrel closed the book and looked at Henry. "That's what the Torah says. What is going on in our country now is a war between an Arab newcomer and a Jew. Blind Jews, in their unwillingness to accept the truth because of their liberal traditions, allowed the Arab cancer to grow deep inside the Jewish State; so now the newcomer considers our land belongs to him.

"I think all Jews have to realize that the only answer is surgery—we have to remove the newcomer from our land. Everybody who is against the normal and logistical solution contributes to a large-scale slaughter between the Jews and Arabs in the nearest future. And this is the main reason the Army ousted the government—not to oust the corrupt people from power, but to save the Jewish State. Two nations who claim rights on the same land at the same time would never live in peace on that land. That's why I beg you, Dr. Ginsberg, help us to regain Eretz Israel." Colonel Barrel stopped talking. Excitement and sincerity were openly reflected on his face; he was nervous.

Henry peered into his eyes—the clever eyes of a clever man, and thought that the first impression had never failed him; he had liked Colonel Barrel from the first glance. "I have to think over your offer, colonel," Henry said standing up the chair.

CHAPTER 68

───────────▼───────────

The next day Henry woke up early. Before giving his answer to Colonel Barrel, Henry decided to go to Jerusalem and to pray near the Wailing Wall. Preparing his morning coffee, Rachel felt that the day would be perhaps the most important day of Henry's life—the Day of Judgment. When Henry sat at the kitchen table, Rachel did not interrupt his silence as he was submerged in his thoughts.

Unexpectedly, his younger son, Baruch, appeared at the kitchen door. Surprised, Rachel looked at her son. "You are an early bird today, Baruch."

Baruch smiled. "There is no sleep, Ma. In a week, I have to check-in to join the IDF." He sat at table, and she poured coffee in his cup.

"Army is necessary, son," Henry said. "All of us served the Army. But have you thought about your life after the service? Who are you going to be?"

"I did, Dad. First of all, I'd like to graduate from a medical school. Then I'm going to enter the rabbinical school."

"Are you going to become a rabbi?" Rachel rolled her eyes.

"A military rabbi, Ma," Baruch said, and then he explained, "We are the nation of priests, aren't we?"

"We are, son." Henry smiled. "I think you would be a great Chief Military Rabbi."

After Baruch left, Henry stood up and came to the window. Rachel joined him and he embraced her shoulders. "Another day has come," he said, looking at a wonderful sunrise behind the window. It was a moment of stillness—the stillness of the first hours of a new day.

At the end of the day, Henry called Colonel Barrel. "Uri," he said, "I accept your offer. Let's roll it over."

About the Author

Edward Schwartz (Eli Besprozvany) has written in a variety of genres, including poetry, drama, detective, essays and contemporary fiction. He is an author of fourteen books, including *A Deep Danger, Rainbow Behind the Back,* and *The White Cliff.* Edward Schwartz grew up in Russia, received a doctorate in Physics from St. Petersburg University, and now makes his home in Forest Hills, New York. Visit his Web site at edward-schwartz.com.

978-0-595-40184-0
0-595-40184-8

Printed in the United States
59962LVS00003B/64-81